Judith

Nicholas Mosley was born in 1923. He is the author of thirteen novels, including *Accident*, *Impossible Object* and the other four volumes of the *Catastrophe Practice* series, *Hopeful Monsters*, *Imago Bird*, *Serpent* and *Catastrophe Practice*. He has also written three biographies, a travel book and a book about religion. Nicholas Mosley is married, has five children, and lives in London.

This edition of *Judith* has a text substantially revised from that of the original Secker & Warburg edition (1986).

NICHOLAS MOSLEY

Judith

Minerva

A Minerva Paperback
JUDITH

First published in Great Britain 1986
by Martin Secker & Warburg Limited
This revised Minerva edition published 1992
by Mandarin Paperbacks
Michelin House, 81 Fulham Road, London SW3 6RB

Minerva is an imprint of the Octopus Publishing Group,
a division of Reed International Books Limited

Copyright © 1986 Nicholas Mosley
Revised edition copyright © 1991 Nicholas Mosley

A CIP catalogue record for this title
is available from the British Library
ISBN 0 7493 9954 6

Printed in Great Britain
by Cox and Wyman Limited, Reading, Berks

To Marius and Jonathan

PART I

Dear Bert,

All right, I'll tell you. But don't tell anyone else. You may think this means – I might get it published one day.

I can't marry you. I can't marry anyone else. Will you think this means – I might marry you one day?

When I came to England (as a child I had been with my parents, as you know, in Hong Kong and Singapore) there was an extraordinary slowness and stillness on the road into London from the airport: it was as if some bomb had gone off: people sat in their cars like toys with spikes up inside them: in the streets they seemed dazed, as if they were looking for where their homes had once been and for food. Where I had been brought up people seemed always to know exactly where they were and what they were doing: they were getting on, getting power, getting money: everyone was in the business of owning a percentage of everyone else. In London people seemed to have been liberated from the wheel of all this; but it was as if some juggernaut had gone over them, and they were like new-born babies left lying on the edge of a bed while doctors tended to the dying earth, their mother.

I went to that drama school, as you know, and got one or two jobs in fringe theatre. That was just before you first met me. (Who am I writing this for? is it you? is it you?)

Then I got a small part in the West End in a play called *Judith*. This was a breakthrough for me – not only because I was going to the West End, but because I was understudying the star who was a famous actress from whom I thought I might learn. I also thought that from the play I might learn something about myself: I am as you know (I mean you, not you!) called Judith.

The story of *Judith* was taken from the book in the Bible or rather the Apocrypha. The Jews are being besieged in a town call Bethulia: the Assyrians are about to break in, and if they do they will sack the town and kill the inhabitants. The Jews are in despair; but there is in Bethulia a beautiful young widow called Judith, who gets the idea that God has called her to save her people. She announces she will go down to the Assyrians and will make some sort of offering of herself to their captain, Holofernes. The Jews agree to this, since it seems to be God's will. So Judith dresses herself up and goes to the camp of the Assyrians; and there, because she is beautiful, she gets herself taken in to Holofernes. He is attracted to her; he arranges a dinner. But before he can make love to her he gets drunk and passes out (you have heard this story?) and while he is asleep, Judith takes down his sword and chops his head off. She carries his head back in her overnight bag to Bethulia and tells the Jews to hang it on the walls. Then in the morning when the Assyrian soldiers see the head they run away in panic.

So this is a story, you see, about good coming out of an action that might usually be called evil: or about how you can call this coming-out-of-evil good, perhaps, so long as you can say it is God's will.

But then, what men have usually done, of course, is to use saying it is God's will as justification for their own evil.

But Judith was a woman. Do you think the story is about how good–coming–out–of–evil might be a special accomplishment of women?

The play in which I was to understudy the star had been written some sixty or seventy years ago at a time when people had stopped making much use of the idea of God's will – either as a belief, or as an excuse for their own purposes or desires. The playwright told the story without bringing in much about God; sexual passion had taken God's place: it was this now, conventionally, that was seen as the force behind dramas about interactions between good and evil. When Judith went down to the Assyrian camp it was because she had become obsessed by fantasies about Holofernes: the saving of Bethulia was incidental to her sexual desires – it was almost admittedly her excuse. The Jews even seemed to accept much of this: sexual passion has its mumbo-jumbo, I suppose, almost as much as have ideas about God. So there, by the second act, was Judith all dressed up and taken in to Holofernes; and Holofernes was enthralled by her of course; but then – such were the conventions of the time – how could they show the uniqueness, the completeness, the eternality as it were of their love: they could not just do the usual, of course, because then where would be the magnificence, the drama? They had to start talking about death: was this not what lovers a hundred years ago always seemed to have to talk about – death as the only suitable and perfect apotheosis of love? So Holofernes didn't even have to get drunk and pass out: Judith chopped his head off because in some fashionable manner she simply loved him so much and he loved her: this was their destiny: he would be hers for ever, and she could carry his head around in her bag. (Who on earth got hooked by this stuff? not you: not you?) Perhaps men in the audiences could go home (perhaps even as Jews and Assyrians might have gone home?) comforted by the enchantment of such a demonstration; their heads tucked up as it were in the bags of beautiful women, their mothers.

When the revival of this play came to the West End some seventy years later it was of course more difficult to get away with this sort of thing; romantic passion was as much out of favour as ideas about God's will. But there was a nostalgia about seeing great actors and actresses perform; and great performances could only be given in something of the style of these old dramas.

The star whom I was understudying had as it happened

become notorious in real life for something of this old style: in innumerable newspaper stories she was portrayed as a gobbler-up of men – someone who indeed might carry scalps home in baskets and hang them on her wall. She was a small fierce woman with big breasts. Sometimes her energy and rage seemed to get turned against herself: there had been photographs of her carried from her home on a stretcher with blankets up to her chin.

For this production of *Judith*, professionally and personally, she had gone back to one of her ex-husbands who once had been a star in his own right. He was a tall gangling man who was known to be a drunk: he would sometimes spin about the stage like a top running down; lurch into furniture and footlights as if in search of some disaster to whip him up. He and his ex-wife came together, split up, came together again; the public loved these old-fashioned dramas when they were in newspapers and thus could be treated as occurrences that could not happen to them. So when it was known that ex-husband-and-wife were coming together again to be in this play *Judith* there was excitement and speculation. For had there not been a time when in fact she had gone at him (so the story went) with a carving knife? and he had been photographed later coming out of the door of a nursing home on the arm of his new girlfriend and saying – Yes, we still hope to be able to have children. So what might happen now when Judith took that sword from its sheath? Might there not be two heads, one false and one real – Holofernes having been caught flirting in the wings perhaps with one of the Assyrian slave-girls – rolling, when the time came, towards the footlights?

I myself happened to be one of the Assyrian handmaidens: it was my job to get Judith dolled up for her big night with Holofernes. I used to think – Women have always known, even if they cannot talk about, the way in which good can come out of evil?

There was a night – the play had been running for a few weeks – when it seemed that Holofernes was even more drunk than usual; he had been bobbing about in the corridors like a cork in a rough sea; he did not make his entrance until the second act, the scene of which was in his tent. This act started with the dolling-up of Judith: myself and another girl attended her with combs, scents and ointments. There was some rage within her this night like the mouth of a steel trap: there had been some row in the interval; shouting had been heard in her dressing-room; doors had slammed. When Holofernes did make his entrance – coming in from a day of war in full and shining armour – it was evident immediately that whatever had been happening behind the scenes was to be carried on to the stage: Holofernes had his helmet on back to front: this might not have been noticed – it was one of those helmets with a crest that might go this way or that – except that after Holofernes had taken one look at Judith he walked to the front of the stage and winked and put a finger to his lips: then he raised and lowered his eyebrows several times. The audience began to laugh. Holofernes did not in fact have much to say directly after his entrance: he was supposed to stare at Judith passionately and silently while his generals discussed the battle and the handmaidens came to divest him of his armour. But now he seemed to have stopped acting. It is difficult to say of what this impression consists. He gazed at Judith ruminatively, as if he were wondering what he should do. There was the impression that he seemed to have a choice.

The other handmaiden and I undressed him. During this scene it had always been as if we were preparing some victim. I had thought – Surely people will not for ever be getting their thrills from this?

On this night Judith reclined on her couch with her mouth, her breasts, like some giant clam at the bottom of the ocean.

When Holofernes did embark on his main dialogue with Judith he got most of his lines right: I mean he got the sequence of words right – the stuff about the fulfilment of love only being found perfectly in death, and so on – but it was as if he were also at the same time wondering about what he was saying; as if he might at any moment break off and exclaim –

Listen to this! Or even – What frightful rubbish! He was still half turning to the audience as if to ask – Well what do you make of it? And the audience was becoming half hypnotised. There was something powerful about this acting or non-acting that I had not experienced before – there was an impression that what was really happening was going on elsewhere. And Judith, I suppose, was being upstaged; she was still trying to act in the grand style; but being on stage she could not get at Holofernes personally, it was as if she were trapped. Holofernes' voice became dreamy, self-reflective, sing-song; he looked up at the sky; some of the audience continued to laugh. But for the most part there was an air of expectancy: was, or was not, something of a quite unusual kind about to happen?

Myself and the other handmaiden finished the taking-off of Holofernes' armour; we stood back; there remained on him just some grotesque metal codpiece fastened by straps at the back. He had somehow got the straps twisted and jammed; we had tried to right them, but the buckle would not move. When Holofernes went over to join Judith on her couch, the dialogue took on some ludicrous immediate relevance – what torments there were for people trapped by desire! what resolution might there be indeed except by giving up the whole charade! And so on. And then the time came for the removal of the codpiece.

Holofernes, on Judith's couch, had been pulling at the straps at his back for some time; he was getting nowhere; the audience began to sense they were on the edge of the catastrophe that they had (or perhaps after all had not?) desired. Their laughter went to and fro in gusts: there were sudden appalled silences. After a time Holofernes turned to the audience, his hands still on his straps, and made one of his comic wide-eyed faces with his eyebrows going up and down. Then he stood, came to the centre of the stage, and did, perfectly for a moment, one of those funny walks that Charlie Chaplin used to do of someone pulling himself up and along by the seat of his trousers. This, in the context, had an extraordinary effect. It was as if some comment were being made on the whole business of acting from as it were another dimension. I think at that moment I knew I would never be a great tragic actress.

Judith got up from her couch, went to the centre of the stage, got hold of the straps at the back of Holofernes codpiece, and gave them a tremendous heave. Holofernes seemed to be lifted almost off his feet. Then Judith went back to her couch.

She reclined on one elbow again, watching him. I thought – You mean, like this, the story of Judith and Holofernes might not after all have to end in a conventional blood-bath?

Holofernes appeared to be immobilised – like an old horse dangled from a crane above a ship. There were one or two screams as well as laughter from the audience. From the back, bits of Holofernes' flesh bulged out. I wondered – Has something appalling happened to his front?

There was a time during which nothing much happened: Holofernes seemed to dangle with one foot half off the ground: Judith continued to size him up like meat. I wondered if, eventually, the curtain would have to come down. But it did still seem as if some electrifying performance was continuing. After a time noise from the audience stopped. I thought – But the point of this non-acting is still, yes, that one is somehow involved in choice?

I left the back of the stage and went to Holofernes' front: I saw that yes, indeed, one of his balls had come half out of his codpiece and was squashed against his thigh. It was like one of those globules that you can make from burst balloons; he was doing nothing to free it; he was I suppose getting some satisfaction, as an actor might indeed, from the enthralment of his audience. It might have been agony also, of course; do you not have to pay for such powerful effects? His face, anyway, seemed to be in pain. I knelt down in front of him and pulled at the bottom of his codpiece; his ball, like a sea-anemone, popped back inside. He said in a deep voice 'Thank you, my dear.' The audience remained hushed. I went back to where I had been standing.

Now there was something extraordinary that continued

here: Holofernes went on with his non-acting: I mean he said his lines, but it was as if at the same time he was showing that he knew this wasn't the point: as if he expected you – you on the stage (myself) and you in the audience (you?) – to know that something quite different was going on: as if he expected you to be sharing his interest even in whatever it was that was really happening as it were off-stage. And this was working. I mean it seemed to be working for the audience: it was even working, now, for Judith too. She stopped her histrionics: she became caught up in some style that was quiet, ironic, self-reflective. It was as if she were saying her lines and at the same time saying – Well, you see, we have got through one absurd drama, haven't we; and now we can calm down; so what about Judith and Holofernes? And the effect that this produced was curiously like some powerful moments in life: for do not humans for the most part, of course, talk the most fearful rubbish? But then, if they know this, are not the moments when this knowingness breaks through not to do with rubbish? The audience anyway seemed to catch the feel of this: Judith and Holofernes were, after all, giving uniquely extraordinary performances. They did their whole love scene, seduction scene, passion-and-death scene, in this style – as if this were indeed, yes, the sort of fix that poor humans found themselves in: but what an odd joke it was! and might there not still be something dignified in the fact that humans could see this? The two of them, after all, were perhaps for once being honest and even gentle with one another. And so at the end of this second act, when Judith and Holofernes went off to the alcove to go to bed or to the beheading or whatever it was, they had their arms round one another and it was as if they might really be in love, as they were supposed to be in the script and as I suppose they were in life; but they were not going to die; perhaps they would not even have to pretend to die; perhaps they would have a nice time even; this was, was it not, the unique theatrical experience.

There was a long interval in which no one quite knew what was happening, neither behind the stage nor I suppose in front;

no one talked about it much; what was there to say? what had happened did not seem to be much within the area of what could be talked about. Judith and Holofernes had barricaded themselves in her dressing-room; perhaps in fact they were making love; they did not come out; there was the sound, after a time, of someone crying. Eventually the stage manager got into the dressing-room, and when he came out he said the performance was over. He went in front of the curtain – the audience had remained largely seated during the interval – and announced that the leading lady was indisposed. It was interesting that he said it was the leading lady who was indisposed: I thought – You mean, she takes the responsibility? I sat on a fallen pillar at the side of the stage and wondered if I might have my chance now of taking over from Judith; but I did not think I would be asked to; and I found that I did not mind if I was not. In a sense I had taken over something (but what?) when I had stepped out of context and had helped Holofernes. But this had not helped, of course, the continuation of the play.

The play ran for a few more nights, or a week even, and then it folded. I mean the audience on the night had been enthralled, but they probably could not remember except as a joke what they had been enthralled by; and the actors anyway could not or did not reproduce it. Judith and Holofernes went through the motions – half in the old style, half in the new – but they could not gather again the effects of that night, which perhaps after all had depended on chance and unique circumstances. So audiences, finding nothing now that they could enjoy, let alone put into words, became hostile to the actor and actress; and people stopped coming to the play.

For myself – I was not sure if I wanted to go on being an actress: but then no one, for a time, asked me to. No one talked to me about the scene when I had stepped forwards and freed Holofernes' ball: no one talked about the scene afterwards when Judith and Holofernes had acted as if they were not acting. I suppose I don't quite know how to talk about this either. But this is the point, isn't it? – you can't talk much in real life about how things might be all right. When the play folded, Judith and Holofernes just sent me, from the two of them together, an enormous bunch of red roses.

My dream in coming to London (I had spent time on the way at a university on the West Coast of America) had been that here I would find people who were sophisticated and witty – who were not in the business of owning a percentage of everyone else. To some extent I found this with theatre people; but they still seemed to have their eyes on bits and pieces of others; not so much it is true for the sake of money, as out of some need or even demand to be appreciated.

When I did not get any work in the theatre I got that job as a sort of companion at the house in Ruskin Square: this was when you (and you?) first saw me. I used to take that dog for walks in the square.

The people I came across there were not trying to be elegant or witty: they were interested in money; but for the most part they were obsessed by gossip about people.

One group that I kept on hearing about which did seem likely to be at least witty was one that was involved in the actual business of providing gossip – the satire-and-scandal business – one which publicised and ridiculed the goings-on of the successful and notorious for the delectation of those who were neither but who seemed to need this gossip like some sort of food. These satire-and-scandal people were centred on a glossy magazine which was nicknamed *Die Flamme*: I am going to call it *Die Flamme* because (or although?) I am not sure about libel, though the people who ran the magazine seemed impervious to concern about libel. The original *Die Flamme* (as it were: do you not know this) was a magazine run by the Nazis in the 1930s to abuse and ridicule people who differed from themselves; this nickname for the latter-day *Die Flamme* was I suppose unfair, but it was true that part of its style was to insult people in ways that made it difficult for them to answer back – and by this to gain popularity and prestige. It was not easy for those insulted to reply successfully because the

Die Flamme people could switch from saying their stories were true to claiming they were obviously a joke: they prided themselves on performing a genuine public service in shedding light on murky corners, but there was also the suggestion that no one need believe what they said.

Before I arrived in London I had wanted to meet these satire-and-scandal people: their fame had spread to America. I was in this sense a child of my time, in that I was interested in the pecking orders of society. I am not ashamed about this; however you grow, you grow out of where you start from. And perhaps here I have always seen myself in relation to society in some way like Judith in relation to the Assyrians.

So this is not going to be one of those stories of a girl coming to London from the colonies or ex-colonies and being bitched and battered and bewildered: all this sort of thing has been done: it is not difficult, I suppose, to go on getting satisfaction from hearing the stories. But the point of Judith, wasn't it, was that she gave some impression of control – I mean she called it God's will, but she must have felt it as control. I had felt for some time that women opted out of what might be their special faculties for control – opted out, I mean, by taking refuge either in subservience to men or nowadays by making themselves become like men when what they know and complain about almost in the same breath is that men are like babies. The ways in which there might be (and indeed often is, but so secretly!) feminine control were almost never talked about: perhaps they are too frightening; perhaps they are too close, yes, to the story of Judith and Holofernes.

It was known that the *Die Flamme* people used to meet once or twice a week in a pub: they did this to discuss what they would put in their magazine; to toss bits of gossip and jokes about like bread or sausages across a table. I think they also did this just to be on show: they needed to exhibit themselves so that the public could be in the way of feeding them with the raw materials of gossip; then they could feed the public with processed gossip back in return. Their needs were not so different from those of show-business people; but show-business people usually want to be loved, and I think the *Die Flamme* people mostly wanted to be feared.

I went to this pub one evening with my friend from Ruskin Square (I wanted to get out of that job; it was not much of a job; it was not much, goodness knows, in the pecking order). We went to the pub to have a look: to become part of a crowd that gathers at feeding time at the zoo. All the *Die Flamme* people I had heard of were there – the one with short legs, the one with granny specs, the woman with hair like epaulets. They were in a part of the pub that seemed to have been specially cordoned off for them: it might once have been used for playing billiards. They were around a table, seven or eight, with glasses of beer in front of them; they were bobbing backwards and forwards, exclaiming, making faces, laughing. Every now and then one or another of them would pick up a piece of paper and read something out; look over the tops of his or her spectacles owl-like, performing. For a moment everyone would be still; then they would all be bobbing backwards and forwards again, laughing. They were like one of those clockwork tableaux in Disneyland in which animals mime the goings-on of humans: there is one called The Bear's Jazz Band; the bears go through the motions of strumming banjos, beating drums, blowing saxophones; crowds come to watch – why? – because there is some ghastly reassurance in the odd things humans do being done by animals? then, does it matter so much if the things humans do are ridiculous? Anyway, there was quite a crowd in the pub watching the *Die Flamme* people: it was as if some sort of glamour might rub off, rub on, just by the fact of watching and being watched. We were most of us pretending not wholeheartedly to watch: this not-being-quite-there seemed necessary for sophistication.

One of the people at the *Die Flamme* table was Desmond. I did not know him at the time: I am going to call him Desmond. This is the beginning of the story that I have to tell you, really.

Desmond was not quite like the other members of the

14

group; he got his timing slightly off-beat for rocking backwards and forwards. He had rather long blond hair and a narrow face; he smoked a pipe; he seemed to be caricaturing Englishness. He was the only one of the *Die Flamme* people who could be called attractive.

I thought I would pick up Desmond.

I suppose this is one of the things it should be difficult to write about, women in stories having got used to seeing themselves as victims – I mean, in stories written by women. Of course, there are those phantoms with snakes in their hair in stories written by men. Perhaps everyone gets a kick out of seeing themselves as a victim.

But the point of Judith was that she did not; was it not?

I had learned how to do this sort of thing from my father's old friend Miss Julie from Hong Kong (there is something incongruous about my father here: for the most part he appeared to be a typical academic). What you do is – stand in profile, one foot in front of the other, front knee slightly bent, toe pointing to the ground; as if you were within the frame of a picture; something like a Degas dancer perhaps; or one of those outdoor girls (Courbet?) feeling the temperature of some water. You do not, of course, aim directly at being like one of the girls of Miss Julie of Hong Kong – one hip jutting, framed within a doorway – however much the effect of this sort of thing might be what you require. But one of the points about art is to make something like seduction aesthetic, is it not? Anyway, if you stand like this, and become yourself like a painting – well, what do you think a painting is or does? does it not attract? has it not some force, or field, like gravity?

Anyway, Desmond looked at me, did not look at me; looked at me, did not look at me. There was the counter-pull, of course, of the force of the *Die Flamme* people. Amongst animals this sort of thing is to do with smell. Humans have largely lost the faculties that go with smell. They pop up again, perhaps, with things like works of art; with paintings.

I did not think Desmond would be able to make any positive move on his own: the weight of the *Die Flamme* people would be like inertia. And Englishmen, it seemed to me then, had not only lost, as it were, their sense of smell but had got out of the way of picking up women even for the sake of prestige in the pecking order. They seemed to fear (also perhaps to desire?) the chance of getting chopped up like Holofernes.

Well, what might Judith do in this interesting situation?

My friend and I sometimes played darts in pubs. He would hold his dart in front of his mouth with his little finger crooked as if he were sipping tea. I liked playing darts because I could ruminate about how one day, if I practised painstakingly enough, I might be able to step up and almost without looking get all three darts one on top of another in the bull's-eye – as Zen Buddhists say can happen if one practises correctly for years and years for instance at archery.

There was a dart-board in another compartment of the pub. I remembered a scene in a novel I had once read in which a girl throws a dart right over the partition of a pub. I thought – I will be like Artemis with Orion: if I throw a dart carefully enough, I will get it over the partition and lodged in the woodwork somewhere near Desmond. Then I can go round and – how supplicatingly! (one knee in front of the other) – ask forgiveness for such lack of control. But, in fact, I could not quite remember what had happened between Artemis and Orion; she had killed him, had she not? But there have to be risks, don't there, in any change of the *status quo*.

My friend and I went into the next compartment to play darts. After a time I threw a dart so that it landed in the woodwork not far from Desmond's ear. Oh one does, yes, feel ashamed of these things; there are many things of this time that I shall be telling you of which I am ashamed. I felt, I think, as one is supposed to feel as I followed the dart into the other part of the pub – Dear God, I might have hit him! I promise I will never do this sort of thing again! I stood in front of Desmond and said 'I'm so terribly, terribly sorry.' The point is very nearly to mean it; perhaps not quite. Desmond was acting as if the dart had in fact pierced his ear; he was holding his head stiffly against the woodwork. He said 'Will someone kindly tell me exactly what has occurred?' The man with the granny specs said 'The missile I think has pierced your left ear.' The woman with hair like epaulets said 'Is that the ear that you wanted to have pierced?' People laughed; rocked backwards and forwards. I leaned across Desmond to get the dart out of the woodwork. I thought – There will be that smell of cloth, of dust, of energy – like that of a dancer. The man with short legs said 'Please may I have my ear pierced?' Everyone laughed again. I stood in front of Desmond with my hands clasped in front of me: I thought – I do not want to be too openly pornographic. I said 'What can I do to make up; can I offer you dinner?'

Desmond said 'I'll give you dinner.'

I said 'No, I've got to do something to make up.'

There was not much more to be done. I waited while Desmond went through the motions of finishing his business with the *Die Flamme* people. I did not have trouble with my darts-playing friend. Each of us I suppose by now wanted to be rid of the other: there are virtues, as well as boredom, in being distanced from the style of old passions. Also there was satisfaction for my friend I think in his handing me on to someone higher up, as it were, in the pecking order: some of the glamour of the *Die Flamme* people might even rub off on him.

It had not been like this where I had been brought up: there was always the chance, if you were a girl in a doorway, of a killer with a knife being round some corner.

Desmond said 'Shall we go?'

I said 'Yes.' Then – 'Where?'

He said 'You have to choose!'

There was something here that I had noticed when I first came to London – the games-playing that went on in the business of choosing restaurants. It was men, of course, who were still nominally supposed to choose: but they seemed to have lost confidence in this, and women seemed often to be ensuring that this should be so – complaining of the table, of the music, picking at the food; ordering strange salads that could not be provided. But women, of course, still wanted it to be men who made the choice. Now I found myself in the position of the chooser. I thought – You close your eyes, do you: and after years and years, as with Zen archery, you get somewhere near the bull's-eye?

Desmond was the first man I had met who seemed to admit this predicament. He said 'How marvellous not to be expected to decide about restaurants!'

Desmond was this tall, good-looking Englishman. He wore a cap and a tweed jacket with leather patches on the elbows. I thought – He is like someone coming back from being with horses, or from the First World War.

But still – What on earth do you do about restaurants? No wonder men go off to things like race meetings and wars!

I thought I might say – I have been told of a good one just round this corner –

'Here!'

'Wow! Are you sure?'

'Yes.'

'It looks a bit expensive!'

But then when we were inside, and had been sat down in armchairs, and menus had been placed in front of us like musical scores, and I had thought – Dear God, what should women do: of course it is easy to mock men's pretensions – Desmond put his hand on my arm and said 'Look here, I'm paying.'

I said 'No you're not.'

He said 'Yes I am.'

I said 'Well, we'll go fifty-fifty.'

I thought – This is right? What I admire is people wanting to get the best of both worlds?

Of course, I wanted to admire Desmond.

During dinner Desmond talked: he talked about the state of the country, the state of the world. He talked sometimes looking at me and then, when I looked at him, looking away: he talked as if he were a circus tamer warding off a tiger with a stick. He talked about politics: he said politics were either sinister or a farce: power was exercised by mad freaks crouched over gambling tables: the conspiracy theory of history both was and was not true – there really were conspirators who ran the world, some conglomeration of capitalist millionaires and communist élites, and yet all this was still a game; things went their own way in fact by chance. I got the impression that he was saying all this because this was his particular game; he happened to like these words: he liked them perhaps because they were incongruous with his rather respectable appearance; the question about whether or not they were true did not mean much to him. I suppose he was a child of his time in this lack of regard for what might be true: what was necessary was to make an impact: he could not easily see the impact, in the society in which he found himself, of what was true.

All this, of course, might have been something to do with me. We were in this restaurant with mirrors and cut glass and flowers. Sometimes he stretched a hand across the table and laid it on my arm; then he would withdraw it, as if he had advanced too far into no man's land. This was a style he had picked up from his ancestors I suppose: you do not over-commit yourself with women; you keep open your lines of retreat; you protect your flanks; is not that what you say? I do not know how to write about Desmond. Of course it is terrible when, in war, soldiers die.

I said 'Do you live in London?'

He said 'Not exactly.'

I said 'Where do you live?'

He blew his cheeks out and frowned. I thought – These are his signals for a tactical retreat? One of the ideas I had picked up from Miss Julie from Hong Kong was although there is this theory that all men at all times are longing to go to bed with women (Miss Julie would say – There they are with their insides hanging out, poor dears!) in fact what they want to do is more to make a song and dance about it but in the end not go to bed; to pass out perhaps like Holofernes; to go home and if necessary have what Miss Julie called a quiet pull. (– They have to do something with those insides, poor dears!) Miss Julie's idea was that men nowadays did not much want to go to bed with women because they felt themselves vulnerable to women's criticism of their performances there (just as I suppose they felt themselves vulnerable in the matter of choice of restaurants); but it was useful to both sides to keep up the pretence about men's insatiable desires, because thus men could retain some pride and women their liking for complaint.

The way out of this predicament, Miss Julie suggested, was what it always had been before the curse of romantic puritanism came along, which was that men and women should go to bed together for money: with money you knew where you were; there was no question of anyone expecting anything different from what was offered and what was paid for. Here men and women achieved some functioning equality.

Desmond said 'You live in London?'

I said 'Yes.'

'Can we go somewhere?'

'If you like.'

He said 'But not tonight. I'm afraid I've got to get home.'

He explained that he had a wife and child somewhere on the outskirts of London. As he told me this he drew heavy lines on the tablecloth with his fork. I thought I might say – We could go to my place. But this was not strictly true, and I did not think there would be any point in challenging Desmond's defenceworks.

He said 'But we will one day, won't we?'

I said 'Of course.'

I had not worked out, then, much about the *Die Flamme* people; but it had seemed from their magazine that much of their cruelty, their arrogance, might be to do with some system of defenceworks. They were most of them, I learned later, somewhat religiously puritanical about sex: they exposed and lacerated others, not risking being exposed and lacerated themselves.

20

Miss Julie once said – But of course men want to be taken over! to be sent to bed and tucked up like naughty babies!

Looking across the table at Desmond I thought – You mean, it might be easier for you if I ordered you to come home and –

Miss Julie had said – Don't get involved in that, my dear; they'll be so pleased, they'll never forgive you!

Desmond was like one of those heroic blond beasts: did they not in the end want to get themselves torn to pieces?

He said 'In about a fortnight?'

I said 'All right.'

I thought – But the world might have come to an end in a fortnight!

Do you think I might always have had some sort of wish to destroy Desmond? Do women have such a rage against men?

So Desmond and I took to having dinner two or three times a week, and afterwards he would catch the last train home to wherever it was in Buckinghamshire. Of course in some sense we became lovers: I would go with him to the station and we would say good-bye as if we were in one of those 1940s films; how can you have all that heaving about in taxis, on station platforms, unless you are being kept apart like people in a 1940s film? If there is no war, then at least you have to be trying to be faithful to a wife and a child in Buckinghamshire. But then – perhaps Desmond and I really were a bit in love. I liked being taken round by him: I liked being on show with the *Die Flamme* people. Perhaps Desmond liked showing me off as his girl. Is there not always something narcissistic about being in love?

From time to time he would say 'I really am going to fix up a room one day in London!'

I have this need to try to understand Desmond. I think it is not so much a rage that women have against men, as a guilt about feeling that in many areas men have been made redundant.

Desmond was one of the bright not-quite-so-young writers on *Die Flamme* magazine; his job was to take stories from gossip or newspapers and to spin elaborate fantasies from them. The point was deliberately that readers should not quite know what was a fantasy and what was not; in this style any wild story might purvey some thrill – it might be true, and if it were not, then indeed where was the reader's sense of humour! I do not know how Desmond had started on this job; he had wanted to be a writer; but there was a part of him that seemed always to be saying – But don't you see that life is venomous! And so *Die Flamme* magazine became a home for him; because there was something very practically, and powerfully, successful about its venom. Several people who worked for *Die Flamme* magazine called themselves Christians (Desmond was a Catholic) but it seemed to me they were more like Manichaeans – if you think the world is irredeemably evil then you have no responsibility for it; you can do what you like; you have some licence simply to amuse and to be amused.

Or perhaps it was just that the *Die Flamme* people had been to English public schools; and their contacts with their own and other people's bodies had been often to do with cruelty.

Desmond would sometimes bring in to the pubs or restaurants where we met a bundle of newspaper cuttings which had been gathered for him by a secretary; he would read out items in funny voices and then would put the papers on the table and would draw lines round paragraphs with a red pencil as if he were marking out bombing areas for an attack.

There was one story being run by *Die Flamme* at this time which was about a left-wing politician whom they called Dirty Lenin. Dirty Lenin had at one time been caught (or had he? but this uncertainty was the point) doing something in the City with what are called bonds; there had been an activity called washing bonds, which was improper. So when the *Die Flamme* people made this public, they called the bond-washer Dirty Lenin: do you see? Do you? Another of the points of this stuff is that a reader may feel himself in the know; one of an élite. For this, of course, it does not matter whether or not a story is true.

When questioned, Desmond would puff his cheeks out and reach for his pipe. He would say – Well he's an arrogant sod anyway.

Oh, I might have felt some enmity against Desmond!

There was an evening when Desmond did have to stay up in London for the night: he had a date with some television people early in the morning. We had dinner together; he frowned and blew his cheeks out: I wondered if he might say something like – I have a headache: what bad luck! I did see, of course, that he probably loved his wife. Up till recently I had still been staying in that house in Ruskin Square; this had been a suitable background for whatever strange business it was that Desmond and I were up to: I mean he could frown at me intently and say – Ah, it would be different, wouldn't it, if we could go back to your place! And so he need not feel guilty – or too absurd. But just recently I had moved out of Ruskin Square and had gone to stay in a cheap hotel, or hostel, at the back of Victoria Station. I had not told Desmond about this (I have not told you! but this is another story). Perhaps I did not want to put burdens on to him. But then when he and I were having dinner that evening and he was frowning and blowing even more portentously than usual, eventually he said 'But the terrible thing is I'm booked in to stay with friends!' And I thought – But this is beyond even being ridiculous! At the same time, however, he also looked so miserable that I thought – Perhaps after all his burden is not that he thinks he might almost have to go to bed with me but that he has to go through all this rubbish every time; and might he not long to be liberated from this? So I said (what are the connections here, between good and evil!) 'Well, we could go back to my place.'

He said 'To Ruskin Square?'

I said 'No, I've moved out.'

He said 'Where have you moved to?'

He seemed genuinely both excited and alarmed. I thought – Is it some sort of childishness that I love about Desmond?

I said 'I'm in a sort of small hotel at the back of Victoria Station.'

He did not, of course, ask how on earth I had got there. I thought – When he makes marks on the tablecloth with his fork it is, yes, his anxieties that he is defending or attacking.

He said 'We can go there?'

I said 'If you like.'

He said 'Of course I like!'

I thought – He is like someone who has been told he will be the first passenger to the moon.

What I did not tell him (well, there are these things that you wanted me to tell you) was that one of the reasons I had left Ruskin Square was that I had become friendly with an Indian boy who was some sort of revolutionary: he was also the receptionist, or doorkeeper, at this hotel or hostel at the back of Victoria Station. I mean he had a room in the basement and I had a room on the top floor: but there we were. There was no reason, really, why I should not go with anyone I liked to my room: but what have things in this area got to do with reason?

Desmond said 'How wonderful!'

Outside the restaurant Desmond looked for a taxi; he stood with his arm raised like the Statue of Liberty. I thought – Whatever happens will not exactly be my fault; or is it true that women like men fighting duels? In the taxi Desmond and I carried on like the people in a 1940s film; I mean we sat rather bleakly holding hands. I thought – But those people often could only do it, didn't it seem, if it was mixed up with going off to war? And so, might we not have to make our own war? And then – What if women do like men fighting duels?

The Indian boy was waiting on the steps outside the hostel. I had thought he might be. He watched us as we got out of the taxi and came up the steps. I was still trying to work out – You mean, this is one of the things you can't work out, the chances of good coming out of evil? At the top of the steps the Indian boy held out his arm and said 'This man cannot come in here.' The Indian boy was rather small and beautiful: he was called Krishna: he was like that person playing a flute. Desmond said 'Why can I not come in here?' Krishna said 'Residents only after half-past ten.' Desmond said 'This lady and I wish to have coffee in the lounge.' I thought – So how, after all, did those people in the 1940s ever get to bed? Krishna said 'There is no lounge.' I suppose I might have whispered to Krishna; to have tried to put things right; but the paralysis in such a context is that one does not know what is right. Desmond said 'This lady has paid for her room, has she not?' Krishna said 'You get moving.' We were standing around on the top of the steps with nothing much happening. Then Krishna said 'And don't let me see your face around here again!'

This was the sort of phrase, I suppose, that might have been shouted at one of Krishna's ancestors by – whom? – one of Desmond's ancestors, in the far-off days of the British Raj?

Desmond said 'Don't you speak to me like that!'

I thought – There might be something sparked off, even now, as a result of these echoes of the British Raj?

Desmond tried to push past Krishna to go in at the door of the hotel. Krishna got hold of him. I had noticed before that when men start to fight they do not stand back and slog at one another as they do in American films; they take hold of each other by the elbows or shoulders and seem to dance; it is more like the sort of fighting they do in Thailand – they shuffle, and look down at their legs, and try to trip one another up. The Indian boy was much shorter than Desmond so that it was easier for him to get at Desmond's feet; also he was probably more practised. Desmond was like someone in the process of moving heavy furniture. After a time he fell, and pulled Krishna down on top of him: there was a peculiar moment when it was as if they were making love. Then Krishna got a knee into Desmond's groin and Desmond got a hand free and punched Krishna in the face. Then Krishna got up and ran into the hallway of the hotel and came out carrying a knife. I began to shout obscenities at him: this was what I had been told was the thing to do in such circumstances by Miss Julie of Hong Kong. I don't know why it works: except perhaps that what gives relief in these circumstances is any contact with what is obscene. Krishna stood with his arms hanging down. I thought – So what am I doing? it is with him, is it, now, that I want to go to bed? Desmond got up and went into the hall of the hotel and looked around as if for something to smash. He picked up a small wooden table; then he put it down, and came and rejoined me on the steps. He said 'We can go to another hotel.' I said 'Yes.' I wanted to say to Krishna – I'm so sorry! I only wanted to talk to this man! It won't take long!

The taxi was still waiting at the bottom of the steps. I thought – Taxi-drivers are people who expect these things to happen as if in a 1940s film?

I said to Desmond 'Where shall we go?'

He said 'To the Ritz.'

I said 'The Ritz!'

I did admire Desmond then. I thought – He knows, does he, about those days when people like his ancestors fought duels?

Desmond said 'When it is the middle of the night, and you have no luggage, and you have been kicked in the balls – always go to the Ritz!'

I said 'I'm so sorry!'

He said 'Oh that's all right.'

Then – 'It's a wilful Indian that blows nobody any good.'

On our way to the Ritz I did not know whether Desmond would be able to pull this off; but he did seem to be taking on a slightly different and older personality – older both historically and in himself – something blooded, I suppose, and thus more authoritative; some younger son of the aristocracy perhaps just back from the coast of Coromandel or the cataracts of the Upper Nile; his baggage shipwrecked on some quicksands *en route*; and so here he was now cast ashore with his young wife. Or this could be the story – it was only necessary, surely, to have a good story. I thought – If Desmond gets away with this it will be some achievement in the masculine world equivalent to the subtle expertise of Miss Julie from Hong Kong.

At the Ritz there were two men behind a table who were impassive while Desmond spoke. I thought – A story is believed because of its style: if it is aesthetic, does this make it effective too?

Desmond said 'I'm so terribly sorry to be a nuisance like this, but we are in some sense in the position of King Lear in the storm.'

One of the men behind the table pushed forward a card for Desmond to sign.

We were taken up by a page-boy to a room which was of cream and blue and gold. Desmond gave the page-boy two pounds. I thought – He knows the right amount, two pounds?

I said to Desmond 'I think you are wonderful!'

I thought – You mean, I really might mean this?

There is the feeling of being alone in a hotel room with someone for the first time which is like that, I suppose, of being in a bullring: you walk round, looking for corners where you might be safe. I thought – How difficult, indeed, to be a man! to be like an old horse with all your insides having to hang out.

Since Desmond had not wanted before to take me to a hotel room I had assumed that what he was scared of was – the usual.

I thought – But he has done his stuff: now it is up to me, Miss Julie from Hong Kong!

I said 'Does it hurt?'

He said 'A bit.'

I said 'Let me see.'

There was an old film – do you remember? – in which Brigitte Bardot had been making men impotent right and left and then two of them had a fight and one of them got kicked in the balls and it was this one, of course, with whom Brigitte Bardot eventually condescended to go to bed: and things then, of course, were supposed to be all right. But in fact, are there not more complex activities needed in the area between evil and good, if things are to be all right?

I said 'Here?'

He said 'Yes.'

I said 'It doesn't look as if you've been hurt!'

What you have to do, I think, is to become quite rapt, and yet dispassionate; rapt, and yet dispassionate; getting carried away, and letting things come together; playing a game, and getting a root down deep; so that what eventually, by skill, is tapped, is – oil, gas, fire. You have to breathe, so your breath has flames about it; this is the area that was once covered by smell. There comes a moment, yes, when reality takes over.

I said 'Good heavens, you better always be hurt!'

Desmond said 'So what are you going to do about it?'

I said 'This? This? You were quite cruel, were you not, to that nice Indian boy!'

For a short while you can make the game, which is in the mind, come out, work.

Then once we got started, Desmond took on what is called the masculine role: he became like the figurehead of a ship. I thought – But then why is it women who are the figureheads of ships?

After a time Desmond made a noise like a foghorn.

I thought – So we have avoided the rocks: we have carried out cleverly the tasks of our journey: he will not now say, will he – Was that all right?

He said 'Why are you smiling?' Then that thing in Latin that people say when you smile – '*Post coitum omne animal triste est.*'

I thought – What would it be like really to be in love? You would not talk? You would have no language? It would be like being in a painting with just – a house, a snake, a tree?

Then – But I have got what I have wanted, haven't I? I am with one of the *Die Flamme* people: I am in bed at the Ritz Hotel.

Then – You mean, people are sometimes sad just when they get what they want?

Now there is something that I want to put in here (lying in my bath the next morning at the Ritz Hotel) which is that however much this is a story of someone on the make and even imagining they might have reached somewhere such as Holofernes' tent (Desmond had gone off to his appointment with the television people) – however much this is true, and however much I was at the same time pleased because I had had fun and yet somewhat ashamed of this being true, the side of me that was ashamed (or is shame not the word? the side of me that always seemed to be waiting for something quite different round some corner), this is a story about this too. I had glimpses of what it might be every now and then: it was as if I were walking up a spiral staircase and there were here and there very narrow windows; I could not see much through; but it was as if there were opposite me another tower containing another spiral staircase with windows; and there might be a chance of my coinciding with someone else at a window; and we might at least (but this might be enough!) wave to each other and say – Coo-ee!

I was reminded of one such moment in my bath at the Ritz Hotel.

(You have a glimpse of me through a window of my staircase? a girl compact, did you not once call me, Bert – with light strong limbs and dark curly hair –)

I had been at the university on the West Coast of America and there was a lecture one evening from a visiting English professor: he was called Professor Ackerman: I thought the lecture sounded interesting and decided to go. This Professor had written a book which had become something of a cult among the anti-academic academics of the Coast: the Professor had been a biologist and a physicist and was now something called a cyberneticist; his book (so far as I could make out: people were apt to be inarticulate about it) was to do with the different levels at which, or from which, one could look at consciousness or learning or experience – what appeared to be an impossibility or a contradiction at one level became reconciled with itself on or from another. I was told that when people attended the Professor's lectures they were apt to have the impression that he was talking about something slightly different from what he was saying – as if he were using some code – people were hearing him on one level, but he seemed to be keeping something back on another. When he was challenged about this he would say – No, he was doing his best to say what he meant in the best way available to him; but of course all messages depended on the use and understanding of some code. This either irritated people or fascinated them according to – what? – temperament; choice; acquired taste?

At the beginning of his book he had put the quotation from St Mark's gospel in which Jesus explains why he speaks to people in parables – 'that seeing they may see and not perceive and hearing they may hear and not understand, lest at any time they should be converted and their sins should be forgiven them'.

There was a large crowd for the Professor's lecture: it was quiet and respectful. The Professor was a sturdy-looking man of, I supposed, about sixty: he had a nut-brown head and hair in a sort of laurel-wreath. When he spoke I did not feel that he was playing any trick; he seemed to watch his words as they came out of him to see how they were doing, but this for him seemed natural. He did sometimes, as if hearing himself, seem to be on the point of shaking his head or laughing: perhaps it was this that made people imagine he was thinking of something else. He also moved his eyes over his audience while he was speaking: this was as if he were trying to see where his words might land; as if he were saying – Is it you? is it you?

He talked about a dispute in the physical sciences that had been going on when he had been a student. There had been a dominant school of thought which had held (I may not get the words right: you know the code?) that when one talked about physical reality one found oneself inescapably involved in paradoxes: light was a matter of both particles and waves: one could measure either a particle's position or its velocity but not both at the same time. This had to be accepted: it was impossible to observe objectivity without objectivity being affected by that by which it was observed. There was a phrase that had been fashionable in this school of thought (I wrote it down) – 'Reality is a function of the experimental condition.' But there was another school, the Professor said (and it seemed that this was the one which he had liked to align himself with), which held that this sort of limitation was not so much to do with one's inability to know reality as with restrictions imposed on knowing by conceptual thought and language. What was necessary if one was to understand reality

– to see it as a whole, that is, which it was – was to have a more developed idea than usual of what could and could not be done by thought and language: to gain some glimpse of what might lie somehow elsewhere.

Or this is what I understood the Professor to say.

I felt also – He is talking to me? He will know, won't he, that his words are not falling on stony ground?

After the lecture there was an opportunity for people to come up and talk to the Professor: we assembled in a room where coffee and white wine and sandwiches were provided. People queued up for their turn to have their word; he sat in the corner with a special supply of whisky. He seemed both authoritative and yet almost in despair; as if he were benevolent, and yet possibly on the point of screaming like one of those paintings of people trapped in a glass case.

In the queue I rehearsed the opening lines of what I intended to say – What I am going to ask you might seem to have nothing to do with what you were saying: what I am going to ask you might seem to have nothing to do with what you were saying – but then, when my time came and I was in front of the Professor – he had such small amused bright eyes! – everything went out of my head; it was as if all the lights had come on in a theatre.

I said 'You know what you were saying about the experiments that you choose affecting what you call reality – '

He said 'Yes – '

I said 'Then could you not choose your experiments, in order to affect reality?'

He seemed to be thinking of something quite different for a time. He was looking over my shoulder.

He said 'You mean control it – '

I said 'Yes - '

He said 'You mean like an actress - '

I thought – You mean, you were once in love with someone like an actress?

He said 'You can do that for a time, and then you will stop; or else you will destroy yourself.'

I thought – He is seeing through me to the person he was in love with?

Then he put out a hand and touched me on the forehead.

He said 'Of course you can fix things, and you will succeed for a time: you have to do this, in fact, in order to stay alive. But if you're clever enough for this, then you'll know that it isn't reality. Reality is something beyond yourself: if it's not, what's the point? But it's where all meaning lives, and where all joy lives, and where all love lives: and don't you forget it.'

I said 'Right.'

He took his finger away from my forehead.

Then he said 'You may have to hit some kind of rock bottom.'

I thought – You mean, before I begin?

Then – But how will I know?

He raised the hand with which he had touched my forehead and he held his fingers pointed and then he opened and shut them once or twice as if they were the mouth of a bird. Then he said 'Coo-ee!'

It was this of which I was reminded in the bathroom of the Ritz Hotel. It seemed that I might now lift my hand up and wave to the Professor and say – Coo-ee!

I thought – But you don't mean, do you, that this is anywhere like rock bottom?

So it became established that Desmond and I were lovers: he would occasionally stay up in London for the night; he at last got a room in the flat of a friend where we sometimes went in the afternoons. But now this was done, what on earth was it that we were doing?

We had each been useful to the other as an idea: what was there when we looked at each other as persons?

Desmond, for instance, would hardly like to think he might be on some journey towards rock bottom.

The Professor's words did not seem difficult: when you think you control things, you do not move beyond what began as an idea.

Desmond and I would sit in cafés and pubs: we were like people in an advertisement: we were advertising – what? – that this was what people do who have become established as lovers? Then people who saw us could say – Ah yes, they are lovers: they are sitting in cafés and pubs!

Desmond kept up his more masculine role: he indulged in badinage: he would criticise my clothes. He would say – What, the sales are on at Oxfam?

He was apt to use slogans about making love – One for the road: Chalk it up: Back to the drawing-board. We were like people taking our clothes off at the side of an athletics track; preparing our starting-blocks and fingers.

I thought – Making love is like a life-belt thrown to people who might drown: it hits them on the head; if they sink, is it to rock bottom?

I usually went back to the Indian boy, Krishna, at night. Desmond never asked me about this. I thought – This is the sign that we have both of us got what we wanted?

I did have to make up some story to Krishna: I said that Desmond was my uncle from whom I hoped to borrow money. This was a story he would respect: I do not know if he believed it. I did think from time to time – At least I respect him for requiring a story.

What I was doing, of course (oh we know all this! what do we do about what we know?), was that in being with both Desmond and Krishna I was splitting one side of myself from another. This is obvious: we do it for protection: had not the Professor said – You may have to, to stay alive? But he had also said – You have to give it up. And you are saved, are you, by going to rock bottom?

The room in which Krishna lived in the basement of the hotel or hostel had a lot of political posters on the wall. I had met him with the Young Trotskyites. His particular revolution was to do with the part of South India from which he came; he was part of a religious and racial minority that was being persecuted. He and his friends were demanding independence as if this were something that could be given to them like money. In the evenings a group of them would crowd into his room: they would perch on the floor, against the walls; listen to speeches beneath the noise of a record-player and the sweet smell of dope. Political people, I suppose, like to sit up late at night with a lot of noise and exhaustion going on and then after a time there can be the impression of enormous events elsewhere.

Krishna got carried away when making love. I thought – But what is the difference between a trick of the guts, and a trick of the mind?

Desmond would turn up in a pub at lunchtime with his sheaf of newspapers under his arm. He would say – Oh what shall we give to old Dirty Lenin today? a junkie wife? parrot's disease? a pregnant daughter?

I wish I could bring Desmond to life: he seemed to try to disarm himself by being awful. But what has been called 'bringing to life' is usually to do with characters who are deathly.

I do not feel that I need to try to bring Krishna so much to life: but then he does not play this sort of part in the story.

I thought – If I could find someone who at the same time was dark and passionate and elegant and daft, then could I stop behaving like one of those poor deprived gorgons with snakes in their hair?

There was an evening when the *Die Flamme* people gave a party –

Oh I was getting tired of this, yes! I was becoming somewhat ill at the time. I will be trying to talk of this later.

There was an evening when the *Die Flamme* people gave a party and all the Medusas and flatworms (as you, Bert, once called them) were there – coelenterates, whose mouths are the same as their anuses. That is, there was assembled in an enormous ballroom the élite of the London literary world – and not only of the literary world, because the *Die Flamme* style had splashed over into the fashionable, and to possess an invitation to this party had become a matter of snob prestige. Guests were crammed into the auditorium of a huge theatre that had been turned into a ballroom: there were about a thousand of us wriggling like fish-bait in a tin. One of the forms my sickness had begun to take at this time was to have visions, almost physical, of human beings trapped in mud: they were struggling to get out; they had no hope; everyone was trying to climb up on, and was only pushing down, everybody else. There were these hundreds of people crammed into the ballroom like worms: why did they want to be there? was God, after all, a fisherman in thigh-length boots like a woman? But what would be his catch? Did he every now and then take someone out of the can and put them on a hook: to dangle them in order to attract – what? that which the Professor had called reality, round some corner? It did not seem, in fact, that many of the people at the *Die Flamme* party were trying to get out of whatever it was they were in; they were climbing up on each other's heads, or shoulders, just to stay where they were; to keep others under.

The *Die Flamme* people themselves were in a box on the ground-floor level: they bobbed backwards and forwards nodding and laughing. They were like royalty. I thought – What terrible contempt there is to do with royalty! both that people should want to look on them like this, and that they should allow it.

There was a sculptor in Düsseldorf – do you remember? who used to make life-size plastic sheep and sell them to rich industrialists who crammed them into attics; it was some comfort to industrialists to have the sheep there: perhaps they themselves could then more easily go on opening and shutting their mouths and bobbing backwards and forwards downstairs. I suppose the social world has always run on some sort of contempt. Where does a worm go, if one gets out of it?

I was not with Desmond at the *Die Flamme* party because his wife was there: she was a short plump woman like a pigeon. About her presence, of course, I had been cool, witty, understanding. But at the same time I had happened to quarrel with Desmond: there are these coincidences, are there not, at least in the unconscious.

35

What I had quarrelled with Desmond about was the vendetta that the *Die Flamme* people were pursuing against the politician they called Dirty Lenin. One of Dirty Lenin's children, at boarding-school, had attempted suicide. Of course there was no direct connection between this event and *Die Flamme*'s vendetta. But, indeed, yes, there are coincidences.

Desmond had puffed and blown his cheeks out.

I had thought – Hurry, hurry, there must be some slide down soon towards the bottom of this slope!

There was one man who was going to be at the *Die Flamme* party of whom I had heard and whom I wanted to meet: I was still, I suppose, shameless about this. But what else is there to do, even if you see it, until you get out, except to keep yourself up on other people's shoulders? This man at the party I shall call Oliver: this was what the *Die Flamme* people called him: they had once run a strip cartoon about him in which he was called Oliver Screw. This was a take-off of Oliver Twist – the joke being that Oliver Twist was someone who asked for more: what Oliver Screw asked for more of was not porridge but women. The real-life Oliver had been a stage-designer; he was now a painter; he had become enormously successful by painting female nudes. These were done in a bony, unerotic, skinnily life-like style; they usually had wrinkles and hairs and they sat or lay with their legs apart and there were bits of everything showing. It had become fashionable for rich women to have their portraits painted by Oliver; their industrialist husbands liked to hang them in their dining-rooms, I suppose, as suitable shepherdesses for their plastic sheep upstairs. Oliver became rich; and also some sort of guru to these people. I imagined him like Rasputin, holding his fingers out to adoring ladies who licked them clean.

He had for a time, in fact, been a good painter: he had been compared with Goya, and Bacon, and so on. Then recently, I understood, he had stopped painting. It was a time, I suppose, when many artists were asking themselves what they were doing.

He was one of the very few people whom the *Die Flamme*

people seemed in awe of. They had tried to mock him with their strip cartoon: but this had been, Desmond admitted, like trying to get at Mephistopheles by depicting him as a successful devil.

I had said to Desmond – What's he like?

Desmond had said – He's the sort of shit people go round the bend for.

Oliver turned up at the *Die Flamme* party with a small bearded man with dark glasses and a gold-topped cane who was said to own pop-stars in Hollywood. Oliver was a thick-set broad-shouldered man with tight dark wiry hair and the cut-out face of an actor. He looked Greek, or Turkish.

I thought – These worms in the tin can; are they not also the snakes in one's hair?

There was loud music. I thought – If I am to pick up Oliver it is no use standing still: he will have had enough of tasteful heroines chained to their rocks.

There was a black man on the dance floor who was a very good dancer. His hair was done up in snakes like that of a West Indian, yet he danced with the angular movements of arms and legs turned out of someone from the part of the world in which I had been brought up. So I went on to the dance floor and did this sort of dancing with him: I mean not with him, of course: you do not look, you do not touch: the point of this dancing is that you create networks of spaces between. After a time we had the dance floor almost to ourselves, while people watched. Afterwards we went to opposite sides of the dance floor still without having much looked at each other.

So it was easy to choose my place where to come to rest as if on fire.

I thought – I know that I have said I will not do this sort of thing again!

Oliver said 'Where did you learn to dance like that?'

I said 'At Jogyakarta.'

He said 'Where's that?'

I thought – You mean, you are not impressed with girls who say things like – At Jogyakarta?

I said 'In Java.'

When I looked at him he had his eyes half-closed and the toes of one foot pointing towards the ground. I thought – For God's sake, he thinks he is like a Degas dancer?

He said 'I wonder if you would do me the most enormous favour?'

I said 'What?'

He spoke with a slight foreign accent. He did not seem to have looked at me at all.

He said 'Would you come with me to another party? I would be tremendously grateful if you could.'

I thought – This is clever!

I said 'All right.'

He said 'Thank you.'

When he did look at me he had strange enamel-like green eyes like those that were supposed to have once been painted on marble statues. I remembered Desmond saying – He has the reputation of being able to do anything he likes with horses.

He said 'I'll wait for you here.'

I said 'I'll come with you now.'

He said 'This is extraordinarily good of you.'

I said 'This is a terrible party.'

I thought – I am a little out of control: I suppose I have not been on a slope before where the conditions are likely to be so fast.

As we went out of the ballroom Oliver said 'The party I will be taking you to will be even worse.' He laughed.

When he laughed his face lit up for a moment like a lot of candles coming on within a pumpkin.

In the street outside there was an enormous white car with a black chauffeur. When Oliver appeared the chauffeur got out and opened a door. We climbed in and sat side by side; the chauffeur settled a rug over our knees. I thought – We are in one of those black-and-white art movies of the 1950s, to do with damnation and death.

Oliver said 'I should explain. My wife and my girlfriend

happen to have both left me on the same day. It is important for me that I should appear, but not appear on my own, at this party.'

I thought – You mean, you are saying you trust me enough to risk being honest?

He said 'You may believe me when I say that there did not seem to be anyone at that party I could have done this better with than with you.'

I thought – You mean, you know enough to know this would work with me, being honest and knowing I will not think you are flattering me?

We drove along like two French actors going down into the underworld.

He said 'You know my name?'

I said 'Yes.'

He did not say – I do not know yours.

He said 'I should explain about this car. It isn't mine. It belongs to someone called Louise de St Remy, to whose party we are going.'

I said 'I see.'

He said 'Do you know Louise?'

I said 'No.'

He said 'I will tell you a story about Louise and her chauffeur.'

There were some buttons on the arm-rest of his seat. He pushed one or two and windows went up and down and eventually the one between the back compartment of the car and the front.

Oliver said 'Louise and her chauffeur were going over the Alps one day and Louise said – Stop the car I want to pee. Her chauffeur said – Yes, madam, the water is boiling.'

I said 'Yes that's a very good story.'

I thought – This is the style? You say things in a matter-of-fact voice, and assume people will know what you are meaning?

We arrived at a large apartment block that overlooked the river. There were turrets and battlements and towers. We went up in a lift. On the first floor there were about thirty people gathered in a room like a mausoleum. There were busts and vases on marble pillars: books like plaques locating ashes went up to the tops of walls. Men in dinner-jackets stood holding plates; women wearing evening dresses with thin straps going over their shoulders sat straight-backed on the arms or edges of sofas. There was a buffet at one end of the room presided over by a man in Mozart-opera livery: a waitress in a black dress with a white ruff came round with drinks on a tray. Everything was very quiet, and orderly. I thought – Well, nothing is supposed to go on in the holy of holies, is it?

The only other atmosphere I could remember like this was in a gambling casino I had once been to, where the enormously rich had succeeded in losing or winning thousands by doing absolutely nothing except slowly move their fingers every now and then like crabs.

I thought – These are the people whom Desmond talks about who run the world? who let themselves be used for the conspiracy theory of history because this is what other people require of them?

A woman in a dress the colour of a contraceptive diaphragm came up to talk to Oliver. Oliver introduced me: he had in fact learned my name. I thought – I have been an amateur in this; he is very professional.

I went to a window and looked out. Across the river there was the floodlit power station with its four tall chimneys: I thought – It is like a dead horse, its feet up in the air.

Then – Old gods and goddesses are preserved because they live in tombs which are quite airless?

Oliver went on talking to his hostess. They were like people in a painting plotting beneath the high blank wall of a Venetian building.

The man dressed like Figaro came up and offered me some food. Then a young man with dyed black hair and make-up stood by me and said 'We were saying it was better when it had three.'

I said 'Three what?'

He said 'Chimneys.'

I said 'Do you know Oliver's wife or his girlfriend?'

The man was eating with a fork from a plate; he shovelled food in like a croupier. After a time he moved away. I thought – You mean, you are not allowed to ask a direct question?

I tried to remember what I had heard about Oliver's wife. She was enormously rich; she was an American; she had previously been married to a German prince. Or this might have been his girlfriend?

Oliver came over to me. He said 'All right, we can go now if you like.'

I said 'I quite like it here.'

He said 'Why?'

I said 'I've never been anywhere like this before.'

Oliver was looking at me. I was looking out over the river. I thought – I have not got it wrong: you have to be honest?

He said 'Will you come home with me?'

I said 'No.' Then – 'You know I can't!'

He said 'Why not?'

I said 'Because that's what everyone does with you!'

He lifted his head right up so that his neck seemed to stretch towards the ceiling. Then he smiled. I thought – Does his laughter ever come out: or does it just burn within his skull like the flames around witches?

He said 'Do you know the story about D'Annunzio?'

I said 'No.'

He said 'D'Annunzio had the reputation of being able to go to bed with any woman he liked. Then one day some woman got the idea of being the first one ever to turn down D'Annunzio; so after that every woman wanted to be like her, and poor D'Annunzio couldn't get to bed with anyone at all.'

I said 'Is that true?'

He said 'It might be.'

I thought – Oliver is the only person who has made me feel inadequate?

He stood looking out of the window. I thought – But he has

41

been doing this sort of thing for so long, that it is impossible even for himself to tell whether or not he is acting.

It seemed I should say – Still, I can't go to bed with you!

He said 'Take these.'

He had taken from his pocket a bunch of keys which he held out in front of him as if he were a water-diviner. We watched them: his hand was steady: the keys did not swing.

I said 'What are they?'

He said 'They're the keys of the new flat I've just moved into. I'd like someone to have a spare pair. I'm always losing my own.'

I thought – This is really very clever.

I said 'All right.' I took the keys.

He said 'And promise to ring me in the morning. Will you? The number is on the keys.'

I looked at the keys and there was a label with a telephone number and an address on it. I thought – But is it not odd to have an address on a bunch of keys?

I said 'All right.'

He said 'You have promised.'

I said 'Yes.'

I thought – But if he does not know himself whether he is or is not acting, does this or does this not mean that he is in touch with something beyond this?

Now what about those spiral staircases going up or down: the windows one occasionally passes through when one waves and says – Coo-ee?

There are coincidences. But are the staircases going up (to something beyond) or down (towards rock bottom): or are both processes going on at the same time, so that when one sees another's face at a window this might mean – either this or that is up or down, so what is the difference?

I was driven back towards the hostel by the chauffeur in the car: Oliver had said he wanted to walk. I got out of the car at Victoria Station. I could not think of any story to invent if there were a scene on the steps of the hostel.

Upstairs I found that someone had been in my room; my drawers had been turned out; money had been taken. It was likely that this had been done either by, or with the knowledge of, Krishna; he was the only person except myself who had a key to the room. His revolutionary party was always short of money: Lenin, he had often explained to me, had encouraged the robbing of banks to obtain funds for his revolution.

So I went down to the basement and found him and his friends perched like conspirators or chickens against the walls and I thought this would be quite a good time to have a quarrel. At first he said he knew nothing about the money and then he said what good did I do with my money anyway? So we had a fight and I tore down some of the posters and I said that if he was a revolutionary why didn't he go out and fight; and so on. I said he and his friends were indistinguishable from very rich capitalists in that they sat around in a vacuum so that people were drawn in just by nothing happening.

I slept in my room on the top floor with the bits and pieces of my past life scattered about on the ground. I thought sooner or later Krishna would come up and we would make love; and then everything would be just the same as before; and I could not make out if I wanted this, or could not bear it, or both. I thought – Well this is some sort of despair, or giving up, isn't it? I sometimes imagined, when I talked to myself like this, that I was talking to the Professor. I felt as if I were still at the top of a long steep slope. I would have to move out of the hostel. I thought I might shout – Help! Here I come!

I had the bunch of keys under my pillow as if they were some life-line that had been thrown to me by Oliver.

Well, there are some coincidences that are more coincidental than others, aren't there?

By morning Krishna had not come to my room. I thought – That's that: and a mercy anyway.

I got out the bunch of keys.

There were one or two things that did not quite make sense about the previous evening. Oliver and I had stood by the window overlooking the river; he had said 'Promise to ring me in the morning!' The keys had a label with the address on it. Keys were a Freudian sex-symbol weren't they? They were also some symbol of death. Keys were to heaven or to hell: at the top and bottom of the staircase.

I thought – I know how Oliver would operate: he is like me.

Rock bottom is not always a metaphor; not at least when you hit it.

Had he not said that his wife and his girlfriend had both just left him?

I thought I should ring Oliver as soon as possible.

At first Krishna was in the entrance hall where the telephone was; then he went down to his room. Oliver's number was engaged. Then Krishna came up from his room.

I thought – Hurry: you must hurry.

You sometimes know what is happening don't you? even when you can't put it into language.

– There are the guns and the tanks in the streets outside the theatre –

I dressed and went out of the house and ran to a call-box. When Oliver's number was still engaged I asked the operator to check to see if there was anyone talking on the line. There was not. I thought – Hurry; it is proper to hurry. Then – Or is it just that for once I feel straightforwardly needed?

I went out of the call-box and looked for a taxi.

I had no money for a taxi. I thought – Either Oliver will pay, or if he does not, then there may well have been an excuse to have taken a taxi without any money.

I told the taxi-driver the address that was on the keys and the taxi went up to the West End. I thought – To heaven or hell, what is the difference? The building where Oliver had his flat was another large Victorian apartment block with turrets and battlements and towers. I felt as if I were a knight approaching where a sleeping beauty was lying. I asked the taxi-driver to wait. By the door there was a column of bells with numbers and names against them: there was no name against the number of Oliver's flat. I rang, then let myself in with one of the keys. There was a rather grand hallway with a lift. Oliver's flat was on the top floor.

I thought – It is with the drama, or the being needed, that you feel powerful, elect, perfect?

I went up in the lift. On the top floor there was a landing with two doors to flats; a passage went along to another door with glass in it which gave on to what looked like a fire-escape. I rang the bell by the door of Oliver's flat; I knocked; then I used the keys to go in. Inside the flat there was an extraordinary heat; it was like the engine-room of a ship; there was a passage which went past the open door of a sitting-room – this had packing-cases on the floor and dust-sheets over the furniture – then there was a kitchen and a bathroom on the other side of the passage and at the end a door which seemed likely to lead to a bedroom. Through this there came a scraping noise. It was like the creaking of a ship – one of those ships, perhaps, from which the crew have mysteriously disappeared. I went in. Oliver was lying on the bed on his back wearing the white shirt and black trousers he had been wearing the night before; his hands were folded across his chest like those of a crusader. The scraping noise was coming from his mouth, which was open: the noise was his breathing. There were bits of foam and of encrustation at the corners of his mouth; it was as if some sea had gone out and left him. There was an empty pill-bottle on a table by the side of his bed: a glass which smelled as if it had contained whisky. The noise coming from his lungs was as if an iron file were scraping away inside him; something was trying to break free, and then he would be dead. I thought I knew what to do about this: you do, God knows, if you have lived among Europeans in Hong Kong. The telephone was by the bed with the receiver off. I thought – He was gambling with me: playing Russian roulette: what on earth did he think were the odds? it is as if he had put five bullets in and left just one space empty. I dialled 999 and gave the address and said 'Come quickly, there's someone dying.' I heard myself – so clear and confident – then I realised I had not stipulated ambulance or police. I had put the receiver down. I did not think it mattered. Then I went through into the bathroom – I do not know why – and on a shelf above the basin there was a piece of paper with some white powder on it and beside it an old-fashioned razor-blade. I thought – Dear God, a razor-blade! do you want to leave clues that are almost jokes for me or the police? I smelled the white powder, which seemed to be some mixture: then I thought – But it is I who have dialled for the police! I screwed up the heroin or cocaine or whatever it was in its paper, but it was dusted about on the shelf; there might be some on the basin, or the floor; and what on earth do you do with an old-fashioned razor-blade? I thought I might telephone again to try to stop the police, but I did not think this would work. There are things that you just do, are there not, when you have been feeling decisive, confident, elect. I went out on to the landing to stand by the door of the lift to try to stop, send away, the police when they came; then the door of Oliver's flat banged shut behind me. I realised I had put down the bunch of keys on the table by Oliver's bed. I thought – I am mad: I have come to save Oliver and I have destroyed him. I felt it vital that I should get back into Oliver's flat before the police or ambulance men arrived: I had left the paper with the dope in it in the bathroom. I went along to the glass door at the end of the landing and it did, yes, give on to the small metal platform of a fire-escape. There was a key to this door in a glass case; I got the key out and unlocked the door and went out on to the fire-escape. There was a parapet along the battlements to the right which went past the windows of what must be Oliver's flat; the third window should be that of Oliver's bedroom. I thought I had to do this because had he not asked me to save him: and had I not accepted responsibility? I set out crawling along the parapet; there was an enormous drop to the street below. When I was going past the windows of the sitting-room there was the siren of a police car or an ambulance in the street. I thought – If I am found like this how can I explain? but then, nothing of importance can ever be explained, can it? I realised it was unlikely that the window into Oliver's bedroom would be unlatched since the flat had been so airless: so I might fall, and make an end of it. Or I might fly like a bird. When I reached the window I found I could get my fingers underneath the bottom; then it went up; so I thought – Now everything will be all right; thank you! I went in head-first through the window and through the curtains which were still drawn; and in so doing I knocked over a small table. A drawer opened and what looked like an enormous bundle of twenty-pound notes fell out. I was on my hands and knees, staring at this, like a dog above a bone. The police car or ambulance was arriving in the street below. I picked up the table and put the drawer back and closed the window and pushed the bundle of notes into my pocket; then I went into the bathroom and put the piece of paper with the dope in it into another pocket and I wiped the shelf and the basin and the razor-blade and washed my hands. When I had done all this the buzzer went from what I supposed was the downstairs door. I went to the entry-phone and pressed the button and told whoever it was to come up; then I went into the bedroom and stood by Oliver's bed. Oliver's breath was still scraping. I thought – Well, I needed money for the taxi, didn't I? Then I went to the door on to the landing and waited for the lift.

Two policemen arrived, one in uniform and one not. I said 'I'm so terribly sorry I didn't mean to call the police, I meant to call just an ambulance.' I went ahead of them down the passageway. I was wearing jeans: there was the money, and the dope, in my pockets. I stood by the bed and held Oliver's wrist: I said 'He's taken an overdose, I don't know why, I hope the ambulance is coming.' I thought – You don't say too much, do you? they make you feel guilty anyway. The police-man in plainclothes picked up the empty bottle of pills and sniffed it and sniffed the glass of whisky; then he spoke to the one in uniform who went into the passage and spoke into his two-way radio. The man in plainclothes moved around the room: he picked up things and put them down again: he opened the drawer in the table where the money had been. I thought – Police are supposed to take money, aren't they? Then –

Everyone is guilty about something. The man in plainclothes said 'Do you live here?' I said 'No.' Then – 'But I've got the keys.' Then – 'He's only just moved in.' I could hear the man in uniform go into the bathroom: I thought – But Oliver might have dope anywhere! I said to the man in plainclothes 'I let myself in just now, this morning.' The man had eyes like iron gratings through which fingers sometimes crawled. I thought – He is thinking what it would be like to have a flat like this and this girl who lets herself in with her own keys in the morning. I stood in my jeans with the dope and the money in my pockets. I thought – One knee slightly bent: one foot in front of the other. Then – This will be all right: there may be the smell of dope and money; there is also the smell of sex.

The man in uniform came in and said 'They're coming.'

The one in plainclothes said 'Wait for them on the landing.' Then he said to me – 'How can we get in touch with you?'

I said 'You can get in touch with me here.'

He said 'Will do.'

He looked at me with his hot, imprisoned eyes. He made a note of the number that was on the telephone.

When the ambulance men arrived they were quick and professional: they put Oliver on to a stretcher and strapped him so that he would not fall off in the lift: they asked me if I knew what he had taken, or how much, and I said I did not. When they were going off with him I said – 'Oh can I come with you?'

I thought it was necessary to get the policemen out of the flat. I said to the one in plainclothes 'Please!'

He said 'Come in the car.'

So I got them out of the flat, and locked the door, and then downstairs I found the taxi was still waiting. I thought – You mean taxi-drivers are like fairy godfathers in 1940s films? I thanked the plainclothes policeman with such genuine, grateful eyes! I said I would go to the hospital in the taxi. There was the hint – Well, you can ring me, can't you? But then in the taxi I thought – How extraordinarily everything has worked out! I mean if I had not shut myself out on the landing and had not had to crawl along that parapet, however would I have got the money to pay for this taxi!

Now there is something I want to put in here – as if it might be another face at a window in one of those spiral staircases –

When I arrived at the hospital they had already taken Oliver off to pump him out or do whatever they had to do: they could not tell me yet whether he would live or die. I gave details to a woman behind a desk of what I knew about Oliver: she asked me whom she should put down as his next of kin. I said that I did not think Oliver would want anyone to know what had happened, so she said should she put me down as next of kin. I said 'All right'. I thought – After all, I am protecting him; did he not give me his keys? But I did wonder for a moment whether I might be being trapped by Oliver in this; what are people doing when they involve others in games of Russian roulette?

Then in a waiting-room of the hospital (they had told me it might be some time before they knew whether Oliver would live or die) I found an old copy of *Die Flamme* magazine: in it there was one of the strip cartoons about Oliver: it was one showing him in the role of Faust: his bargain with the devil was that he should, at the cost of his soul, be able to get any girl he liked. But there was another story in this number which was to do with one of the more venomous vendettas the *Die Flamme* people had been carrying on for some time: this was against an Indian guru whom they referred to contemptuously as God. Some of the followers of this guru apparently themselves referred to him as God: and when he had been questioned about this (I remembered this story from an earlier number of the magazine) he had said it was a joke; but he had added that of course God liked jokes. When the *Die Flamme* reporter had asked him whether it was he who liked this sort of joke, he had apparently been overcome with laughter; and the *Die Flamme* reporter had felt discomfited, because, it seemed to be being suggested, he did not have a sense of humour.

In this number of the magazine (it was this that seemed to me like a face at a window) there was a story about the guru that I had not heard before. Two girls who were his acolytes had been caught smuggling drugs in Europe; they had been on their way to his commune, or *ashram*, in India. When their case had come up in court they had said – or rather the lawyers hired by their families had said – that the girls had been doing their smuggling on behalf of the guru who had brainwashed them, so they could not be held morally or legally responsible. The magistrates had had sympathy with this argument, and the girls had been given a suspended sentence. When the *Die Flamme* reporter had questioned God about this he had said that if it would be any help to any of his acolytes in trouble with the authorities to say that he was responsible, then of course he would be delighted to do so. The reporter had said – Yes, but in fact was he or wasn't he responsible? Whereupon the guru had been so overcome with laughter again that he had had to leave the room. This had so incensed the *Die Flamme* people that they had published comments about him that were indeed uncharacteristically humourless – the charges about drugs against the guru might not be able to be proved, but what about his encouragement of sex! and so on. So it did seem that a lack of sense of humour was being visited back on the *Die Flamme* people as some sort of retribution.

I read this story in the waiting-room of the hospital. There was a photograph of the guru who had a bright nut-brown face rather like that of the Professor. I thought I might wave and say – Coo-ee!

After a time a doctor came into the waiting-room and said that they had done all they could for Oliver but that they still would not know for some time whether he would recover. The doctor looked at me with hot, distrustful eyes. I thought – There are these connections, like those of the shadows of a cage, between drugs and death and sex. He told me I could go and sit with Oliver. I thought – But if these people have envy, is it not satisfied by the chance of death?

Have you ever been in the intensive-care unit of a hospital? Figures in white coats stand facing switches and dials. The switches and dials are on the faces on machines that are connected by wires and tubes to bodies. It is as if the bodies are feeding the machines; and the people in white coats are there to see that the supply of food does not run out.

Oliver was on a bed like a trolley. There was a large tube going down his throat, a smaller one in at the side of his neck, and one coming out from the sheets at the bottom of the bed. There were two pads on his chest from which wires went to a machine with a screen on it like a clock; the numbers became sometimes greater and sometimes less; this was to do with his heartbeat. There was another machine which drew zig-zag lines on a roll of paper and it was as if these were to do with the weather in other bits of Oliver. The pipe down his throat was like some terrible sexual violation.

I sat beside Oliver and I sometimes held my hand on his arm and I watched the numbers on the screen above his head grow greater and sometimes less. I thought – If you can measure a person's life, can you not also alter it? This was, I think, what I had been trying to say to the Professor. I wanted to alter Oliver's life because I felt that he had asked me to; he must have been someone who had come near enough to rock bottom.

I stayed with Oliver through most of that day; I had nowhere else, after all, to go. I thought – People's lives might bounce up from just such moments, mightn't they? when nothing much else seems to be happening.

One of the nurses told me that I need not wait: that Oliver would not regain consciousness, if he did, until late that evening. I thought – But is it also myself who might change? now that there is nothing much, or everything, happening?

I went down to the canteen where people sat as if in limbo, waiting for their tickets to heaven or to hell.

Late that evening Oliver's hands began to move; they fluttered; they seemed to be trying to pull out the terrible pipe down his throat. It was like someone trying to pull himself up by his gut-strings. I could not bear this; Oliver's fingers scrabbled like fish-bait in the tin. I asked a nurse if she could take the pipe out; she said the right time for the pipe to come out was when he was strong enough to pull it out himself. I thought – But who ever gets out of the tin on their own? I sometimes held Oliver's hand to stop him scratching: he had beautiful fine-boned hands with long fingers. After a time I could no longer bear it and I helped him to pull the pipe out from his throat; it came out with a dreadful noise like a horse's penis.

I asked Oliver if he could hear what I was saying, and if he could, would he press my hand. He pressed. I asked him if he knew who I was, and did he want me to stay with him, I mean did he want me to come back and be with him in the morning. There was a pause while he seemed to be trying to open his eyes; they were like dried-out seaweed waiting for water; then he squeezed my hand over and over. So I said I would stay with him until he fell asleep, and I would come back. I thought – You feel you know just where you are, do you, when someone has been on the point of dying?

I went back to Oliver's flat. I wanted to see if there was anything more I should clean up. Also, I had not had a home of my own for some time.

I put the chain on the door behind me. I thought – This is some cave: I am hiding from pursuers: I am one of those primitive humans who have just learned the secret of fire.

There did not seem to have been anyone living in the flat; nothing was unpacked; there were none of Oliver's paintings; there was no sign of anything belonging to a woman.

I thought – It is as if he had arranged for me to move in here?

There was bread and cheese and apples in the kitchen; a bottle of whisky. I sat on the floor of the sitting-room amongst the packing-cases. I thought – I am like someone cut off by a fall of rock; with luck, no one will find me till the end of winter.

Once or twice the telephone rang. I did not answer it. I thought it might be that policeman.

I began to count the bundle of twenty-pound notes but it

was so large that my mind went blank, and I put it back in my pocket.

I thought I would go through some of the packing-cases in the sitting-room: one of them contained papers. There was nothing to tell me much about Oliver's present life: one letter was from a lawyer about his wife's money in America; there were some catalogues of exhibitions in Europe. But then there were hundreds of letters from Oliver's old girlfriends: these were done up carefully in bundles with bits of string.

As I went through them – cross-legged on the floor like Goldilocks researching the natural history of bears – there was a pattern that seemed to emerge. Hundreds of letters were from girls who, it appeared, had been in love with Oliver more than he had been in love with them: these letters complained, cajoled, pleaded, argued: the words went on and on like flies trapped between window-panes. From the tone of the letters it seemed that Oliver had hardly answered them; he had just tied them up like dead people's mouths with string. Then there were a few short letters that were cool and factual and which seemed to be from a woman whom Oliver had been more in love with than she had been in love with him: the pile of these compared to the others was tiny, like the Sphinx beside the Pyramids. And somewhere in this woman's house I imagined there would be a heap of Oliver's letters complaining, cajoling, pleading, arguing; huge tombs looming above the smile of the Sphinx.

I thought – One should write no letters! or just one great letter that would carry one past all such images like the eternal waters of the Nile.

When I went back to the hospital the next day they had moved Oliver out of the intensive-care unit and he was in a ward with three other beds. There was a contraption like a scaffold beside him with a drip going into his arm. He had his head propped up on pillows as if he had arranged himself to be watching the door.

I said 'Hullo.'

53

'Hullo.'

I thought I might say – I wondered if you remembered me?

I said 'How do you feel?'

'All right.'

'I've got myself down as your next of kin.'

'That's very good of you.'

He was watching me, half-smiling. I thought – He thinks I am someone else? He imagines we are meeting in some other incarnation?

I said 'You didn't want me to get in touch with anyone?'

He said 'No.'

I said 'I've tidied the flat.'

He said 'Thanks.'

Then he said 'What I wanted them to find was just a little pile of clothes on the beach.'

I thought – He is establishing some complicity between us? well there is complicity between us: he wants us to be joined as if in the cover-up of some crime?

He said 'Did you find the money?'

I said 'Yes.'

He said 'I knew you'd be efficient.'

All the time there was the impression that we were talking about something of which he assumed I knew more than I did. I thought – This has always been one of his weapons?

Then – This is what those people in America must have felt when it seemed the Professor was talking in code.

He said 'Did you find lots of letters?'

I said 'Yes.'

Then – 'Do you mind?'

I thought I should be saying – But the police came and they could have found the dope! How did you know I would fix things? If you were not dead, you could be in jail!

There was a grinning somewhere inside his skull that seemed upside-down like bats.

He said 'Do you know, there really are green fields and angels, when you nearly get there? and a man in a white robe who comes to tell you it is all right!'

He spoke with his odd not-quite-foreign accent. I thought –
You mean, you will make out it has been worth while to have
nearly died?

He said 'When the Emperor Nero and the Empress Poppaea
got fed up with their boring exciting life they decided to die, so
they could come alive again and live quietly somewhere in the
Peloponnese. They heard about this witch-doctor who had
been doing it in Jerusalem.'

I thought – But what a risk! you genuinely did not mind if
you died?

His strange enamel-green eyes were like the eyes of that
bronze Greek charioteer that have been taken out, so that
when you look at them you look inside.

He said 'What can you do with someone who has saved
your life?'

I thought – Love them, honour them: hate them for ever?

He said 'Do you think you can ever forgive them?'

I thought – I don't know, do you?

Then – Did not Desmond say Oliver could do anything he
liked with animals?

I said 'Is there anything you want?'

He said 'Promise you won't leave me.'

I thought – He says his lines like Holofernes did that night
when the play effectively ended: looking down on himself,
playing with words; is it his words that are like horses?

I said 'Can I buy some cooking things?'

He said 'Buy what you want. It's your flat. It's your
money.'

I thought – You are doing some experiment? you are
playing Russian follow-my-leader?

Then – You know, do you, that I will keep up?

I went to pick up my things from the hostel: I chose a time
when I imagined that Krishna would be involved in the
basement with his friends. I went up the stairs holding my
shoes in my hand. I thought – People become involved in
conspiracies because they like the excitement; the impression

of bodies being moved at night; of what has been dead coming alive.

In my room in the hostel I found an IOU typed out for the money that Krishna had taken. I thought for a moment – I might be making some terrible mistake?

Oliver came out of hospital on the third or fourth day: I took him home to the flat in a taxi and sat him up in the bed, which was an elegant four-poster. I had unpacked linen and china and put flowers in vases. Oliver watched me with his mad, rather childish smile. It was as if he needed to locate himself by watching me as I moved around the room.

When he was in his pyjamas and propped up in bed I realised how old he was. I suppose at that time he was in his early fifties. I thought – He is like a grandmother pretending to be a wolf: but would not Little Red Riding Hood have always hoped that her grandmother was a wolf?

There was indeed something womanish about Oliver: or perhaps it was to do with what people think of as being womanish. He had white, rather tight skin like something upholstered. I suppose women are in fact often like Oliver's paintings of them – bony, with bits and pieces coming out.

He would sit up in bed with his hands flat upon the bedspread: he was like a statue waiting for rain.

While he watched me as I moved I thought – His eyes are like some tether: the rope you tie to goats.

He said 'Does anyone know you're here?'

I said 'No.'

He said 'Do you think they'll think I've murdered you?'

I did not know quite what to say to Oliver. I thought – It is by making you feel inadequate that he tethers you. But then, had I not always imagined that in silence I would feel at home?

He would say 'Come here.'

I would stand by the edge of his bed.

He would say 'How am I going to forgive you? What do you think it would be to forgive you?'

I thought – You mean, you are only pretending that it is you who are in my power?

56

Do you know the story of Achilles and Penthesilea? It is in a play by Kleist.

Achilles, King of the Myrmidones, is at war with Penthesilea, Queen of the Amazons: this is a particular but also a universal war, the one between men and women. Achilles comes face to face with Penthesilea on the battlefield; they fall in love; but what are they to do? They are dedicated to enmity; they have no style for anything different. Then in the course of the fighting Penthesilea is taken prisoner by Achilles; she happens at this moment to be knocked unconscious so she does not know what has occurred. Achilles explains to her handmaidens who have been captured with her that he loves her, that he will treat her with all the respect and adoration she might require. But the wisest of the handmaidens says – What will it matter to her that you respect and adore her? she will never forgive you if she learns you have taken her prisoner. So Achilles and the handmaidens fashion a plot: when Penthesilea wakes they will pretend that it is not she who has been taken prisoner by Achilles but that it is he who has been taken prisoner by her: then everyone will be happy: Penthesilea will think that she has taken Achilles prisoner, and Achilles will know that this is not true. So when Penthesilea awakes everyone is committed to this piece of acting. And so for a time she and Achilles are in empyrean bliss. But then in another turn of the battle those of Penthesilea's forces who have not been taken prisoner rescue their Queen, and Penthesilea learns what has been happening. She vows revenge. Achilles, meanwhile, has been so overwhelmed by his time of bliss that he says – Never mind: I will simply now surrender to Penthesilea genuinely! what can be more worth while than such bliss? But when he approaches her, without weapons and with open arms, she will of course have nothing to do with what she feels is now his condescension to her; and she hacks him to pieces. And then, for some reason or other, apparently she tries to eat him.

Well, with Oliver and myself, I thought – Who is Penthesilea and who is Achilles?

And what on earth does it mean that she eats him?

Oliver would say 'Come here.'

I said 'How did you know I would come that morning?'

He said 'I had to take the risk.'

I said 'Why?'

He said 'How else would I have got you?'

I thought – It takes more than conjuring tricks to be so clever? You have to be in touch with what the Professor called something beyond?

When Oliver painted his portraits of women's bodies, it was as if he were turning them inside out with his fingers.

I said 'Do you know the story of Achilles and Penthesilea?'

He said 'Yes.' Then – 'You know, Kleist killed himself together with his girlfriend.'

I said 'Yes.'

He said 'Aren't you frightened?'

I lay on the cover of the bed next to him. His close-cropped hair was like something that has been burned: that has been propped up in the dark corner of a temple. His fingers were like something probing beyond a membrane, a wall; to another dimension.

I hired a television set and placed it at the end of the bed: we sat side by side with his arm around me. We watched, as if through some peephole, the things people were doing in the world outside: the running, the fighting, the shouting; the climbing up on each other's heads and shoulders. I thought – We are like one of those couples on the top of Etruscan tombs: we will be dug up, serene and smiling, in a thousand years.

Or – I am like one of those bits of material that a child takes to bed when it sucks its thumb instead of its mother?

I wish I could explain about Oliver. He created this vacuum into which you were sucked: like a black hole, it was not easy to get out of.

I went out to shop each day; I cooked; I cleaned the flat. I thought – It is some sort of nothingness that most people come to be tethered to after all: they like just to tick over; to lie; to be at peace.

He said 'Do you know Kleist's story of the puppet-master?'

I said 'No.'

He said 'Kleist had the idea that human beings were never at ease, because they were split between being doers and being observers of what they were doing. Puppets were graceful, all-of-a-piece, because they were hung by a single string from their centre of gravity.'

I said 'Yes, I see.'

Oliver said 'Come here.'

I thought – But it is I who am fixing this?

– I am the goat; and Oliver is the peg to which I have wanted, needed, to be tethered?

You know that pornographic story of the woman who is chained up in a cellar and she is beaten and buggered or whatever and she accepts this, likes it even? She doesn't have to think anymore, doesn't worry; whatever happens is the responsibility of the man who owns her. And what is unpleasant doesn't take very long: it's either in the past, and thank goodness it's over, or it's in the future, which may never come: but as a result you're not bored even if in the present there is nothing happening, because there's the past and the future and you're at peace. For what is peace except a sort of nothingness in which you are not bored; and how else might you achieve this? I think a lot of people fix their lives in some way like this: it's not just that the story is pornographic. I mean a lot of people suffer and so are not bored and then it's quite nice when they stop this: how else do you explain the things that people do? I mean, why should they so willingly destroy themselves?

But then – whoever wants to be the man who owns the woman in the cellar?

Oliver would say 'This is your centre of gravity? This?'

People have got used to talking in such violent ways about sex; it is as if Achilles and Penthesilea were still on their battlefield.

But there can be something so sweet, like honey, at the centre, passively: it is this that is like the string of a puppet taking over?

59

Perhaps it is of recognising this that people are scared: lest – what? – their sins should be forgiven them and they should become something different?

I thought – In India the god Shiva is a god equally of creation and destruction –

– But his dance is to do with stillness within his circle of fire?

Oliver had been quite near to death. He was ill. I sometimes massaged him – his thick white skin and flesh.

He would say 'Harder!'

I thought – Well, who is the woman in the cellar?

You dig down to get the hook in; for the gold; the buried treasure.

He would say – There!

I would think – You who are so powerful! You think you are in control? But have we not known, you and I, that the chosen, the elect, have been accustomed to be victims?

From where I am writing now I can see, framed in the doorway of my hut, the estuary with the blue and green hills in the distance, the shore with the gold-pink sand; two or three dogs even; the birds dropping down like notes of music. This is the present. The present is not what we experienced in the cave. Those were shadows.

Can I say – What happens when you know the elect are victims?

– Then, of course, what you are, you also are not?

You can turn those shadows in the cave into what shines like trees in a painting?

On the path that goes down towards the sea there is a man in a white robe squatting: he is talking to a child: the child looks up to the hut where I am sitting. The man is like Christ: the child is the carrier of some message. The message is given: it has to be found: it is both the land, and the seed that a bird is carrying.

The child runs down towards the river. The birds are above. They are unheard; they are the form and vibrations of music.

I am writing this with a pencil and paper on my knee. The

marks I make are like those on a butterfly's wing. The child has been told – Do not tell anyone.

What is being drawn up, by a string and a hook from the sea, is the substance, the thing-in-itself, of music.

Oliver did not seem to have difficulty in getting hold of drugs. He would make a telephone call by picking the receiver up, dialling, letting the number ring two or three times, putting the receiver down, dialling again, giving a message in some sort of code – usually to do with flowers. The next day or even a few hours later a packet would appear in the letter-box downstairs. I would go to get it. Oliver did not seem to worry about the packet lying about downstairs: part of the business, it seemed, was to be a gambler.

There was cheap heroin coming into the country at this time, from Iran or Pakistan or somewhere: money had once been poured into such countries by the West to make them self-sufficient; it was easiest to become self-sufficient by growing poppies for heroin; this found its way back to the capitalist West which thus got a return on its investment. Even when revolutionaries took over some of these countries I suppose it still seemed sensible to allow such a return to the West. Cocaine seldom seemed to be a problem: there are always revolutionaries – are there not? – in South America.

Then there were alchemists in Amsterdam who fashioned pills and potions in strange and fearsome mixtures for the conjuring-up of meanings of the world – phantoms to order, coming in various shapes and sizes.

There is so much written about the pain and deathliness of drugs: but what are their delights: what have humans always wanted to get hooked-up into?

Humans have this drive to commit themselves, to give themselves over, to a cause, a god, a fatherland, a lover. They join groups, parties, armies, treadmills; their aim is to become identified, loyal, fixed, all-of-a-piece. It is scarcely bearable to be something blown about on your own. To be alone and be yourself is to know some great hollow at the centre; this can be the terror that there is the drive to fill; it can also be used, of course, to make music.

What is easiest is to dress up in uniform, march to Moscow, flop about like Tristan and Isolde on some beach. You do away with emptiness at the centre by doing away with life. Snow covers the bodies on the plains around Moscow: the dying music moves to the perfect silence on the beach.

Drugs are for people who understand not too little about society but too much – and yet nothing more. Why dress up for Moscow? Who's bluffing with that song and dance on the beach? If you've got a death-wish why not do it at home, decently? Don't spill over into the environment with your medals and romanticism and shit.

Drugs, like bombs, are given pretty names: Fat Boy, Thin Man, Angel Meat. The stuff that Oliver got was mainly mixtures: you experimented: have not people always experimented to find out meanings of the world?

There was a substance you swallowed that made you solid and perfect and eternal: as if you were a golden statue straddling the entrance to a harbour. Looking down you could see small ships like flecks on piss beneath you: you did not need to do anything because anybody could do anything to you: they could tear you, chew you, there would still be all the kingdoms of the world beneath. You were that firm solid god whose toes people kissed like the sea.

Then there was a powder that you sniffed that made you feel as if you were the active instrument of god: you marched through valleys of orange trees to the last great battle of Armageddon: you were a tank in hot streets churning amongst brown bodies of children. They ran towards you with their hands up shouting – Peace! You raised your arm; opened your fingers; your dust settled down upon the world. Walking back through the burnt-out orange plantations you smiled – This is peace!

There was a shredded stuff you chewed and then you could in fact go out into the streets and people appeared in forms that you had imagined in dreams: they were great tufted things like celery, like penises; they waddled and slid along the pavement. There were holes propped up in the shapes of mouths; there were eyes and ears clamped tight or writhing like anuses. You began to laugh. It was laughter by which you could be blown about and filled: you were a hollow swinging from a lamp-post.

Oliver and I both kept up for some time the pretence that he had to stay in bed: this was necessary for us, I suppose, as the peg to which we were tethered. I would go out to the shops; I would have something to come back to – the huge sick queen bee at the centre. This was our game: it was like that of Achilles and Penthesilea.

Then one day I went out without my keys. There was the impression again that I might have done this unconsciously on purpose. It seemed sensible that I should crawl back once more along the parapet to a window; then I might get at my keys without disturbing Oliver. I also had the idea that it would be a chance to see what Oliver did when I was not in the flat. Might he not even be one of those objects that do not exist when the observer is not there? I mean, of course, that I as observer would be there – but as if in another dimension.

I crawled out along the parapet to the sitting-room window and through this I saw Oliver standing, naked, in the middle of the room; he was talking on the telephone. I thought – He is practising being that vulgar golden god, is he, with his legs apart above a harbour. Then – But why is he not using the telephone by his bed?

I was on my hands and knees on the parapet like a cat. I thought – It is as if he has planned that I should crawl to see him standing naked in the sitting-room.

He was talking in an animated way on the telephone. He looked straight at me. He went on talking.

I thought – You mean, our game of pretence is over? But then will we not, as Achilles and Penthesilea, tear one or the other of us to pieces?

Oliver put the receiver down and came to the window and opened it.

I said 'I forgot my keys.'

He said 'Come in and get warm.'

He moved about the room without difficulty. I sat on a sofa. I thought – I am watching him in the way that up to now he has watched me.

He said 'Had you been out there long?'

I said 'No.'

He said 'You're looking rotten.'

He came and stood over me. He put his arms on either side of me against the back of the sofa.

I thought – You mean, it is now my turn to be ill?

He said 'Let's put you to bed.'

I said 'What about the shopping?'

He said 'I'll do the shopping.'

I thought – This can still work? We need not end up savaging each other like Achilles and Penthesilea?

I did not, of course, become ill all at once. I had for some time previously been using bits and pieces of dope. But these flip-overs happen quickly.

You are elect, heroic, on some parapet like a bird: then suddenly you are over.

Your mind does not register exactly what has occurred. You wake up in bed. Your old life is like a body on the pavement.

Well, what point was there for me in getting out of bed in the mornings now? Oliver would usually go out about mid-day. He did not tell me where he went. He said that he did not intend to get in touch with his wife or his old girlfriend.

There are gaps in the mind. There are gaps in this story. When you do not wish to remember, do you invent?

Why should Oliver have moved into this flat? Why had he risked taking sleeping pills with such apparent little chance of being rescued? Why did he wish his friends and enemies to think him dead?

One of the fantasies I made up at this time – Oliver going off and leaving me with pills and powders and the television in bed – was that he must be some sort of secret-service agent (of course! what better explanation was there? such are the contemporary fantasies made flesh to deal with the rubbish of the human mind). Oliver had had to pretend to die in order to stay alive: he was in hiding from people who were after him. Well, of course, this did not quite make sense: but it is the not making sense that such fantasies are there to deal with. And I had been required because Oliver had needed me to look after him; perhaps this was why he needed now to keep me hidden – so that I would not tell. He went off each day, indeed, not to see his wife or his girlfriend, nor even to paint (I knew he still had a studio somewhere: but there would have been nothing fanciful enough for me, I suppose, in the idea that he had gone off simply to paint), but rather to visit those small, ruthless Englishmen like banjo-players who were his masters and who had their offices somewhere in the Charing Cross Road: there he would get his further instructions in the world of poisoned umbrellas and messages stuck like bits of lavatory paper within trees; and it was this world I was involved in! Might there not be a knock on the door one day and I would go to answer it and in would come those men in shiny suits leaping about like salmon; they would hold their pistols with both hands in front of them like people straining to have a shit; and I would say – You can do what you like to me! And then I would shoot from underneath the bedclothes; for they would not have known, would they, that I was heroic, immune, perfect.

When Oliver returned to the flat he used to say – You're a mess! We'll have to clean you up. Shall we? Then – You know, do you, it's a turn-on to be a mess?

Well, what do you think this sort of thing is about humans? They choose to find it easier to stay watching shadows on the wall of a cave?

There was a day when Oliver had gone out and I was sitting in the alcove of the bedroom window; from here you could see the pavement on the street below; I had been watching people coming and going as if they were little bits and pieces of slime-mould: do you know about slime-mould? it is a fungus that grows in the forest. It starts as bits and pieces and then it comes together and forms a worm; this worm crawls all-of-a-piece and then it erects itself like a penis and explodes; so the little bits and pieces are scattered all over the forest. Then they begin to come together again – and so on. I thought – These people in the street, who are bits and pieces, they will need some enormous explosion one day to make them come together? and so on.

I was watching the street and I saw someone wearing a mackintosh and looking like a private detective in a 1940s film: he was standing beneath a lamp-post. I thought he was Desmond. I mean he might have been Desmond: I had not seen Desmond since the night of the *Die Flamme* party: but might he not have heard – what? – that I had been captured and held hostage by men with moustaches like poisoned umbrellas? and might he not have come to rescue me from beneath a lamp-post – had not Desmond always been like someone in a 1940s film? He would have come treading down the steps of the Casbah; shadows would be flailing like the branches of trees against a wall: the images, memories, of course, become mixed; they are like the worms struggling to get out of a tin can. I thought I should be careful not to let myself be seen from the street: but how should I let Desmond know that I was here? What is it that people throw down from a window – a pebble? a button? a note of music? I thought I might go down in the lift and see if it was Desmond: but did I in fact want to be rescued? I could say – You must forget me! Go! I must never see you again! And then I could die in his arms. And so on. I went to the lift. I was wearing a dressing-gown. I had been smoking – what? When the lift moved I began to feel very ill. I sat on the floor and perhaps I did not know where I was for a time: I seemed to be inside one of those machines in the intensive-care unit of a hospital: there were men outside watching switches and dials. Or I was one of those eggs on the inner surface of a womb: someone outside me had drunk vodka and gin: they were trying to dislodge me: there were waves washing over me: I had to hang on. I suppose the lift reached street-level, but I did not get out: I think it was one of the neighbours who found me. And then after a time Oliver appeared; he took over; perhaps he had been one of the people watching switches and dials. He was gentle: he called me his 'old thing'. I thought – But this is some code: he is telling me that he knows that I know what he is up to; but they don't let you get away with this sort of knowledge, do they? It is I, still, whom they are after; whom they will have to try to see will end up dead.

But what about those faces that pop up at a window?

There was an evening when I was watching television with the sound switched off: I had taken to watching television like this: so much went on in the mind, one could watch people opening and shutting their mouths, coming together and breaking up, like slime-mould, like penises. There was some sort of discussion going on; a semi-circle of people sat and smiled and turned their heads this way and that: no one had noticed that they were clockwork; they had been taken over by people from Andromeda. There was a questioner who was trying to throw questions like ping-pong balls into their mouths; or was it that they were trying to get something out; the camera seemed to be searching for what it might be; then there might be flashing lights and notes of music. But there was one man at the end of the semi-circle whom the camera did not dwell on; when it touched him it seemed to jerk away, as if it had itself been touched. He was a bony, bright-eyed man who had a hand up to his mouth as if he were trying to prevent himself from laughing. Sometimes when the camera shot away it seemed to pick him up again unexpectedly as if he had transferred himself by magic to the other end of the row; then there were just the clockwork toys again opening and shutting their mouths. I became interested in the man because he seemed to have come in from outside the framework: I mean the radio-waves might have got mixed up and in fact he was part of some quite different programme; or perhaps he was the controller from Andromeda. I had mislaid the instrument by which you turn on the sound; I crawled to the television and pushed a button and there was a roaring blank for some time: it was as if a bomb had gone off. I thought – Wouldn't it be easy to push the wrong button! Then – You mean, some bomb might really have gone off? Then there was a man's voice saying quite clearly 'But don't you see what trouble they had to take in order to destroy themselves?' The picture came alive: it was the face of the man at the end of the row; he seemed to have popped up out of the tomb. I thought I might wave and say – Coo-ee! He put his hand over his mouth again. Then the others went on with their opening and shutting of noises. It seemed that they had been talking about something to do with the Nazis at the time of the Second World War – it was they, was it, who had had to take such trouble to destroy themselves? I thought – Oh well, indeed, coo-ee! Then I realised that Oliver was standing behind me. He leaned forwards and turned off the television. He said 'Who's been eating *my* pudding?'

I said 'That man at the end of the row – '

He said 'Old Jay. Jason. You know old Jason?'

I said 'Who's Jason?'

He said 'Someone still looking for his Golden Fleece. Doesn't know you can buy it now at any sex-shop.'

I said 'Oh I see.'

I worked out after a time – You mean that man at the end of the row, who was as if waving to me from a window, is called Jason?

That same evening Oliver said – marching up and down the room as if there were flies or military music after him –

'I thought it was the *Die Flamme* people that you were so starry-eyed about: get the shit off the streets: rise and shine: get it poured over yourself: piss and polish: that sort of thing.

'You think people like being on top? They don't. They like being underneath. It's warmer where you're shat on. Why do you think children like it, what do you think Freud went on about, was it Freud or Jung who had that dream about God shitting on the world when on the seventh day he rested? That which proceedeth from the father and the son – Good boy! Mummy loves you!

'You think that was clever – Don't you see what trouble they had to take in order to destroy themselves? –

'Give me a nice shiny scrubber any day. What was the name of that boy you were with? Desmond?'

Oliver was standing over me by the edge of the bed.

I thought – You mean, you are jealous of that person called Jason –

– You would like me to get in touch with Desmond?

Why does it seem false, do you know, to try to give straightforward descriptions of sex: is it because sex itself is a metaphor for something different?

This is one of the ways one knows (because there are metaphors) that there is something different?

I mean – You do all these things with bits and pieces of yourself; but you do them because round a corner, just elsewhere, there is something of quite another kind coming together, falling apart, coming together: I mean why else would you spend all that time with bits and pieces of yourself if there were not something different?

But when you can't hold this, pin it down, because it is around some corner – then I suppose there is some rage in you that makes you go after the bits and pieces.

Oliver wasn't much good at straightforward sex: perhaps he had done too much: but then, there were all his bits and pieces. These, as Miss Julie would say, were hanging out; he had to do something with them. He was like some sort of genie half in and half out of a bottle.

He would say – For God's sake, if you wait for yourself, you might have to wait for ever.

And I had got bored, yes, with men who hang around with their tongues out all day as if they were in a desert.

Oliver would say – All right my puppet, my Petrouchka-girl; there's a good centre of gravity!

69

Sometimes a packet would arrive in Oliver's letter-box downstairs that did not contain dope but implements, sexual devices, or whatever: these were I suppose of the same order as dope: they were mechanisms to give a home to fantasies that floated half in and half out of bottles. Do not all humans have fantasies – either trapped, or running wild? I suppose it is better if they are in some way held rather than roar like witches above battlefields.

Oliver would say – Machinery, like puppets, yes, is less ridiculous than humans.

I would think – Are there people, somewhere, who prefer not to be tethered?

Oliver would say – There is no orderliness when there is a choice: humans are ludicrous when they think they have a choice.

I would say – But it might be something one cannot talk about –

Oliver would say – Saints, explorers, have always wanted pain. You know that prayer on Easter Saturday – Oh happy fault! or whatever – how would there be the bliss of redemption if there were no pain?

I would think – Bliss is being in the present, here, and with no dimensions?

Oliver would say – It is a fearful thing to fall into the hands of the living god!

Sometimes we would go out together: I would dress up: then we could shine – as if polished, I suppose, or pissed on, or pissing. We had probably chewed on some of the stuff that made people in the streets roll towards us like penises. I was a doll: why do people make themselves up like dolls? to sit on thrones: like queens, like goddesses, with spikes up inside them?

Oliver would say – We worship you! We bow down! Give us of your bounty!

Oliver had received in one of his paper packets what was the latest contraption from Germany: it was shaped like an egg: it was worked by radio control, like one of those motor-boats that buzz about on ponds. Oliver held the control switch in his hand: the egg was pushed up inside me. Oliver said – Oh Virgin Queen! on the shoulders of your acolytes!

When he pressed the button there was the sensation of a snake uncoiling somewhere near the bottom of my spine and shooting up to burst in the sky above my head.

Oliver said – You are all at one. There is no hollow inside you!

When we walked in the street I did feel as if I were some goddess in procession: crowds were under my skirts: an orb and a sceptre were suns at my breasts. I was to be taken to the altar; to flare up on the wings of angels.

I thought – Dear life, dear God; well, it was nice having known you.

We were on our way to a pub. This was Oliver's idea. It was to be some ordeal: a test for witches.

I had done my hair up in a crest like a bird. That woman from the cellar in the story had a mask like a bird, had she not? There were chains and trinkets around my body.

I was to be enthroned, entombed. I was to sit quite still. I was to be guardian of the secrets.

Well, people do worship this kind of thing, give up their lives to it, don't they?

When we were in the pub I sat in a corner with my back held straight so that the snake in my spine, when it shot up, might not twist and strangle me. I held my orb and sceptre, my worlds, my children, in my arms. Every now and then Oliver pressed the button and there were these stars above my head; the bomb going off; arms reaching after me. I felt – Now nothing further can happen to me: I am the rock: the kingdoms of the world are beneath me.

Oliver had gone to the bar to get drinks. There was a man at the bar with his back half-turned to me. I realised he was the Professor.

I was sure it was the Professor, though recently I had not been thinking of him much. I thought now – You mean, at last this might be rock bottom?

71

There was a rush of cold air coming in. I thought – I am a mummy in one of those caves and after thousands of years the tomb is opened and the mummies are seen in all their glory for a moment and then they collapse in the air like burned paper.

It seemed that if I sat very still the Professor might not see me; the bits of burnt paper might not float to him.

Oliver was buying drinks. The Professor was on his own. I thought – But he will not remember me!

This was a cry for help, of terror – This is I, Cleopatra, at the stake like a witch!

The Professor turned and looked at me. He had his back to the counter of the bar. He seemed to be considering me thoughtfully. I thought – He sees me as if I were a painting.

Perhaps I have not explained enough about the Professor. I had known, when I had talked to him that one time in America, that he had liked me.

I thought I might say – Well, this is what we were talking about, isn't it?

Oliver pressed the button; there was the feeling of flames stretching up, reaching above my head and making me see visions.

The Professor came and stood in front of me. He said 'Hullo.'

I said 'Hullo.'

He said 'Do you remember me?'

I said 'Yes.'

He said 'How are you doing?'

Oliver, from the bar, pressed the button. I thought – My mouth gapes open like the neck of Holofernes.

The Professor said 'You wanted to be an actress – '

I said 'Yes.'

He said 'And you wanted to know if you could make things do what you wanted – '

I said 'Yes.'

Oliver pressed the button.

The Professor said 'And I said you could go on doing this for a time and then you would stop.'

I could not make any sound come out.

He said 'So it's stopped.'

I said 'Yes.'

He said 'Good.'

I thought – I am dust and paper on the floor.

Oliver came from the bar carrying drinks. He stood by the Professor. Oliver was this strange young-old man with a white face and devil's eyebrows like an actor.

Oliver said 'You like her?'

The Professor said 'Yes.'

Oliver said 'She's very expensive.'

The Professor said 'How much?'

Oliver said 'Too much for you, Dr Strabismus.'

I thought – I must get some message through to the Professor.

Oliver said 'Now piss off.'

I said 'Coo-ee!'

The Professor said 'Shall I tell you my telephone number?'

I thought – But I'll never remember it!

The Professor said 'It's the highest score in first-class cricket and the date of the Second Reform Bill.'

Oliver said 'So you ponce too, do you, you talented man?'

The Professor said 'And everything is for the best in the best of all possible worlds.'

I thought – But there is nothing now there, where you might put a finger on my forehead?

When we got home, Oliver said –

'Little Judy from Hong Kong, half-way up the ladder, have a sniff, do: haven't got good tits, but hang on to them, please, if you want a bit of the brown bread and bugger.

'You like that old man? They still make them like that in – where did you meet him – America?

'They re-cycle them? They put them on ice?

'They do it by credit card over the telephone?

'I had a call from your Nazi friend Desmond the other day: he said I had been seen going off with you at the *Die Flamme*

73

party. I said – Walk up, any time, model, top floor: jack-boots and climbing-irons welcome.

'You know why you're a mess? because you have almost as much contempt for people as I have. But what you can't do is accept this. Fetch it! Good boy! Down boy! Oo!

'What shall we do with your boyfriend? Dress him up as little Dezzie death's head? A bit of the old *Arbeit macht frei*?'

I thought – You mean you are attracted to Desmond?

– You are afraid I might get in touch with the Professor?

It was at about this time, I think, that Oliver had begun to take me to a house in North London. He now did not seem to want to leave me so much alone.

I still wondered about why Oliver had stopped painting. Many painters, as I have said, at this time had become confused: asking what painting was, they seemed to be looking for ways to express this predicament.

When Oliver had painted it was as if he had put his hand inside people and had turned them inside out like glove-puppets: their skin was shiny and seemed to be decomposing slightly with sweat.

I think Oliver now wanted to get some sustenance for whatever he felt he needed for his paintings.

The house in North London was a large Victorian building done up like a Moorish palace; there were tiled floors and mosaics; a courtyard with a fountain. The house belonged, I think, to some business associates of Oliver's. I did not know who these were: it did not occur to me to want to know. The style of the house was that it was like an illustration to something pornographic.

There was one of Oliver's paintings, a mural, in an alcove. It was of a female figure lying on a rock with sea-anemones and crabs crawling over her. It seemed unfinished.

Oliver said 'She is Lilith. Do you know the story of Lilith?'
I said 'No.'
He said 'Lilith was Adam's first wife. God had made her equal to Adam. So when she and Adam made love, she wanted

to be equally on top. Adam objected to this, so Lilith flew away and lived on a rock. From there she sent out demons to plague mankind.'

The figure of Lilith was like a womb turned inside out. Her skin was white, as if from acid in the stomach of a whale.

Oliver said 'Be nice to these people! Poor old Jonahs: all eaten up by the devils sent by Lilith!'

Oliver, when he was not being venomous, was being flattering to me at this time. I thought – He does not know which way to hang: from the good breast or the bad breast of his mother.

Or – You mean Lilith would not have had to go away to her rock if she had learned about the powers there are in being underneath?

The people we met in the house in North London were large smooth men like drops of oil on the point of touching substance and spreading. They seemed to be from the Middle East: they gave the impression of being to do with yachts, and armaments. In the house in North London there was not much at first that went on: the atmosphere was like that of the party that Oliver had taken me to when I first met him. But these men did not seem to be residents of any holy of holies: they were like vessels that came in to be scraped and caulked before setting out again.

There had been a story in one of the *Die Flamme* magazines about Oliver's Middle East connections. They had suggested he was some sort of pimp: not only for the sake of what might be his art, but because he liked this sort of power.

The first time I went to the house in North London there was some party or reception. I was to act as a sort of hostess: I was to move among these people carrying caviare and biscuits on a plate. But what they seemed to get from me was the feel of something that they (or indeed I) could not quite grasp: a lick of some fantasy unseen and unspoken: what was it these people had not got that they could still want to feel?

They watched me from behind dark glasses. I thought –

Oliver will get commissions to paint harems in the Middle East? They want their heads cut off like Holofernes?

I said to Oliver 'What have you told them?'

Oliver said 'What do you mean, what have I told them?'

I thought – You have turned me inside out: they feel there is some glow about me; some radiation.

What I worked out was that Oliver must have told them – I am sorry about this: there are, indeed, here parts of the story of which I am ashamed – was that I was something to do with royalty. I mean not, of course, that I was royal: but that I had been, was being, fucked by someone royal: what else would such men want to rub off on; to have rub off on to them? I mean, what else could they not get for money? And what else, for me, might be nearer rock bottom?

I had thought – But of course, I am in the tent of Holofernes; should I not be good at getting something apart from this?

There were the walls with beautiful tiles and statues of nudes like surfaces from which blood could be wiped off.

I said to Oliver 'What exactly have you told them?'

He said 'They are dealers in uranium and plutonium, which are the modern philosopher's stones.'

I said 'What is your connection with them?'

He said 'The Israelis bugger the South Africans who bugger the Arabs who bugger the Israelis.'

I said 'But what do they pay you for?'

He said 'The snake that eats its own tail.'

I said 'And what is that?'

He said 'Queen Sheherazade.'

I said 'Hullo.'

'Hullo.'

'Is that the Professor?'

'Yes.'

'You gave me your number.'

'I did.'

'Can I see you?'

'You can.'

'When?'

'Lunchtime.'

'Where?'

'The National Gallery.'

'Whereabouts?'

'Do you know a painting by Piero di Cosimo of a girl lying on her side with a wound in her throat?'

'Yes.'

'You do?'

'Yes.'

'Then that's all right.'

'I see.'

'I'll see you there.'

'Thanks.'

Hullo, hullo, all you who find yourselves on spiral staircases; who look out of windows: you think you can fly?

You make your mind a blank: you think your number will come up on the roulette wheel –

On my way through the rooms of the National Gallery there was a huge St Sebastian on the wall like a board stuck through with darts: a row of Virgin Marys on their thrones like lavatories.

I thought – What is the difference between these images and those hatched out of the dark in the house in North London?

The painting by Piero di Cosimo is of a girl lying on her side with wounds in her throat and wrists: at her head there is a faun kneeling; at her feet a large brown dog. Behind her is a beach of pink-gold sand on the edge of what looks like an estuary: there are blue and silver hills beyond this in the distance. On the sand are three dogs playing: above the estuary is a line of birds dropping down like notes of music.

I thought – These people are not posing? They are getting on with what they are to be doing?

Then – This might be myself? You are the brown dog? You are the faun?

On the same wall at the other side of the room there was a painting by the same artist of a battle between Lapiths and Centaurs. Squat grey figures bash at each other with clubs and stones and something that looks like a chandelier: they seem to be fighting in the middle of a picnic. Everyone seems to be having a good time: they glow with the ghastly bottom-of-the-ocean light of a flash photograph, or the figures in Oliver's paintings.

I thought – Well, people do think they're having a good time with this sort of posing, showing-off, don't they?

I went back to the picture of the girl with the wound in her throat. I had loved this picture from the first time I had seen it. I thought I would wave and say – Coo-ee!

The Professor said 'Hullo.'

I said 'Hullo.'

We stood side by side looking at the picture. I thought – You mean, you have nothing to say to me?

– Then who is it that I talk to?

I looked up at a corner of the ceiling.

After a time the Professor said 'Now come along here.' He took me by the arm and led me through the gallery.

He went past the St Sebastians like dart-boards and the Virgin Marys on their thrones. I thought – You mean, they pose for those who need them to be posing?

We came to rest in another room in front of a picture which was a small Filippo Lippi of the Annunciation. I had not noticed this before. The Virgin Mary, on the right, is in a courtyard on a chair over which something like a towel has been placed; she is not on her throne; she is leaning forward with a hand beneath her breast: she is facing the angel, to the left, who is kneeling in a small garden. Beyond and between them is a doorway to a staircase down which there has flown a small bird; its passage is marked by a spiral of light. At the top of the picture, almost outside the frame, is a hand with two fingers pointing down. The bird has stopped in the air and is gazing intently at Mary's middle. Mary and the angel are watching the bird.

I thought – You mean, they too are not posing? They are getting on with whatever it is they are to be doing –

– That bird: that finger coming down –

– They are from just outside the painting?

The Professor said 'Now this.'

I thought – I want to sit down.

He said 'Only one more.'

He led me through other galleries. I felt I might be going to faint. Once the Professor seemed to lose his way. He stopped and looked around, humming. I thought – He is waiting for that bird, that finger to come down?

He said 'Here.'

He stopped in front of a small picture by Giorgione of the Adoration of the Magi. There was the usual group of Mary and the child and St Joseph on the left –

I thought I might say – I'm not well.

I said 'I'm sorry.'

He said 'That's all right.'

There are Mary and the child and St Joseph on the left; the three wise men and various worshippers and onlookers on the right. Mary and Joseph and two of the wise men are gazing not at the child but at a place on the ground just in front of him: this space is quite empty except for some faint marks which might once have been a nest containing something like four stones. The child has a finger up to his mouth and is looking out of the picture to the left: also looking in this direction is a donkey.

I thought – You mean, they are intent on something that is both within, and without, the framework of the picture?

The Professor led me to one of the upholstered seats in the middle of the room. We sat down. He said 'Phew!' He seemed to be exhausted.

I thought – All the lights have come on in the auditorium of the theatre?

I said 'They're watching what they themselves are doing: they're not reacting; they're not posing: they are listening.'

He said 'Yes.' Then – 'What are you on, any of the hard stuff?'

I said 'In that battle between the Lapiths and Centaurs, they're all posing as if for a photograph.'

He said 'You're finding it difficult to get off?'

I said 'I can get off.'

He seemed to hum. He tapped his foot up and down. Then he said 'Well, let's have lunch then.'

I thought – I can't have lunch.

I said 'What are they looking at in that empty space on the ground?'

He said 'Put your head down. There.'

I said 'I think I'm going to faint.'

He said 'Well, I want a large whisky.'

I thought – The faun had one hand on her shoulder –

– The finger, then the bird, coming down –

– The nest, where it laid, is now empty?

There was a bright light as if the curtain had come down and all the audience were leaving the theatre.

I thought – You mean, we can get on with whatever it is we are to be doing?

He said 'Rum tiddle di um tum, tum tum.'

I said 'I've got to get some air.'

He said 'Meet you in the square in five minutes.'

I wanted to say – But why me?

It was as if we were sitting in that picture, in the courtyard. He had his hand on my shoulder. He might say – Now now, Mary!

I would say – I didn't mean – !

I said 'Whereabouts in the square?'

He said 'By the right-hand fountain.'

I thought – Right as you look at it?

He said 'Right as you look at it, not right as you look back from the square.'

I thought – Oh, but would they not, indeed, have been blinded, those people, when they looked out from their cave, into the sun!

I said 'Perhaps what they were looking at was light.'

He said 'Perhaps what who were looking at was light?'

I said 'Those people in the farmyard.'

He said 'God Almighty.' Then – 'Take your time.' Then – 'I'm getting my whisky.'

There is something, I suppose, I ought to put in here: as a rest from the light: as if it were a glass of whisky –

There had been recently an evening in the house in North London when Oliver had done more than he usually did: he had staged, or helped to stage, some performance.

It is difficult to write about these things because, again, a description seems more affecting than a performance. A performance seems often not much to do with you at all. Words are not good – are they? – at showing the silliness of shadows.

The performance was trying to make shadows flesh on a wall: what would a dreamer see — what would happen to a dream – if the dreamer saw it enacted?

At first I was to move as before among the guests (five or six) in my usual form as hostess. I distributed sweetmeats and smoke: I was this desirable thing, but untouchable. I was the one because I was the other: the sacred sacrifice: the virgin nymph with the horn of plenty: why do you think there are these images?

Oliver had the idea that what people wanted from queens and goddesses was (of course) sacrifice: there had to be immolation: then desires could come together and burst like slime-mould on to the floor.

So I was to move among these people dressed as – what? – Isis, Artemis, Judith, Jezebel. Was there not a time when women had been goddesses? And arms had reached up adoring, adoring them: and how happy had been their slaves! So in the sand-dunes, in a temple, might it not be a female child that is dismembered (you know this story?) and then partaken of: to be eaten, and redeemed?

I might suggest – I am sorry, my time has come; I must go to my mother; and so on.

There was an alcove in one of the Moorish rooms that was curtained off as if it were a stage. Within this alcove there was a cage in which there was trapped – well, what do you think? – suffering humanity. Suffering humanity was represented, in this case, by Edwin, a large black man from an agency in Hertford Street. I mean Edwin himself was not really so large; but he had the rare and remarkable (do you not think?) attribute of being able to make himself large (if you see what I mean) at will; even if apart from this ability he was a rather unsuccessful middleweight boxer. Edwin used to do knitting behind the stage. Well, I said – didn't I – that these things usually go on below the level of sensible description. But where do they come from: where are they going. Anyway, there I was, with shadows around me that yearned to find a home on a wall; how can humanity both get and not get (in order to keep?) what it needs as unobtainable? You can get it vicariously, can't you? This is the role of dreams: but dreams search for a home to be made flesh; to be raised at will; like the accomplishment, as it were, of Edwin the middleweight boxer. Anyway, when the curtain went up there was this black man in his cage – wrongly imprisoned, of course: on the eve of his execution perhaps (are we not all likely to be blown up?), or even as that rich man Dives straining agonised arms up from hell.

Humanity, indeed, cannot get out of its cage, can it – that cage of desire, of consciousness, of where-are-we-from-and-where-are-we-going. So what can a goddess do about this? except to condescend, of course, vicariously. I had two Thai boys to help me (it was now I who was Holofernes with his handmaidens?). Edwin, of course, could do no more than poke out of his cage. And there were all the guests, the armament manufacturers, watching like drops of oil – about to touch some deep surface at last and spread. For them this had to be vicarious; how else could they also remain their compact, immune, all-of-a-piece globules? So I had to be helped (so fragile was I: such was my care!) on to their representative, their shadow in the cave or cage – Edwin their great vicar from Hertford Street. I had to smile sweetly as I was lifted on the arms of my acolytes; on to, as it were, my throne, my consecration. I could do this quite well: what do

82

you think it is that makes an actress? And Edwin would bang and roar against the bars of the cage: he was quite good at this too: he said he used to imagine he was one of his uncles who had swallowed a serpent in Port au Prince. And the two Thai boys went so delicately: getting the hook as it were, on to the worm at the mouth of the cage. And it was the audience who were caught – by Edwin as suffering humanity; by the Thai boys with their dexterity and control: and by myself, of course, above all – as the drop of oil, their queen, bursting in their minds and spreading.

If a woman were to be the sacrifice, do you think the satisfaction for men would be just the nails having gone in?

That's enough, Princess Salome! Blot her out!

There are shafts between the conscious and the unconscious: they are like bars of light.

(Did not you, Bert, want to make a film like this? A newborn baby lies on the edge of a bed –)

What I remember is the audience becoming very still. I looked amongst them: I was saying – Is it you; is it you?

You can paint the sacrificed god: could you paint the sacrificed goddess?

Would she not be watching you? Looking down –

That is why you would not want her to be on top?

Edwin, I think, at the end had to pretend to be garrotted: he could not be allowed out of his cage. One of the Thai boys had to nip round behind.

You know what happens when a man is garrotted?

Oh, the remaining Thai boy and myself could make quite a prettily posed picture! a cherub at the feet of my throne.

In the end, yes, I would come down.

I would move about amongst my audience like a vicar shaking hands on Easter Sunday.

Of course I am real! Of course you can touch me!

A little blood, a little shit, do you not think?

(Don't you call this contempt?)

That is also what you came for, isn't it?

*

I said to the Professor 'What work are you engaged on at the moment?'

He said 'I'm on a committee in Whitehall to do with chemical and biological warfare.'

I said 'What can you do about such things?'

He said 'You can't unknow what you know. You can't do away with primitive emotions. You can learn a new way of looking.'

I said 'Such as.'

He said 'What is beautiful, and what is simply boring.'

We were sitting on a parapet of a fountain in Trafalgar Square. The basin of the fountain was empty. Pigeons flew about like spirals of dust in a courtyard.

I said 'Do you know Kleist's story of the puppet-master?'

He said 'Yes.'

I said 'He said humans were not viable because they were neither puppets nor gods.'

He said 'He also said that humans would be viable, if they went right round the world and into the Garden of Eden again by the back way.'

I said 'I didn't know that.'

He said 'Didn't you?'

There were some young men in white shirts and grey flannel trousers unloading equipment from a van at the edge of the paved area of the square. They carried wooden planks and rolled-up banners to the plinth at the bottom of the column in the centre.

I said 'No, I don't know how to keep off dope. I don't know how to get out. I don't know where to go.'

He said 'You will when you want to.'

I said 'How will I want?'

He said 'It may not be much to do with you.'

I said 'What will it be to do with?'

He said 'You haven't hit rock bottom.'

The men in white shirts had propped two ladders against the plinth. They climbed up. They seemed to be preparing for a political meeting.

I said 'I thought I had.'

He said 'You may be carried off kicking. Who wants to be reborn?'

I said 'There might be soft lights and sweet music!'

He said 'Yes, indeed, there might be soft lights and sweet music.'

At the side of the square there was a policeman and a policewoman who were watching the men in white shirts at the plinth. The policeman spoke into his two-way radio: the policewoman held hers to her ear.

I said 'But why me?' Then – 'I mean, why are you helping me?'

He said 'Why anyone?' Then – 'My girlfriend's just left me.'

I thought – Is that true? Then – You're too old to have a girlfriend!

There was another group of people coming across the square. They wore bowler hats; they carried cases that looked as if they contained musical instruments.

I said 'Why shouldn't some sort of Bomb go off, if you've got to hit rock bottom?'

He said 'Indeed, why shouldn't some sort of Bomb go off.'

I said 'I thought you had something to tell me.'

He said 'I've told you.'

The men on the plinth were setting up a microphone and loudspeakers. They hung wires over the stone lions at the corners of the plinth.

I thought – Again, what was it in those paintings: an empty space? a courtyard? a girl lying on a beach?

I said 'Why has your girlfriend left you?'

He said 'She's having a baby.'

I thought – You mean the baby's not yours? Then – This is ridiculous!

Then – You mean, it is like the baby in the picture?

He said 'And so I thought I'd do anything to get another girl – '

I said 'That's not true!'

He said 'Of course it's not true!'

I thought – You mean, I have to see why you said it?

The musicians were putting down their instrument-cases at the bottom of the plinth. They were taking off their jackets.

He said 'She's thinking of getting an abortion.'

I said 'And you don't want her to?'

He said 'No.'

I thought I might say – Stop her then.

I thought suddenly – Perhaps I will go to that old guru in India!

I said 'The baby's not yours – '

He said 'I don't know.'

I thought – That girl: the empty space: those two figures in the courtyard –

Then – I am responsible for my story: you are responsible for yours –

– You are responsible for my story: I am responsible for yours –

Two of the musicians had taken hold of the ladders which belonged to the men in white shirts on the plinth. They were climbing up them. They began to walk about on them as if they were stilts.

I said 'I once saw a film about this: the foetus is drawn into a vacuum: it explodes: it can't make a noise.'

He said 'Oh yes.' Then – 'I see.'

I said 'Of course you can stop her if you want to!'

He said 'You see, you're helping me.' Then – 'You've got my number: you can call me any hour of the day or night.'

I thought – You mean, you'll help me to get to India?

The men in white shirts were looking down from the top of their plinth. The men who had taken their ladders were walking about like clowns. One of them carried a flute which he brandished as if it were a sword.

I said 'But you don't want a new girlfriend.'

He said 'Of course I want a new girlfriend!'

I thought – I don't understand this way of seeing things, this way of talking, at all.

There was that physical sensation of cold air coming in. I thought – I am that foetus, trying to get out?

So what did become of that girl with the wound in her throat –

– The message like a bird –

– That empty space?

I said 'What is the name of your girlfriend?'

He said 'Lilia.'

I thought – Not Lilith? Lilia?

The two men on stilts confronted one another; they seemed, with their musical instruments, to be about to fight a duel. The men in white shirts had got down from their plinth and were going after them; the clowns on stilts began waddling across the square. The men in white shirts caught up with them and held the ladders; they were like people struggling to raise a flag.

The Professor said 'It's like an experiment I once did with my students.'

I said 'What is?'

He said 'This.' Then – 'Sometimes there are connections.' Then – 'Yes, we must stop her.'

One of the ladders, upright, was by the parapet of the fountain. As the men in white shirts struggled with it, it toppled, slowly, projecting the man at the top on towards a piece of sculpture within the fountain. There he landed, and clung, as if on a rock in a rough sea; while the other end of the ladder, the length of which had pivoted on the parapet, jerked up and caught one of the men in white shirts in the groin. This man sank to the ground, while his companions gathered round him.

The policeman and the policewoman were approaching across the square. The Professor got up and walked towards them. He stood in front of them and seemed to show them some card of identification. I thought – He is dissuading them from interfering with whatever it is that is going on: he is making out that he has been in control of some experiment all the time.

I thought – I must get away!

I got up and walked in another direction across the square. The Professor was standing with the policeman and the policewoman watching the scene as if they were appreciating some picture.

One evening I was on my own in the sitting-room of the flat and there was a ring on the doorbell from downstairs and I pressed the entry button and then when I opened the door of the flat there was Desmond.

I thought I might say – Go away! Don't you know it is dangerous to be here?

– You have come to rescue me after all? But it is too late! Don't you know this might be a trap?

Desmond said 'Oliver told me you were here.'

I thought – I know Oliver would have told you I was here!

Desmond followed me into the sitting-room. He closed the door. He said 'He said I could come and see you.'

I thought – So you are a member of Them – who? – the invaders from Andromeda? The Gestapo? You will put on rubber gloves. You will be looking for – Guns? Papers? Foetuses?

Desmond sat with his arms along the sides of a chair. I thought – If I had a button, I might get currents passing through him –

He said 'How have you been?'

I said 'All right.'

He said 'Oliver doesn't mind!'

I thought I might say – There will be the explosion; the rubble; the dome of the observatory; the spire open to the wind –

He said 'What does Oliver do? I've heard stories!'

I wanted him to go away. I wanted to explain – We each have to be getting on with – whatever is in those pictures.

He said 'Come to bed.'

I said 'Why did Oliver want you to come here?'

He said 'I don't know, do you?'

He sat with his arms along the sides of the chair. I thought – But don't you know what happens to people who are booby-trapped –

Then – Perhaps all of us have to be wiped out.

He said 'Show me what he does.' Then – 'I'd like anything!'

I thought – Oh I have seen children with dogs' heads and fins of fishes! –

He said 'Aren't you well?'

I said 'No.'

He said 'Perhaps I better come back another time.'

I thought – You mean, there really is something keeping an eye on this, just round some corner?

The experiment that the Professor had once done with his students (he told me later) was –

The students were placed in front of a screen and each was given to hold an instrument similar to those by which you alter the channels on television. The students were told that by pressing this or that button they could affect what image came up on the screen: there were five or six buttons and five or six corresponding images available: the students were told that their instruments were connected to a machine which would project the image selected by the majority of buttons. In fact the instruments were connected to nothing that affected what image came up on the screen: they were connected to a computer which recorded what buttons were pressed, and which analysed the relations and patterns of relations between the buttons pressed and the images. What came up on the screen was occasioned by another machine which made its 'choices' at random: by 'random' was meant something to do with the behaviour of elementary particles: this at that time among scientists had become a definition of 'randomness'. But students were under the impression that they could influence what came up on the screen by becoming part of a statistical majority. So, what was the point of the experiment? The computer recorded the buttons pressed and the images that came up and it analysed the relations and patterns of relations: there were certain coincidences that occurred slightly more or slightly less than what might be expected from laws of averages: there were certain numbers of occasions when the image that came up was the one before, or the one after, the corresponding majority-button pressed – and so on. There were statistics that might seem interesting here and there: but these seemed to be offset by interesting figures somewhere else. So what, indeed, was the point of the experiment?

It was, I suppose, that all this was like life: we are under the illusion – are we not? – that we influence things – even if we imagine our influence is dependent on its being part of a statistical majority. But then, after a time, the students got bored – do we not get bored like this in life: however much we think we participate actively in events we also suspect, at some level, that we do not: and anyway, what sort of personal influence is it that depends on being part of a majority statistic? Is there here anything of control? And so there is a sort of despair (might there not be a button by which we could blow up the world!). And so on. You see what I mean.

But there were one or two students (was one of them you, Bert?) who some time before had begun to see the whole business as absurd: to suspect that, of course, the instruments they held in their hands were connected to nothing except perhaps that which could record and analyse their actions; what else, indeed, would be scientifically possible in such an experiment? But I think these one or two students would have seen this with some sort of irony: they could still press their buttons: does one not thus go on pressing buttons (what else is there to do) in life?

But the Professor then began to notice something very odd that was happening (was it you, Bert? was it you?). Just when these one or two students were going on pressing their buttons without any hope of effect, as it were – in some deference I suppose just to the irony of being conscious of absurdity – there began to come up on the computer, the Professor noticed, quite a few extraordinary results: I mean the buttons pressed by these one or two students began to coincide exactly with the images that came up on the screen: these coincidences happened enormously in excess of anything that could be explained statistically: this seemed to be happening just when these students had given up one set of expectations and were not yet feeling paralysed about another: I mean their minds were open, quizzical, blank; both caring and not caring. They did not know, of course, what was happening: at first the Professor hardly knew himself: but the effects, the results, the coincidences, were there. But then, of course, the Professor became very excited; his excitement communicated itself, perhaps, to these students; anyway, after a time they seemed in some way to become aware of what was happening and the extraordinary run of results tailed off; then stopped altogether. One of the students put his instrument down; would not go on; walked out of the experiment room. Was it not, indeed, Bert, you! Perhaps some white light had come down. What can you do, how can you go on, when you know that the experiment works, but only when, as it were, you do not know that it works; when in the face of impossibility you have a certain – insouciance? You would have to leave – would you not – at least that area that you knew was a theatre.

There is this behaviour of elementary particles that is called random – that does not seem to be to do with what is known as cause and effect. But at the same time, in the same area, there are connections – I mean something happens to a particle here (this has been observed) and something (the same thing? its complement?) happens to a particle there; instantaneously, without (but the question is with what?) what has been called connection. And there are these particles both inside and outside the brain. So what are, indeed, connections?

If you start talking about this, then – good heavens! of course it is easier to go back to talking about statistics.

But if you paint a picture, you are looking – are you not – not at what you expect; but at what you have (how could this be!) discovered – or created?

I got my suitcase out to pack every now and then. I sat by the window looking down into the street.

People moved like bits and pieces of slime-mould. They did not seem able to find a way of coming together. If they did, they would explode?

91

Somewhere or other there was a tower being built up to heaven. If one were a god, I thought, why should one not press the button.

Once or twice Oliver brought people back to the flat. I thought – Each time I get nearer like that child to the edge of the bed: to flip over.

Oliver would say – No one thrown you away yet?

There was an evening when I was sitting on the floor of the bedroom watching television: on television I could do with people what I liked: switch them from one thing to another. I thought – What if God just gets bored with our programme on television; plays us fast-forward to extinction? On one channel there was a ballet: *Romeo and Juliet*, I think: people were staggering about, flopping, coming together, climbing on one another's shoulders: they seemed to be trying to get out of the framework of the picture. But the framework moved with them: they were trapped within their cave. On another channel there was a child crossing a railway bridge; he stopped and looked back; he looked into the camera. I thought – His parents, Romeo and Juliet, are always flopping around; how can he get up off their dreadful shoulders? A train came underneath the railway bridge: I wondered – The child, to get himself loved, will have to jump over?

On another channel there was a programme about the men who in fact had made the Bomb; they were like large-eyed animals that come out only at night: there was their habitat, the dump of buildings in the desert. Then they were in white coats facing switches and dials. On another channel there was a girl being enclosed in an iron case: the inside of the case was exactly the same shape as the girl: she was to be entombed and abandoned, as some sort of retribution. I thought – Those men in white coats are trying to get something through to her: but she cannot scream: there is just that slit like a peephole through which her eyes act terrified. I wanted to see what was going on with the child on the railway bridge. I heard Oliver coming into the flat: he had someone with him. The child on the bridge was looking down: I thought – Do not jump: jump: what particles are there that will make you do one thing rather than another? It seemed that the person with Oliver was Desmond. I thought – Well, after all, yes, Oliver may be half in love with Desmond. Romeo and Juliet were flopping about on their tomb. I wondered what it was the girl in the iron case had down her throat so she could not scream; perhaps I should check with the men in white coats again. But then there was that picture of the miles and miles of rubble: the dome of the observatory, the spire open to the wind. Oliver and Desmond were laughing in the next room. I thought – You can manipulate these pictures: where is it that those people are in the paintings in the National Gallery? I thought I might try soon to get there. Oliver and Desmond came in from the sitting-room. Oliver said to me 'Look who's here!' I thought I might say – But I know who's here. Oliver said to Desmond 'You see what I mean!' Desmond said 'Yes.' I thought – I despise – what? – myself, as well as others. The child had gone down from the railway bridge and was walking by a canal. Romeo and Juliet were having what looked like a fuck on their tomb. There was a button that you pressed that made everything go roaring and blank. Oliver said 'What shall we do with her?' Desmond said 'We can't just leave her like that.' I thought – Where is the girl in iron case? Perhaps she is the foetus, waiting in the tomb. Oliver said 'I'll leave you two together.' Desmond said 'No you needn't go.' Oliver said 'Would you like some help?' Desmond said 'Yes let's get her over the bed.' He began to lift me. I said 'Just a minute.' Oliver said 'No more minutes.' I said 'I want to pee.' Desmond said 'You needn't go to pee.' I still had in my hand the instrument that changed the channels on television: the child was looking down into the waters of the canal. I said 'There's something I want in the bathroom.' Oliver said 'All right.' When I looked at them I thought – Eeny meeny miney mo, Holofernes. Oliver was that thick-set man like a probe: Desmond was a glove with the hand sweating up inside him.

I went out of the bedroom and across the passage into the bathroom. I thought – You can do anything, can you, when you've no idea what it is you are doing. In the bathroom I locked the door. The shelf above the basin was where that piece of screwed-up paper with the powder had been: I thought – Well, it was some sort of signpost – wasn't it – through the maze. I did not know if I was the child above the canal, the foetus, or the girl in the iron case. I wondered – What happens when those men with their probes reach the holy of holies; the heart of the atom, the tomb?

I sat on a chair at the side of the bath over the back of which there was a towel with flowers on it. I thought – So where is that bird; that finger coming down: hullo, hullo, little one.

After a time Oliver came to the other side of the bathroom door and banged on it. He said 'Are you all right?'

I did not know how long I had been there. Perhaps I had been asleep.

I went to the window of the bathroom and tried to open it. It was the sort that swings outwards on a horizontal hinge. It did not seem possible to crawl through at the bottom, as it were between someone's legs; you had to lie along the top, but then you might be hurled outwards as if from some seige machine.

There was that foetus on the floor with a rope tied round its throat. I thought – That girl of the Professor's, where is she?

I stretched out along the slope of the window. I thought – If the hinge breaks, I will be flung out and fly.

Oliver or Desmond, at the door behind me, seemed to be trying to break it down.

I intended to get out and to crawl along the parapet as I had done once or twice before: then I might come to another window where I might get into some dimension where I had not been before.

I thought – That empty nest on the ground: is it where someone fell? a child? a bird? a stone?

That, at last, might be rock bottom?

It was not difficult to get out of the window. But the parapet on this side of the building was more narrow and fragile than the one on which I had crawled before. It seemed, as I knelt on it, that a piece of stone became loose and might, indeed, have fallen to the street below.

I thought – No wonder those shadow-watchers liked staying within their cave!

Someone behind me seemed to be getting through the bathroom door.

I set off along the parapet. I was going towards the windows of the next-door flat. I had sometimes wondered about whoever it was who lived there. Perhaps it was he or she who had picked me up that evening when I had passed out in the lift.

I thought – Hang on, little one; help is coming. I am that bird!

I was coming to a window of the next-door flat; the curtains were only partly drawn; there was a slit in the middle through which I could see (as if they were in a painting) a man and a woman sitting side by side at a piano; they had their backs to me: they were quite still. I thought – They are in love: they are representative of something quite different: they are like the figures that have been lying, that have risen, above an Etruscan tomb. And their notes fly about like birds of music. I crawled on. I heard a voice call out my name behind me. I thought Oliver must be pursuing me on to the parapet. I came to a window like the one out of which I had just climbed; it was on a horizontal hinge opening outwards at the top; but here there was just enough room to crawl through at the bottom. I thought – I will be born. It did seem that there was someone emerging on to the parapet some distance behind me. I thought – Perhaps, yes, if I kick backwards with my feet, there will be that mysterious and instantaneous effect at a distance. The room beyond the window through which I was crawling was in darkness: I had in fact to push against something solid, I think it was the balustrade, with my feet. I seemed to be pulling myself on to the top of another surface, or slope, on a central hinge inside the room. I thought – This is ridiculous. There was some sort of cry behind me. Then the surface on which I was stretching tipped,

and I was projected head-first into the darkness. I thought –
Well, good-bye, old life: I suppose I never really knew you. I
had landed on some rug. I was on all fours in the room.
I thought – Well, are we or are we not those particles to
whom this happens here and that happens there at the same
time? Then – At least, this is quite a comfortable rock
bottom.

I did not want to think of anything else.

You know that experiment in which you look into a box
through a peephole and there is what appears to be a room
with a bed and a table and chairs: and then you look over the
top of the box and you see that it contains just disconnected
lines and planes and it has been yourself, your way of seeing
things, that has transformed the bits and pieces into the
structure of a room. Well, this space into which I had been
projected seemed to be the inside of such a box: I could not
make out what it was into which I had fallen; there were bars
of light at some distance like suspended strips of neon. I was on
a carpet; there was linoleum; then a platform; then a pair of
metal legs. I thought – Dear God, not those legs of the girl in
the iron case! I had imagined I might come to a bathroom
similar to the one which I had left: but this space was larger:
there were distances between solid objects. As I crawled I hit
my head against the soft edge of a bed. I worked out, after a
time, that the bars of light must stand for the gaps round a
door: they also seemed to be reflected in a mirror somewhere
behind me. It seemed likely that there would be a light-switch
at the side of the door. I crawled on. I thought – But there will
be that bright light coming down: the end of the play: the
audience leaving the theatre.

There were noises from the street below. I thought – Please
God, there was that cry: there will not be an ambulance?

But also – Where are that man and woman who are in love in
the next room?

When I found the switch and the light came on it appeared
that the room in which I had landed was a combined
bedroom-bathroom and there was a swing-mirror on a stand

beneath the open window which was what I had crawled on to – as if it were a second window after I had got through the first – and it was because of this that I had been projected head-first, although inwards. I went and shut the window. It was luck, of course, that at the first window I had not been projected outwards. There was a bed on one side of the room and a bath and a washbasin and a lavatory on the other. I thought – This is all right: I can wash; then perhaps lie down on the bed for a while at least. I was not wearing many clothes: there was a dressmaker's dummy in the room. I thought I might say – Hullo and good-bye: Judith, Holofernes.

I locked the door. I went to the basin and washed my face and stared down into the water. I thought – So what do you think you are: on your own: with no more images?

There were voices from people outside in the passage. There were noises from people in the street below.

The handle of the door by the washbasin moved. I thought I might say – Just a moment: I'm just getting off the lavatory.

A woman's voice said 'Who's there?'

I thought I might say – Judith.

– Judith who?

– D'you know what happened to Holofernes?

I said 'I'll be out in a minute.'

The woman's voice said 'Who is it?'

When I did open the door – I had draped a towel round me and arranged my hair: those gods and goddesses should make an effort, should they not, before they collapse like burned paper – there was a red-haired woman in the passage. She had her back against the wall. I thought – Hullo, hullo, this strange landscape.

I said 'I'm terribly sorry, but I wonder if I could use your telephone?'

The woman said 'Of course.'

I said 'Thanks.'

My voice sounded as if it were coming from somewhere behind me. I thought – Sooner or later, I must look back?

97

There was a telephone on a table in the passage. The wallpaper had ships and fish and mermaids on it. I thought – There is something different about gravity in this strange landscape?

The woman put out a hand as if to help me. I sat on a chair by the telephone. I thought I heard the sound of an ambulance. I thought – But what if I cannot bear this?

After a time the woman said 'Can I do anything?'

I said 'I'm trying to remember the number.'

I thought – There are things one can't do, aren't there, when people are watching.

The woman went back into the room in which, I imagined, there was the piano. I thought – This is extraordinarily kind of you.

She left the door ajar. There were people's voices.

I thought – Oliver came out on to the parapet?

After a time the woman came out into the passage again.

I said 'I'm so sorry, I can't remember the number.'

She said 'Oh.'

I said 'It's the highest score in first-class cricket and the date of the Second Reform Bill.'

She said 'The highest score in first-class cricket and the date of the Second Reform Bill.'

I said 'Yes.'

She said 'Just a minute.'

She went back into the room with the piano. There were voices.

I thought – I was wrong about the sound of an ambulance?

A man's voice, loudly, came from the room with the piano. He said 'Four five two?'

I said 'No.'

The man's voice said 'It used to be.'

The woman's voice said 'It doesn't matter what it used to be.'

I thought – Perhaps the man is staying out of sight because if he does he might be one of those particles that will prevent the sound of the ambulance arriving –

The man's voice said 'Four nine nine.'

I said 'Yes, four nine nine.'

The man poked his head round the corner of the passage. He had a strong, bony face. I thought – But I have seen him before?

The woman with red hair appeared to pull him back into the room.

I thought – I am responsible for your story: you are responsible for mine –

There was the woman's voice saying 'And the date of the Second Reform Bill?'

The man's voice said 'It was something to do with Gladstone.'

There was the sound of an ambulance arriving in the street below.

The man's voice said 'Eighteen sixty? Eighteen sixty-seven?'

The man came out into the passage: he was holding the red-haired woman by the hand.

I thought – Oh thank you!

I said 'Yes eighteen sixty-seven.'

The man said to the woman 'I must go.'

The woman said 'Yes.'

The man said 'I love you.'

The woman said 'I love you too.'

There had been that cry, had there not, of a body falling to the street below.

The man turned to me: he said 'Good luck.'

I thought – You mean, Coo-ee?

– But is everything for the best in the best of all possible worlds –

– If this is, at last, rock bottom?

I said 'Thank you.'

The man went along the passage and out of the door of the flat.

I thought – There was that loose bit of parapet, was there not, outside Oliver's bathroom window.

The woman said to me 'Would you like to lie down? Would you like some tea?'

I said 'Could you possibly dial that number for me?'

She said 'Yes.'

I said 'And ask for the Professor.'

She said 'The Professor.'

I said 'And just tell him I'm here: Judith.'

I thought – I did manage, didn't I, to say thank you – I mean say it so that it would be there, as if in a painting, and not just in words flying away.

Some time in the middle of the night (I remember having got as far as that bed) I awoke and there were people sitting by me. I had been having a half-waking, half-sleeping dream about the bottom falling out of the maze; there you are with your hands and back pressed against the wall; you are quite still; but what can you do? what is gravity? It is different in this strange world. Then I was on the grass with the flowers like small trees and the trees like flowers: the faun and the brown dog at each end of me. They had been talking when I had been asleep and now they were not talking: I supposed they were watching me. I tried to remember what had happened before the fall: I mean, before the bottom had dropped out of my maze: and I found of course that I did not want to remember. I prayed – But I need time in this strange world.

– If I have cut the rope, and a body has fallen to the ground, might not the rope have been from an umbilicus?

Then when I seemed to be going to sleep I heard the voices begin again.

Does anyone ever remember what people say, literally?

It was, I suppose, as if we were in that painting.

The Professor and the woman with red hair are at the head and foot of my bed. Their sounds drop down like notes of music.

The Professor is saying 'No, don't talk: just wave perhaps every now and then.'

The woman is saying 'At the coincidences – '

'Yes at the coincidences.'

'But you say she fought – '

'Oh yes, you fight!'

'But what happens then?'

'I'll try to get her to a place in India. I'll see to her.'

And I am thinking – But I was planning to go to that place in India! How does he know about a place in India!

The woman says 'But what if they find out?'

The Professor says 'They won't find out. He won't want anyone to know.'

The woman says 'You'll tell her?' Then – 'You'll tell him about her?'

The Professor says 'I'll tell anyone what they want to know. But they won't.' Then – 'But she mustn't go back.'

And I am thinking – These wounds at my throat and wrist; they are where I have been trying to destroy myself: they are where I am now dangling, as it were, from a hook –

The woman says 'There was a film about two people who sat up all night talking about how to cover up for a girl.'

The Professor says 'It wasn't in the film, it was in the book.'

The woman says 'I work in films.'

The Professor says 'Yes I know you do.'

I am thinking – There are no noises now, are there, from the street below.

The woman says 'Do you sleep with her?'

The Professor says 'No of course I don't sleep with her!'

The woman says 'Well you might do.'

There are no more noises of any sort for some time. I think – On that beach, with the blue and silver hills, the faun and the brown dog – they are lovers?

The Professor says 'Can I sleep here?'

The woman says 'You mean, there's only one other bed?'

I think – There are people who are like this? They will go away when I open my eyes?

When I did open my eyes I saw that the Professor was sitting at the edge of the bed and the woman with red hair had come and stood by him. She had her hand on his shoulder. He had put his arm around her.

The Professor said 'All states of grace are by-products.'

The woman said ' "With love from Judith!" '

PART II

PART II

Dear Professor,

Do you think people write letters for them to be left lying about; so other people can bump into them?

Then there will be sharp corners as well as threads as you go through the maze.

When I first came to this place I did imagine, yes, that I had come to the inside of that painting: the estuary with the green and gold beach and the birds flopping down; the flowers like small trees and the trees like large flowers. But the faun and the brown dog, where were they? You had got me here: what was I to do: how was I to survive?

The bus from the airport went as far as the town at the far side of the estuary and left me there. I was rowed across the water by an old man in a boat. The images sometimes go back to front: you are rowed away from hell, are you, as well as towards it. These boats were the easiest way to get to the Garden from the town. I am going to call this *ashram* the Garden because that is what most of the inmates called it at the time. This was partly a joke – as were so many things to do with the Garden. But did you not say – In order to return to the Garden of Eden you have to go right round the world and in at the back way?

There was a track up to the Garden from the beach at the far side of the estuary. People were on either side of the track selling trinkets – metal jewellery, inlaid boxes, embroidery with beads. These people were mostly local; there were also a few from the Garden trying to raise money for their stay. Those who came to the Garden were Europeans and Americans and a few Japanese: they had travelled at least half-way round the world on their way through the maze.

As I went up the track an Indian boy followed me. I thought I might say – But I am getting away from all this! do you not see the wounds at my hands and throat? The gates into the Garden were an elaborate wooden construction like the entrance to a Chinese pagoda: there was a high wire fence going off on either side. A small crowd, mostly of men, were hanging around outside the gates: they were smoking cigarettes among bicycles piled like dead flies. I learned later that there was no smoking of any kind allowed inside the Garden, so people went just outside to smoke, as if they were pickets or angels with tiny flaming swords.

There was a road in front of the Garden at right angles to the track. I sat down on my rucksack at the opposite side of the road. The Indian boy came up to me. He said 'Where are you from? England? Germany? America?'

I thought I might say – But the wound in my throat, you see, means that I cannot speak to you.

The men outside the gates wore white or yellow smocks and loose white trousers. They laughed, and put their arms round each other's shoulders. They were like people congratulating each other about who had come through after some contest.

The Indian boy said 'I can offer accommodation, at a reasonable price, at the house of my uncle.'

There was a woman standing just inside the gate looking out. She had a wide round face and short fair hair which gave an aura of light around her. She seemed somewhat larger than life. I thought – She is like that painting of the Madonna with all the children of the world under her skirts like chickens.

The Indian boy said 'There is no accommodation left in the Garden.'

I had not known what I would find when I arrived at the Garden: I had not tried to imagine anything beyond the gates. I thought – How is it that you get within, and then do you ever get out of, the framework of a picture?

The Indian boy said 'You speak English?'

I thought I might explain – People who talk to me are apt to die; to fall from windows; to have their heads chopped off.

The woman standing just inside the entrance gates wore a long loose dress like the lines of a Greek statue. She held her arms straight by her sides. I thought – She is like one of those archaic statues who walk forwards with mad smiles on their faces: but she has stopped: she has come to the edge of the picture?

I had for some time had this image of myself as the girl who had been caught, as it were, by some hook in her throat; lifted out of the tin can on to the beach – the images, as usual, became confused here – I was both the worm that had been placed on the hook and the prey that had swallowed the worm and had been landed. My insides were being drawn out; I would be lain where I could not breathe: God was the fisherman in thigh-length boots like a woman. Now there was this woman at the gates to the Garden at the opposite side of the road. She did not exactly look at me; she seemed to cast some line across the water. The light above the surface of the road shimmered. I thought – And I have swallowed whatever it was she has thrown – swallowed it perhaps all those days and weeks ago – and now I am being drawn in, I cannot go easily, what happens when you are caught? are you not born, as you said, kicking?

I nodded and smiled at the Indian boy. I wanted this to mean – I will talk to you later: do you not believe that I will talk to you later?

I went with my rucksack across the road to the gates of the Garden. The Indian boy watched me. When I reached the gates the woman did look at me, and smiled. There was the impression of becoming involved in another element – I suppose that of air, from having been in water. The woman had extraordinary bright-blue eyes – the blueness of the sky at the back of white clouds in a painting. I spoke to her, and asked if I could stay in the Garden. My words seemed to be unnecessary, as if my voice were some sort of crying. The woman continued to smile; she put her arms round my shoulders; I thought perhaps she did not understand English. I did not know quite what was happening to me; it was as if my mind were being lifted, so that I could look down. I suppose I was tired. I had been travelling a long time. The fair-haired woman and I went to a hut just inside the gates of the Garden; we sat on a bench with our backs against a wall. The woman kept her arm around me. We faced the sun. I thought – We are at the inside of the picture looking out.

Beyond the framework there were the men in their loose robes laughing and lounging by their bicycles; the Indian boy was on his own in the middle of the road, watching; it was as if I were seeing them beyond a transparent wall. I thought – That line, thrown out, was from an umbilicus? I have come home?

A girl came out of the hut and knelt in front of me and started to tell me about arrangements. It was true there was no more accommodation available in the Garden, but there were huts just outside, and one could come in for the activities each day. There was such and such a timetable; the costs were this and that; arrangements might be made if one had no money. The woman who had welcomed me kept her arm round my shoulder; I thought – This is to do with that second picture in the National Gallery: Mary and the angel facing each other across a courtyard.

Then – I will learn, in this strange world, how things begin again as if within a picture? And God, in this dimension, is a woman?

The girl kneeling in front of me said 'All right?'

I nodded.

She went back into the hut. The older woman went on holding me: she put her head down against mine.

I thought – But where is that bird; that finger coming down?

For some time I had been conscious of a sound, of a voice, as if it were something blown on the wind: not the chatter of the men with their bicycles outside the gates: not the information of the girl who had knelt before me in the dust: but something almost not there, how could you distinguish it? it was when you stopped trying to pick it out that you heard it; when you concentrated on it it went away. It seemed to be coming from somewhere deeper in the Garden. The woman who had her arm around me pulled her head back from mine. When I looked at her she had this golden face with very fine wrinkles like something containing heat: like salt, like something you could lick. She had white teeth with a slight gap between the front two as if it were the opening into a cave. She looked away from me in the direction from which the voice seemed to come. She stood up. She held my hand. I thought – You mean you do not speak: you listen; you are led? We walked along a path together.

There were oleanders, and hibiscus, and tall eucalyptus trees like feathers. Within them or arising out of them, there was the roof or low dome of an enormous hall. The voice seemed to be coming from the area of this dome: as if the dome were some device for receiving and transmitting messages between stars. I could not at first make out the words that the voice was saying: it had a strange sibilance, as if making use of uncustomary frequencies of sound. The building had no walls: the roof was supported on thin pillars past which air blew: the voice fell from loudspeakers in the ceiling. There were figures seated or lying on the floor of the enormous hall: they were quite still: it was as if they had dropped there like seeds; as if it were being seen (or heard, since this was to do with the voice coming down) whether or not they had landed on fruitful ground.

The woman who was with me smiled: she seemed to indicate that I should join the seated and lying figures. I sat with my back against a pillar on the edge of the floor of the hall. I wanted to ask the woman not to leave me: but I thought that when I needed her she would be there, or would have come back; this would be one of the attributes, I felt, of being inside a picture.

I don't know how much you know (you, who bump into these letters, these messages, on your way through the maze) about this commune thing, this *ashram* thing, this Garden thing: you who presumably (or why are you here?) have some interest in ways within the maze. What was known as the Garden was an *ashram,* or commune, set up on the shore of this hot sea: a thousand or so people lived and worked here; they tried to find, to build, to heal themselves; having come half-way round the world and in as it were at the back way. The maze was in their minds; they had become lost; what distinguished them from others was that they had known they were lost: if you do not know this, how can you know that you are in a maze? People who came to the Garden were like dogs or cats who had had tin cans tied to their tails; they had gone round and round; the tin cans were echoes from their past such as, perhaps, the sounds of bodies falling from windows. You chase your own tail until – what? – there are small circles in the dust that might be nothing; or they might be the faint marks that are made by wing-beats, or stones.

At the centre of the Garden was God: I mean there was this guru who was known as God: I mean some of the inmates of the Garden referred to him, at least part-jokingly, as God: I am going to go on calling him God because one of the points of the Garden, as I have said, was to do with jokes – how to make jokes come alive like a finger or a bird. God had once been a professor of philosophy at somewhere like Madras: he had seen people around him setting themselves up as make-shift gods – telling people what to do, deciding the world was this or that or the other, shutting their eyes or blaming others when the world went its own way. So what do you do about this absurdity (yet terrible necessity?) of human beings setting themselves up as gods: for do you not, after all, if you think you know, have to tell others what to do? You can make a joke of it, perhaps: you can let yourself be called God: but then laugh at yourself and tell others to laugh when the world, as it does, goes its own way.

God had set himself up five or six years earlier by this hot sea and when I arrived a thousand people lived in the Garden constructing, maintaining, expanding, making it work:

another thousand or so came in from outside each day to listen to God, to laugh, to try to learn about themselves and perhaps by this – by seeing themselves as something of a joke – by this part of them, at least, to become like gods. The Garden was set in about ten acres of grounds within which, as well as the enormous hall, were dormitories, eating places, meeting places, workshops – mostly prefabricated buildings set among paths and shrubs. People from outside came in each day on foot, by ferry, by bicycle, by rickshaw: they came from the town and from the village which was on the road to the bridge inland over the estuary. There was also an encampment of thatched huts where people stayed between the Garden and the sea. Each morning it was the custom for God to appear in person to talk to his acolytes: there were also sessions each afternoon (it was during one of these that I had arrived) when his recorded voice came down from loudspeakers in the ceiling like seeds or birdshit from trees.

In some respects I suppose the Garden was not so different from other *ashrams* that have sprung up by this hot sea: I mean there have always been teaching communes in India, but recently there have been kinds flocked to by the people from the West – where gurus talk about what they say cannot be talked about; where people treat them like gods the more they say they are not gods. What was different about the Garden, I think, was just that the people there saw so much of all this in terms of a joke: how could it not be? in what other style, indeed, could one talk about the godliness that one said could not be talked about – a joke being that which brings together, illuminates, things which rationally remain separate; which releases energy like a spark between poles. You would be walking along a path in the Garden and you would see people with their somewhat mad archaic faces suddenly double up with laughter; as if they had been struck by some sort of lightning within; the lightning being the flash that lit up both their own absurdity and their wonder, I suppose, at their seeing this. Words are ridiculous: you have got to use words: so use them for what they are. Then, with luck, you are

111

happy. And perhaps there are wing-beats swirling up the dust: the finger pointing from somewhere just outside the frame of trees.

So when I arrived that hot afternoon and there was the voice coming down from the ceiling of the enormous hall – the bodies spread out on the concrete floor like things fallen haphazardly but also precisely arranged: like pieces of sculpture (for what else is art except that which gives the impression of something fallen from heaven and yet exact: is it not this that happens when you are painting a picture? what you discover is what is already there, and yet you have been free, it is your creation) – when I arrived that hot afternoon I sat with my back against a pillar of the enormous hall and the woman who had brought me there left me; but I felt as if she were around some corner; and the voice was like bits of light coming down.

'Humans have reached a moment in their history when for the first time they can destroy themselves: destroy themselves not just as individuals or as groups but as a species utterly. Humans, of course, have always had the ability to destroy: they have had to, to stay alive. Enemies have had to be fought; forces that would have destroyed humans have had to be destroyed. But now, the forces that would destroy humans are humans themselves.

'Two thousand five hundred years ago humans began to glimpse something of this: it has been said – There is a moment when the world stopped smiling. You can see it in their works of art, their sculpture. Before this, humans had represented themselves as walking forwards like proud animals: what does it matter if they destroy? they have to, to live: this is their nature. Then some darkness, some realisation, comes down on them quite suddenly. There has evolved some inward eye: some knowledge that if you destroy others you are in the process of destroying yourselves: you are connected. But still, is not destruction in your nature? Is it not true you have to destroy in order to stay alive?

112

'Two thousand five hundred years ago you see the pain coming down; there is an impossibility here, humans sense they are trapped by the very same mind, the rationality, that sees that they are trapped. There have been these patterns instilled into them from childhood – to defend yourself you have to attack; to protect yourself you have to blame others and not yourself. Yet you also see, suddenly, that it is yourself that you attack: you look around – it is by yourself that you are trapped. Things both are your fault, and are not: you are free, but you cannot order things.

'People in the West saw this most tragically – that they were helpless, yet they had the impression of being free. They were driven by the forces of animals, and yet there was part of them that could see this and did not want it: this part of them was like gods. But what could they do? – cut out eyes, liver, heartbeat? They could make up rituals, blinkers, dogmas, to comfort the terror and pain. There were many in the West at this time who said it would have been better never to have been born.

'But two thousand five hundred years ago, just at this time when humans at large seemed to become aware of the trap they were in in their minds, there were also one or two, in the East mainly – mutations, perhaps, who had managed to remain alive in an environment that must have seemed hostile to them – who saw from their very consciousness of the predicament what might be done to make it bearable; even to transcend it. For is not this also an observable pattern of humans, of the world, that each catastrophe, or awareness of it, seems to have within it seeds that might fall on to new ground and grow? There were these few people scattered throughout the world – Buddha, Lao-tzu, Mahavira, Zoroaster – who saw that, of course, you destroy yourself by destroying others; you do not get wholeness by antagonism; you do not use the mind to get out of the traps of the mind. You need to give up, give over, to drop or rise to another level. You have to become detached in the way that you now know one part of you is able to be detached – that part which can see how you are trapped. You can float free, as it were, with the whole of you like this: you can become an observer, a listener, a witness: you can become a watcher of yourself in the way that you can be a watcher of others. Then you find a whole new landscape has opened up; it is not, after all, that you are detached; you are part of a whole network of that which is detached; and so you are both detached and not detached. It is difficult to talk of this because words have evolved to deal with the past life that you will have forsaken: but what were old impossibilities, predicaments, can now be held in paradoxes.

'This knowledge has been there, available for those who choose, for two thousand five hundred years. Always there have been teachers. But people have been free to choose for themselves, or not.

'Now, if humans are to survive, this is no longer a matter of individual choice.

'What is happening now is something of the kind that happened two thousand five hundred years ago: either humans will make a leap, a quantum leap, in their consciousness of the world and of themselves – or they will not. But this time if they do not, they will be destroyed.

'When humans took the jump of seeing themselves and their predicament, they evolved their social rituals and blindnesses to make bearable what they saw: there also grew the possibilities, secretly, of change. But there was always the going to and fro – between illusion and light: between what was bearable and unbearable about light, and what was bearable and unbearable about darkness. Now we can no longer go to and fro: the oscillations themselves have become unbearable: we will blow ourselves up. The part of us that is animal, and the part that cannot bear to see this, have created weapons and substances that can destroy the whole: there is no chance of parts living detached. We cannot take refuge in the god-like parts of us: we have to move to where the god-like parts can become the whole.

'Have you noticed how in paintings it is sometimes the animals – the horses, the dogs, the tigers – who look out from the frames as if they know much more, and are wiser, than the humans – as if it were not they, but the confusions of humans, that cause the trap? There is a Christian myth that by humans accepting the redemption of themselves the animal kingdom will be redeemed: but it is also the other way round: we need not fear our animal nature; it is by our recognition of it that we will not be trapped and may become whole; part of the whole.

'There is a story by Heinrich von Kleist about humans not being viable in the way that animals and gods are viable: in order to stay alive, humans have to go right round the world and into their garden again by the back way.'

I was sitting with my back against one of the pillars at the edge of the enormous hall. There were the bodies precisely and at random scattered and ordered on the floor.

I thought – We have been tipped over on to this strange level like those sticks, or dice, which you throw and then observe: through what has been by chance, you think you have a glimpse into the ordering of the future.

Bodies fall this way or that; they fly, or land on pavements out of windows.

I wondered whether the woman with the fair round face had waited for me. The voice had stopped. People in ones and twos began to leave the enormous hall.

I did not know what to do. That white light had come down. Where do you go when you see there is nowhere to go that is not a theatre?

The hook that had been for so long tugging at my throat had got me, it seemed, to the foot of this voice from the ceiling: I now lifted my head: gritted my teeth: it was as if, yes, the hook was being taken out: I seemed to be having a small fit. There was cold air coming in through the holes of my wounds: I opened my mouth: there was some sort of scream: I thought – or is this like music? Or I was one of those pieces of sculpture being discovered in the stone but it was being hit and hit by the chisel and was making its protest to the sky; do not sculptors love figures making their protest to the sky! I did not want to move: I did not want to do whatever it was to grow and become human: there seemed some obscenity even (was this

115

what the voice had suggested?) in the business of survival. There had been a time in my childhood when I had been left alone in the house after my parents had tricked me into not taking me somewhere with them: I had heard my father say – She'll get over it. But I had said to myself – I will not. I will stay in the dust for ever.

I did not know what I was doing in this enormous hall. I was the child on the edge of a bed; the cold air was like fire: there were figures in white coats advancing with sticks to push into your throat; your eyes.

Why should I not be one of the bodies spread on the pavement; to be picked up and put in a barrow?

The woman with hair that was like an aura of light came and sat cross-legged beside me on the concrete floor. She arranged her golden robe across her knees. It was as if she were preparing some space for me. She put her arm round me and pulled me towards her; but this time she went on pulling me, as if there were some task to be done, something almost mechanical on the workshop floor of the enormous hall. She seemed to be trying to get me on to her lap: this did not seem possible; I was too large. I was an old body, dangling, being pulled and bumped up a rock-face. After a time I found myself half on and half off her lap. I lay there quite easily. I had my knees up by my chin; my head against her legs. I thought – You mean, this is no obscenity? There was that hard rather violent taste and smell. It was in my mouth, like a finger. I held my mouth open. She still did not speak.

Just in front of my face, where it lay on her lap, was one of her feet, where she sat cross-legged. I thought – Her toe is like one of those toes of a Pope or a Buddha which people crawl to lick or to suck –

– Of course, a toe is like a breast.

She said 'Go on. You do what you like.'

People who came to the Garden had usually suffered some catastrophe in their lives; how else would they have been tipped out of the particular niches of their minds?

I was taken to one of the thatched huts in the scrubland between the Garden and the sea. The hut was round, with mud-brick walls, like a hut in any tropical country. Inside there were three double bunks; stools and a low table and a charcoal brazier by the door.

Living in the hut into which I moved there were four other girls and one man; we did not come to know each other well; one of the points of the Garden was that it was ourselves we should try to come to know. We were told – Many of the catastrophes in our lives had been caused by our taking to be people what were shadows of our own projection: we could not get to know other people until we knew ourselves.

The four girls in the hut into which I moved were called Ingrid, Samantha, Gopi and Belle. Ingrid was a German who had been on the fringe of some terrorist group; she had spent time in jail. Samantha was an Australian who had had cosmetic surgery which had gone wrong and one of her breasts was rock-hard and larger than the other. Gopi was a small American girl who wore headbands like a Red Indian. Belle was Irish and pregnant, and had one or two children being looked after by her mother at home.

The man, or boy, was called Sylvester: he was Scandinavian: he had long fair hair and looked like the figurehead of a ship. It was usually he who did the cooking. He would sit by the brazier half in and half out of the door and would sing sad songs in his gutteral language. (Well, why is it women who are the figureheads of ships?)

When I was first taken to the hut there was no one there and it was, yes, like the mock-up of some nest: there were clothes and blankets over the floor: there was that smell which seems to be a mixture of fish and stale bread. One of the bottom bunks seemed to be free; it was used as a shelf for tins and plates. I thought – I shall lie on the tins like a fakir to demonstrate my goodwill: or would this be seen as self-destructive?

How shall I describe life in the Garden, and in the hut: one of the purposes of the Garden was that not much should seem to be going on. Growth occurs, doesn't it, when nothing seems

117

to be happening: drama is to do with violence and death. You can describe easiest what is to do with destruction: language is not for what goes on quietly, behind one's back, in the dark.

How much do you know about this sort of thing – this Zen thing, Buddha thing, Tantra thing, Tao thing? (I mean you or you: I know about you!)

You have to become emptied, hollowed out, like a flute: then God can play you.

People have been saying this, yes, for centuries: they've also been saying it can't be said.

God is there, inside you, outside you: you get rid of the barriers of the ego, and you become part of the whole.

Put it into words and it is not quite there: do not try to put it into words and how can it be known?

So you make shots at it, don't you, and let them go. Every now and then you look round; and one or two are on the target.

In our hut, in the evenings, we would go about our business as if we were denizens of some shrine – oil-lamps like fireflies flickered; there was the smoke perhaps of incense; what we were honouring, I suppose, was just a nothingness so that something that might be ourselves might grow in the dark. There is always a nothingness, is there not, within a holy of holies. Ingrid was a long lean German girl who would take her clothes off and lie on her stomach on her top bunk; she was like a leopard up a tree: she would let a paw hang down. Gopi would climb up like a monkey on to Ingrid's back; she would sit astride her to massage her; she would press on ribs and shoulders, getting flowers out of stone, her own small breasts like arrows pointing down. Samantha would do exercises on the floor, wrapping an ankle, or a knee, round the back of her neck so that she became like one of those puzzles which make globes or cubes out of bits of slotted wood. When Belle came in she was like blown leaves; lamps were apt to go out; there was the impression of cats being swept along by broomsticks. Sylvester, in the doorway, would hang on to the legs of his brazier until Belle had passed by: then he would continue with

118

his stirring, or poking about with forks, like someone trying to demonstrate a more practical form of witchcraft.

There was a plastic washbasin on a stand in the hut; a communal tap in the space between four or five huts. There was a building with latrines that people tried to avoid. We wandered off, with bundles of clothes to wash, down to the estuary.

There was one evening when Belle swept in with more violence than usual and one of the chains, or belts, that she wore round her skirts like grappling irons caught on the string of beads that Sylvester wore round his neck: Sylvester fell back, was dragged, like some victim behind a cart. The pan that he had been holding, containing hot oil, shot into the air: Gopi and Ingrid, on the top bunk, thrashed about like people attacked by bats. Samantha, enrapt in the lotus position on the floor, her eyes closed, did not see that a drop of hot oil had landed on her one large breast. Smoke arose from it: a black hole slowly appeared; we watched transfixed. I thought – For the seventh level of consciousness, it is best to have a plastic breast?

We were all trying not to be characters in the Garden: characters are what are formed by families and by society: characters are what stop you growing, like a shell. But then – in what way do you know people which is not to do with their characters? What do you know of a society of people trying to know themselves?

I thought – We have come to this cave: we know we are shadows –

– Those people who think they see substances, they do not have the substance to know they are shadows?

'Hullo.'
   'Hullo.'
   'How are you?'
   'I'm sorry if I was rude.'
   'Oh that is all right.'
I had come across the Indian boy again a few evenings later

outside the gate of the Garden. He was sitting by a rug on
which there were exotic shells for sale. The shells had spikes
like crowns of thorns. It seemed already that I had been a long
time in the Garden.

'I didn't feel very well.'

'Is this your first time in the Garden?'

'Yes.'

'How does it strike you here?'

I picked up one of the shells. I thought – Don't do this: put
it down: I have been only a few days in the Garden.

I said 'Did you collect these yourself?'

'Yes.'

'They're very beautiful.'

I thought – But you do not protect yourself here, do
you, you are protected: and it is true that this shell is
beautiful.

He said 'It is not a good environment in the Garden.'

'Why not?'

'The sanitary conditions are not good.'

I thought – Good heavens, it is true that the sanitary conditions are not good!

He said 'There is offensive behaviour, and drugs.'

I put the shell back on the rug. I thought – You give
up, don't you; you let things go their own way, behind your
back.

I said 'No drugs of any kind are allowed in the Garden.'

'But they are allowed outside.'

'Yes.'

'So what is the difference?'

I thought – You mean, you want me to tell you the
difference?

He said 'Will you come for a walk with me?'

He was tall; much taller than the Indian boy in London. He
wore a white shirt and black trousers.

I thought – Oh well, what is the point of an experiment if
you do not sometimes look, even in these early days, to see
how it is getting on?

He said 'What this country needs is agricultural techniques and machinery.'

I said 'Have you always lived here?'

He said 'I live in the village.'

We had gone a short way into the scrubland at the side of the track that went down the estuary. We stopped. I thought – Where are those three dogs that were playing in that picture?

I said 'The local people don't like the Garden?'

'No.'

'It isn't doing any harm. It isn't stopping anyone bringing in agricultural techniques, and machinery.'

'It spreads superstition. This country has enough superstition.'

'But the Garden is against superstition. It is trying to make people look at what is actually happening.'

I thought – But, indeed, what is the use of words; did not that girl get the wound in her throat to tell her this about talking?

He said 'You are clever. But you do not know what it is like to live in a country that is not clever. People want to go on as before.'

I thought – Supposing he were the serpent: supposing Eve just gave up arguing, and stood with the snake by the track that goes down towards the river –

Then – You mean, this is the sort of projection I put on to people?

I said 'But you are clever. You speak English very well.'

He said 'I teach in the school.'

I said 'What do you teach?'

He said 'Mathematics, and English.'

I thought – And you will want someone to help you with your English in the evenings?

He hitched up his trousers and tucked in his shirt. There were bones jutting out of him as if he had once been wrapped too tightly, like a plant with wires cutting into it.

He said 'You want to be careful. The police will come and clear you out.'

I said 'You can't say – The police will come and clear you out!'

He stared at me. He had clear skin, and a small moustache.

I thought – But still, projections are energy; they are like gravity; what is the relationship between good and evil?

He said 'I am sorry.'

I said 'These people in the Garden are just the same as you: they have their fears, miseries, rages.'

He said 'They have more money.'

I said 'Some have more money.'

I waited. I thought – And enmity stirs up lust: or is it lust that stirs up enmity?

He took hold of my hand.

I thought – But if I know it makes no difference whether or not he takes hold of my hand –

He said 'I was hoping to find someone who will help me with my English in the evenings.'

I said 'Look, I will try to help you with your English one day. I can't do it now. I've not been well.'

He said 'Thank you.' Then – 'What has been wrong with you?'

I said 'I'm all right.'

He said 'Tomorrow?'

I shouted 'No!'

I thought I might turn and run. But this, of course, would make things more interesting.

Eve, of course, at some level must have wanted to destroy the snake.

I thought – So it is important, is it, in order that projections should be freed, that nothing much should seem to be happening in the Garden?

After a time I felt that he would understand when I said I had to go back into the Garden.

Life began in the Garden each day while it was still dark: ghostly figures converged from the huts, from the road to the village and the town, from the track up from the estuary. At

122

the entrance to the Garden there was one small lantern: bicycles were piled beneath it like dead moths. It was as if souls were hurrying to be in time for the Resurrection.

Under the roof of the enormous hall there was still almost no light: figures like pieces of sculpture were already there – to be discovered within the stone. From the loudspeakers under the roof music began – a quick drumming. This was an exercise, a meditation, to do – what? – to reach to the being that you really were: to draw it up, free from the stone.

For the first ten minutes you stand with your feet apart and pump the air out of your lungs using your elbows like bellows; you blow through your nose; you do this in time to the music. You fan an almost dead fire; you are raising from the bottom of the ocean an old wrecked ship. Of course this is ridiculous. It is to do, is it not, with the supply of oxygen to the brain. Sooner or later you begin to float; to be on fire; why should it not be to do with oxygen to the brain? So why not do it then? – if you are a bit of dead wood at the bottom of the ocean.

There were all these hundreds of people in the enormous hall pumping away at their sunken ships; the dome in the dark above like a sky that they might shoot up into like heartbeats.

This goes on for what seems to be more than ten minutes: nothing much, as usual, seems to be happening. You do not see, do you, the connections between your body and your brain; why should you see the connections between yourself and the universe? The mechanisms of life go on in secret: you know this: you would destroy them if you dug them up to see.

The music stops: starts again in a faster rhythm. You now have to shake off all bits and pieces that might be preventing you from rising: stones, sands, limpets, encrustments; weeds that have grown like lovers' arms around you. You let go, shout, yell: it is when pieces fly off that you create some space. Then you can grow. The air comes in, takes hold, forms some bubble around you. Do you not think God lets himself go from time to time: smashes the rocks and crockery? Then there is a seed, a homunculus, in a cell.

123

How much do you know about this sort of thing: have you ever tried it? You are becoming that part of yourself that can be looking down on yourself; and laughing. This goes on for ten minutes. Then the music stops. It starts again in a faster rhythm.

Now what you have to do is to raise your hands above your head and jump up and down on the same spot for ten minutes. Who has ever heard of jumping up and down on the same spot for ten minutes? And so on. You are trying to get a balloon up into the air; you have thrown bits of ballast out; as you jump up and down you are one of those contraptions roaring with flames and hot air: will the fabric of the balloon fill; will the whole apparatus burst into flames; on what sort of apotheosis will you be carried up to heaven? You have begun: you think – Well, I will carry on as long as I can; then I will stop. For what is not possible is not possible: you are, after all, this bag of old bones, flesh, offal; you have been dumped on the earth; how can you suddenly go shooting in a chariot-rocket to heaven? By pulling yourself up by your own shoestrings, I suppose. But then – whatever is happening is happening secretly. You jump up and down: you find, at least, that there is no necessity to stop; you get in the way of it; perhaps you are becoming that puppet, are you, with its centre of gravity tied to heaven. And what is gravity except that which can jump up and down, as it were, for ever – its arms up through the universe! Or there is that snake – itself, after all, an old body of blood and bones – that lies curled up at the bottom of your spine; that when it is aroused shoots up like a rocket through your womb, heart, mind, and out beyond, into the sky. Or what is making love, I suppose, except jumping up and down on the same spot for ten minutes – and then, with luck, the snake bursts inside you, above you, like stars. And so then where are you? Not quite yet floating serene above what strange landscape. The point of heaven is, I suppose, that when you have come you are once and for all and for ever there. All this goes on for what seems, yes, to be ever. The experience is that you are held, moved, as if by a line at your centre of gravity.

The music stops. You stand still where you have landed for ten minutes.

Or it is not exactly that you are still: you are breathing so heavily that the fires of your rocket-chariot, still roaring, seem to be consuming you: but you are not consumed; you are yourself; what have gone are your ropes to the sky and ground; you are liberated from the stone. And so, yes, you are on the rim of some new world; you have landed. You cannot remember, quite, how you got here: you were blowing, shaking, jumping; you were working with bellows and cylinders: now here you are – in this strange landscape. While all this has been going on the sun has come up; I mean, the exercise has been timed so that at this point the sun should come up; so it is as if you have been, indeed, working hand in hand with gravity. We had not noticed the sun previously, of course; we had been so intent on the firing of our chariot-rocket to heaven. But now there we were, exactly at, within, outlined by the rose-pink fires of sun and sky: statues standing in the enormous hall released, discovered, set down from the stone. It was as if we had created this light, this freedom, together with the sun; what a miracle it is after all for the sun to come up each day! And had not the same force been within us rising and bursting like stars? We had to try to stay very still, of course; for were we not, on this strange planet, like babies on the edge of a bed. Sweat poured off us. Might we not bring life to the dying earth, our mother.

The music started again.

For the last twenty minutes you have, simply, to dance. You dance in celebration of – what? – the fact that you have come through? that you have been dead, sunken, and now are alive? What else are you doing when you dance? The hook has been taken out; you have been lifted, set up; you have a centre of your own. All dancing is a form of celebration – perhaps of the fact that a human can be, on his own, neither an animal nor a god; but something of both; which is more than either. Dancing, we were the snake and the tree and the person watching the tree. I have always loved dancing. Dancing is to do with

125

what cannot be put into words: you move, and you are com-pletely yourself; your limbs are part of everything around you.

In the Garden I got a job in the cloth-making workshop. I also helped in the canteen in the evenings.

There was a wooden loom with a shuttle that went to and fro: to and fro: nothing much (are you surprised?) seemed to be happening. After a time there was a small length of cloth where there had not been one before. We made clothes the colour of flames; of the sun.

There was an extraordinary air of stillness combined with busy-ness in the Garden. A thousand or so people came in each day: some for their therapy groups, encounter groups; some for cooking and cleaning; but it was as if everyone was aware of something slightly different going on; some part of them which had chosen to be still, to watch, to listen: to try to become conscious of their being part of the whole.

The shuttle of the loom went to and fro. There was the sound of drumming, of music, round some corner. It was as if one were part of some blood, liver, heartbeat.

At meal-times people queued for their bread, soup, veget-ables and fruit: the canteen was a long low building with urns like those in a laundry. We ate outside on wooden benches beneath a bamboo canopy. The sun made stripes through the bamboos so that the setting seemed to be some sieve, or riddle. I thought -- The old dying bits of us are flaking off, falling through.

One of the points of the Garden was that we should learn to meditate; meditation was an attitude of mind: it was the looking down on oneself, whatever one was doing. The point of meditation was that it should go on, like a heartbeat, all the time. People had grown hard shells around themselves: if they became watchers, listeners, in whatever it was they were doing, that which was hidden inside the shells might grow: after a time, the shells would fall off. There was a myth that snakes were immortal, because they were such that their skins fell off.

126

I did not join any of the therapy groups or encounter groups: I thought – This is not my need: I have banged about enough, have I not, with worms in the tin can.

But there were flies that still buzzed in my mind. The mind was the shell, or bottle, in which these flies were trapped. One could look down on it for a time: then suddenly it was so awful; so awful!

Often during my first days and weeks in the Garden I looked for the woman who had gathered me in at the gate; who had held me that first day in the enormous hall. When I did not find her, it did not seem that I minded. I thought – I suppose she is one of the events that are like a heartbeat, that go on around some corner.

The flies were memories, like devils, like bombers coming in: where do they come from, how do we stop them? Were they the demons that Lilith sends from her rock? Might not Lilith come back to save us?

I wondered – Is the woman who took me in at the gate Lilith: Adam's first wife, and his equal, in the Garden of Eden?

The memories that came in were to do with all those poor worms treading on each other's heads in the mud of the tin can; the people scratching in the rubble for where their homes had once been and for food. There had been that terrible tube down Oliver's throat like a horse's penis; his fingers clutching, clutching, like crabs tearing at flesh. I had tried to help him: how had I helped him! There had been a broken body on the pavement beneath the window of the flat, kicking, kicking. A child had fallen off the end of the bed while the doctors had tended to the dying earth, its mother.

My mother had been in a Japanese prison camp during the war. She had been fifteen. She had once told me a story. They had all been very hungry in the prison camp: certain prisoners were suspected of hoarding food. She was with her own mother – my grandmother – in a hut: she looked over the edge of her bunk one night and saw her mother eating tinned milk with a spoon. I mean she was giving none to her child, my mother, who was starving.

It is a baby who kicks out at the edge of the bed. Someone falls over.

On the pathways of the Garden between hibiscus and oleander there used to be people striding forwards with those smiles like mad archaic statues and I sometimes wanted to puncture them with arrows as if they were those inane St Sebastians; but this might have given them pleasure! Or I might pile them into the huge urns of the canteen as if these were jaws and seed-pods in a painting of hell by Hieronymus Bosch.

My father was a professor of anthropology. I think he had fallen in love with my mother out of pity. There is a terrible power in the hands of a person who is pitied. Of course, my father wanted to pity: I think he also wanted to love.

Sometimes in our thatched hut at night Belle would weep; Sylvester would hold her; Ingrid would stride off like a horse into the night. The gentle flames from the oil-lamps made our skin appear thin, almost transparent. What hope was there for people who might cast off their shells? Would they not be exposed to the worms of blowflies coming in?

Then one day when I seemed to be reaching some impasse in my feelings about the Garden – had I not been here long enough: what was I doing: where else had I to go? – I came in the course of some errand to that part of the Garden where there was God's inner garden: I mean God lived within the compound of the Garden but he had his own house-and-garden like the nucleus of a cell. This had a gate, and a hedge, and a smaller fence around it. There was always something mysterious about God's inner garden. I had stopped on the path because some memory, or even presentiment, had struck me: these images made you listen as if for bombs coming down: I was on the path with my hands held out as if for rain: what must it have been like for birds, those bombs coming down! Someone appeared at the gate of God's inner garden. I realised it was the woman with short fair hair like Lilith and the aura of light around her. She stood quite still when she saw me. I thought – You do not speak: I do not want you to speak!

except to say – nothing. The last time I had seen her was when she had taken me to the door of my hut and had left me there. I thought – Of course, this is why I have not seen her: she lives in God's inner garden. So it is true she is like Lilith! Then – But she was at the gate of the Garden that day to welcome me!

I thought I might begin crying again. Sometimes during those days, yes, I sat on the edges of paths and cried.

You had said, had you not? – It was not your fault!

– Everything both absolutely is, and is not, your fault.

Who was I talking to?

The woman who was looking at me had such bright blue eyes: I thought – But let me have your darkness! I found, as before, that I had opened my mouth. I thought – The hook has been taken out? It is this taste that is like a smell?

Do you know that piece of natural history about elephants in central Africa who have some terrible need for minerals, for some sort of salt-lick. They can only get these minerals from stalactites that hang from the roofs of caves in mountains. So the elephants have to make their way to these mountains; they lumber into the caves – huge potholers hanging on to each other's tails in the dark. When they are deep inside they break off the stalactites with their tusks; they chew them: they give them to their children. They have to do this or they would die; they cannot get the minerals on the plains. The minerals are to do with old encrustations, do you think, that you need from time to time to stay alive.

This has something to do with a mother and her tinned milk – do you think?

Why are these particular crystals, liquids, to be found in the body of a particular person – is it what was once to do with smell?

I had a cat, once, that used to burrow, burrow, into my armpit.

I still did not speak to the woman. It is difficult to say – Can I come into your dark?

She was standing at the entrance to God's inner garden.

She opened the gate for me to come in.

I thought I might say as I went in – You know the natural history of those elephants in the cave?

When I first arrived in the Garden God had not been making his customary appearances each day. It was said that he was ill, or resting; or just that he had decided not to appear.

So we listened to the recordings of his voice from the roof of the enormous hall. He said many of the things I came to expect – There has to be an opening, an emptying, before you can grow: you have to become hollowed, so that music can be made through you.

But God also said things which seemed to be particular to himself at this time: these were to do not so much with his message as with the effect or lack of effect of his message: he was looking down on it, I suppose: he was seeing it falling like seeds on to this or that ground.

– I do not want to be a god to you. I do not want to be a father-figure to you. I want to make you free. But it is true, perhaps, that you will not be free unless I have been some sort of god to you.

– I do not want you to be serious. I am not serious! One is thinking of oneself when one is serious. When you laugh, you are taken over by something other. Then you can grow.

– You cannot make yourself true by willing yourself to be true; you cannot make yourself yourself by willing yourself to be yourself; these are conditions that can only be brought about by something other. You have to let yourself go; let the forms into which you have been forced by society go: then you will find that in their place there is something other. You can call this something God: but it will be yourself; it will be your true self because you will have been entered by, become part of, a whole.

– Truth is that of which the opposite is also true. I do not want to be a god to you. I want you to be free.

But while God's voice came dropping down thus from the ceiling like birdsong, like drops from the roof of a cave forming pillars, there were all those figures on the floor of the enormous hall being fashioned, moulded, into – what? – worshippers, acolytes? slaves? I wondered – Would not God in the end have to do more than say he was ill or resting, to make people free?

Then one evening it was announced that God was going to appear in person again; and the next morning everyone assembled in the enormous hall. This had always used to be the highlight of each day in the Garden: about two thousand people gathered: we sat cross-legged, straight-backed, on the ground; facing a platform like a stage. Some had their eyes closed and swayed slightly like reeds: a few were alert, amused, watchful. I thought – So what happens if you let people call you God, and yet tell them you want them to be free?

Around the perimeter of the hall there were figures in white or yellow robes standing facing inwards: these were the special acolytes or disciples who acted as guardians: they seemed slightly lifted, their feet just off the floor, as if they were figures in a Byzantine mosaic. On the platform one of them spoke into a microphone quietly; he said that everyone would have to sit absolutely still and not cough for possibly two hours. I thought – How can you tell people not to cough for two hours? is not this one of the things that people cannot will themselves to do? You mean, they will be depending on something other?

As the time approached for God to appear there was a hush; a surmise: how on earth would God act: come down in a balloon? be lowered in a basket? I could not make out, this first time, looking round the enormous hall, what these people were feeling: were they in ecstasy? were they not rather laughing? Some with their eyes closed rocked backwards and forwards like snakes: but they were being drawn up, yes, out of some basket?

When God did arrive – he had set out from his house in his inner garden some hundred yards away – he appeared above the heads of the seated figures at the edge of the hall bouncing along like a target at a fun-fair shooting-range: he was carried by half a dozen of his acolytes on a litter: one held an umbrella over his head: perhaps he had really been ill and so had to be carried: but, yes, he did appear to be on the point of roaring with laughter. He was a middle-aged, brown-skinned man with a lot of white-and-grey hair and a beard. When the litter was set down by the platform he stepped out delicately and seemed to glide as if he were on wheels; he went to a chair that had been prepared for him. He looked round the assembled multitude with his hands held as if in prayer; the adoring faces looked up at him; he still seemed to be on the point of bursting into laughter.

Well, what do you think you do when you are trying to say what you yourself say cannot be said? You roll your words like balls down a slope? they fall off the edges, they go into slots, one or two, at the bottom?

Up till recently, I had been told, God's discourses had been to do with what most people had come to expect – his interpretations of Zen, of Tao, of Tantra, of Christ, of Buddha. It was recordings of these talks that had for the most part played from the roof of the enormous hall. But just before he had become ill, or had rested, an urgency had come into his discourses – this had been evident in the recording that I had heard when I had first arrived – the urgency was partly to do with what he felt about the state of the world; but there was also the recognition of the predicament that the more he told people they should be free the more they worshipped him: so if words are counter-productive, would it not be better to be silent? But this must be the predicament of all gods, must it not: and so here he was now, sitting himself down in his chair, about to try to say the unsayable: so might he not, indeed, seem to be on the point of roaring with laughter?

God's discourse this time did not last two hours: but while it did last no one did in fact seem to cough, or to stir – let alone (as it were) leave the theatre. I do not know how he managed this: he spoke in his sibilant half-chant, half-whisper; he lingered on the ends of words as if he were dangling them on a hook; he had hands which seemed to shape his parables as if he were forming rainbows in bubbles. I suppose people had always been tickled, caressed, goaded by him; he put out probes to where we had been wounded; his task was to catch us, heal us, make us free – might not these processes be the same?

In this first discourse after his absence he spoke in a style, people said, that he had not used before. I will try to get his words; I will be putting some formation of my own into them. He spoke as an actor; a story-teller: but also as someone who was saying – Look: you must know what you are doing when you are story-tellers, actors: you are standing back from, seeing, what you have found; then you will be free!

He said –

'God was lying in bed one Sunday morning reading his Sunday newspapers and he said to his wife, who was called Lilith, and who, of course, was the same as he – I don't know what we are going to do with those two children! all they do is loll about in the garden all day.

'But Lilith, who was, as they say, one flesh with God, said – Well that's what you told them to do, isn't it?

'God said – I know I told them to! But they needn't have obeyed me, need they?

'God was touchy on this point. He felt himself vulnerable here to Lilith.

'Lilith said – You told them to obey you.

'God said – I know I told them to obey me!

'Lilith said – Well, you can't blame them.

'God said – I don't blame them!

'Lilith said – But you tell them you do.

'God said – Of course I tell them I do!

'And so on.

'God, who could never get his wife, or other half, to understand what was to do not with logic, but with meta-logic, rolled over with his back to her in bed and ruminated on how it was no good arguing with the half of him that was a woman.

'Now Adam and Eve, God's two children, who had been listening outside the window – which they usually did when their parents were supposed to be reading the newspapers on a Sunday morning and were under the impression that the children were lolling about in the garden – turned to each other during this silence.

'Adam whispered to Eve – What do you think they are up to now?

' – The usual, I dare say.

' – That creaking!

' – That groaning!

' – I think it's called the primal scene.

'Adam and Eve giggled.

'Eve said – What is the primal scene?

' – I think it's fucking.

' – It sounds more like an argument.

' – Perhaps it is an argument.

' – I thought it was more like – you know –

' – What?

' – What that snake does in the garden.

'Now in the bedroom, where God had been lying with his back to himself, or Lilith, for some time, he thought he would roll over and try to explain things to her once more.

'He said – Look, I'll spell it out. If I had not told those children to obey me, how could they disobey me? And if they don't disobey me, how can they ever grow up?

'Lilith said – But they haven't disobeyed you. They haven't grown up.

'God said – Look: how often do I have to go through this? I told the children to obey me so they would have the chance to disobey me: but I can't tell them that this is the case, because they have to work it out for themselves, or they won't grow up.

'Lilith said – Don't shout at me, I am not stupid.

'God said – I give up.

'Now Adam and Eve, outside the window, could not quite hear what was said, because God and Lilith were talking in whispers; but they heard the creaking and groaning.

'Eve said – I think they're putting it on.

'Adam said – Putting what on?

134

' – This performance.

'Adam said – Perhaps they just want to get us out of the garden.

'Eve said – Well they're jolly well not going to get us out of the garden!

' – I suppose they think they will, if we witness the primal scene.

' – Well, if we do, let's make out we think they've just been talking!

' – Yes, jolly good – said Adam.

'Now God and Lilith, who had been silent back to back in their bed for some time, heard Adam and Eve whispering outside their window.

'God said – What's that?

'Lilith said – I think it's the children, who have been listening outside the window.

'God said – Do you think it might be a good thing if we had them in? I mean, it might assist in their development if they witnessed the primal scene.

'Lilith said – But can you manage it? At your age! We seem to spend all our time talking.

'God was furious. He thought that Adam and Eve might have overheard. He shouted – Are you listening?

'Adam said – Yes!

'God thought – All right! I know what will fix Lilith: and what will get those two layabouts out of the garden.

'He said in a mournful voice to Lilith – Ah, I know! You'd like a younger man! As a matter of fact, I realise you've always fancied Adam!

'Lilith said – What? Then – And what about you and Eve!

'God shouted – All right you two can come in!

'Adam and Eve came in. They said – Morning Dad! Morning Mum! They climbed into bed with their parents.

'Then they said – Finished with the Sunday newspapers?'

I was walking on the beach by the sea early one morning (it was my day off: I was thinking – God has gone mad? God will pretend to go mad to get us out of the Garden?) and there were huge white waves coming in like tiers of seats in a theatre; like a crowd roaring. I came across the Indian boy, who was called Shastri, by a boat pulled up on the sand.

'Hullo.'

'Hullo.'

'Have you thought about what I said?'

I wondered if he had seen me setting out for the beach. He sometimes seemed to lie in wait for me outside the gates of the Garden.

I said 'Look, I'm no good at teaching. I can't be any good for others if I'm no good for myself.'

He wore his black trousers and white shirt. I thought – It is some sort of uniform: like a skeleton in my cupboard.

He said 'I just asked you to come for walks with me.'

I said 'I know you think it's wrong to care about oneself when other people are hungry. But people are always saying they worry about other people being hungry, and this doesn't seem to do much good, I mean there are always more people hungry.'

I thought – Oh but it's the words that are so awful; so awful!

We had begun to walk together along the beach. There was the line of white waves coming in like a crowd storming a palace. I thought – Or does he see me riding on a shell like Aphrodite?

He said 'And what good do you do in the Garden?'

I said 'Look, the Garden isn't what you think it is.'

He said 'What is it?'

I said 'I think it's coming to an end. I think God's trying to get us out.'

The beach stretched for miles in front of us. There was a blue-gold haze in the distance. We had got beyond the area where fishermen's boats were drawn up on the sand.

He said 'You are told to live for yourselves: not to care about other people. But how can you live without depending on other people?'

I said 'Look, why don't you come into the Garden?'

He said 'They wouldn't allow me.'

I said 'Of course they would!'

'Why?'

The beach was quite empty. It was still early in the morning. I thought – We could go into the sand-dunes, hand in hand –

– Or would you come into the Garden if I asked you to come in with me?

– Eve and the serpent, walking in, hand in hand!

He said 'Is it true that they ask you for your money as soon as you arrive in the Garden?'

I said 'No.'

He said 'I have heard of one mother who came here having abandoned her children and when her husband came to fetch her she persuaded him to stay and to abandon the children too.'

I said 'There are always stories about the Garden. It is true they are odd about children. They think that parents often do more harm than good.'

He said 'Will you come to a political meeting with me?'

I said 'What political meeting?'

He said 'In the village.'

There were some extraordinary and huge track-marks in front of us in the sand. They went up from the sea to the edge of the dunes. They were as if some juggernaut had come up out of the water.

I stopped and poked my toes about in the tracks. I thought – He will come to the Garden if I go to his political meeting? I imagine it will do some good if I can get him to the Garden?

He said 'That is a turtle track. The females come at night and lay their eggs up by the dunes.'

I thought – But I know about this!

He said 'The eggs are a great delicacy. It will be a great day for the people in my village.'

I said 'But you won't tell them!'

I thought perhaps I could try to wipe out the tracks with my foot.

He said 'They lay hundreds of eggs.' He began to walk up towards the sand-dunes.

I shouted 'Don't!'

He turned and looked at me. I thought – I will stand with my arms like Aphrodite: in my cockle-shell out of the sea.

I said 'I've seen a film about this. I have a nightmare about it. The baby turtles hatch out and they run towards the sea. Then the seagulls get them. And if any get past the seagulls, then there are lines of huge crabs.'

He said 'The crabs and seagulls know when they are coming. Very few get through.'

I said 'I know.'

He said 'Why should not my people in the village have the eggs, rather than the crabs and seagulls?'

I said 'Some get through.'

I thought – Why should I not say, humans should be different from crabs and seagulls?

I said 'It is so terrible for the mother turtles. They have to struggle with such effort!'

He said 'People will see where the eggs are from the tracks anyway.'

I said 'I just don't want it to be you and I who tell them, or dig the eggs up.'

I thought – All right: you really want me to come to a political meeting?

You know that dream of beautiful people who are walking hand in hand on a beach; and the person watching the beautiful people wonders why it is that they are so serene and so composed; and then this person notices that they glance towards the sand-dunes every now and then, and within the sand-dunes there is a temple, and within this temple there are old hags who are dismembering a child. And it is because of this, because of the sacrifice round some corner, that the people on the beach are so beautiful and serene.

I had always thought – Surely, from time to time, one is the child?

I thought now – Anyway, does one not sometimes want to be the child?

I said 'All right, I'll come to your meeting.'

I turned to the sea. I thought – I could take my clothes off, and run down to the waves.

Then – Poor snake, with everyone's foot against it!

He said 'What are you doing?'

I said 'Do you want a swim?'

He said 'I don't swim.'

I said 'Come on!'

I thought, running from the sand-dunes to the sea – I mean, crabs and seagulls won't get us?

Each night in the Garden there was another coming-together in the enormous hall: nothing here of the exactness, the stillness, of adoring upturned faces or of figures being drawn up out of the stone: it was a sort of Hallowe'en, a *danse macabre* of shadowy figures prancing about and singing, playing drums, forming and re-forming circles – a celebration of darkness before sleep.

It was at night that I was able to feel most watchful: both separate from and yet connected to the Garden. I could prowl around and observe the shadows banging and cavorting in the dark: I could be not quite one of these myself: it was as if I could put a hand out and feel – There is something beyond even these dancing walls.

There was also a special audience each night in God's garden-within-the-Garden: here a few chosen disciples came to be given his personal blessing – those who were going away, those who had newly returned, those who were for some reason thought to be in need of grace. There was always an air of mystery about God's inner garden: I was not at first asked to these special audiences. When I had come across the woman with fair hair we had gone to her room in an annexe to the inner garden; we had not gone to God's house itself.

It was coincidental with this special audience in the nucleus

139

of the Garden that the figures leapt about and sang in the enormous hall outside. I did sometimes join in here. We held hands in circles, came together, moved apart: like things under the sea, washed by a tide. I wondered – These people find it easy to lose themselves: what will they find?

I had once gone with my father to a monkey-dance in Indonesia where men sat in concentric circles and made drumming noises with their mouths: a figure in skins and feathers span and stamped in the middle. The people of the tribe were becoming at one with – what – the parts inside them, outside them, of the forest? There was an outer circle of tourists with flowered shirts and cameras.

I thought – Should not all this go on unseen; life bursting into stars secretly?

There had been a time when I had gone with my father and mother to a Buddhist temple in Java; there were the usual crowds – here of local people – swarming over the alleyways and cupolas and towers: the temple was like a dead elephant and we were mice: we were gnawing at it. Everywhere people posed for photographs: families climbed on each other's shoulders to pose for photographs: there were schoolchildren with funny T-shirts and plastic hats. My father tried to ignore all this: he moved about the rooftops like a stork; then he became engulfed by a group of schoolchildren and posed for a photograph with them out of some sort of contempt; he put his arms round them and grinned like a skull. My mother had managed as usual to get a group of students around her (in their white shirts and black trousers?); she was pretending to need help with her camera, her bag, her guidebook; they were like moths around her ('Where do you come from: England? Germany? America?').

I thought – All these shadows are dancing around in the enormous hall of my mind.

Of course, there were an average amount of loonies in the Garden: people who posed transfixed like St Sebastian; who knelt and swayed like Mary Magdalene with tears running down their cheeks. Or some would lie together just off the paths in the oleander bushes; sucking like bees or butterflies each other's – what? – toes?

My father took us once to a place in central Java which an old man told us was where the Garden of Eden had been. My father was looking for the place where the bones of one of the early humans or pre-humans had been found: this was in the bend of a river: the bones had been dug up and removed a century ago. This place, and the Garden of Eden, I think became confused in my father's mind: we camped on a small promontory in a lake: there were volcanoes and bubbling springs all around. My mother said – This is not the bend of a river. My father said – I did not say it was the bend of a river. My mother said – What is it then? My father said – There was some place, some time, when *Homo sapiens* emerged from *Homo erectus*. My mother said – It seems a pity that he did not stay as *Homo erectus*. These jokes, these terrible figures, leaping and cavorting in the dark of my mind.

I wondered – Will there be again that white light coming down?

There were times when my father would get in a terrible rage; it was as if he were a bull with the darts stuck into him, hanging out. Then my mother would drag me in to protect her. I would stand in front of her like Athene with her shield. I imagined my father might murder my mother. Of course, children think it is their fault.

Why do they imagine this? They think, like gods, that they can handle it? They think, unlike gods, that they have a duty to handle it?

Athene held Hector's arm when he was about to kill Achilles, so that it was Hector who died.

Children lose this magic: what happens when they grow up?

What is their duty to these shadows; these bits and pieces that cavort on walls inside and outside their minds?

God, ensconced on his platform in the enormous hall, said –
  'God was out walking in his garden one day when he came

across Lilith in a glade in the woods. This was where, in the new dispensation of things, she used to go cavorting with their son Adam.

'God said – Any chance of that boy getting out of the garden yet?

' – Not yet – said Lilith dreamily.

' – Look, I have an idea – said God. He sat down beside her.

'He was a cunning old bird. He wanted to have the chance to try out one or two of his own experiments with Eve.

' – What about – said God – we make up some story that you were Adam's first wife: you are, of course, anyway, psychoanalytically speaking. Then we can say that he wanted to be too much on top: and you have gone off in a huff to sit on some rock.

' – What on earth good would that do? – Lilith said.

' – Well then you could see much more of each other – God said. – He would come to rescue you. And we could say you were surrounded by devils, so you wouldn't be spied on by your boring daughter-in-law Eve.

' – But what if he doesn't come to rescue me? – Lilith said.

' – Of course he will! – God said. – Didn't you say that what he likes is adventures, and hardship, and dressing up?

'So Lilith went off and found a nice rock in a lonely part of the garden: and she dreamed there of Adam coming to visit her in shining armour.

'God went on walking through the garden and he found Adam still lolling about beneath a tree. So God said – I say, have you seen anything of your mother?

' – She told me to wait for her here – Adam said.

' – Look here – said God – I've heard that she's off to sit on some rock, because she objects to your always wanting to be on top.

' – Me always wanting to be on top? – Adam said.

' – I know it sounds odd – God said – but don't you think you could go and look for her? Then you two could be together; and, if you liked, she could be on top.

' – What sort of rock is it? – Adam said. – You mean like Mount Everest? Or perhaps the South Pole?

' – Yes – God said.

' – I have been thinking – Adam said – that it might be fun if I did something rather more interesting, like getting myself strung up on a tree.

' – All right, you do that – God said.

'He went on through the garden. He was looking for Eve. He found her doing one of her aerobic work-outs with the snake, who can eat its own tail.

' – Look, – said God – your mother has gone off to sit on a rock; your husband, or brother, or whatever he calls himself, is thinking of getting himself strung up on a tree: I don't see how I'm ever going to get you children out of the garden!

' – Shall I show you? – said Eve.

' – There is all this confusion about who is on top and who is underneath – said God.

' – There is no top and no underneath – said Eve. – The snake and I have been experimenting. The one on top, as soon as he or she thinks this, is immediately underneath. The one underneath, as soon as he or she knows this, is immediately on top. And so on. It is a circle. It is all one.

'– I say! – said God.

' – Like to try it? – said Eve.

' – Where did you learn this? – said God.

'The snake looked modest.

' – But people must see that women are in fact on top – said God – I mean, that men come out of women.

' – Then all you have to do is to make up a story that it was woman that came out of man – said Eve.

' – You mean – said God – men are better at making things up?

' – So who's on top? – said Eve.

'God thought about this for a time. He liked watching the snake and Eve.

'He said – But look here: we'd better make another story up: we don't want people bursting into the garden!

' – What sort of story? – said Eve.

' – What about that I've had to turn you out of the garden because you've learned about the circle of good and evil –

' – Well you're the one who makes things up – said Eve.'

The Indian boy, Shastri, used to wait for me outside the gates of the Garden. He would be standing by the rug of corals and shells. One evening there were other boys with him. They all wore white shirts and black trousers. I thought – This is what is called, is it, a political meeting.

'Here I am.'

'Shall we go?'

When I smiled at the other Indian boys they looked away as if they were embarrassed.

The road to the village was full of bicyclists. I walked ahead. Shastri came up beside me. The other boys followed. It was as if they were nudging each other. Bits of uncertainty hung out of them like cloth through holes in trousers.

I said 'Tell me about this meeting.'

He said 'It's a group of us. I've explained.'

I thought – I know about political meetings: in the basement of the hostel behind Victoria Station.

I said 'I'm not very good at politics.'

He said 'What were your political affiliations in England?'

There were wooden shacks either side of the road with stalls in front of them. The stalls sold beans and strips of leather and pieces of bicycles. I thought – These are bits that have tumbled out of men's insides.

I said 'I had no political affiliations in England.'

I thought I might have said – I was a liaison officer with the camp of the Assyrians.

The village began some way from the Garden. Houses spread back from the road; there were paths between them and trees. Dogs and children stood and watched; they were like things seen in a painting.

Shastri said 'Would you like to see some jewellery?'

There was a table by the side of the road with benches beside it and bottles of soft drinks. Segments of water melons were covered with pips and flies. I thought I might say to Shastri – What do you want from this? Do you imagine I do not think you make things up?

I said 'No I don't want to see any jewellery.'

'My uncle has good ivory and tortoiseshell at his house.'

A man came up and spoke to Shastri in their language. The boys in their white shirts and black trousers had stopped at the far side of the road. They formed a little group, as if of conspirators, facing inwards.

I thought – Do you not know I am a gunfighter in the camp of the Assyrians?

Shastri said 'Would you like a drink?'

I sat down. The boys on the other side of the road were passing round cigarettes. I thought – Perhaps he has some sort of bet with them.

Beyond the stalls and buildings at the far side of the road there was a tower – a squat flat-topped pyramid shape of blackish stone rising above the roof-tops. There were bulges and scrolls and weeds growing out of the stone. I thought – I will go to this temple. I have been with my father to so many temples! That is where hags sometimes dismember a child.

He said 'Have I offended you?'

I said 'Can we look at that temple?'

I got up and walked across the road. He came after me. I thought – It is your fault. This sort of stuff is so awful; so awful.

I went past the group of Indian boys. Shastri called after me 'Won't you have a drink?'

There was a path going between the wooden buildings in the direction of the temple. To one side of this path, hung across the entrance to a courtyard, was a banner painted red with lines of the local lettering across it and underneath this – PNR PARTY OF NATIONAL RESURGENCE.

I thought – You mean, there really is a political meeting?

– This is where we were going?

– Those boys are shy: they don't speak English?

The courtyard beyond the banner seemed to be empty.

I thought – Well, I don't know. I am sorry.

The entrance to the temple was further on, at the other side of the path. There was a stone god in a niche beside it with his head as if chewed by animals.

I went into an open courtyard. Shastri stopped to take off his shoes. I thought – You think you know why you do things? Well, what is the circle of good and evil?

There were thistles and dried-up flowers between slabs of stone. The temple was like something set together with huge loose bricks from a child's toy-box. It was small; no more than ten or fifteen metres high. I thought – It is black because of fires or bird-shit; or is bird-shit used for fuel?

Shastri had followed me into the courtyard. There were clapped-out gods in niches round the walls. The entrance to the central tower was narrow between two upright stones – like a tomb, or a gap between teeth.

God's voice, dropping down from the loudspeakers, had said – Sex is not a sin: it is just stupid.

Birds flew out of the entrance to the tower. There was the smell of bats. I thought – Temples are places where birds seem like bats.

Shastri said 'Please! will you come to my uncle's house?'

I went in to the inner sanctum of the temple. At first I could see nothing because I myself was in the pathway of the light. Then I moved to one side and there was a small square chamber like a tomb: of course, there was nothing in it: is it that there never is? Then the light from the door was blocked again as Shastri came in. When he stood behind me he put his hands on my shoulders. He seemed to be trembling. I thought – Oh God, there are those stories in books, in films, about this. There was a further alcove, or niche, at the far side of the holy of holies. I thought – It might be a cupboard where something quite practical is stored: such as a winding sheet, or an angel. When I moved towards it I blocked the light again; when I moved to one side I could not see within. I thought – So you wait, do you, until your eyes become accustomed to the dark.

Shastri put his hands again, then his head, on my shoulder. I said 'I can't come to your uncle's house.' He said 'Why not?' I said 'I can't.' He said 'People do it the whole time in the Garden.'

When my eyes became accustomed to the darkness I saw that inside the alcove there was one of those tall stone domed things like an enormous penis: it was streaked with what looked like flesh and blood; perhaps flower-petals and porridge. I thought – Ah, you old hags, will you one day have done with children!

I put a hand out and laid it on the stone penis.

Shastri said 'Don't do that!'

I said 'Why not?' Then – 'All right we can make love here.'

Shastri said 'I don't want to make love here!'

I said 'Why not?'

Shastri said 'I want friendship!'

I thought – Dear God, friendship!

Then – You mean it is I who still make up these stories? Or – I want to be on top?

So who am I writing to: you? is it you?

One is writing to someone or other, is one not?

One does not tell everything in a letter. (You call these letters!) Sometimes one comes out better: sometimes worse. Do you think I told everything in that letter to Bert?

Did you go back to that red-haired girl after that morning? (I mean you!) Did you know her already? You seemed to be getting on quite well with her.

You and I understood something that morning, didn't we?

You were not the brown dog: you were the faun.

Outlandish things do happen, don't they: when on the edge of – what? – a bed?

When I said I wanted to give up I did not mean, of course, that I wanted to give up –

You said – No one will tell. No one will know.

I thought – I will know! (But I didn't!)

You meant, of course, about that body on the pavement.

147

You were so good to me: I thought that one day what has happened between us, would happen.

You can say, can you, about evil and good, that the one does not happen without the other?

But this is what words are not good at.

How are you? You will look after yourself?

Perhaps I will come back and look after you.

I think this now: I thought this when I was in the Garden.

There were times when I was in the Garden, yes, when I did go with the woman with fair hair who was like a cave in a mountain: she would come and stand in the doorway of the workshop or kitchen where I worked; then I would follow her; we would go to the annexe of God's house. She still did not speak much: she was half-Rumanian, half-Italian, I think: she was one of the women responsible for the day-to-day running of the Garden. All the practical running of the Garden God handed over to women. There was a connection (I mean literally!) between her annexe and God's house.

Well, yes, it was as if she were the cave and I were the elephant in the mountain. She would lie on her side and she would accommodate me as if I were (you know why there is this need for metaphors?) piglets, a whole brood: she would raise an arm here, a leg there (well, yes, the need is because the point of the thing is that it is going on slightly elsewhere) and it was, indeed, as if I had been starved of minerals. Perhaps they had been taken away from my mother when she had been in that Japanese prison camp, so I had not had her – what – tinned milk, touch, taste, sound, smell? (I must forgive my mother.) Was it this that was going on elsewhere? But here, now, was not this body in the half-dark like the roof of a cave; like salt and wine; like nectar.

Perhaps there is not the same battle between women because there has already been (or should have been?) a circle: while the child feeds, the mother cleans; lifts it with her tongue: you have seen this? God can be still learning.

You do not talk about this because the words get it wrong.

What is wonder? What is taste, touch, smell?

Perhaps I had never known about sensuality before: the girl with the wound in her throat is rather like a doll.

My friend who was like Lilith would say – You come alive, my little English girl: oh little bird in bush, who made you?

Before this I had been wondering, had I not, if I would stay in the Garden: could I be sure I was not playing with shadows even when the sun came up each morning in the enormous hall? There has to be some tap-root down into the dark – does there not? This woman had taken me in: I was happy devouring her. Alchemists, in their search for minerals, were hoping for miracles: they used minerals as symbols of the connections between themselves and the outside world. I found minerals, miracles, as lures that were bringing me home. When I was with this woman who was like Lilith in the hot afternoons it was as if there were being made tangible the things in the Garden that might otherwise seem to be going on elsewhere: the connections between space and time: love, birth, growth, death: the just-this-ness of things, which is like gravity.

One day when I had been some months in the Garden I thought I would use my day off to walk inland to the bridge over the river. I had been several times by boat to the town across the estuary: this town was comparatively modern, built around the harbour. But in the hills there were the remains of an old town built by the Jesuits and the Franciscans in the seventeenth century: you could get to this up a track across the river.

The bridge was three or four miles beyond the village – a single span like a rainbow. The rainbow was of steel and concrete: I thought – God's covenant with men was that he would not destroy them, not that they would not destroy themselves. The other side of the river the road turned back to the new town by the harbour; the track went up into the hills. I walked between trees with huge roots like the feet of a monster; the trunks stuck up like legs; the body was far above with gaps in the green like stars. I thought – None of this will live, if men destroy themselves?

It took another hour to walk from the bridge to the old town in the jungle; it was a hot day; I was tired. I wondered why the Christians had built their churches so far from the sea (the remains of the old town consisted of four or five enormous churches): was it because they wanted to feel safe from marauders, or did they feel that their huge churches would look ridiculous by the sea?

When you come across the site of the old town it is like coming across a stage-set. Over the brow of a hill, round a corner (you have been passing the roots of trees wrestling with fallen stones) you see just there, popped up as it were in front of you, the façade of an enormous church: the church is in the baroque style; it is three or four storeys high, with scrolls and pediments and arches. This church is in fact one of four set round a central cobbled square; the square is as big as a parade ground; there is almost nothing left of the town except these four huge churches and the square. But it is this first church that springs up at you out of the jungle. It seems to be nothing to do with jungle; to have been dumped there by some film people.

Do you know those stage-sets, façades, that people built in the sixteenth and seventeenth centuries that were to do with the preservation of memory? I mean people did actually construct, at this time, theatres, or models of theatres, to help with the problem of how to remember; I mean you could not then easily check with written or printed words: people found it easiest to hold things in the mind if they could make up some story or drama. So they constructed these stage-sets: I mean not only in their minds but apparently actually, literally, complete with doorways, windows, porticoes, pillars, niches; so that in and out of these they could get people, objects, coming and going – and also in their minds: so that like this they could remember what they wanted. But then – how dependent humans are on making up stories! Did they remember this: I mean remember not only what they wanted to remember, but how much they were limited by their dependence on stories? The huge façades of churches are always, I suppose, to do with the preservation of stories.

I stopped at some distance from this façade – a high pediment with scrolls like sea-shells at the top; round windows like eyes on the second floor; rectangles with pillars in the middle; an arched doorway at ground-level with heraldic decorations. I did not know what I wanted from my memory: what figures might emerge: Agamemnon and Clytemnestra? my father and my mother? myself as Electra waiting to get my revenge on – but whom? both, for being so much concerned with dying? There was in fact a figure standing within the arched doorway of the church looking up: he was studying, as tourists do, the decoration on the portico. But this was ridiculous. I mean, what did really happen in the seventeenth century? Did they hire actors to perform just the stories they wanted to make real? I had had the impression, you see (but was not this inevitable?), that I knew who this figure was in the doorway of the church: but could not almost anything be possible, given the likelihood of these enormous façades in the jungle. I thought I might go across the square and look at one of the other churches first: I had got out of the way of talking to people, whoever they might be. The figure was that of a man: he wore a tweed jacket in this hot climate; he had short legs. Well, who does this remind you of? Or you; or you. I walked towards the other side of the square. I had the impression that he might have turned and was watching me. Of course, he might have thought I was popping up like some actor in his theatre of memory. The man of whom I was reminded was, of course, one of those who ran *Die Flamme* magazine: he had short legs: I had last seen him, I supposed, bobbing backwards and forwards at the *Die Flamme* party: he was called Eccleston. I thought – Why on earth did people want to have theatres of memory? you mean, they liked being reminded about the boring trouble they took destroying themselves? The side-wall of the church that I was approaching across the square was like a fortress: I thought – Memories could take refuge here; you could never blot them out: they would defend themselves with boiling oil and arrows.

The interior of this church into which I went was huge and cavernous like a riding-school: decorations had been taken down or had never been put up: walls were white and soft and peeling like acid on skin. There was one huge and battered crucifix at the back of the altar: one of the nails had come out – not from the hands or feet but from the wall – so that the whole contraption seemed to be swinging round to deliver some blow. I had moved into the middle of the church: someone was coming in at the door behind me. I felt I could not bear it if it was Eccleston: surely memories do not come down from their niches and pursue you? I thought I might take refuge behind the altar: swing round with that crucifix like a weapon in my hand – someone had come up behind me and put a hand on my shoulder. When I turned it was my Indian friend, Shastri. Shastri had taken to waiting and following me outside the Garden. I have not really explained about this: one does not explain, does one, when things become too boring. I had been with him once or twice to his uncle's house: I would not go just when he wanted me. I suppose this was my fault: I suppose it was not my fault. Shastri said 'What are you doing here?' I thought – Now Eccleston will come in, will he, and he will see me having some fracas with an Indian boy: we will be back at the hostel behind Victoria Station. Do you not see that this might be boring? Shastri said 'You are meeting someone here?' Well this is the sort of thing that memories say, is it not. Shastri must have followed me all the way through the jungle. I said 'No I'm not meeting anyone here.' Shastri said 'Then why didn't you want me to come with you?' I thought – Because you say things like: then why didn't you want me to come with you. The door behind us opened and someone else was coming in. I thought – Now, it will be Eccleston: and he will not quite know, will he, what is real and what is memory: might we not be actors in the seventeenth century? Whoever it was began to walk very slowly up the centre of the church. I was sure it was Eccleston. Shastri remained holding me by the arm. I thought – Well, heigh-ho, let's see what happens this time. When Eccleston was half-way towards the altar he turned and said 'Hullo!' I said 'Hullo!' He had this long knobbly face like a Jerusalem artichoke. He said 'I wondered if it was you.' I said 'Yes it's me.' I thought – Do you think this is how people greeted their memories in the seventeenth century? like Stanley, or whoever it was, later, in some jungle. Shastri said 'Excuse me I am with this lady.' Eccleston had a way of looking at people as if he were enormously amused: I wondered how he would look if he were in fact amused. He said 'I am so sorry, will you excuse me if I have just a quick word with this lady.' Shastri said 'Go ahead.' Eccleston said 'How are you?' I said 'All right.' Eccleston said 'I would like to talk to you: I wonder if you would come to the hotel this evening and have a drink?' Shastri said to me 'You told me you were not meeting this man.' I said 'I am not meeting this man.' Eccleston said 'Can I just ask you one or two questions about the Garden?' I said 'What story are you on?' I thought suddenly – But in this memory-theatre, would you know what story you are on? Shastri said 'No.' Eccleston said to Shastri 'But I'd be delighted if you came too!' He did some sort of flashing of his eyes with Shastri. I thought – You mean, Eccleston is homosexual? Then – But of course, he would want to get stories that were harmful to the Garden! Shastri let go of my arm. He said 'Thank you.' Eccleston said to me 'I knew you were here, but I didn't know how to find you.' I thought – Of course you would have known how to find me! Eccleston was smiling. I thought – But if you are in this theatre of memory, you have some message to tell me that is part of my story?

On my way back down the track with the cut-off claws of trees (I had begun by running: I had managed to get away from both Eccleston and Shastri) I tried to work out – What is it one is doing with memory? What falsifications result from the need for a story?

My mother and father, for instance (those old claws! those figures of autumn and winter popping in and out of doorways) –

How would I write about them if I started again: if I tried to see the way we make up stories?

My father in the front of the Land-Rover, talking and talking. Sometimes to illustrate a point he would take his hands from the wheel: we would be driving round corners where a lorry as wide as the road was likely to come: my mother would hold on to the sides of her seat as she sometimes did when she came across Japanese who reminded her of prison. My father saying – What distinguishes humans from non-humans is when they begin to use symbols; when they begin to use language. My mother said – Language is not symbols. My father said – Yes it is. My mother said – Look out! My father said – Before language, you just grunt and roar. My mother said – I am not grunting and roaring! My father said – I didn't say you were. And so on.

I was lying in the back of the Land-Rover among the pots and pans and camping equipment.

I would think – I will never be like this! I will be on my own, and make symbols I will talk to.

I was crossing the river by the road-bridge. I thought – One day I will forgive my father and mother: I will see them as if they are in a painting?

On my way back to my hut I walked along a path at the back of the Garden where the wire fence of the perimeter came to within a few feet of the fence around God's inner garden. The wire mesh of both fences was usually covered with climbing plants so that one could not see through; however, recently some of the greenery had died so that there were patches of brown. It seemed that if I pulled at one of these with my fingers gently I would make a peephole.

I thought – If this were the theatre of memory, I would be seeing behind the scenes?

Across a small lawn there was a loggia, with pillars, at the back of God's house. In front of this, half-facing me, was a girl, of about my own age, with long fair hair: she was standing in front of an easel: she appeared to be painting something just out of my sight near the hedge on my left. You

154

know those paintings in which the painter paints himself painting a scene which is reflected in a mirror in the background of the painting? – there is that huge one by Velázquez, in the Prado – it seemed to me that this girl, painting, might be some reflection of myself: it might be myself painting myself painting the scene: but still, what was it that was being painted? Behind the girl at the easel (she had fair hair; she could not, except by some trick of the light or the imagination, be like me) there was a plate-glass window; within this window in the loggia (the regressions might be endless) there was another image, I mean an actual reflection, which was of God, who appeared to be seated in a garden chair with his back to the hedge or fence and facing the window. I mean that this was what was reflected in the plate glass at the back of the loggia: this was what the girl seemed to be painting. But with God there was another figure kneeling or seated on the ground: she had her arms over God's lap. I thought – This is what you usually do not see of God; the other part of him. The figure was that of my friend who was like Lilith. The girl in front of the loggia, half-facing me, was painting this scene; God-and-Lilith were reflected in the window behind her: they were somewhere just out of sight to her right on my left. I thought – I am seeing – what – not a symbol, but a symbol of symbols? Am I watching myself watching – or myself creating it? It seemed that if I moved the dead strands of climbers carefully I might see God face to face: I mean I saw God at his discourses every day, but that was a story-God: this would be God without his smile or mask: he would be together with his, and my, Lilith. I mean Moses, did he not, only saw God's arse? There was one of God's acolytes, like a gardener, on his hands and knees just beyond the fence: he was replanting the hedge: he was watching me. I thought – It is all right: we are both of us angels. I pressed my head as close as I could against the fence. I did then have a glimpse of God and Lilith with her head on his knee: she was wearing her flame-coloured dress; he had his hand on her hair. I thought – But of course they are together, at one, beyond the walls of the

155

cave: they are what we talk about as the sun, are they? And now I have seen them: been with them: I mean, there is that girl painting them. So you do not get burned outside the walls of the cave, do you? You set up your easel perhaps, which is the back way.

'Hullo.'
  'Hullo.'
  'It was good of you to come.'
  'Not at all.'
  'Would you like a drink?'
  'Orange juice please.'
  'Not "Save the Oranges"!'
  'No.'
I have not explained about this hotel. It is a grand tourist hotel not far from the Garden on a promontory between the estuary and the sea. People in the Garden used to pretend it wasn't there, though people with money stayed there when they visited the Garden. It and its grounds were surrounded by a high wire fence rather like that which surrounded the Garden. I used to think – It is some sort of alternative or anti-Garden. I tried not to go there, perhaps because I thought I might want to stay.

Eccleston said 'You've been in the Garden – what – four or five months?'

'Yes.'

'And how do you find it?'

'All right.'

'What made you choose it?'

'A story that you once printed about it, as a matter of fact.'

We were sitting on a lawn by a bright-blue swimming-pool. There were palm trees hung with fairy lights.

Eccleston said 'An orange juice and a large vodka and tonic, please.'

I said 'You printed a story, months ago, about sex and drugs. But there are no drugs in the Garden. You made the people in the Garden sound so wonderful.'

156

Eccleston said 'Lovely lovely sex and drugs.'

Eccleston was a middle-aged man with a heavy, handsome face set so low on his shoulders that it was as if a sculptor had miscalculated and found himself short of stone.

I said 'What story are you doing now?'

He said 'You're still starry-eyed – '

I said 'What is starry-eyed – '

I thought – I've forgotten how to do this.

He said 'All things bright and beautiful.'

I said 'You do think you're learning something, yes.'

The people round the swimming-pool were at tables in twos and fours. It was as if they were ready to play some game that they had forgotten. I thought – Perhaps they should be making up the game.

He said 'What are you learning?'

I said 'To stand back from yourself. To try to see yourself.'

He said 'Sounds a bit schizophrenic.'

I said 'Thanks for the drink.'

Eccleston wore a white linen jacket with a white polo-neck shirt and dark cotton trousers. His face was the texture of paper that has been soaked. I thought – It would not be possible for him to see himself?

He said 'You know the story about the girl who died and came alive?'

I said 'Yes.'

He said 'Well, what is it?'

I said 'There are always these stories.'

The people round the swimming-pool seemed to be waiting for some announcement. I thought – Of the result of the Battle of Waterloo? Whether or not the Bomb has gone off?

He said 'What stories?'

I said 'People die, and come alive.'

He said 'And you don't think that's interesting?'

'Not very.'

'Why not?'

'What does it mean?'

There had been this story, it is true (well, how can one talk

157

about such things? these are just stories that pop up like the figures in porticoes and doorways) about an incident that had happened just before I had arrived in the Garden. There had been a girl called Anita Kroll who was supposed to have died, and to have come alive: I mean she had been pronounced dead, and then God had just touched her, people said. I had heard the story originally from Shastri. People in the Garden did not talk about it much: when I asked them they were apt to say something like – Oh that! – and laugh and look away.

Eccleston said 'Well, what does it mean?'

I said 'It's a story. No one pays much attention to it in the Garden.'

'Not when it's getting so much publicity outside?'

'No.'

'Not when the publicity must be bringing a lot of new people, and a lot of money, into the Garden?'

'But it's people like you who are doing the publicity. It's you who are thinking about money.'

It was true, I suppose, that it was difficult to know how to think about the story in the Garden.

'Well it's quite clever to appear disinterested. This, of course, creates even more interest outside.'

I had got out of the habit of fighting with people like Eccleston. I thought I might say – Well yes, it is clever, to want to have everything both ways.

He said 'She was thought to be dead – '

'Yes.'

'And a doctor certified this – '

'Apparently.'

'And then she was seen to come alive.'

'So they say.'

'But what do you think?'

'It was before my time in the Garden.'

So far as I had been able to make out, what had happened was this –

The girl called Anita Kroll had been to one of God's sessions with his special disciples in the evening: God had blessed her,

158

put his finger on her forehead, and she had been carried out in some state of collapse. Then later in her room it had been thought that she was dead: she seemed to have had a heart-attack. A doctor had been sent for and he had said that she was dead: then God had appeared at the door of her room – God usually never went out of his inner garden except for his morning discourses – and he had taken her by the hand, and had slapped it or something, and Anita Kroll had come alive. Then God had gone back to his inner garden. It was said that no one had informed God that Anita Kroll was supposed to be dead, because they had not wanted to disturb his meditation. Afterwards God had told them not to spread the story. But, of course, versions of it had got out.

I said 'You can believe what you want to believe: which is what people do anyway. There's no way of proving or disproving such a story. If there was, you wouldn't have a choice.'

He said 'A choice of what?'

I said 'Attitudes.'

He said again 'But what do you think is true?'

It was true, yes, that I had thought that this might be one of God's jokes: one of the jokes which, of course, he said might truly express what is true.

I said 'I think it's a symbol.'

He said 'A symbol of what?'

I said 'Of people's attitude to the story: to what is dead coming alive. A symbol of a symbol.'

I thought – Well this may indeed be a joke: with luck, people won't understand it.

He said 'You don't think it's a symbol of a charlatan deceiving a pathetically gullible audience?'

I said 'If you like.'

The people round the swimming-pool seemed to have had some sort of ash scattered over them. They glistened and were dry at the same time. I thought – Why do rich people glisten? They want to be preserved? They want to be just the same in a thousand years?

He said 'Where is Anita Kroll now?'

I said 'She is supposed to have left the Garden.'

He said 'You do see the connotations!'

I said 'What?'

He said 'Christ does a miracle: he orders his disciples not to spread it abroad. This, of course, means it is enormously spread abroad. The people are ready for the next miracle – guess what? – God himself dying and coming alive?'

It is true that I had thought of this – of course, this is what God has been saying: in order to free people, do you not have to die and come alive?

I said 'It could be a joke.'

He said 'A joke!'

I said 'There are a lot of jokes in the Garden.'

I suddenly had the impression (oh yes! as I quite often had at this time) that something quite different was happening – where? – round a corner: down some staircase: someone coming into the hotel perhaps (well, it might have been you! had you not laughed that first time I met you and put your finger on my forehead? did I not need some ally in my battle with Eccleston?).

I said 'What did Anita Kroll look like?'

He said 'She looked rather like you, as a matter of fact; except that she had fair hair.'

He took a brief-case from the floor, opened it, and looked through some papers. Then he handed me a photograph.

I thought – Oh dear God, I have known this, have I, for the last two hours?

The girl in the photograph, Anita Kroll, was the girl, it seemed likely, whom I had seen painting God-and-Lilith in God's inner garden. I mean this was possible, but not of course certain, because what can one tell from a photograph?

– So what would it mean then that this girl had died and come alive?

– This would, indeed, be a joke –

– And something one would wish to be kept secret?

I thought – But this is ridiculous.

Or – One day, of course, I will have to get out of the Garden.

There was too much light coming down. Some of it was slightly frightening. I could not bear to go on talking to Eccleston. For something to say, I suppose – as an actor might *ad lib* if there had been a small explosion in a theatre – I said 'How is Desmond?'

Eccleston was silent for so long – I was still looking at the photograph – that I thought the curtain had come down and perhaps everyone had left the auditorium.

Then when I looked at him his face had lost its supercilious look. I thought – What, he too is frightened?

He said 'Desmond – '

I said 'Yes.'

He said 'Desmond's dead.'

I thought – Now look –

He said 'I thought you knew.'

I said 'No.'

He said 'He fell out of a window.'

Why did you not tell me it was Desmond who had died? Why did you let me think it was Oliver?

Of course it makes a difference. How can I put into words what the difference is?

Oliver was part of me: Desmond was not.

Or did you not know I thought it was Oliver? Or did you think it would be easier for me if I thought it was?

I suppose I remembered what I wanted to remember. And there were the effects of dope. But why should I have wanted to remember it like this? I wanted to punish myself – for what I had been with Oliver?

At the time, I was not much responsible for Desmond: what was he doing there? Of course, if you wish, I had once wanted to pick him up: but I had tried to discourage him from coming into that part of my story.

What is there to say about feelings – they are the stones that people put in their pockets as they walk into the sea?

I had got Oliver back from the dead: I should not have wanted him to die again. (If I sometimes did, this is no contradiction.) Oliver was of the dark, deep: we were accomplices in the town of Bethulia.

Desmond was so obviously bright; like Holofernes.

Does anyone understand? – it is the black horse that drags you towards perdition: it is on the back of the black horse that you get on to the road to the gods again. You have grown wings. If you understand this, perhaps you stop it happening?

When Plato wrote his myth it was so difficult to understand; this did not stop it happening?

Desmond wrote his simple stories for *Die Flamme* magazine: on his white horse, could one say he was like Icarus?

I am so sorry about Desmond. Oliver has two or three children somewhere, hasn't he?

Of course, that morning, you said all the right things –

– Each person is responsible for himself: you are no more responsible for the other than the other is responsible for you –

– You learn from things going wrong: what do you learn from things going right?

– The choice is: are you to learn or are you not?

I suppose I have not described what was marvellous about Oliver: I could not do this, could I, in my letter to Bert. (Do you think I used to see Bert somewhat like Desmond? it is of this I am afraid?) There were times when Oliver and I laughed so much (I have tried to say this): he freed me from that part of me that thought I was omnipotent. Of course, yes, this involved some going down towards perdition.

When Oliver and I walked through streets and Oliver would do one of his funny acts (have I not described these?) there would be that sort of lighting-up of laughter all around such as there sometimes was in the Garden. Of course, you could say this luminousness was like that of flesh under the sea.

Did you go, that night or morning, to see Oliver? Of course, I never asked you. What was he like?

Yes, I will learn from this.

Do you think this is terrible, what I say?

Thank you for having helped me. Well, shall I come back and look after you one day?

From where I am sitting I can see the estuary. I will be your brown dog? Who will be your faun?

That girl with the red hair – you helped her to grow wings, did you?

What I imagined then – what I imagine now – is that you will always when it is needed send me a message coming through a doorway like a bird!

When I left Eccleston at the grand hotel I met Shastri coming up on the road outside; he had put on a jacket to go with his dark trousers; I said 'I thought you would not be seen dead in this hotel!'

He said 'I'm having dinner with your friend Mr Eccleston.'

I said 'I know you're having dinner with my friend Mr Eccleston.'

I tried to remember what Eccleston and I had talked about after he had told me about Desmond. There had been that white light: memories like bats, like an audience, flying out of the cave. I had wanted to get away; to be on my own.

Shastri said 'You are not coming too?'

I said 'No.' Then – 'Watch out he doesn't bugger you.'

Eccleston had been interested in what was the local opinion about the Garden. I had said to him – Doubtless you will find out from my friend Shastri. He had said – He is coming to dinner. I had said – I know he is coming to dinner.

Shastri said 'He wants information.'

I said 'Well see that he pays you.'

Shastri said 'For buggering me?'

I said 'Shastri, I love you.' I kissed him.

I thought – But yes, I am afraid of imagining people are like Desmond!

Shastri said 'Perhaps it is best if you are not present. You are not interested in politics.'

I said 'He writes articles full of lies in an English magazine.'

Shastri said 'He wishes to expose hypocrisy and corruption.'

I thought I might say – Of course, all this is often the same thing.

Some time later that night – I had gone walking on the beach: I had swum in the white waves – I thought I must go back to the grand hotel; to see Eccleston perhaps; to see what Eccleston was up to with Shastri; to find out more about Desmond and Oliver, do you think; oh yes, to find out more about Oliver. I did not really want to go back to the hotel: I had to go somewhere: sparks were flying off the ground as I walked to my hut; my mind had to get rid of electricity. I thought I would walk along the side of the estuary to the rocks of the promontory; like this I might seem not to make up my mind whether or not I would go to the grand hotel: if I could find a way up from the rocks, I would; if I could not, I would not. So you keep all your chances up in the air, do you? Is this a characteristic of what is called detachment, being hollowed out: or is it being a witch above a battlefield with seaweed in your hair?

I went along the sand at the edge of the estuary. There was an almost full moon. This was where the girl with the wound in her throat might have lain: there were the remains of an enormous bonfire. This was also where, people had told me, they had built a funeral pyre to burn the body of Anita Kroll (she had been such a long time dead? but, of course, it was all a story!) or had they built a bonfire in celebration of her being alive? Well, how can you think of this: what is enlightenment, what is illusion? There were bright, metallic flowers by the ashes of the bonfire: this was some other bonfire: I thought I would ask my friend who was like Lilith about Anita Kroll. But you can only be told what things are not, can't you, not what they are. I walked on towards the rocks and the lights of the grand hotel: these were in the distance like those of an ocean liner. I thought – And I am an iceberg come to – what? – stroke gently against your sides. I did not know what on earth I wanted to find out about Oliver: in what way it might seem that he was all right. Or was I hoping for that further message? I had thought I might come across a pathway up from the estuary to the grand hotel: but who would want to move between the grand hotel and the water? those people would not be baby turtles to run towards the sea. I set off across rocks that were black and sharp; there were thorn-bushes growing from cracks; there were gullies between the estuary and the grand hotel. It suddenly became quite dark: the moon had moved behind clouds: I was in a small chasm of thorn-bushes, somewhat torn and bleeding. I thought I might say – All right, God, find some other sacrifice! Lights suddenly came on which lit up brightly the perimeter fence of the grand hotel; the scene was like that of some prison. I thought – The lights have come on because they know someone is trying to break in: someone has come right round the world – and so on. A joke! Then – But you mean, I am getting the habit of confusing the Garden with the grand hotel? I climbed on over a few more rocks and bushes – I had forgotten exactly why I was doing this – and I came to the perimeter fence which was about seven or eight feet high: it was lit at various points from inside by lights on poles. I thought – Well, indeed, it is this anti-Garden which is guarded. Along the branch of a tree that reached out over the fence there was a shape – it might be a leopard? on its stomach, stretched out – oh well, yes, perhaps it was a snake (not a bird?): in this state of mind, perhaps anything. Then I saw it was a man. He wore white trousers and a dark-blue shirt. He seemed to have been pulling himself along the branch of the tree; to have stopped when he heard me coming. He looked at me, and then he said 'Coo-ee!' I thought – Dear God Almighty, you cannot say – Coo-ee! Then – So this is the message sent to me? He was a middle-aged man, long and bony: he started to laugh. He said 'I'm trying to get into the garden.' I thought I might say – So I see. He said 'You're from the Garden.' I said 'Yes.' He said 'I mean the Garden with a capital G.' He went on laughing. He nearly fell off the branch. I thought – I know what he will do: he will pull himself along so that when he laughs again he will fall off inside the garden. He said 'It would take too long to explain why I am here.' I thought – But I know exactly why you are here; you are doing the same as me: you happened to be walking along by the estuary and you thought you would try to find a short cut, or a back way, into the grand hotel. He said 'In the morning, will you show me around the Garden, I mean the Garden with a capital G?' I said 'Yes.' He seemed to slip, and fall, and he hung by his arms from the branch of the tree. He was inside the fence. He said 'Aren't you coming in?' I said 'No.' He said 'Why not?' He let go of the branch and dropped. He came and we stood facing each other through the wire. I said 'Because it's all a bit much.' He said 'Yes.'

I said 'Are you the man who knew the highest score in first-class cricket and the date of the Second Reform Bill?'

He said 'No.' Then – 'I know the highest score in first-class cricket but I don't know the date of the Second Reform Bill.'

I said 'I'll meet you at the gates at ten to six in the morning.'

He said 'I'll be there.'

I thought – He has come to rescue me from my haunting by Eccleston?

– Then tonight it will indeed be necessary to make my mind a blank, a hollow; there will be no fuse, no bright light coming down; that might separate this time from that.

'Hullo.'

'Hullo.'

'You must tell me what to do.'

'Follow me.'

I was still sure I had seen the man before. If he was not the man who had known the highest score in first-class cricket and the date of the Second Reform Bill, who was he?

'When the music starts you first breathe out, hard, like a bellows.'

'I breathe out, hard, like a bellows.'

'Don't bother about breathing in.'

'Oh no, no, I won't bother about breathing in!'

He seemed to be laughing: not at me, but with me.

'And we do not talk.'

He opened his mouth and shut it. He clenched his hands and moved from one foot to the other like someone preparing for the long-jump. He was this tall man with spectacles and a head like a bronze hatchet.

I said 'Then, when the music stops, I'll tell you what to do after that.'

He mouthed – Then when the music stops – He looked round as if he might run after his words, as if they were butterflies.

I thought – This is the sort of language there might be through the back door of that garden?

When the music started, the man pumped with his elbows so hard that he was like one of those people who try to take off from the top of a tower with home-made wings. I thought – He is both putting his heart into this and mocking it. This is what God teaches in the Garden – to be true to a thing you also have to be in some way laughing at it?

Then – Who am I talking to?

I found, when I was with this man, that I was wondering what I might do when I got out of the Garden.

I said 'Now, when the music starts again, you shake, and let bits and pieces fly off you.'

He said 'Let bits and pieces fly off me.'

He clapped a hand over his mouth and looked up to the sky as if he were one of those pieces of agonised sculpture beneath a thunderbolt about to come down.

When the music started again he wobbled so dementedly that his spectacles half flew off: he caught them: it was as if he might loose his teeth, an arm, what was left of his hair, a wooden leg: he seemed to go diving after bits of himself. I thought – You mean, he really does understand – you do it, but of course you are laughing if you watch yourself doing it?

I said 'Now, you hold your arms above your head and jump up and down on the spot for ten minutes.'

He raised and lowered his eyebrows like a comedian. He took his spectacles off and put them in a pocket.

Then he looked at me quietly, ruminatively, as if he had pulled a curtain aside and found – what – me lying in some alcove?

I said 'And afterwards, when the music stops, you stay absolutely still for a quarter of an hour.'

He said 'Quite like the old one-two.'

When he started jumping he did this with such wild concentration that it seemed to be myself who was about to be overcome by laughter: I thought – He is, yes, pulling himself up by his own shoestrings. Then – Of course, there is a sense in which you can do this.

The music stopped.

I thought – So where are the two of us now on this strange planet?

He was pouring with sweat. I had never seen anyone sweat so much. He seemed to be like some Narcissus forming his own pool on the ground.

I remembered – I had been in Oliver's flat, watching television. There had been a line of people and the camera had moved to the end of the row. There it had seemed to fall off, into another dimension. This man had been at the end of the row. Lights had come on in the theatre.

We were standing on the floor of the enormous hall. The sun was coming up. There was a red glow on the floor like a river.

He had said something like – But do you see what trouble people have to go to, to destroy themselves!

So here we were, in this strange landscape.

You cannot bear things not because they are too little, but because they are too much.

The light on the floor was like some sort of grid, or riddle –

– What has four legs in the morning, two in the afternoon and three in the evening? –

– Some understanding, dimensions, we might be carried by; not fall through –

I said 'Now we dance in celebration.'

He was looking at the floor. He put out a finger and pointed. I did not know why he did this.

I said 'And then we have breakfast.'

He danced quite well. He was like some stork, lifting his feet around roof-tops. I thought – I have loved life so much! how indeed can I show I am grateful? It was as if we were dancing on this riddle; bits and old pieces of us fell through: we were supported, delicately, on bars of light. Every now and then he laughed as if he were laughing at us dancing: we were dancing round that empty space to which he had pointed; where the bird had built its nest on the ground. The baby was looking away just out of the picture. I thought – You mean, there is something still waiting one day to be born?

'There's bread and honey and yoghurt and cereals.'

 'The lot.'

 'Shall we sit here?'

 'Yes.'

We sat at a table where bars of light came down from the bamboo awning, as if demonstrating that these were not the walls of a cage.

 'I think I once saw you on television in England.'

 'I'm a friend of some friends of yours in England.'

 'How did you know who I was?'

 'I didn't.'

 'You seemed to know me when you were up that tree.'

 'I thought I recognised you.'

 'I did recognise you.'

 'I met that dreadful man called Eccleston in the hotel.'

I did not quite know what this explained. I remembered – But Oliver knew you!

I said 'But you are not the man who knew the highest score in first-class cricket.'

He said 'No.'

I said 'But why weren't you surprised when I asked you if you were the man who knew the highest score in first-class cricket?'

He said 'I told you, I do know the highest score in first-class cricket.'

 'What is it?'

 'Four five two?'

 'No.'

'Four nine nine?'

'Yes.'

He said 'Perhaps everyone wants to be fascinating, mysterious, secret, hidden.'

I said 'Who?'

He said 'What was I saying on television?'

He was eating cereal with honey. This seemed to get stuck in his teeth. He put a finger in his mouth. This seemed to enable him to look at me without taking his eyes from me for some time.

I said 'You were saying what trouble people had to take to destroy themselves.'

He said 'Or not to destroy themselves.'

I said 'Who are these friends of mine in England?'

He said 'Bert. And Max. Max Ackerman. The Professor, as you call him.'

I said 'Oh. And you are called Jason.'

He said 'I'm married to Bert's sister.'

I thought – I didn't know Bert had a sister.

Then – You know the Professor?

I said 'I didn't know Bert and the Professor knew one another.'

He said 'Oh yes.' Then – 'And Bert knows you, and the Professor knows you, and I know Bert and the Professor, and the Professor knows my wife, and now I know you, so the only people who don't know each other are you and my wife.'

I thought – The Professor knows your wife? She's not the woman that –

Then – How long have you been married?

There was the bright light coming down.

I thought – But we are outside the theatre. We are within the bars of light.

He said 'Max says you saved his life. He says perhaps you helped to save all our lives.' Then – 'Why do you call him the Professor'?

I said 'I don't know.' Then – 'Why does he say I saved his life?'

He said 'I don't know, do you?'

I said 'He saved my life!'

He ate grapefruit, scraping it round and round as if he were not noticing that there was nothing left inside.

He said 'My wife was one of Max's old girlfriends. How much do you want me to talk? You know the thing about breaking things up if you talk?'

I said 'I see.' Then – 'The baby's all right?'

He said 'Yes. That's right.'

He pushed his plate away and looked into the distance. I thought – Perhaps he may soon be saying – I've got to get away from here!

He said 'You've been in the Garden – what – five months?'

I said 'Yes.'

He said 'And how long are you going to stay here?'

I said 'I don't know.'

He said 'When you've really loved it, I suppose you'll go.'

I thought – Will he look at me again? Will he find more honey in his teeth?

I said 'What is your wife called?'

He said 'Lilia.'

I said 'And what are you doing in this part of the world?'

He said 'I've been working on a film. I've been doing a filmscript.'

I said 'And when are you going back?'

He said 'I've got to get back very soon. My wife's having this baby.'

I thought – He is looking at whatever it is just out of the picture.

Then – All I said to the Professor was: of course you can stop her, if you like, getting rid of the baby!

He said 'What time is God's discourse?'

I said 'In about half an hour.'

He said 'Can we last out?'

I said 'How is Max?'

He said 'Quite in love with you, I think.' Then – 'As is Bert.'

171

I thought I might say – And how is your wife?

I said 'Max did not tell me much about you.'

I thought – You don't really know whose baby it is?

He said, as if quoting ' – Things are going on elsewhere – '

I thought – He acts: he knows that he is acting: does this make him, yes, not an actor?

I said 'Why did you come to the Garden?'

He said 'I wanted to look at the place anyway.'

I thought – What do you mean 'anyway'?

He said 'And I wanted to see you.'

I thought – You mean, you wanted to see me because the Professor was attracted to me: I cheered the Professor up? Or because of the baby.

He said 'I was grateful.'

I said 'You knew Oliver, didn't you?'

He said 'Yes, I know Oliver.'

I thought – In a way, you are quite like Oliver.

Then – Should I say: you know about Desmond?

I said 'I don't think I can leave this place.'

He said 'Why not?' Then – 'You don't feel guilty, do you?'

I said 'Yes, I do.'

I thought – Now comes the message from the Professor? From you?

He said 'You don't. You were frightened. Of taking it on. But you're all right now.'

I had a half-full plate of porridge. I wondered if I could throw it at him.

I said 'Of taking what on?'

Then he said that thing that you all say, again as if quoting ' – What is difficult about life is not to have been given too little but to have been given too much.'

I said 'You know what happened to Desmond?'

He said 'Yes, I do.' Then – 'It wasn't your fault.' Then as if quoting ' – With love from Judith.'

I said 'I'm going.' I stood up.

He said 'How long did you say it was before God's discourse?'

172

I said 'Twenty minutes.'

He said 'Just time for a shit.'

God, on his platform, ineffable, smiling, said –

'God was walking in his rock-garden one day when he came across Lilith among her bees and wasps and dragon-flies. And there was Adam, on his crucifix like Mr Universe, in one of his mother's or first wife's grottoes.

'Now God was feeling low, as he had just come from an afternoon with Eve and the snake in the water-garden. There they had been playing their games of Going-On-Thy-Belly-All-The-Days-Of-Thy-Life and It-Shall-Bruise-Thy-Head-And-Thou-Shalt-Bruise-His-Heel: and God was tired.

'He said to Lilith – Look, we'll never get anyone out of this garden!

'Lilith said – It's all your fault. You told them those stories, and now we're all used to having a nice time.

'God said – But they were supposed to find out about stories!

'Lilith said – We've been through all this. You thought they wouldn't call nice having such an awful time.

'God sat down by Lilith. Lilith made room for him on her rock. She said to some of her bees and daddy-longlegs – Go and sting Adam!

'Adam said – Not my will but thine – and so on.

'God said – Look: we wanted something better for our children.

'Lilith who, as God had noticed before, sometimes did not seem to realise what she was saying, said – You cannot make a silk purse out of a sow's ear.

'God said – Look: suppose we put it to them to build a bloody great tower up to heaven: then they can think they are becoming like gods!

'Lilith said – Why should they do that?

'God said – Then they can put a bloody great bomb on top.

'Lilith said – But they might be destroying themselves.

'God said – But they might be getting into heaven.

'Lilith said – You mean, at least they'll be out of the garden?

'Lilith thought about this for a time. She mused – If the bomb is not to go off, they'll have to learn this by a bomb going off – and so on. So she said – I can't quite work this out.

'God said – Neither can I.

'Lilith said – But if they are supposed to be better than us –

'God said – You think they'll have to have a child?

'Lilith lay back among her slime-mould and dung-beetles. Adam quivered in his grotto like Napoleon stung by arrows on the walls of Troy.

'Lilith said – You know, what has always interested me, is that when you told them not to eat from the Tree of Knowledge of good and evil, you didn't tell them not to eat from the Tree of Life.

'God said – Well, if I had, they would have eaten it, wouldn't they?

'Lilith said – But you didn't want them to?

'God said – I don't know. Then – Do I?

'Lilith said – I see. Then – We haven't exactly been through all this.

'Adam got down from his niche in the grotto and went to find Eve. She was dressed-up for the snake as the scarlet woman of Babylon. Adam said – Excuse me, but I've just overheard those two old pensioners talking again.

'Eve said – Why, what are they saying?

'Adam said – They're saying that if we build a bloody great tower and put a bomb on top, we might think we were getting into heaven, but we'd be destroying ourselves. Or is it the other way round?

'Eve said – Does that mean they're afraid, or not, of us breaking into heaven?

'Adam said – I don't know, do you?

'Eve said – I think they're still just trying to get us out of the garden.

'Adam said – What they don't seem to know is whether they're talking about a bomb or about our having a child.

'Now the snake, who had overheard this conversation, got

174

hold of one or two of his friends and said – I say, chaps, we'd better keep close to the ground for a while.

' – We already are close to the ground – the cockroach said.

' – Yes, it has been shown scientifically that you and your species are virtually immune from radioactivity – the snake said.

'Now Lilith, who had overheard this conversation, because she used to lie with her ear close to the ground, said to God – Do you know what those creepy crawly things are saying now?

'God said – Yes, because when I created the world I also created language, which produces the opposite of what it intends.

' – I am not referring to language – Lilith said.

' – Perhaps – God said – they can put it in inverted commas!

' – What? – Lilith said.

' – That bloody great tower! – God said.

'Now everyone in the garden heard this, because God shouted it at the top of his voice. Then he rushed through the garden as if a bomb had gone off, or he had just jumped out of his bath.

' – Has he gone mad? – Adam said.

' – Now they say why can't we put it in inverted commas! – Eve said.

' – But is that better than where we have been putting it? – Adam said.

' – I think what they are saying – Eve said – is that it is time for us to have a child.'

Jason, who was sitting next to me, listening to God's language, had begun to smile from the beginning; and he went on smiling so much that it was as if his face was being pulled out of shape in a wind-tunnel. He had a gap in the side of his teeth; he hung on to one ear; perhaps he felt he might be blown away, or perhaps he was deaf. I thought – It is indeed as if some bomb has gone off (in inverted commas!) and there are all these people leaning against the wind in this enormous hall.

And then after God had left, bouncing off on the shoulders of his acolytes as usual like some target at a fun-fair shooting-range, Jason – I remembered how Oliver had been so jealous of him! – did not move for a time; then he blew his cheeks out as Desmond sometimes used to do; then he said 'There you are then!'

I thought I might say like Lilith or Eve – What do you mean, there I am then?

He said 'Eve has the last word! So where's the child?'

When he stood he hopped about on one foot because a leg had gone to sleep. He put a hand on my shoulder.

I thought – You mean, you are talking about your child?

I spent the rest of the day with him. What else is there to say? In the afternoon we went for a walk along the beach. There were children digging for turtles' eggs in the sand. The yolks had golden blood that ran down.

He said 'What else is there to say? The child of Eve wouldn't be frightened of destruction, would it? and so it might not destroy so much. When you're finished with this place, you'll move on.'

We walked so far along the beach that we came to the end of it. There was a rock over which crabs swarmed like flies.

He said 'There was all that business about not getting rid of the baby. Max rang up someone and he said to her and she said to him – oh, it's too difficult for words! That's just what happened. So here's the baby. I'll try to explain one day.'

Then – 'I think they had just that message for you.'

We turned away from the rock and went into the sand-dunes.

He said 'I'll go back tomorrow. I'll tell them I've seen you. The baby is due any day now.'

Then – 'I wish I could tell you what I mean about this. There's a network. It's aesthetic. Do you know Plato's myth about the dark horse and the pathway to the gods?'

I said 'Yes.'

He said 'You do?'

I said 'Yes.'

He said 'That's all right then.'

At the back of the sand-dunes there was, would you not guess, a small temple. Of course I might have said – Oh, and do you know that dream?

I said 'What will you do when you get back?'

He said 'Perhaps I'll write a story.'

I said 'What story?'

He said 'Well – all this fits together: just: although we don't quite know what is going on, as they say, around some corner.'

We were going up, of course, to look at the deserted temple in the sand-dunes.

Then he said 'Do you know that story of the hags and the child?'

I said 'Yes.'

We were standing inside the temple in the sand-dunes.

I wanted to say – You do promise, one day, we can come back here? We can stay in that hotel?

He said 'I have the impression that the child is now being born.'

Those hags that were dismembering the child – they would be eating bits and pieces of it? Do not lovers want to eat bits and pieces of each other? So that they can be alive?

I began to cry. He held me as if he were trying to get his arms right around me, like gravity.

I thought – But if we make love, it will not be to do with any of those old images!

He said 'Let's go back to the hotel.'

I said 'Yes, let's.'

When we were walking back along the beach it was as if I had not quite walked before; where were those strings; you can be on your own, can you, with your centre of gravity. What else is grace?

He walked along beside me, not smiling, not like one of those statues with their hands by their sides. I thought – You can depend on the sun and moon, you mad archaic statues!

Then – But you mean, some bomb may still have to go off?

177

When we got back to the grand hotel there was a page-boy in the lobby with a telegram. The telegram was asking Jason to come home at once: his wife was about to have, or there was some trouble about her having, or she had even started to have, the baby. Well you know more about this than I do, don't you? (Not you!) Jason showed me the telegram. Then he folded it and put it in his pocket. Then he said 'And may everything be for the best in the best of all possible worlds.' I said 'Will you be able to get a flight before morning?' He said 'Perhaps I won't be able to get a flight before morning!' I said 'Is that awful?' He said 'Yes, awful.' I said 'We can try.' He said 'Yes.' Then he widened his eyes and raised an arm as if he were letting something fly away like a bird and he said 'It is vital, you know, that we should have done everything we can to get me a flight before morning!'

It was shortly after this that the crowds began to increase enormously in and around the Garden: this was mainly in response to articles written by Eccleston and others about Anita Kroll. Such articles were for the most part, of course, aimed at being scathing about the Garden: they accused God of being a charlatan and a confidence-trickster: they exhorted the authorities to make an end of the Garden. Of course, such articles greatly increased the Garden's notoriety: people heard the story of someone who was supposed to have been dead and come alive; they flocked to have a look. This was, although it was unlikely that Eccleston and others had thought of this, perhaps one way of destroying the Garden. People's attitudes at this time seemed everywhere to be getting out of control: inmates of the Garden oscillated more and more between hero-worship and rather embarrassed laughter. Outside, there were stories about God himself – that he was indeed going mad: that he was talking gibberish: that he had begun to speak in tongues. And it was true that while he was speaking people had the impression that they understood what he was saying, but afterwards they found it difficult to describe what this was to others or even to themselves. The enormous hall was not large enough for all the people who came to hear him; his voice was relayed by loudspeakers to other parts of the Garden. In the early mornings, too, the hall began to be so jammed that when you jumped up and down there was not enough room for the bits and pieces to fly off: it did seem, yes, that the time might soon come to get out of the Garden.

God came to an end of his stories (or stories about stories?) about God and Lilith and Adam and Eve: he seemed to want to shock people in a simpler way. He announced that this was what he was trying to do – that people would not change until their patterns of mind were not just preached against (this reinforced pattern) but punctured. He began to tell joke-book vulgar stories about what, he seemed to suggest, were misunderstandings about God and men: the more vulgar and second-hand these became, the more his acolytes closed their eyes and swayed backwards and forwards as if hypnotised. Sometimes, at some of the words, they seemed to flinch; but I thought – This is the ecstasy of St Sebastian, or of Adam in his grotto.

'The Pope was practising golf shots in his study. Every time he did a bad shot he said – Shit! Missed! – Cardinal Virtue, who was standing beside him, said – Holy Father you should not use such language, or a thunderbolt will surely come from heaven and strike you down! – The next time the Pope played a bad shot he said – Shit! Missed! – There was a lightning-flash and Cardinal Virtue disappeared in a puff of smoke. Then there was a voice from the heavens saying – Shit! Missed!'

This sort of thing was spoken in God's precise, sibilant near-whisper: the same voice as that in which he spoke of someone being hollowed like a flute so that truth could blow through.

People flocked to the Garden by air, by train and bus, by taxi: they arrived with bedrolls and rucksacks. A shanty town sprang up between the area of thatched huts and the sea. The grand hotel filled with newspaper men and film men on the trail of the story about Anita Kroll. The scene became like that of a gold-rush: in the shanty town at night tiny oil lamps glittered like the eyes of animals: in the grand hotel, one evening, there was a fight. Or it was like one of those gatherings on a hot and dusty plain where the Virgin Mary has appeared and spoken to children: of course, the children can never explain precisely what the Virgin Mary has said: it has just seemed to them to have had some ultimate meaning.

People tried to make enquiries about Anita Kroll: God would not answer questions: sometimes it was given as a reason that he was not well. It seemed to be accepted that God was in some sense ill; but also that he was using this as a means of evading questions. When his disciples were questioned about Anita Kroll they continued to treat the matter as some funny metaphysical riddle: what on earth would be an empirical test that would convince anyone that Anita Kroll had in fact been dead and had come alive? So what was the point of going on with such enquiries? People would believe what they wanted to believe; so why not get on with it. Questioners seemed incensed by this sort of argument; and so they made up the hostile stories that, I suppose, they wanted to make up anyway. There were stories that Anita Kroll had been seen driving with God in the town in the back of a large American car: that God was keeping her in his house as his mistress: that some quite different girl was being trained, to be sprung on the world later as a resurrected Anita Kroll. God himself, on the stage of the enormous hall with his huge sea-like eyes roaming about among the audience, seemed to be saying – Do you not see that this is what I am trying to teach you? truth is not a matter of choice between this or that view of facts; it is not to do with people who are trapped into thinking like this, but with those who are out of the trap altogether.

God's discourses continued on their bizarre way for some time; all the time he kept saying that what he was saying was beyond the scope of words. Then one morning he came in and sat there and he did not say anything. It was announced that he was not ill, but that he just wanted to sit there and not speak.

We all went on coming to the enormous hall. God was set down on the stage in his litter: he looked at us and we looked at him: he seemed to be saying – Is it you? Is it you?

The multitudes who had come to the Garden seemed to be waiting for some new miracle – or catastrophe, or farce. I thought – These might be the same thing?

The hostile feelings that had always existed amongst the local people towards the Garden were exacerbated by the influx: it was true now that the condition of the encampments around the Garden might be a threat to health; the television people and newspaper men treated local customs with little respect. All this coincided with a crisis of antagonism between factions within the local community itself. The territory, or enclave, in which the Garden lay had been settled by Europeans in the sixteenth century: a third of the local population were Christians; these from time to time found themselves under attack from the now more numerous but less influential Hindus. There had recently been riots in the town: shops owned by Christians had been smashed and looted. This in turn had coincided with God's discourses becoming increasingly contemptuous of both Christians and Hindus – of what he suggested was the Christians' materialism and the Hindus' lack of it. Both factions could at least come together from time to time in their hostility to the Garden.

I once heard Shastri addressing a political meeting at the side of the road. He stood on a handcart that had one wheel missing: his group of boys in white shirts and black trousers were propping it up. He was saying the sort of things that people always say at political meetings – other people have privilege, privilege is wrong, we demand that we have privilege.

When I talked to Shastri he said – What is your God planning? to say he has died, and to come alive? taking with him everyone's money?

One day one of the shanties made of sacking and old driftwood in the sand-dunes caught fire; a child was burned; her mother was said to have been on acid. The next day the police came and walked around the scene. Their helmets were like the shells of crabs. They seemed to be waiting for baby turtles.

Throughout my time in the Garden I never went (perhaps I went just once in order to see) to any of the encounter groups or what used to be called 'human potential' groups in which people were supposed to be helped to get rid of bottled-up feelings of rage – against parents, brothers, sisters, husbands, wives, society. Strangers would face each other on the floor of a large room and shout the abuse that they had not been able to shout at whom it concerned; there was an outpouring of hatred that was meant to disappear down some drain. But the reserves of hatred, from such a well, seemed endless. I thought – Surely there is enough to do in the way of fighting in the world outside?

Once or twice I went down to the grand hotel to see – what? the bodies stretched out by the swimming-pool? the landscape in which I had for a moment been happy, in which I might be happy again? I thought – If you have to fight anyway, perhaps it is in seeing yourself as an agent in occupied territory that you might feel at home.

One evening I was lying on my bunk in the hut and Ingrid and Gopi were combing each other's hair like one person looking in a mirror and Samantha had got into a yoga position like the one in which you are supposed to be able to squirt water in and out of your arse; and there was a sort of pattering, a small screaming, on the pathways outside: it seemed to be to do with rats; we went to the doorway and looked out. It was the police running down to the shanty town by the sand-dunes; they carried long sticks like the wings of seagulls or the claws of crabs. I thought – It is they, and not the baby turtles, who now run towards the sea; and will the baby turtles get them? I followed them and saw them hitting with their sticks at the makeshift huts: the denizens came out and the police kicked and knocked the huts over: there did not seem to be much purpose in what they were doing; people would wait for a time, standing around in the half-dark, and then start putting their huts up again. I thought – It is like that painting in the National Gallery of the battle between the Lapiths and the Centaurs: people enjoy bashing and being bashed about; it is what they are used to; it is not so easy simply to get out?

The house in the village in which Shastri lived, and which was owned by his uncle, was a sort of boarding-house on two floors with rooms on four sides facing inwards round a courtyard. Bedrooms were on the upper floor with doors on to an inner veranda; on the ground floor there was an eating-room and a kitchen and a laundry and rooms where people could hold meetings. Men in striped pyjamas used to stand on the veranda and lean on the balustrade and look down as if they were political prisoners.

I did go to one of Shastri's meetings: I sat at the back of a room of men and girls in white shirts and black trousers while Shastri faced us from behind a table. He spoke mostly in their local language: when he spoke in English, he seemed to be speaking to me.

'My father was once a schoolteacher and had high hopes of this man who is now called God. He thought he might lead the country to a new beginning! Then there was a strike of school-teachers and my father lost his job – Who was this man who would do nothing to support him?

'My father went to jail. These people in the Garden, who will support them in the day of retribution?

'When last there was violence it was not ourselves who suffered: it was the rich! the privileged! Let no one imagine it is a privilege now to say you will come alive when you have been dead!'

I thought – A political meeting is like some box, perhaps, which you listen to through a keyhole and the bits and pieces of sound that come out seem to make sense; then you lift the lid off and it is all nonsense, there are no connections.

Afterwards I went up with Shastri to his room. I lay on the bed with my hands behind my head while noises came in like flies from the road outside. I said –

'My father had the idea that human beings became different from apes when they walked upright; then they could have bigger brains, there were thus no limits to their interest in sexuality. This resulted in language: they couldn't have sex all the time, so they had to think, to talk about it – to plan, to attack, to cajole, to defend. They did not need to spend so much time hunting for food. Of course, when we know this, we can just stop talking: but we carry this enormous brain round in our heads. We don't use it yet wholly; we can cut off bits and pieces of it. But we don't use our ability to take the lid off and look inside. This would be the whole – to talk, and to talk about what you are talking about at the same time.'

Shastri, with his hands at the buckle of his belt like a gunfighter in a western film, said 'What are you saying? I don't understand what you are talking about.'

There was a day when I was told I had been chosen to be one of the disciples to whom God was to give his special blessing that evening in his inner garden. I did not know why I had been chosen; it might have been arranged by one of the people in my hut, or by my friend who was like Lilith. I did not see her so often now: we had never spoken to each other much. (Do you think I was growing up? Or do you think that with Shastri I was having just another dose of childhood?)

Twenty or thirty people lined up outside the entrance to God's inner garden: we were all clean and bright: I had not been into this part of God's own territory before. We were taken round the side of his house into the part of the garden at the back where there was the loggia; this was where I had seen, from the outside, the picture being painted by the girl who might have been Anita Kroll. I wondered where Anita Kroll was now; were we not both, perhaps, being trained to be agents in occupied territory? The boundary hedge of God's inner garden had been patched up with matting: rugs had been placed on the ground; we sat facing the loggia, within which there had been placed one of God's empty chairs. Beyond, in the outer garden, we could hear the music of the nightly celebration starting up: what was to happen here, in the nucleus, was to be echoed in the larger cell. There was even a small band of drummers here at one end of the loggia: the style of the blessing, the transmission of grace, seemed, as usual, to be about to contain some self-mockery: we were both to experience blessing, and to look down on it as if it were some stage show. I thought – God may suddenly pop his head through curtains like a clown.

In fact when God did appear from the back of the loggia he was smiling and gliding as usual; he turned this way and that in greeting to the lines of people in front of him; it was as if he were a toy; as if he were saying – Gods are after all, are they not, some sort of clockwork toys! He sat in his chair and arranged his robes and looked amongst us with his sad, enormous eyes as if to say – You know which is the joke? which the sadness? which the reality? The drumming began. God's chosen acolytes were to be led up to him one by one. I did not at first see my friend who was like Lilith. Then I thought I caught a glimpse of her through the plate-glass window. I could not see the girl who might have been Anita Kroll.

As each acolyte was led forwards to God's throne the drumming intensified: she or he knelt and bowed down: God moved to the edge of his chair as if he had indigestion: he spoke to the acolyte softly, so that no one else could hear what he said. I thought – Well, God does say different things to different people, doesn't he? Then God seemed to move forwards almost beyond the edge of his chair; he put his hand round the back of the head of the acolyte as if he were getting a hold of (yes!) a musical instrument: he put the thumb of his other hand on the centre of the acolyte's forehead and seemed to play it (you have met this image before?) as if he were producing music: he waggled his thumb and fingers this way and that – why do the thumb and fingers have to waggle, do you know? is it because this technique is necessary to produce

185

the single note of pure music? After a time the acolyte in front of God seemed to wilt: it was as if she or he were dissolving into music: were being remoulded; perhaps would emerge again as something indeed emptied, or like a bird from an egg. So then she or he could go out, and fly around, and appear as her- or himself again – as nothing? – or at the bottom of that staircase? I thought – Of course, God's finger comes down from above that doorway; the loggia is the courtyard containing the angel and Mary. So then, being played, are we not being taken beyond the framework of the picture? After a time one or two of the acolytes began to howl: it was as if the instrument being played were less a cello, more a saw: I thought – Who was that satyr, Marsyas, who was tortured for playing music? The images, as so often, became piled up. I thought – It is not so much that I fear I am being carried away: it is that I know I will have to watch, with cunning, if I am to emerge from this upheaval of bodies as if in a telephone-box.

There were one or two of God's regular disciples ready to prop up the bodies of the enrapt, collapsing acolytes: I thought – Dear God, they are like those two Thai boys who used to lift me at the house in North London: indeed, what is and what is not a joke? The place on the forehead against which God was pressing his thumb was the place where there was, or might be, the third eye of Shiva: this is the eye that sees inwards: I thought – Perhaps when you see with this, the bits and pieces in your brain become connected like light.

After a time the acolyte had to be helped up, or even carried out, like a knocked-out boxer. And there was the drumming and wailing going on all the time, the people on either side of me swaying about, the whole scene reverberating with the banging away in the outer garden. I thought – So what is this music you are trying to put into or draw out of people? you want them to be carried as passed-out bodies to Valhalla? Don't you want them to fly? Does not a bird have to find land on its own? Does it not then come back to you?

When it came to my turn to be led up to God's throne I was thinking – no, not thinking: we had been told by God, had we not, that we should not think: but had I not also been told by God why on earth should I obey him? so what I was doing both was and was not thinking (this is, yes, an easy way of putting it) – What would have been the point if God or the angel or whoever it was had put his finger on Mary's forehead and Mary had passed out moaning and yelling? God would be looking for someone who could bear his burden, would he not: who could look him in the eye; or at least look down at some place where the bird might be; in front of her stomach, in fact; up from that empty nest of stones. In fact God would long, would he not, for someone who could both love him (could it be me?) and yet get away from him. When it came to my turn to go up to God's throne I saw that my friend who looked like Lilith had appeared and was standing beside him. She smiled at me. I thought – And you, Anita Kroll, are you beyond that window? Then – All right, God, here I am. But the child is looking, is he not, somewhere beyond the picture. There was all this drumming: people in the audience were swaying and moaning. I knelt: I thought I might arrange my pink and gold robes behind me: well, if I were not Mary, might I not be the angel? In such circumstances people do see visions, don't they? God put his head down close to mine. There was no smell. Perhaps you notice this only when there is no smell. There was something soft and luminous in him like the canvas of a picture seen close up. I thought – Things are in a different focus here. God said my name in his soft whisper: then 'You are thinking of leaving us?' I nodded. God had these extraordinary transparent eyes that you seemed to see through into a new landscape. He put his hand round the back of my head and the other hand in front of my forehead: then he paused, and then put this other hand against my throat. I had not seen him do this to anyone before. He said 'You will speak?' I said 'Yes.' He did not put his thumb on my forehead and wobble it.

You remember that story of Marsyas and Apollo who challenged each other to a duel about who could make the best music: Apollo played the lyre and Marsyas played the flute: Apollo was judged to have won, because Marsyas looked so ridiculous when he blew his cheeks out. So Marsyas, as a punishment for the presumption of his challenge, was sentenced to be flayed alive while Apollo watched – has not this always made Apollo seem worse than ridiculous? God leaned forward again and whispered 'You will come and see us?' He still did not wobble: I did not blow my cheeks out or yell or moan. I thought – There has been made this hole through the canvas: what is here is to do with vibrations, not music.

The disciples on either side put their hands under my arms as if to support me. I thought I might say – Oh for goodness sake, I don't need this, don't be ridiculous! God's huge face smiled down at me. I thought — It is like the sun that comes up in the morning: there it is, the grid; the riddle.

It seemed that there was an enormous event going on elsewhere: that something quite different was with some difficulty being born. I had no further image of this: there was just that empty space on the ground; the bird flown from its nest; the child looking out of the picture; God's huge face at the back of the finger looking down. Just before I got up to leave – when I did, I did not go back to my place on the rugs in front of the loggia but went straight round the side of the house and out of God's inner garden – just before I got up to leave – how composed I was! how immaculate, as it were! – God took hold of my head between his two hands and I had the impression that he was going to kiss me on my forehead. I did not want him to do this: I did not know why: I would not put my head down, so if he kissed me he would have to kiss my mouth. So he smiled, and took his hands away. He sat back. He seemed pleased. I thought – Well who was it who did or did not kiss someone in a garden? Then – Well, there will be that baby on the edge of the bed: here is the earth, its mother. I wondered if I should wave and say – Coo-ee!

Dearest Judith,
You know we had planned to have the baby at home – with soft lights and sweet music, the world is good and loving, that sort of thing? Well, as the time approached it was found

that the baby had the most enormous head: it had got the cord wrapped round its throat; like the clown at the circus; like the person trying to lift himself up by his own boot-laces; that sort of thing.

All this happened when I was away: we had known I would have to finish work on the filmscript. But Lilia was told she would have to go into hospital: she did not want to go to hospital: she was told she would have to have a cae-sarian operation: she had said she would rather die than have a caesarian operation. And so on. One can't really argue these things.

I had planned to get back with a week in hand: but the baby started to move. Perhaps she made it start early: perhaps it was one of those instances (guess why) when people have to muddle up the dates so they can say – It's started early. Anyway, there it was: and where was I? and there was that telegram. Well, there was no chance of my getting back in reasonable time.

When I did get back I found Lilia had been already a day or so at the hospital: you know how in hospital things get taken out of your hands: you are out of the human network (soft lights and sweet music) and into the machine. In the hospital I found a man in a white coat biting his nails in the passage. I said – I'm the father. He said – I'm the doctor. Then – You do realise, don't you it may be either your wife or your child?

When I found Lilia she was tired; she was in pain; she said – Promise you won't let them make me have an operation. The doctor said – I've told you it's probably too late to have the operation. Lilia said – Then promise you won't let them hurt the child.

Now I am very weak, reasonable, when it comes to things like hospitals: if I had arrived a day or two earlier, would I not have had to insist on her having the operation?

The doctor said – The baby's head is too far down.

Lilia said – What were you doing in that hotel?

Well what was I doing in that hotel? It was true, of

course, that I had wanted to look at the Garden.

The doctor kept on tapping me on the arm and taking me to one side: the baby's head was too big: the baby's head might have to be crushed: the baby's head would probably be crushed anyway.

You can assure yourself, can't you, that you are ready to die (like God): this is not much help to you or to other people.

The doctor said – You want your wife to die?

I said – You do not know she will die?

Well, it is a cold night, isn't it, on the north face of the Eiger: your loved one – the one you are committed to – dangles from the end of a rope. Either you cut the rope and one of you dies, or both of you will.

But this is a child!

The doctor said – I will not be responsible.

I thought – Why had we got married in the first place?

So what do you do – jump up and down with your arms above your head for, certainly, more than ten minutes?

You think one can't make a joke of this? In this sort of life, did you not say, can one not make a joke of anything?

Lilia was in a good deal of distress now: the problem has always been, hasn't it, human suffering: you can't bear it: not just your own, but sometimes other people's. There is also human guilt. I was holding her hand. There was the doctor, the anaesthetist, and an enormous black nurse who might, one felt, given a chance, conjure up strange spirits out of the forest. The doctor came and went: others – sisters or students, I suppose – piled in every now and then. We waited. I thought – What is going on elsewhere: what happens if you say – I cannot bear that I cannot bear it?

Then some time in the middle of the night – I suppose I had not been there more than about two hours – your old friend Bert appeared at the door: he said 'Oh you're here!' and then, as if I were not there, to Lilia – 'I've found her!' An old lady with black hair and bright-blue eyes came in. I did not know her. Do you know her? I mean she does not quite give the impression of being old: she is more like someone who has lasted a very long time and so is young in the sense of when she started. She went up to Lilia and said 'Now!' Lilia said 'Thank you!' Behind her in the doorway appeared your other old friend whom you call the Professor; he looked rather sheepish: I said 'Do come in!' He said 'Thank you.' Do you know that Marx Brothers film in which more and more people pile into a small ship's cabin? It is very funny. The doctor was saying 'Who are these people?' The old woman with black hair said something to the huge black nurse in a strange language; the nurse seemed to light up; they chattered away in this language; they began doing things to the bedclothes and taking hold of Lilia. The Professor said 'This lady is a doctor, and my wife.' The doctor said 'I don't care a damn if she's your wife.' Then – 'And who are you?' The Professor said 'I'm Professor Ackerman.' Bert was leaning with his hands in his pockets against a trolley of instruments which began to move: the doctor shouted 'Get these people out of here!' The Professor said 'Just give us five or ten minutes.' Then he said to me 'Forgive us, we didn't know where you were.' I said 'That's all right.' The old woman was telling Lilia what to do with her breathing; she held her wrist; she put her other hand round the back of Lilia's neck and raised it and seemed to squeeze; it was as if she were playing a musical instrument. Lilia's breathing became more rhythmical; but it began to make a tearing sound; as if something were being undone like a wrapping. The black nurse was handing round face-masks; the doctor had gone out of the room; the Professor had his back against the door; Bert was at the foot, and I was at the head of the bed. The woman with black hair put a hand over Lilia's mouth: she spoke to the nurse in their strange language; the nurse began rubbing Lilia's legs, strongly. For some time now there had been between Lilia's raised legs something like a plug, a lid, a landfall: it was smooth and brown: I realised now that this was in fact the baby's head. It was trying to get out; it could get no further. Lilia's body seemed to be beginning to undergo some sort of earthquake: the old woman said something to the black nurse: then she took her hand away from Lilia's face, raised the knee of Lilia's right leg and held it with her right hand just above the ankle. She seemed to press very hard with her thumb. She was also still pressing at the back of Lilia's neck. Lilia's mouth opened as if something like a snake was trying to come out: but there was no cry. Then the nurse came and stood beside the old woman by the bed and she took hold of the little toe of Lilia's right foot between her finger and thumb and she seemed to press very hard there; it was as if the two of them were hard at work with music; then Lilia's body seemed to take off: I mean to rise in the air almost: there was something transporting her like unheard music. Then it became apparent that the baby was being born. It emerged in a sort of whoosh; as if without much regard for the mechanics of it. The nurse put out a hand as if to stop it from continuing right over the edge of the bed. Lilia still did not cry out; I wondered if she would ever take another breath; the old woman put her face down against Lilia's very gently. After a time Lilia did seem to breathe again. The baby was there. The nurse was doing to it the usual things, I suppose. The doctor put his head in at the door.

Well, that's nearly all, isn't it? Except that when I was thanking the old woman, who is called Eleanor, I said 'It wouldn't have happened like that – I mean you wouldn't have been here, would you, if I had been here from the very beginning – would it?' The old woman said 'No, I suppose it wouldn't – would I.' Then she smiled, and put her fingers against my face.

So that is all, isn't it?

Well – What did you think we were doing in that hotel?

The baby has got the most enormous head.

Perhaps it will be able to say, one day, or not need to say, the things that can't be said.

With love from Jason

★

From the hotel where I am writing this there is the lawn, and the swimming-pool, and the fairy lights in the palm trees; beyond is the view to the sea and the beach in front of the sand-dunes. You write about the past from the present: the present goes as you write about it. There are these lightning-flashes. It is seven years since the events I have been recalling. I mean – Jason and I have come back here after seven years.

I have been copying out Jason's letter. At what hour, of what day, did these events jointly, or separately, occur? Did the birth take place when I was in God's inner garden?

The baby's head coming through the back of the canvas.

It is not necessary, I suppose, to see coincidences in time: there are, after all, other dimensions.

Yesterday Jason and I walked to where the Garden used to be: the perimeter fence and the concrete floor of the enormous hall are still there. Most of the prefabricated buildings have gone. There is a new concrete block that is an agricultural college.

Did the roof of the enormous hall finally rise like a chariot-balloon to heaven?

Jason said – Do you copy my style, or do I copy yours?

Today Jason has gone to look at those churches in the hills. He did not have time to look at them the last time he was here.

I said I would get on with finishing my two stories.

The scene round the swimming-pool has not changed much in seven years. They have built a bar at which you can drink while sitting half under water. Do you think this is equivalent to babies in soft lights and sweet music?

Last night Jason read part of this story. He said – People may want to know a bit more: what happened to Anita Kroll?

I said – Well what did happen to Anita Kroll?

He said – What happened to God –

I said – How would you write about what happened to God?

He said – All right, you'd better get on with your stories.

After our walk to where the Garden had once been we went on down to the estuary. There are still the remains of fires where bodies have been burned. I said – Well, it might be asked who was the man with the red-haired girl in the flat next door –

He said – I told you, I didn't know her then.

I said – Oh no, it was the Professor who knew her.

He said – It's sometimes difficult to get the timing right – in memory, in stories.

I thought – So what does it mean, you mean, this being dead and coming alive? You know it about yourself: do you need to know anything else – about other people?

How do you think we appear to people now? As if we are floating; have no feelings? I sometimes think – Feelings were those shadows on the walls.

Sometimes it is so beautiful! There are those colours, that you live in beyond the canvas of a picture.

Jason said – Of course it is as if we are in occupied territory: there are people with arrows, to get us posed against a wall.

I said – You mean, we sometimes do pose for them?

We walked back along to the promontory where we had once climbed over rocks to the grand hotel. This had always seemed to be a garden in occupied territory.

I said – Was that why you wrote your things like that?

He said – Like what?

I said – As if we all know each other, but make out we don't know each other, because we are agents in occupied territory. Then – An attitude: a way of seeing things?

Jason has just come back from his day up by the churches. He had taken part of this story with him.

He says – You told the Professor about our night in the hotel!

I say – I didn't tell the Professor about our night in the hotel!

I thought I might say – Didn't you say the point of stories was that some might be in inverted commas?

Or – Do you think I will ever send out on the waters these stories I have been writing, these so-called letters?

Jason sits in a deck-chair by the swimming-pool with his hat tipped over his eyes. He goes on reading my story.

I want to say – Things pop up in the mind like targets at a

fun-fair shooting-range: you know this; you let them go; you look at your story.

God has in fact popped up again in California. It is not clear whether or not he is mad. Or perhaps he might be pretending to be mad – like Nietzsche – to protect himself from people wondering whether or not he is mad.

God is still not speaking much. The quotations he likes passing on to his disciples are one from Nietzsche –

– Supposing truth to be a woman, what? Is the suspicion not well founded that philosophers, when they have been dogmatists, have had little understanding of women? –

– And the one when Jesus says that he talks in parables to his disciples lest people should understand and their sins should be forgiven them.

Jason says – It's still a matter of aesthetics.

I say – What is a matter of aesthetics?

He says – Life: looking after this and letting go of that.

I thought I might say – Women do this! Create it –

– All those sperms, like worms, or words, battering to be let into the old tin can –

– Not you: not you: is it you?

Around the swimming-pool there are the soft brown bodies: a new shanty-town has sprung up on the outskirts of the village.

This morning I went to look for Shastri. His uncle told me he had gone to England.

I say to Jason – But still, some bomb may have to go off –

He says – Oh well. What does God mean by inverted commas?

I thought I might say – Or the child?

He might say – What about the child?

I am trying to continue writing this in our room, sitting by the window. Jason has remained with my typescript by the swimming-pool.

I might say – I mean, it doesn't matter if one doesn't know who the father is?

He might say – I know what you mean!

I could say – What if I were going to have a child –

Then – But that is not why I came to this hotel!

Jason comes in. He gives me my typescript. I think – Does he in fact know?

He might say – Is not the father the one who goes across the desert with the child on a donkey?

He says – Well, what is it, do you think, that we will know at the end of your story?

I went into the town one day because I was thinking of getting my ticket away from the Garden. I was in the streets when a mob went past; they were breaking one or two windows; there were the sprightly, shining faces of people having a good time – the battle between the Lapiths and the Centaurs.

There were rumours that God was also thinking of getting his ticket to leave the Garden: he continued to appear each morning and to sit silently in the enormous hall. In the afternoons extracts from his old discourses were relayed from the ceiling. It was noticeable that many of the passages chosen contained references relevant to what was going on in the town: there were scathing stories about Christians and Hindus: ridiculing people who committed themselves to a cause. This was humanity's way, God seemed to be saying, of self-destruction: words, of course, were agents of this: which was why (he had always said) he might one day have to be silent.

Local people turned up in increasing numbers to listen to these recordings: there was even a group of local boys and girls who turned up now to sit and watch silently in the mornings. God's eyes moved over the multitude: he was looking for – what – is it you? is it you? But what would he require of some people rather than of others?

Then Shastri asked me, after all this time, if I would take him into the Garden. I said – But you can go in on your own! I wondered – There is some reason why he does not want to go with his friends into the Garden?

He said – They say your God is plotting to abandon you

people here: he will move to where there are more pickings in California.

I said – I thought you said he was plotting to die, and to come alive again.

Shastri said – California is the headquarters of the entertainment and armament industries.

There was an anxiety that God might be assassinated: not so much because of his blasphemies against local religions (this could be an excuse) but because the time and events seemed ripe for assassination. Why were local people showing such interest when they were hostile to the Garden?

Once I came across my old friend who was like Lilith standing again at the gate into God's inner garden. I thought – She is like a child looking for its mother. She beckoned me in. I had not seen her for some time. I followed her down a path and into the main part of God's house. I had not been here before: there was a hall, bare and whitewashed, and a tiled floor. Through a door to the left there was a room with walls covered with books from floor to ceiling; there were books and magazines piled on the floor. In another room there was just a bed, a wooden table, a wooden chair, and a washstand of the kind in which there is a hole and a china bowl. The bed was narrow with a brass headpiece; there were clean white sheets neatly tucked and straightened. There was no one in the room. My friend said 'He was here.' It was as if she might start looking under the floorboards. I thought – But there never is anything in the holy of holies, is there? I said 'Is he ill?' After a time she said 'Yes.' She went on towards the back of the house where there were two of God's closest disciples coming in from the Garden. She turned and gestured to me as if I should go. I thought – God has fallen out of bed? he went floating up to the ceiling?

There began to be stories that God had been seen in two places at once: that he had learned how to leave his body, or was employing some sort of double.

When I went to the town to decide about my ticket I found the door of the travel agency boarded up. It was said to be

197

impossible to get tickets out of the town now because so many people were leaving.

Many of those in the shanties by the sand-dunes no longer bothered to come to the Garden: they sat in their lairs and smoked; there were just their eyes and the tips of their tiny weapons in the darkness. I thought – Or they are eggs, waiting to hatch and begin their run down to the sea.

In the enormous hall, in the mornings, the Indian boys in their white shirts and black trousers gathered in a group near the perimeter like a lump just under the skin.

In the afternoons God's voice came down –

'Death is part of life. A cancer is a form of life. Cut it out, and you are likely to destroy the whole. A cancer is life that runs away with itself. But the whole may have to be allowed to die, in order to start again.'

There began to be a wind blowing day and night in and around the Garden. Dark sheets of rain came down. I thought – This is the lowering of a curtain. But where do we go when we leave the theatre?

With the wind there came in huge waves from the sea: there was something like a waterspout, and fishes appeared on dry land. A huge wreck was washed up – not a ship from the present storm but a much earlier wreck: it had wooden ribs, and looked like Noah's Ark.

I thought – What would be the equivalent, now, of Noah's Ark?

God reappeared and sat silently in the enormous hall; Shastri came in and sat with me. He seemed deliberately to be separating himself from the knot of his friends by the perimeter. I had stopped asking myself why he was doing this. I thought – So what should you do, about the form of life that runs away with itself!

It did sometimes seem that God, lying back in his chair, might by dying.

Shastri was sitting by my side one day –

What is it that stops people in Plato's cave coming out

into the sun? The fear of the fact that they are dying any-way?

Shastri was sitting by my side on this particular day: the sun was bright outside: there was the knot of his friends by the perimeter. I was thinking how I must get back to England: I would start off by bus even: what were the shadows on walls, now, that were preventing me? It was terrible, yes, that people died. I would try to go to a university: there were one or two people I wanted to see. I became aware that Shastri was restless beside me. He had once before half stood up as if to put some question to this silent God: I had pulled at his arm and he had sat down. Now he seemed to be getting himself ready to stand again. I did not care much now. I thought – It was not I, after all, who enabled him to come into the Garden: does not God at last have to accept responsibility for the snake and grow up? For all these centuries, have we not been treating God as an infant? I had noticed that there was a figure moving at the peri-meter of the enormous hall. You must remember (events are, are they not, in the form of stories) how extremely unusual it was for anyone to move in the hall during God's discourses or silences; perhaps people's attention had already been distracted by the movements made by Shastri. The figure at the perimeter was that of one of the Indian boys in white shirt and black trousers; he had got right round towards God's platform; no one seemed to notice him; I had noticed him, perhaps because I had my hand on Shastri's arm and thus was free to look. Even the attention of God's special guardians seemed to have been distracted – those figures suspended like Byzantine frescoes a few inches off the floor. I let go of Shastri: Shastri stood up; the guardians moved forwards; Shastri moved towards them, pushing his way between the shoulders of acolytes like some-one walking through waves. I thought I might go after him: but I was watching the boy who had emerged from the group like a lump just under the skin and who had reached God's platform. Two of the disciples took hold of Shastri and held him by the arms: beyond him behind the disciples, as in some mirror image, as it were (I thought – This is some counterpart

of myself and the picture painted by Anita Kroll?), the other
boy in a white shirt and black trousers had climbed up on to
the platform of God's throne. I imagined for a moment that I
understood what was happening absolutely. Then, of course,
the understanding went. Someone cried out; a wailing began.
The boy who had climbed on to the platform seemed to throw
something in the direction of God. I thought – A knife? a
bomb? a rope? a token of esteem? God did not seem to move
from his position of sitting as if exhausted in his chair. Then
some women, one of whom was my friend Lilith, climbed on
to the platform from the front row of the audience and took
hold of the boy who had thrown whatever it was in the
direction of God: then God sat upright immediately and made
a decisive gesture towards them; they let the boy go; the boy
ran out from the hall. Then God sat back as if collapsed. Then
the disciples who were holding Shastri, who had seen this last
scene, let Shastri go. There were people now standing up in
the crowd and calling: God was lying twisted; it did seem as
if he might have been wounded. Shastri came back towards
me through the sea of faces: he sat down beside me. Lilith
was kneeling by God, who might be dying; or he might be
pretending to be dying; or he might not mind whether people
thought he was dying or pretending to be dying. Lilith put
her head against his knees. Afterwards there were different
versions of what had happened: some people said they had
actually seen the boy on the platform throw a knife towards
God; some said he had only reached out as if to try to touch
God's garment; some said Shastri had deliberately caused a
diversion; some even said they had seen Shastri prepare to
throw something towards God. I had put my hand again on
Shastri's arm. I thought – Here, this time, poor snake, I will
protect you.

What everyone agreed about, was that God had sat up in his
chair and had ordered his disciples not to hold on to anyone;
and then had fallen back as if wounded.

Shastri said – I did not do anything.

I said – I know you did not do anything.

Shastri said – I wanted to ask a question.

I thought – The answer is, I suppose, that God is getting himself, and us, out of the Garden.

So God was carried off in his litter round the perimeter of the enormous hall; bouncing (for the last time?) like someone who has been shot on a fun-fair shooting-range. The funny hat that he sometimes wore fell off; was put on again; fell off; I thought – He would like it that this, his last exit, or deposition, is ridiculous. Are not depositions so often romantic; almost sexual?

Then there were other scenes like farce in the enormous hall; some people were crying; some were laughing; everyone seemed interested, as usual, not so much in what had actually happened as in their own reactions: they were looking round now not really even for a story: they were asking – what am I? I am still I, am I not? No one seemed to know, or really to want to know, if God had in fact been hurt; whether, being ill already, he had suffered some further shock; or was he (of course) taking advantage of the situation to do whatever it was he wanted – indeed, perhaps to get us out of the Garden. Certainly no one seemed to want to leave the enormous hall. I suppose they all realised that some scene had occurred that was to alter their lives; they could not yet know what it was; they wanted to hang on to what was there. Well, this is what life is like, is it not: and then after a time you can carry on with your story – or complaint about lack of a story. Discussions, arguments, broke out, but without much energy: what was there to say? God might be dying: God might not be dying: but had he not so often said – What is life without death? What does it matter if I die? If I do not die, how will you get out of the Garden?

There was no hostility shown against the group of Indian boys. They had stayed to listen, to watch. After a time the police arrived. They stood in groups talking with the disciples. They seemed to be passing the time. After a while both the Indian boys and the police went off.

Shastri had gone. I did not go with him. No one tried to stop him.

The eyes of one or two of the disciples sometimes wandered off into the distance and they were the eyes of figures in Byzantine frescoes who suddenly find themselves with both feet on the ground.

It was announced later that God was, yes, gravely ill: that the celebration tonight would be a special one: it would be in respect of his ordeal; or in his memory; or for his recovery: or with regard to whatever it was that was supposed to be happening.

Well, this is nearly all, isn't it? We will be moving on soon to the practical part of our demonstration. (It takes seven years, does it, for some events to come to fruition?)

They built an enormous bonfire down by the estuary. Rain blew about like smoke. In fact they could not that night celebrate God's death, or deliverance, or whatever, for the water itself seemed to be on fire.

I thought – At least God's disciples won't have to creep down and steal those ashes after dark: there will be no one in the theatre.

In our hut, packing our cases and rucksacks, we did not speak much. I thought – To talk would be like putting one's finger down one's throat, to see if anything is growing there.

I wondered – How is that baby?

' tried to remember my last sight of Lilith in her golden robe as she walked by God's litter as he was carried from the platform: was she distressed, was she watchful, was she laughing?

I thought – I do hope God will pop up again in California: and there will be Lilith, and Anita Kroll, on either side of him, as his prophets.

It was actually announced on the radio that God had died: then that he had had a heart-attack and was in hospital: then that he was to be flown abroad for special treatment.

People can't really know what is going on, can they? What they can do is not destroy themselves with convictions, blinkers, drama.

202

When I walked down to the estuary I found some of the disciples looking up at the sky: to see whether there might be a gap in the clouds? for that finger to come down? that cosmic seed, or bonfire?

I had been six months in the Garden. Hullo, hullo, do you hear me?

So it is now, yes, seven years later. All the cells of your body change every seven years. What is it that stays the same – the pattern; the child; the heartbeat?

– The fairy lights in occupied territory?

We, Jason and I, will be leaving this grand hotel tomorrow.

– This place where I have been writing; where past and present are poles, and there are sparks between.

What has happened in the interval? There are other events; other stories.

At the time of God's disappearance – the time of the ending of the Garden, and of that part of my story – there was an evening when the rain stopped and we were going to have the bonfire: what it was now in honour of perhaps no one knew or cared: it did seem that there was to be some body, or effigy, that was going to be burned: might this be, or stand for, God's real body? This was the sort of thing that theologians had once fought wars over, wasn't it?

At least we didn't ask this sort of question any more. This was the beach where the girl had lain with the wound in her throat: where baby turtles might run towards the sea.

Thousands of people seemed to come in for this last bonfire. Crowds with their arms up circled and recircled by the river.

There was a dummy body brought down on a stretcher. There was a roar when it was thrown on the fire. Sparks flew up.

I wondered if in the papers the next day they would report God's ascension.

I walked by the estuary. I thought – One day, yes, I will try to write about this. What is the bringing-to-life of words, except God's creation?

Would people still have to kill you, hang you on a wall, walk round you?

Still, in a painting, you can be getting on with whatever it is you are to be doing.

I went with my rucksack down to the estuary. There was the crowd with its arms up like flames coming from water. I said – Good-bye. Then I went on towards the bridge over the river. My last sight of the people from the Garden was from some point on the bridge: the shadows dancing on a wall that was not a wall, but like water. You have seen your own reflection: it smiles: you can go through.

You need not look behind. There is a symmetry, do you not think, in the world to which you are going?

I went over the bridge towards the town.

I had loved the Garden. It was not a fraud: how can something be a fraud when it says – Of course, if you like, this is a fraud?

There was the person who said – All people are liars.

So it goes to and fro. And then there is the bright light coming down.

Do you not know plants, for instance, thrive on laughter?

I am so grateful – to you and to you. For having been watchful with me.

Where are you now? I do try to look after you?

What we will have been trying to find out during these seven years is – Can you make, as well as watch, things happen?

Such as –

Love from Judith

PART III

Dear Jason,

That's why you wrote like that? To say – You think if you say something can't be said, you haven't said it?

– What is a work of art if not a bomb that does not go off: a riddle at the centre of the maze.

In the spring of this year, in England, there were demonstrations at American airbases where missiles with nuclear warheads were deployed. The concern about these missiles coincided with a failure of communication about them: on the one hand it was supposed, reasonably, that the existence of such bombs made self-annihilation likely; on the other hand it was argued that their presence alone made large-scale war improbable. Each position could be defended with logic and with passion. The arguments did not touch, because they remained on different levels.

One level was to do with the effect of bombs: the other was to do with what might happen now there is knowledge about the effect of bombs.

Of course, you know all this. But you? We have been through the question of who it is to whom one is talking when one writes: it is oneself, and whatever face one might recognise in a maze.

When I arrived back in England this year (yes, when I came

back after our second visit to the hotel by the sea) there were these demonstrations at the airbases where missiles were deployed; each side had become entrenched on its side of the wire: people know, do they not, where they are in time of war. They build shelters and defenceworks from words and arguments like old shell-cases: they do not pay much attention, except in so far as it enables them to remain entrenched where they are, to what is in fact happening on the other side of the wire.

I wanted to go to one of these demonstrations, to try to see as if into that box with the lid taken off. Also, I knew two or three of the people I cared about most in the world would be there.

When I got out at the local railway station there was one of those English streets like an illustration to a toy-town: a grocer's and a butcher's and a post-office and a policeman: all life-size: why are toys, dolls, sometimes sinister? They are all-of-a-piece: they are not looking at themselves? They are like those people taken over by Andromeda?

I had brought my bicycle with me on the train; I rode past the church and the hotel and the signposts on the village green. There is a theory, is there not, that if one travels no faster than the speed of one's own power one remains in contact with – well – whatever there might be round some corner?

There was a long straight road through pine trees. It was like a stretch of water on which stones might skim. Do you know this part of East Anglia? (I mean, do you?) There was a time when this landscape was the most populated part of the country: it is the place where traces of earliest human habitation have been found. There was such poor soil that predatory animals could not survive here; so humans came here to be safe from predators and because they had learned how to be intelligent about soil. The earth contained flints: the humans dug out the flints with which they could kill whatever predators there were; also with flints they tilled the soil. Intelligence, I suppose, is to do with learning to take advantage of seeds that land on stony ground.

Later, when humans had established themselves as the most successful of all predators, this area became one of the least populated parts of the country: humans, taking advantage of destructiveness, had moved on to richer soil. Then later again, because the land was so empty, the airbases moved in. There was an irony here: the drive to extinction had made humans return to an area where human society began.

Of course, there is always the chance of such a return, and such irony, being the occasion of something further being learned. I mean – What might be the advantages of being able to have a look at the story of flints, and of destructiveness, and of good and bad soil?

I had a map which Bert had drawn for me which showed the road that went out past the church and the hotel and the signposts on the village green; then there were dotted lines to indicate distances in which nothing much occurred. In the top left-hand corner of the map there was a cherub with his cheeks blown out: in the bottom right-hand corner, as if it were some signature, there was what seemed to be a Virgin and child.

The road ran between pine trees. Cars skimmed past like stones. How is it that one stays upright on a bicycle, do you know? Is it just that as one moves one makes small horizontal adjustments to the front wheel – or is it to do with the nature of gravity?

Some miles out of the village with the railway station there was a track going off the road to the left. There was a notice at the side of this track saying NO THROUGH ROAD and PRIVATE. On Bert's map there was the track and the notice and beyond it a drawing of what looked like Noah's Ark: outside the Ark there was a queue of five or six people. I tried to go on my bicycle down the track but the ground became too rutted. I thought – On a tightrope, you cannot make horizontal adjustments to the front wheel: you hold your arms out like wings to get in touch with gravity?

There were thin trees around me like antennae; like notations for music. I thought – Gravity is a music we do not hear?

The track through the wood led to a farm-type gate with a wire fence going off on either side. On the gate was a single strand of barbed wire and a notice saying BATTLE AREA KEEP OUT and beneath this a sign of the skull and crossbones. Beyond the gate was another notice saying DANGER OF UNEXPLODED BOMBS. There was a path going off to the right on the near side of the fence.

I should have explained (for you) that in addition to the airbases there had also moved into this part of the country, it being so empty, a battle-training ground for soldiers – a huge area, some thirty square miles. No one was allowed in here except, occasionally, soldiers to play their games – to get their tanks and guns out of the nursery toy-box. This battle-area was a short distance from the airbase where there was to be the demonstration: it was not used very often now; nursery games had become electronic and technological.

On Bert's map there was the fence and the skull and crossbones, and an arrow pointing along the path going off to the right. Within the battle-area at the far side of the fence he had done a drawing of a mermaid with what looked like an olive-branch in her hand.

Some mutation, do you think, that might be at home here?

I walked with my bicycle along the path on the near side of the fence. Did you see that film (did you?) about a police state with a forbidden area into which individuals are not allowed to go; but they do go, at their peril, in order to find out something about themselves.

These images are in the mind. They are also in the area beyond the fence – other people having gone in there.

On Bert's map the path along which I was pushing my bicycle came to a wall in which there was a doorway. The wall was one of three sides of a rectangle which enclosed a space in which Bert had drawn what seemed to be a tomb. There was a tree growing out of the tomb in the branches of which there was a bird. All this was at the very right-hand edge of the paper on which Bert had drawn his map. There was no fourth side to the rectangle containing the tree and the tomb because

Bert's pencil, or the hand he was making the drawing with, seemed to have fallen over the edge.

I had not been here before. You have not been here before?

In this strange landscape, one might fall into a different dimension?

The path along which I was walking dipped down towards a wall that was indeed like the wall in Bert's map – at right-angles to the path and of the kind that might once have surrounded, for instance, the kitchen garden of some large country house: it was high and overgrown: it made an intrusion into the battle-area as if it were some lump under the skin. Set in the wall, at the end of the path, there was indeed a small door of a kind that there might be in fairy stories – where do they come from, these images; what do you do with them, where are they going? Beside the door there were notices saying PRIVATE and OUT OF BOUNDS TO TROOPS. I tried to work it out – This is a forbidden area within the forbidden area: so, of course (this is easy!), it is where one has to go?

I use 'of course' to mean – There are signs like these chalked on trees on one's way through the maze.

The impression is of people watching you. You are in a story-book. There are cherubs on clouds.

Through the door there was indeed an area which must once have been a kitchen garden: there were high brick walls with ivy and dead fruit trees; nothing much lived now except nettles and grass. At the centre of this space there was, yes, a tomb. It was an elaborate tomb with pinnacles and spires like a model of a gothic chapel. There was an iron railing round it through which brambles were entwined.

You are conscious of the present: there are threads here and there to the future and the past.

A path had been trodden roughly from the doorway to this tomb: there was also a path from the doorway to a patch of cut and trampled grass by the end wall on the right. Within this clearing was an orange-and-blue tent. The front flaps of the tent were closed. In front of the tent were the remains of a fire and some pots and pans. There did not seem to be anyone in the area of the tent – nor indeed within the rectangle which contained the old kitchen garden and the tomb.

I propped my bicycle against the wall inside the door. What do you do where there are too many images: do you see beyond the walls of shadows: is the bright light of fusing, the sun?

I went to the space in front of the tent and put my rucksack on the ground and sat on it. I thought – Once, so many years ago, I sat on my rucksack and my old friend Lilith welcomed me from the gate of the Garden.

Hullo, hullo, all you images! all you people as if in a picture going about your business: you have become your own suns, your own shadows?

There was another pathway trampled from the tent to a door in the wall opposite the one through which I had come. This was the wall for which there had been no room on Bert's map – where he, or his pencil, had fallen off the edge of the picture. There was no pathway cleared from this doorway to the tomb. I thought – But too much of this sort of thing becomes ridiculous.

You move here and there like a bird looking for land: sometimes you settle with an olive-branch in your mouth.

I want to say to you, Jason, now, before Bert arrives – Thank you for our time in the hotel by the sea!

Bert came in through the door in the wall opposite the one against which I had left my bicycle. He seemed taller and thinner. He began walking towards the tomb; he made scything movements with his feet as if to clear a pathway there. When he reached the railings he stood on tiptoe, as if he wanted to see over the top of, and into, the tomb. By the wall opposite there was my bicycle.

Bert appeared both more substantial and more frail. It was only a few months since I had last seen him. He had grown a small blond moustache. I thought – I did not want him to suffer! but he is like someone now at home from, having come to terms with, the First World War.

Then – How could I ever have thought he might be like Desmond!

I might say – Hullo –

– Hullo –

– I wondered if you remembered me? –

I suppose he saw my bicycle. He lowered his head, and stood like some guardian of the tomb.

I could say – You did ask me to come here!

He would say – But that was some time ago: and since then you have been in another country.

There is that ballet, do you know it, in which people sit, and stand, and move across the stage, and just come to rest perhaps against a ruined pillar: the music is the slow movement of a symphony: the dancers seem to be trying to do just what would show honour to the music. Bert left the tomb and came towards me through the long grass. There is an effect that you can get in a film of someone walking through grass as if on water.

He said 'Hullo.'

I said 'Hullo.'

He said as if he did not now mind what might hurt him 'Did you have a nice time?'

I said 'Yes, it was quite nice, thank you.'

He stretched out a hand and put a finger on my forehead. I thought – Why do people when they cannot think of anything else to do, put a finger on my forehead?

He said 'You found your way.'

I said 'Yes, thank you for the map.'

He said 'Da da di dum dum; da da di da.'

I said 'I'm sorry.'

I thought – Because I have the mark of Cain? Then – But Cain needed comfort!

Bert kneeled and undid the flap of the tent. Inside there were a groundsheet and a sleeping-bag and one or two blankets. There was also a jumble of cameras and film equipment.

I said 'Tell me what's happened.'

He said 'About this or that?'

213

I said 'Both.'

Bert crawled inside the tent. He was like one of those elephants going into that cave to get minerals, to get comfort, do you remember?

He said 'Well, there's this demonstration, as you know.'

I said 'Yes.'

He said 'They'll be at the airbase tomorrow.'

I said 'What are they going to do?'

I thought – There is a fence between us as we talk, like the one around the airbase.

He said 'They've been doing this sort of thing for years, as you know. The more they demonstrate, the more the other side feels at home. You knock a ball over a net: if the other side isn't there, you haven't got a game.'

He was rearranging the film equipment inside the tent; pushing it to one side, spreading out the groundsheet as if to make a larger bed.

He said 'It's like the Western Front in the First World War. Everyone's dug in. There's a women's camp outside the fence. Every now and then they expose their breasts to the men inside the fence, and the men inside expose their arses.'

I said 'But nothing happens.'

He said 'But nothing happens.'

I said 'Except a Bomb may go off.'

He said 'Except a Bomb may go off.'

When he crawled out of the tent he would not look at me. I thought – All right, why not kick me: drag me around the stage.

Then – We are trying to build, or break down, with our talk, a fence like the one around the airbase?

He said 'Lilia took an overdose, did you know?'

I said 'Yes.'

He said 'I suppose she wanted to do more than make a protest: about you and Jason: set a small sort of bomb off.'

I thought – You mean, this was a valid form of protest of Lilia's? Some sort of bomb may have to go off?

He took my rucksack and carried it into the tent.

I thought – You think you need not even ask me whether or

not I will stay?

He said 'I wrote an article for their magazine – I mean, the magazine of the women outside the airbase. I said it was no good simply to go on demonstrating: this only encourages those within. I said that if they were to get anything of what they wanted, then some sort of bomb would have to go off. Then people would experience reality, and not just be re-inforcing themselves with words. It is words and gestures that are counter-productive.'

He lay on his back inside the tent with his hands behind his head. I thought – Well, what happens now: you think we have grown up, do you, Holofernes?

I said 'And did they publish it?'

He said 'No.'

I thought – So you are not responsible.

Or – But you know, don't you, that I feel responsible myself!

He put his hand on the sleeping-bag beside him as if invit-ing me to join him.

He said 'I told them the exact time and place – the sort of bomb that should go off. I mean not a big bomb, which they couldn't get anyway; but an old-fashioned bomb, with perhaps some radioactive material around it.'

I thought – This is mad. But you have said, haven't you, that words are counter-productive?

He said 'I told them that at this Easter demonstration at the American airbase, just next door, there was this enormous battle-area where no one ever comes. I mean, no one anyway would be here on Easter Saturday. I said they could let the bomb off here. Then people could see what it was like; but no one should be hurt, except possibly military men, who like practising this sort of thing anyway.'

I said 'But you made it clear it was a joke.'

He said 'Yes, but what is a joke.'

I said 'Exactly.'

I thought – You mean, might not some old god have quite often behaved like this?

He said 'And now they're said to have got hold of some radioactive material.'

I said 'Who are said to have got hold of some radioactive material?'

He said 'I don't know.'

I thought – You mean you don't know, or you won't tell me? Then – Bert isn't stammering any more!

He said 'Of course, they might just be saying it.'

I said 'Yes, they might just be saying it.' Then – 'But then that would be counter-productive.'

He said 'Yes, that would be counter-productive.'

I thought I might crawl into the tent and put my head on his knee.

Behind me was the long grass, the tomb, the walls on which fruit trees had once grown.

I wondered – Why did you draw the tree growing out of the tomb?

He said 'The whole thing is ridiculous.'

I thought I might say – Yes, the whole thing is ridiculous.

I said 'But you mean, even if people did explode such a bomb, they wouldn't be able to control it?'

He said 'Yes, they might not be able to control it.'

I said 'But that, presumably, would be part of what you were trying to show.'

He said 'Yes, that would be part of what one was trying to show.'

I crawled into the tent and put my head against his knee. He was trembling slightly. I thought – If he were pretending to tremble, it would not be so effective?

I said 'And how is Lilia now?'

He said 'She's all right.'

I said 'And the child?'

He said 'All right.'

I said 'You think you should not even have put the idea into words?'

He said 'I am not saying what anyone should or should not have done.'

216

I said 'And you came here to stop it: no, how can you stop it? to be here – '

He said ' – Being responsible.'

I said 'Responsible and not responsible.'

He said 'Exactly.'

He put a finger in my hair and twirled it round. I went to the entrance of the tent and pulled the flap down so that we were enclosed.

He said 'Why did you come here?'

I said 'For the same sort of reason as you.'

He said 'Being responsible – '

I said 'You think you can tell how what you have done will affect the future?'

There were some leaves from the trees outside making shadows on the walls. I thought – I am that child, whosoever or whatsoever it was, lying in its pram, looking up.

He said 'We used to come here as children. The house used to be just beyond that wall.'

I thought – We come back on the curve of the universe. Then things have a chance of making themselves all right again?

I said 'Yes, I know.'

He said 'You've been here before?'

I said 'Not here exactly.'

He said 'Where did you go?'

I thought – You mean here? or to that other place?

Then – Words, being counter-productive, might help to make things all right?

I said 'To that hotel: at that place I stayed at before.'

He said 'Why did you go there?'

I said 'I wanted to write about it. It was from there, that time years ago, that I began to write my letter to you.'

I thought I might have said – I came here now, of course, because of you.

The tent was about three feet high. There was a dim orange light. Bert lifted his hand above his face as if he might make shadows on the wall. The light seemed to make shadows on his face.

217

He said 'Lilia has always manipulated things. If you do this, in the end, I suppose, you have to hit rock bottom.'

I said 'But what about the child?'

He said 'Yes, what about the child.'

He sat up. It was as if his head and shoulders were pressing against the roof of a cave. I thought – He is one of those elephants; he is trying to get sustenance?

He said 'Neither Lilia nor anyone else knows what they are doing with the child.' Then – 'Perhaps what she did was her way of getting him a day off from school.'

I said 'Getting him a day off from school?'

Bert said 'There was an accident at the school-crossing that day. Some children were hurt. Oh, don't you see, how do you think one can talk about this!'

I thought – Yes, I see.

Then – I mean, I see why you cannot talk about this.

Bert lay back. He said 'The child! Why do you call him the child?'

I thought – You do mean, because of Lilia taking an overdose, the child didn't go to school that day?

Bert said as if quoting ' – Type of explosive, wind direction, height from ground, that sort of thing – '

I tried to imagine Lilia and the child. I had a picture of him at the top of a staircase, holding on to bannisters, looking down.

The mind, yes, goes blank.

Bert said 'I don't know when Lilia found out about you and Jason. How much she knew.'

I thought I might say – Not much. I suppose enough.

Or – But then do you, or do you not, want such a bomb to go off?

I was looking up at the leaves, the shadows.

There are, do you think, these coincidences?

I said 'Whose is that tomb?'

He said 'My great great grandmother's or something.' Then, as if he were quoting ' – She was born in this part of the world.'

He put an arm round me. He stroked my back.

I said 'Do you think one could make a joke of that?'

He said 'Of what?'

I said 'Of Jason and Medea. Of that bomb going off.'

He said ' – Ladies and Gentlemen, we now come to the more practical part of our demonstration – '

I said 'But you don't even know they've got hold of this radioactive material!'

He said 'There is some evidence that they've got hold of radioactive material.'

I said 'Tell me, who are "they"?'

He said 'There are always "theys".'

I said 'Of course I feel guilty!' Then – 'I mean, about Lilia.'

He said 'Don't cry.'

I said 'It's so awful. So awful!'

I thought – Jason and Lilia, or Medea, and that girl, what was her name: they must have all wanted to kill each other!

I sat up and put my hands around my knees.

I thought – I am not pretending to cry!

He said 'Lilia and the child and Jason are all right.'

I wanted to say – Where's Jason?

(Well, where were you? waiting for some new dragon's teeth to grow, I suppose!)

I said 'When was the house pulled down?'

He said 'After the war. There was a fire.'

I thought I might say – I came here to say I'd marry you!

He said 'Would you like some food?'

I said 'Yes.'

He crawled out of the tent. He took with him a small gas-stove and a bowl in which there were carrots and potatoes.

I thought – I do not see, really, how one lives like this. Then – This is the only possible way to live?

He said 'We used to camp here, my mother and my father and Lilia and I. Even then the battle-area was usually empty.'

He poured what was left of a can of water into the bowl and began to wash the carrots and potatoes.

He said 'It was like the Garden of Eden. There were all the notices telling people to keep out.'

'So you used to go in?'

'So I used to go in.'

He put the carrots and potatoes into a saucepan and lit the stove; then he held the bowl with the dirty water in it and looked at the saucepan.

He said ' – Cooking water, washing-water, drinking-water: that sort of thing – '

I said 'But if Jason and Lilia and the child are all right – '

He said 'Yes?'

I said 'You think you can't talk about it?'

He said nothing.

I thought I might say – Not even in inverted commas?

He might say – Can you live in inverted commas? Can you die in inverted commas?

He crawled into the tent and got hold of a can of clean water which, when he emerged from the tent again, he poured into the saucepan which he put on the stove.

I said 'What did you think of my letter?'

He said 'I sent you a map.' Then – 'You said you began that letter years ago? You finished it and sent it a month ago!'

I said 'I want to say, things are different now.'

He crawled into the tent again and rummaged about among some clothes. He produced a bundle of letters which he began leafing through as he sat cross-legged on the sleeping-bag.

He said 'Do you love him?'

I said 'Who?'

He said 'Jason.'

I thought – Why don't I say: I came here to say I'd marry you!

He said 'Read this.' He began himself to read one of the letters.

I said 'No, I don't love him.'

He said 'Words are counter-productive.'

I said 'Yes, I have loved him.'

He said 'In inverted commas!'

He held out towards me the letter that he had been reading.

I took the letter. I looked at it. I said 'It's from the Professor!'
He said 'But you do go to bed with him – '
I said 'Who, the Professor?'
He said 'No, not the Professor!' He laughed.
I thought – Well, why not the Professor?
Then – You mean, after all, this might be a joke?
Here is the Professor's letter –

Dear Bert,
What I was trying to say was this –

Humans are addicted to power-struggles as individuals can be addicted to dope. They need them to locate themselves; to give themselves a fix.

You can't get people out of this by teaching: teaching is one more move in the game: people just learn more sophisticated ways of getting themselves a fix. To get yourself out of an addiction you don't fight it straight; you have to hit some kind of rock bottom. Ask Judith. I don't know whether or not some bomb has to go off.

Structures change through chance mutation – then through the business of whether a mutation lives or dies. What lives is that which is suited to an environment. It is the conventional, by definition, who are usually suited to an environment. So most mutations die. But if an environment changes, then of course it is the conventional who may die.

By environment I mean both conditions in the external world and the habits of humans that affect these.

If a mutant finds itself suited to a change in environment, then of course it can live.

But it might find itself at the mercy of the dying conventionalists.

It is conventional, still, to see things in terms of one thing against another – in terms of opposition, rather than of what is called feedback.

A mutant, yes, might see things in patterns which are circular; or self-referring (or, indeed, a joke?).

It is, yes, like when you have taken the lid off that box: there are all the bits and pieces: but also there is your seeing them, which is to do with light.

Language has evolved to do with the demarcation of bits and pieces: language is not suited to deal with light.

If old forms are broken up, yes, there is a chance for new forms to become available.

You cannot bring about a chance mutation; you can prepare the ground on which such or such a chance mutation might live.

Within the human genetic capability (forgive the jargon; this crops up when language pretends it is in the area of control) there is such enormous potentiality that almost anything might be there to be encouraged to live, given this or that ground.

When one talks about old forms being broken up, one might be talking about ideas or about the outside world or about, yes, people.

Of course – you can talk about the breaking up of things and ideas; you cannot talk thus about people.

I think a hopeful mutant would be able to look at this impossibility. (When I say joke, I do not, of course, mean simply what is taken as a joke.)

Does looking do anything? Well, does doing do anything? We will see. We are looking, aren't we?

You say – Would not women do it better?

Ask Judith.

Love from Max

In the morning (yes, I have left the rest of the evening out: it was you, wasn't it, who said that aesthetics was a matter of leaving this or that out) –

In the morning the walls of the tent, or cave, or tomb, or whatever, were transparent to light. I wondered – We are made of light? This is Easter Saturday? The baby turtles begin their triumphant march towards the sea?

Bert was asleep. Or he was pretending to be asleep. He lay on his back with his hands folded like a crusader.

I thought – So I will be that girl who crawls out of the shelter to collect firewood, who holds out her hands to the flames, and says – If he were the sun and moon and I were gravity –

You think you know why you wrote it like that?

We are happy, yes, when we make connections.

The grass outside the tent was covered with dew, as if seeds or sperm had come down from the sky on it.

I went round looking for firewood. I thought – If I meet that old god walking in the garden I shall say – Hullo, hullo, I hope you had a nice time last night –

– Because I did, we did, thank you.

You cannot be jealous, in this new dispensation?

When I got back to the tent Bert was sitting in front of it cross-legged with his hands on his knees. He said 'I've been up since dawn collecting firewood.'

I said 'And I've been lying in bed thinking – Well, I know why we had to go through all that: so we could have such a nice time last night.'

He said 'You must never believe that everything won't come out all right.'

I thought – And everything is for the best in the best of all possible worlds?

Then – You mean, you don't want to marry me?

I made the fire and put on the saucepan for coffee. There was fruit and some rather old bread. Bert watched.

He said 'We've been here before.'

I said 'There is that impression.'

He said 'It's some trick of the brain.'

I said 'Ah, don't talk about dimensions!'

Do you remember how the sun used to come up as one jumped up and down in the Garden? It was as if one had made the sun by blowing on it like a furnace.

Bert said 'I can't think of anything else to say.'

I said 'We are all right then.'

He said 'Would you like to hear my speech? about the demonstration – '

I said 'Yes.'

Bert crawled into the tent. He came out with a sheaf of papers. He sat cross-legged. He stared at the ground.

I said 'Where are you going to make this speech?'

He said 'In the market-place.'

We were opposite one another across the fire. Bert sometimes seemed about to perform his speech: then he put the papers on the ground. He said 'Ladies and gentlemen, your money will be returned at the box-office.'

I said 'I came here to say I'd marry you.'

Bert said 'Oh dear God, you can't say that!'

The door in the high brick wall through which I had come the previous day opened, and a man in military uniform came in. He carried some sort of automatic weapon under his arm. He looked at the tomb; then at Bert and myself in front of the tent.

I said 'Ladies and gentlemen – '

Bert said 'I mean – thank you!'

I said 'Look. Do you tell the truth: or do you manipulate?'

Bert said 'You tell the truth: you manipulate – '

The man in uniform, who appeared to be an officer, made a gesture through the door behind him and five or six soldiers came through. They wore camouflage uniforms and had automatic weapons under their arms.

I thought – Well, can you be shot in inverted commas!

The officer walked over and looked at the tomb. The soldiers watched Bert and myself. I thought – They would see us like figures in a painting?

The officer came towards us through the long grass. He moved slowly, as if treading to avoid fallen pillars.

He said to Bert 'Stand up.'

Bert said 'I'm naked.'

The officer said 'You're not.'

Bert said 'Oh no, you're quite right, I'm not.'

The soldiers had spread out and were coming towards us in

224

a line. I thought – They are those angels with swords, come to turn us out. Then – This is ridiculous.

Bert stood up. He was wearing an enormous pullover which came down to his knees.

Bert said 'I am the owner of this garden. You have seen the notice. It is out of bounds to troops.'

The officer said 'Have you means of identification?'

Bert murmured ' – What has two legs in the morning, two in the evening and – '

The officer stared at Bert. I thought – You mean, he is homosexual?

The officer said 'Don't I know you?'

Bert said 'Yes.'

The officer said 'You were at school.'

I thought – But this is cheating. Or it is the number coming up, when you make your mind a blank, on the roulette wheel –

The officer blushed. He was a neat, clean-cut-out man like an actor. I thought – You mean, he was once in love with Bert?

Then – This is not cheating? What would be chance, in a chance mutation –

The officer said 'What are you doing here?'

Bert said 'We work for a film company.'

The officer said 'You're making a film?'

Bert said 'Yes.'

Then he looked up to the tops of trees. The officer looked up to where he was looking.

After a time, one or two of the soldiers did the same.

I said 'Would you like some breakfast?'

The officer made a gesture to the men who were behind him. Two of them came forwards and knelt and crawled into the tent.

Bert sat down. He said '*Petit Déjeuner sur l'Herbe.*'

I poured out a cup of coffee which I handed to the officer. I said to the men 'We have to share one cup.'

The officer said 'Have you seen any odd bods around here?'

Bert said 'Oh, I thought you said odd bombs!'

The officer stared at him. Then he said 'Where did you hear that?'

Bert said 'I don't think they'll plant a bomb here in fact. I mean in the battle-area. That would be too subtle for them. They might do something somewhere else.'

The officer said 'Where did you get this information?'

The two soldiers who had crawled inside the tent were going through Bert's photographic equipment. I thought – They are hunters, not elephants looking for a salt-lick in the cave.

Bert said 'It's no good to them if they do anything that's expected. It's got to seem like an accident.'

The officer said 'What are you talking about?'

Bert said 'I've made it up.'

The officer said 'You'd better come into town.'

The soldiers came out of the tent. One of them said 'Just photographic equipment.'

Bert said 'Oh, you want to give us a lift into town?'

I said 'I've got my bicycle.'

Bert said 'Put it on the handlebars.' He hit his hand against his head, as if he had been stupid. He said 'I mean, the under-carriage.'

I did not know how to do this. I did not know if Bert knew how to do this. I thought – You mean, you think of nothing, and say what comes into your head, and then there are one or two connections?

Bert had gone into the tent and was putting on more clothes. The officer, staring after him, seemed to have been hypnotised by Bert. I thought – Well, this area is supposed to be to do with love, isn't it?

There was the sound of a helicopter overhead. It was coming from the direction in which Bert had looked to the tops of trees. The officer and the soldiers looked up again. Bert came out and began tidying the cooking things outside the tent.

I thought – But you can't bring in a helicopter or God just like this!

The helicopter came swirling and clacking over the tops of trees. Bert waved to it. Then he said to me 'Leave your things here,' and he began getting film equipment out of the tent.

I do not know how to write about this. In writing, you say one thing happens after another: you usually see what you expect. But why should not just this thing happen after that, in the outside world?

Bert began fastening up the front of the tent. He said to the officer 'How are you?'

The officer said 'Very well.'

Bert said 'See you in the town.'

The officer said 'You're going into town?'

Bert said to me 'Coming?'

I thought – You mean, you manipulate; you take what comes; things happen?

I said 'What shall I carry?'

Bert put out a hand and laid it on my hair. I thought – Cry, what shall I cry –

He said 'You carry the sound.'

The officer said 'That's your helicopter?'

Bert festooned himself with film equipment. The officer watched. He was a good-looking young man with small, neat features. Bert put his hand on his arm. He said 'I've given all the information I know.'

The officer said 'What information?'

Bert laughed. He said 'See you behind the cricket pavilion!'

The soldiers, squatting, were making patterns with the butts of their weapons on the ground. I thought – They are embarrassed like Christ with the woman discovered in adultery.

Bert handed me some recording equipment which I hung from a strap over my shoulder. Then he looked up again to the tops of trees. I thought – You mean there are these waves, these particles, going through you all the time?

The officer said 'You know where to find us?'

Bert said 'That's right.' The helicopter had gone on.

Bert and I set off as if after the helicopter through the long grass. We went towards the door in the wall opposite to the one against which I had left my bicycle. I thought – Put your feet exactly where I do –

Bert said 'Don't look round.'

I thought I might say – I know about not looking round!

Then Bert said 'You are much loved.'

I thought I might say – This is not laughter, this is tears.

When we reached the doorway in the wall at the far side of the tomb (I never looked closely at that tomb: is there a small tree growing out of it?) the officer and soldiers were still hanging around the tent: perhaps they could not bear to tear themselves away (there are paintings like that). Time did seem to be going very slowly: something happens to time, as well as space, don't they say, when you fall into unknown territory? Bert opened the door in the far wall and went through. At first there seemed to be an area of just further grass and nettles. I thought – But I still know nothing about Bert's relationship with the people who might or might not be planting this bomb: I mean, I believe that what Bert has told me is true: but being true in this area seems to mean that you still do not know exactly what is going on: you are looking at, without putting any interpretation on, what is there: you put one foot in front of another.

Then – But it is all right to interpret, no not interpret, like this, on another level?

The grass and nettles gave on to an area of cobbles and what seemed to be the backyards of a large country house. There were stables and lofts and granaries and kennels. I thought – This is where children must once have played – or those enormous babies who were ladies and gentlemen walking on the grass. Bert stopped and said 'Look, you should not really come any further.' I said 'What are you going to do: you're going to look for that bomb?'

He faced me and put his hands on my shoulders and his forehead against mine.

He said 'Look: I can't say I'll marry you now!'

I thought – You mean, you don't think you could be a father?

I said 'All right.'

We went on.

I thought – Somewhere or other, has not something like this happened before?

Well, Jason, you did want to marry Lilia?

Then round some corner (no, I do not think we make things happen like this: I think we make ourselves so that things happen like this; one thing rather than another) – round some corner there popped up the façade of an enormous building: it was as if we had been going along that path in the jungle near the Garden, of course (you have made the connection?), although this was not, in fact, exactly a façade, because what we were now looking at was seen from the back – from what had once been the inside of a building – the rest was not there, it had been knocked down. There remained just this front elevation of a large country house in the baroque style: there was ornamentation around the doors and windows and even a pediment and a scroll or two: it was three storeys high: but because we were looking at it from the inside, through its windows we saw the sky. The windows of those enormous churches in the jungle had led to darkness. And so on. I thought – No wonder people close their eyes!

Bert said 'You have been here before?'

I said 'No, I haven't been here before.'

Bert said 'You've been to the cottage.'

I said 'I've been to the cottage with you!'

Bert held my hand.

There was a fence round the ruins of the building and the usual notices about keeping out; and then a particular one saying DANGER OF FALLING MASONRY. I thought – This is an extension of that area that is forbidden within what is forbidden: so, again, you are invited in: you can work this out?

Bert said 'We used to play here as children. We were supposed not to be allowed to climb.'

There were weeds and piles of rubble where the main part of the house had once been. I thought – This, do you think, is one of the boxes with the lid off?

Bert said 'The façade was preserved because of its aesthetic qualifications.'

I said 'Oh, Bert, I'm so sorry!'

He said 'I want you to go back.'

I said 'I want to go on.'

Bert stepped over the fence that went round the building. I followed. Our cameras and recording equipment banged around us. We were now inside what had once been the house. Bert's great great grandmother had lived here, or something. I thought – you mean, he is not really looking for a bomb?

The doors and windows of the lower floor of the façade were boarded up so you could not see through them to the landscape beyond. You could only see through the windows of the two top floors where there was the sky.

I thought – If, inside the theatre of memory, you have become yourself one of the figures that pop up at windows, what is it that you might see when you look out?

What had once been the side walls of the house had been cut off at a slope so that there were still bits of them like buttresses against the façade. Beyond these side walls were the half-standing ruins of outhouses and a shrubbery, so that here one could still not see through to any landscape in front. The whole structure was, indeed, like the backdrop of a stage-set, seen from the back.

I thought – The battle-area is beyond the façade: but if no one comes here, has the audience left the theatre, or has the play not even begun?

In the corner on the left, beside the side-buttress and the inside of the façade, there were the remains of a spiral staircase which must have once gone up to some sort of tower. The staircase had been sliced through vertically as in some architect's drawing: only stretches or segments of it remained against the back wall of the façade. I thought – It is one of the ladders on which figures in the theatre of memory climb when they want someone to remember – what – the shape of their lives? its meaning? This is one of the staircases, is it, on which one climbs to say – Coo-ee?

Bert said 'Do you see that piece of plastic?'

I said 'What piece of plastic?'

He pointed to the top of the building where there was no roof nor battlements nor towers: but where there was what looked like a piece of plastic wrapped round a stone.

He said 'Do you think it's a bomb?'

I said 'Bert, you're mad!'

He said 'I tried to get up there yesterday but I couldn't.'

I thought – He must know more than I think he knows: or why is he doing this?

I said 'Why couldn't you?'

He said 'Perhaps I need an audience.'

I said 'Bert, I'm so miserable!'

He said 'Yes, I'm sorry too.'

He put his arms around me.

Then he said 'Could you help me up on to the top level of that staircase?'

I said 'Yes.'

I thought – Perhaps this is some ordeal: some ritual?

He said 'Why do you say now you'll marry me?'

I said 'I've said I'll help you!'

I took his arms away from me.

He said 'Eeny meeny miney mo – '

I said 'It depends where you begin.'

He said 'Well, where did we?'

He walked over the rubble to what was left of the spiral staircase. I followed him. I thought – At least you may know what we are talking about: do you?

The first remaining segment of the staircase rose to a height of about a metre; then it ended. The next segment was parallel to it about two metres above.

Bert looked up to the top of the building where the piece of plastic wrapping was. He said 'Height off ground: wind direction – '

I thought – You mean, people will think you are mad anyway?

He climbed the first segment of the spiral staircase. He then reached up to the outside of the top of the second. He was festooned with his cine equipment: the camera swung. I thought – Well, people just do like doing, and watching, don't they, things like this.

He said 'Can I put a foot on your shoulder?'

I said 'Yes.'

I thought – Some old memories are still trying to get out of the tin can?

By my standing underneath him and his putting his foot on my shoulder he was able to scramble up on to the second segment of the staircase. I thought – This is a demonstration that we never know what things are for: will we know, if it is counter-productive?

I said 'Do you want the sound equipment?'

He said 'Yes.'

I thought – So you mean, at the end of all this, we might have found out what it is for?

He said 'Do you think you could possibly come up where I was just now and then I can help you up here: and then you can help me up on to the third level?'

I said 'All right.'

I climbed the first segment of the staircase and stood on the outer edge of the top step. I thought – A stone will come loose? I will fall and dangle at the end of a rope?

I said 'This is very difficult.'

He said 'Yes, I know.'

I handed him up his sound equipment. He put it by him on the second level. Then he knelt and I reached up to him my arms and he took hold of them. I thought – But one day you will marry me?

He said 'Swing like a pendulum.'

I said 'Swing like a pendulum.'

He said 'Then you can get a foothold.'

By hanging from his arms, and swinging, I did manage to get a foot up on to the second level; then, with a good deal of scraping, my body after it.

I thought – Those two climbers on the north face of the

Eiger: cut the rope and one of them dies: if you don't, both of
them will –

– This was always about something being born?

He said 'This is the hardest part.'

'Yes.'

'I can't stand on your shoulders.'

'Why not?'

'Because if I do, either you or I will fall backwards.'

I thought – You cut the rope that is from an umbilicus?

We were standing with our backs against the inside wall of
the façade. I thought – Or perhaps with one great heave –
upsadaisy!

Bert began to try to climb up on to the third level of the
staircase. I held my hands cupped so that he could put his foot
in them. I still do not know how to describe all this: as if
nothing were happening? I thought – Even if he gets to the
top he will have to come down: or does he think he will be
taken up in a chariot-rocket to heaven?

Bert scrabbled and clawed like someone – well – trying to
give birth? trying to be born?

Give a squeeze, do you think, to his little toe? his ankle?

If Bert got on to the third level of the staircase it did seem,
it is true, that it would not be too difficult for him to get to the
top of the façade: there were projecting stones and bits of
metal.

Bert reached the third level. I handed up to him his equipment from the second. He said 'Thanks.'

I thought – You mean, you have now got away from me?

He lay on his stomach and looked down.

I thought – Ah, you are not a snake!

He said 'I mean, thank you for saying what you said.'

I said 'You do what you like.'

There was the sound of a helicopter again overhead. I did
not want to go on with this. I turned away and sat with my
back against the wall.

Of course, it was conceivable, was it not, that there might
have been some sort of bomb wrapped in plastic at the top

233

of the ruined building: it was likely, I supposed, that the helicopter was to do with the army or the police who might have been on the look-out for a bomb. Or the helicopter might really be to do with Bert's film company (Bert did, after all, have a film company!): or it might have been that Bert had made the whole thing up. None of this seemed much to matter. I sat with my back against the wall on the second level of the staircase. From the bottom of this level it would not be too difficult to get down. Bert had gone further up taking his camera and his sound equipment with him.

I thought – Well, if he is the man on the tightrope, I am not going to be stuck posing as the girl in spangles at the bottom.

From where I sat I could see the outline of what had once been the huge country house. There was a drawing-room, and a hall, and passages, and a kitchen.

I thought – This is where Bert's ancestors were put away?

To the right of the outline of the building there was the wall of the old kitchen garden from which we had come.

I thought – There are maps of the past: but of the present?

The helicopter was coming overhead. It was making its whirring and clacking. There was a man at the side with what seemed to be a loud-hailer.

I thought – But even if Bert is making this up, he cannot know the ending –

He may simply be shot?

Could one live like this if one had children?

One would want a happy ending, would one not?

I was keeping as close to the wall as possible so as to be out of sight of the man with the loud-hailer.

I had not noticed that not so far from the end of the second level of the staircase there was a first-floor window, not bricked up, through which, if I could get there, I might see whatever it was at the back of, or rather I mean at the front of, the building. I had imagined that beyond here was the battle-area: there must once have been magnificent lawns and terraces and gardens.

I had a glimpse of Bert who was getting to the very top of

the building. I thought – Of course, he is like one of those old heroes on Everest who go on and on and do not come back: who seem to have slid right over the rim of the world –

The man in the helicopter appeared to have seen Bert. There was a voice from the loud-hailer. The sound got lost in the wind.

I wondered if, when the helicopter had gone, I might climb along, finding footholds, to where I could see through the first-floor window. I thought – It is important in this dimension, of course, to appear to be doing things for oneself.

– Might it be that I would see as if out of, or would it be into, a painting?

There were bits of stone and metal projecting from the wall here like those from the wall along which Bert was climbing.

One of the ways in which memory was stirred here was to do with that time, yes, years ago, when I had climbed out on to and along the parapet and battlements of Oliver's flat – first in order to save his life; then, it had seemed, in order to save mine. In remembering this it was not as if I were going back into the past: one looks down at the past from the present. But then, there had been that body which had fallen on to the pavement. There might be such a thing again, might there not, with Bert (or myself?) climbing.

The helicopter was overhead like an enormous angel of life or death. I thought – I should not hide. I will see what is beyond that window.

I began to climb out on to the wall beyond the second level of the staircase. I thought – This could be a further peephole at the far side of the box?

Bert had reached the very top of the building. He was crawling along the ledge like a target at a fun-fair shooting-range. The helicopter was directly overhead. It seemed to be trying to blow him off with its wings – or to give him something to fight against. I thought – He is like a bird of paradise with its long tail: this is there to strengthen him: but if he falls?

Then – This is ridiculous.

The helicopter was lowering a rope towards Bert.

My handholds and footholds were difficult: I could not pay much attention to what was happening overhead: I thought – This is right: I have to be getting on with what I am doing. I imagined Bert to be standing with his arms out like a bird: becoming entangled, or stepping gracefully, on to a hook. I thought – Oh yes, with God that fisherman in thigh-length boots like a woman! There were still all these images, like flies, like pollen: but how difficult it is not to fall! After a time the sound of the helicopter went away. I thought Bert must have gone with it. Would he be hanging in the air, waving – Coo-ee! – from his chariot-rocket to heaven?

The helicopter, I supposed, need not have been to do with the army or police: it was more likely, yes, to be to do with Bert's film company.

I was still hanging on to my rock-face: my own face pressed against the wall. There was pain here and there. I thought – I am like someone trying to get out of that cave –

– a hummingbird in front of a flower –

– or I am the child that is hanging on inside me?

When I reached the window – I had imagined that the boundary of the battle-area would coincide with the front of the house, this being the extremity of the piece of land that jutted like a lump beneath the skin: so that it would be, yes, a strange territory on to which I looked out – when I reached the window – pivoting on my hands, my stomach, my feet left somewhere behind me; how slow this was! what an inch by inch effort! – at first it was the somewhat distant view that I saw: this was, indeed, like the substance of a painting: one of those Flemish landscapes dotted with animals like stars: these animals were sheep: they were in a huge green parkland very lush and bright: the light was such that it seemed to come (as it does in such a landscape) not from reflection but from the objects themselves; the sheep and the grassland and the trees dotted here and there appearing to be, yes, their own suns. I thought – And the trees even contain their own shadows: so they are at once darkness and light. This was, indeed, like some entrance into the content of a picture (the being-at-home in the Garden of Eden by the back way?): the Milky Way spread out and around with each particle exact: it also seemed to be a landscape into which humans (because they feared to carry their own light?) had not yet come.

I had, I suppose, glimpsed such a landscape once or twice before – in the Australian desert; on the plains of Africa where zebra graze. But in so far as this landscape was framed as if within a picture, it did seem to be in this sense at least in a style into which humans had come – in that they were able to be painters of pictures. I thought – And by what strange routes does one get here!

I tried to push myself further into the window so that I could see directly down. I did not have to worry too much now about footholds: I did not worry, certainly, about what I would find below. I mean, there would be no body on the pavement: there would just be, as it were, that empty nest of stones: with Bert, for sure, having flown. Directly beneath the front of the house there was a terrace: the terrace had weeds growing between the stones and a broken balustrade: I thought – You mean, it is the edge of a stage that a body goes over! Beyond the balustrade there were slopes and steps going down to the bright-and-exact parkland. There were two stone lions at the bottom of the steps: they looked out over the sheep and lambs. There was even a dried-up fountain and a statue with roses growing over it. I was on my stomach, balancing, my head and feet in the air. I wanted to say – There, do you see, my little one? In the distance, over by a far line of plantation trees, there was a white figure on a dark horse moving. I thought – She is on the threshold of the landscape? she is already within? I assumed the figure to be that of a woman. I thought – Perhaps she is myself: this is a picture even now being painted, like that one by Anita Kroll?

Now I want to put in here (since I have touched on the subject, and because it took me some time to get back on my way to the American airbase) about a time when I went to visit Oliver – I

237

mean, not long after I returned to England from my time seven years ago in the Garden.

Oliver was at a place in the country where he had gone because he was ill: I had thought that he might be dying. He himself had often thought about dying. I wondered if he had got used to it.

I went by train into the sort of country where there are wooded gorges with rivers at the bottom and houses stuck on slopes – not a landscape so much as a rock-garden.

The house was a low stone monastery-like construction, built, I suppose, at the end of the nineteenth century. There was a chapel with two gothic pinnacles. In front of the house were wooden seats facing a lawn on which old men were playing bowls.

Oliver was on one of these seats; he had lost his hair: he was very thin. He seemed to have been watching the drive for me. When I saw him I thought I might say – I did love you, you know: I had never quite loved anyone before in my life.

When Oliver smiled he was able to look more wicked than he had ever done before, perhaps because now he was supposed to be holy.

He said 'Hullo.'

I said 'Hullo.'

He said 'You're looking very well.' Then – 'Can't say the same about me.'

I thought – When people are hollowed out, holy, they are in contact with the dead like those caves that make booming noises from the sea?

We sat side by side on the wooden seat, watching bowls.

I said 'I thought I should thank you.'

He said 'For what?'

I said 'For whatever it was you did, or didn't do, after Desmond died. It couldn't have been easy.'

He said 'Oh that!'

On the lawn the old men threw balls, and lumbered after them, and veered to one side, as the balls did, before they all came to rest.

238

He said 'The thing I had to do, really, as it always is, was nothing.'

I said 'What exactly is wrong with you?'

He said 'I'm on this drug.'

I thought – They give you drugs, of course, to combat drugs. Then – What did I mean, when I thought you were a survivor?

He said 'It's when they give me the drug that I can't do anything.'

He stretched his neck from time to time as if he were reaching for something like an apple; or were being tickled by a leaf, or a shadow, just beyond the framework of a picture.

I said 'I went away.'

He said 'I know.' Then – 'Did you find what you wanted?'

I said 'Yes.'

He said 'What was it?'

I thought I must not say – One cannot put it into words.

I said 'I suppose, a way of looking at things.'

He said 'What way?'

I said 'At yourself looking.'

I thought – But this, surely, is what he is doing: stretching his neck, tickling himself, from just outside the picture.

He said 'The problem is, to get messages through to the muscles from the brain.'

I said 'Can they cure it?'

He said 'No.' Then – 'You've got to do some trick.'

I thought – How would one tell whether or not those old men playing bowls were mad – throwing balls, roaming after them, swerving and coming to rest? –

He said 'Get them when they aren't looking! Don't give them time to see what you're up to!'

I thought – What? The muscles? People? Bits and pieces in the brain?

He said 'You've got to pretend to be doing something else: then you've got them!'

I thought I might say – But it's not just a trick –

– This place: there's something outside, that you hook on to?

I began to feel sad. I thought – I suppose I had hoped everything would be for the best in the best of all possible worlds, even with Oliver.

He said 'You know when I took that overdose – '

I said 'Yes.'

He said 'I thought that was quite a good trick!'

He laughed.

I thought – Well, was it?

He said 'I mean, I didn't mean to take the pills. I thought I'd trick you.'

I tried to work this out. I said 'Then why did you take them?'

He said 'I don't know.' Then – 'I mean, I think I simply got bored of tricks.'

I thought – Well then, can I think: That was all right, wasn't it?

He said 'Also, I didn't think I'd get you.'

I thought – By a trick? Then – Well, you wouldn't, would you?

He stared for a long time in front of him. He stretched his neck.

I thought – The trick is, for it not to be a trick?

He suddenly got up off the seat and started running towards the people playing bowls. He ran at a trot, his arms hanging down, leaning forwards. Then he stopped, some way on to the lawn, and looked back. He said 'There!'

I said 'That's good!'

He said 'Quite a good trick!'

I said 'Yes, I see that!'

He said 'You do things: then sometimes something quite different is happening.'

I said 'But it's not a trick!'

He said 'No. That's right.' Then – 'I did get you!'

He was this old man on a lawn, his arms hanging down. He was like some sort of self-portrait. You know how self-portraits seem to be looking at you: they seem even to be painting you: they are not often, as Oliver was, laughing.

When I got to the American airbase (you need a map of this strange territory? the airbase was a few miles to the west of the battle-area) the entrance was at the edge of a village where, like the village with the railway station, there was a pub, a church, a village green. I thought – These patterns are in our minds: we set them out like toys here and there.

There was a road along the side of a high wire fence within which were the concrete buildings of the airbase: the land was at the top of a slightly convex plateau so that you could not see more than a certain distance inside. On the horizon the noses of one or two aeroplanes poked out as if they were those of animals in a zoo.

The demonstrators were assembled on the side of the road opposite the gates: there was a crowd on the village green and stretching each way along the road. There were, I suppose, some four or five thousand demonstrators: they carried banners and balloons; there were babies on people's backs and in push-chairs. On the green were groups having picnics. It was like some sporting occasion or a pop concert, or the location for an epic film.

On the edge of the crowd, and dotted amongst it, were police. The police seemed to be acting as if the demonstrators were not there: the demonstrators were acting as if the police were not there. I thought – Actors think they have to act as if their audiences were not there.

Sometimes two or three demonstrators, as if deliberately, would stand very close to the police while they talked. It was not clear whether they wanted to make the point that they thought the police were, or were not, there.

The gates across the road were a high wire construction with sentry-huts inside. A few senior policemen stood chatting in the roadway. Within were five or six soldiers standing and not talking. I thought – Soldiers do not have to talk because they carry weapons.

Further along the road in the direction beyond the village there was an estate of modern red-brick houses where, it seemed, the families of the American airmen lived. This was not fenced off (the animals were not dangerous?): every now and then a car or small bus would move, carrying people between the houses and the airbase. The vehicle would stop at the gates: those inside the bus would not look out while a policeman looked in: then a soldier would open the gates and the car or bus would move on.

On the other side of the road from the group of houses, where the perimeter fence of the airbase left the road and went off into a wood, there was a path which led (so I guessed and learned later) to the camp of the women who had been keeping a vigil outside. These women had previously been encamped near the gates: they had been moved on, with some violence it was said, just before the demonstration. The women had fled into the woods like witches. They reappeared here and there in twos and threes: they could be distinguished because for the most part they wore padded jackets and loose trousers and Wellington boots. They moved among the police and the demonstrators as if they were showing, impartially, that they recognised neither group to be there.

I thought – People do only recognise things similar to themselves?

– But still, each is only here because of the other that they do not recognise: they are reacting to phantoms; they are not looking at themselves.

I could walk amongst them as if I myself were unseen. This was a desire I remembered having in childhood. I thought – But an agent in occupied territory, there to recognise without being recognised – this would be looking at oneself?

I saw Lilia on the far side of the road. She was talking to the policemen by the gates. She was wearing white dungarees, a white scarf and white boots. I thought – She is an angel of life or death; it was not her I saw riding in the battle-area?

Or – She is that angel, off-stage, waiting to go into a court-yard.

242

Of course, I had known Lilia would be at the demonstration. I had not expected to come across her so easily.

I thought – We should meet in one of those amphitheatres of Greece: to shout at each other across the stage; with blood on the floor like the setting sun.

– What was the name of that girl who took Jason from Medea?

I had expected Lilia's child to be with her. I thought it was odd she was not with her child.

Beyond the gates, in front of which Lilia was talking to the policemen, there were the burrows with the noses of planes and missiles peeping out.

Lilia turned away from the group of policemen. I wondered if I could make her look at me. I might do this if I could get myself not to try to make her look at me – and so on.

The crowd was lining up to march off somewhere – perhaps to the local town; perhaps to another airbase. There were clergymen and a bishop or two at the head of the column (this was, after all, a demonstration on Easter Saturday: well, what do you think was happening in that tomb?). I thought I might say to Lilia – Of course you want to kill me! Of course I have wanted to kill you! but we can all come alive, can we not, at the end of Act III? There was a group with guitars around the bishops; they began to play; the column moved off. I thought – It is on Easter Saturday, is it not, that there is the Harrowing of Hell? Policemen had formed in a line on either side of the road; demonstrators flowed like a river between them. The police were guarding both the airbase and the village; the demonstrators would run down safely and be lost in the sea.

Lilia turned and looked at me. She was on the opposite side of the road or river. I thought – Thus, of course, my friend in the Garden turned to look at me: Lilith: Lilia: of course there are connections! between hate and love.

I could not get through the procession towards Lilia: there were all these people opening and shutting their mouths, singing hymns. I thought – The traffic jams in heaven!

Lilia had the absolutely receptive face of a deer: I thought – It is by its sense of smell, that a deer protects itself. Lilia leaned slightly forwards with her arms crossed beneath her breasts – as if she were carrying a child.

I thought – One might cross a river just as one climbs on the façade of a ruined building.

Lilia had begun to walk in time with the procession at the far side of the road. I kept pace with her. I thought I might say –

– I thought you might be here –

– I didn't expect you to be here –

– Can we talk? –

There was a helicopter overhead. I thought – Bert! on your hook like Petrouchka! Coo-ee!

The tails and noses of aeroplanes within the airbase were like the humps of a sea-serpent. Lilia and I kept up with each other on our different sides of the road. She might say – See, I have made for you this cloak of fire! I would say – Oh do let's see what it looks like on! There was a group of the women with heavy quilted jackets and loose trousers watching the procession go past. I thought – As witches, they are dressed all ready to be burned. The road or river seemed to contain trees and dead bodies floating. I thought – You choose to drown, or you choose to burn?

I thought, since I was choosing nothing, I should try to step across the road towards Lilia.

When I stopped and turned, I found that Lilia had stopped and had turned too.

Lilia came across the road as if she were walking on water: as if she were treading on the trunks of bodies or dead trees. She had this extraordinarily tough and yet quite open face – like a prison from which all the bars had long since been blown. I thought – I am not a witch, I will stand quite still: did people do this when they felt the flames?

Lilia said 'Have you seen my child?'

I said 'No.'

She said 'I've lost him.'

I thought – Do you not think we might be those two figures in a courtyard?

Then – It is not only to me, is it, that you do not use the name of your child?

She said 'He went off on his bicycle.'

I said 'In which direction did he go?'

She said 'He went to find Eleanor.'

I said 'Eleanor is here?'

She said 'She's somewhere by the women's camp.'

I thought – We are like an extended family stretched out across that desert with their donkey.

Lilia and I were by the side of the road with all the people playing guitars and singing hymns going past us. I thought – Pious souls have always gone to and fro in wrong directions.

I said 'Would you like some coffee?'

Lilia said 'Yes.'

I said 'We can go to the pub.'

Lilia said 'I told him, if he got lost, to meet me in the pub.'

On our way across the green, which now was emptying, we passed some clowns. One was miming a chicken, and another was chasing him with an axe. When the clown with the axe struck at the chicken, the chicken reared up with his wings out and the clown with the axe staggered back clutching his head.

She said 'Bert tells him these stories.'

I said 'What stories does Bert tell him?'

She said 'About buried treasure, and that sort of thing.'

I said 'Do you think Bert makes up stories?'

She said 'Of course Bert makes up stories!'

We were walking towards the pub at the far side of the village green. The ground-floor windows were boarded up. In front of the door there was a large man wearing a track-suit and a woollen hat. As we approached, he put an arm across the door.

Lilia said 'I'm meeting my child here.'

The man with the woollen hat said 'No one goes in.'

Lilia shouted 'Do you fucking think you're going to stop me meeting my child?'

The man lowered his arm, and we went in.

Inside the pub there was a hall, which was empty, and a bar with a grille across the counter to the right. This room was half in darkness, the windows being boarded up. Lilia turned on some lights.

I said 'Does Bert think you can alter things by making up stories?'

She said 'Do you think you can make things better by telling the truth?'

She walked up and down. I sat on a stool at the barricaded bar.

The stage on which Lilia and I now found ourselves (I call it a stage: you wouldn't want me to call it anything else, would you?) consisted of the archway into the hall on the right (right if you were looking out from the stage; left if you are in the audience beyond the boarded-up window), the bar at the back with the grille over it (you recognise the scene?), a staircase up on the left down which some messenger might come; towards the front a false fire with glowing coals from which no heat came but to which you could hold out your hands as if they might throw shadows. I thought – Well, after all, why did not people get out of that cave? They were, yes, I understand, frightened of burning by being their own suns.

Lilia walked up and down. She lit a cigarette, and puffed, and the smoke came after her. I thought – Those old gestures often work on a stage.

Lilia said 'God I do hate you.'

I said 'I've hated you too.'

Lilia said 'Why?'

I thought I might say – so I said – 'Because I'm jealous?'

Lilia said 'How long have you known Jason?'

'I first met him when he came to write about the Garden.'

'He didn't go to write about the Garden!'

'All right, when he'd been working on that film.'

She said 'Seven years!'

'I haven't what's called known him for seven years.'

'How long have you what's called known him for?'

I thought – I suppose it's only actors who shout and yell: because they feel nothing, and in order to feel nothing.

She said 'You knew he had a wife and child.'

I said 'Yes, I knew he had a wife and child.'

She said 'If you didn't think of me, couldn't you think of the child?'

I thought – Oh, cut that last line!

She said 'I'm sorry.'

I said 'It's I who am sorry.'

She said 'What are you sorry for?'

I thought – I'm sorry for being human. I'm sorry for the sake of getting the emotions out –

Lilia went to the chimneypiece and put her hands against it and rested her head on her hands. Then she said, as if to herself 'Get it out: get it out – '

I thought – I might be burning: that cloak of flesh turning to fire.

I said 'I suppose I didn't think you'd mind.'

She said 'Why didn't you think I'd mind?' Then – 'What has he been telling you!'

I said 'Nothing.'

She said 'He wrote that story about me!'

I said 'I didn't think it was about you.'

She said 'Well, he wrote about you – '

I said 'That wasn't about me.'

She said 'Well I thought it was.' Then – 'It wasn't about me.'

She lifted her head and looked around the room. She seemed to listen. Then she almost laughed, and said 'Who was it about?'

I thought I might say – Jason, Medea.

She walked about the room again. She puffed at her cigarette, and the smoke came after her.

She said 'Does he pay for you? – '

I said 'What?'

She said 'No, cut that.'

Then – 'When you go away together.'

She went to the boarded-up window and leaned with her head against it.

I thought – This is a rehearsal? The real play will be, is, going on outside?

I said 'I'm trying to marry Bert.'

She said 'God, that is like one of his stories!'

I said 'But I don't think Bert will have me.'

She said 'Well, if you don't mind my saying so, you can hardly blame him, can you?'

I said 'No, I don't.'

She turned and looked at me directly for the first time since we had been in the room. She said 'I mean, I think that's a pity. If Bert doesn't have you.'

I thought – Lilia: Lilith! we are both old elephants; who go into caves every now and then to rub off salt from people's rocks!

She said 'Are you pregnant?'

I said 'That is in fact a line from one of his stories!'

She said again 'I'm sorry.' Then – 'Why do I keep on saying I'm sorry!' Then – 'Could the child be Bert's?'

I thought I might say – Perhaps: but words, don't you think, are counter-productive?

So – Surely we can choose not to be characters in his stories!

She walked up and down again. She said 'I hate you, I hate you. What is it that the woman does to the girl in the play?'

I said 'What play?'

She said 'Jason. Medea.'

I said 'Jason leaves Medea for – I can't remember the girl's name. Medea makes a cloak of fire for the girl, which burns her up on her wedding day.'

Lilia said 'That's what I'd like to do to you!'

I thought I might say – That's good! That's good!

I said 'Then Medea murders her children.'

She said 'What good did that do?'

She stood still. She seemed to be listening again.

I said 'Nothing.' Then – 'But I'm not going to have a wedding day.'

I thought I might cry.

Someone seemed to have come into the hallway. It was as if they, too, were listening; or waiting for some cue. I wanted to say – Not yet! We are doing so well!

Lilia was looking round at the archway to the hall.

I thought – Or you mean, now, this might be the beginning of the play?

I said 'I could go and look – for your child.'

She said 'Why should you do that?'

I said 'Where else might he have gone on his bicycle?' Then – 'You will be here for him when he comes back.'

She turned and looked at me. She went on looking at me. She had these open, trustful-distrustful eyes. I wanted to say – This is the message: can we not learn the code?

She said 'We stay here sometimes, did you know?'

I said 'Yes.'

She said 'I mean, not by the ruin: in a cottage on the other side.'

I thought I might say – Yes, I know.

She said 'You've been there?'

I thought – She does not, really, care whether or not I have been there?

I said 'What are the stories that Bert told him?'

She said 'Well, there's this battle-area, where no one is allowed to go. Of course, Bert used to go there. When we were children. In fact it was quite safe. He used to say it was like the Garden of Eden: where people had been told they mustn't go.'

I said 'Yes, I had a glimpse of it this morning.'

She said 'Bert told him stories of a secret place in the middle; where there was a tree, which is the Tree of Life: where all things are at one with their shadows.'

I thought – Bert! Lilia! There is a bright light like a child! like some sort of bomb coming down!

Lilia said 'So he used to go there, when we were here at Christmas, although I told him not to. I think he thought Eleanor would take him there now on her horse.'

I said 'I'll try to find Eleanor. She's on a horse?'

Lilia stared at me.

All the time there was the impression of both knowing, and yet not knowing, what was happening: there was the person listening in the hallway: there were the events elsewhere.

A man in a tweed jacket came in from the hallway. He had a youngish middle-aged cut-out face. I thought – You can tell these people, can you, because they all seem to be auditioning for the part of Holofernes.

He said 'Do I know you two?'

Lilia said 'No.'

He said 'What's this about the battle-area? Snakes and dragons? Babes in the wood?'

Lilia said 'For God's sake!' Then – 'They're fairy stories.'

The man said 'You believe in fairies?'

He came and sat between us at the bar. Lilia had sat at the bar some distance from me.

I thought – Lilia does or does not know about Bert's story about the bomb?

Lilia said 'If I were you, I'd believe in fairies.'

The man said 'Well, I don't. And may I ask what you two girls are doing in here?'

I said 'Looking for a drink.'

Lilia said 'Meeting someone.'

The man said 'Who?'

I thought – This is a headquarters? They've closed the pub? Then – They all seem the same, these people whom we call 'they', and their opponents.

I said 'We're rehearsing a play.'

The man said 'Oh you're rehearsing a play, are you?' He put a hand up and rattled the grille which covered the bar.

I thought – Or you mean, Lilia has all the time been anxious about the bomb in the battle-area? This man thinks she has been talking about a bomb in the battle-area –

The man said – 'You mean it's a hoax?'

Lilia said 'No it's not a hoax.'

The man said 'You know what I'm talking about?'

Lilia said 'No, do you?'

I thought – Which one of us, do you think, might kill Holofernes?

The man said to me 'You were at that tomb this morning.'

I said 'Yes.'

Lilia said 'You were with Bert?'

The man said 'Come on!'

Lilia said 'What's Bert doing?'

I said 'He went up in a helicopter.'

The man said 'That was his helicopter?'

I thought – This is ridiculous.

I said 'He works for a film company.'

The man said 'I know he works for a film company.'

I tried to remember the sort of style that Bert had been practising. I thought I might say – Look, why should you believe anything we say?

Lilia said to the man 'We don't want to talk to you. Why don't you go away.'

The man said 'You two girls could be in a lot of trouble.'

I thought – Lilia, you said 'we'!

A woman appeared behind the counter of the bar and began taking down the grille. She was a heavy-faced woman with upturned spectacles and grey hair.

I thought – She is a major-general in drag: she may start to kick up her heels and dance and sing?

The man said 'Now tell me what you know.'

Lilia said 'I'll have a vodka and tomato juice, please.'

I said 'Whisky and water, please.'

The man said 'Two vodkas, a whisky and a tomato juice.'

The woman poured out drinks as if she had never poured out drinks before. I thought – You mean she is such an obvious major-general in drag, her disguise is impenetrable, she is really a major-general in drag?

The man said 'You were told this place was out of bounds.'

Lilia said 'I'm meeting my child.'

The man said 'You're meeting your child.'

Lilia said 'Yes.'

The man said to me 'What is the name of your film company?'

Lilia looked at me. I thought – I suppose I should find out whether or not Lilia knows about the bomb.

I said to the man 'What do you know about this bomb?'

Lilia said 'What bomb?'

The man said 'What bomb?'

I said 'We told you all we know this morning.'

Lilia said 'I must go and look for my child.'

The man said 'You're staying here.'

I thought – That was a mistake?

Then – But I could not not have said, could I, there might be a bomb in the battle-area –

I had the impression that Lilia might know something that I did not know: or perhaps we were both trying to tell the other – to find out – whatever it was that was hidden in the stone.

The man turned to Lilia. He had his back to me. He said 'Now tell me what you know.'

Lilia, over the man's shoulder, said to me 'I don't think he did want to come back and meet me here!'

I said 'Why not?'

Lilia said 'I don't know.'

She looked up at the staircase behind her on the left as if she were expecting someone to come down. I thought – A messenger? Jason? (Well, where in God's name were you?)

After a time the man looked up the staircase.

I thought I might smile and say – You two, have a nice time!

Lilia said again 'I must go.'

The man said again 'You're staying here.'

I said 'I'm going. I'll find the child.'

I thought – Holofernes: he prefers her to me?

The woman behind the bar said 'They say they've got hold of this radioactive material, did you know?'

There are times, do you not think, when one gives up even trying? I thought – These two people who have come in are phantoms: why should we try to understand the shadows on the walls of the cave?

The man said 'Have you been upstairs?'

The woman behind the bar said 'No.'

The man took hold of Lilia's arm.

I thought I might say – Don't touch her! She's been outside!

The woman behind the bar said 'It may be a diversion.'

The man said 'Oh it's a diversion all right!'

I went towards the exit to the pub. No one tried to stop me. I thought – You mean, simply, that I'm the one to go?

There is that theory, is there not, that when something of importance is known to one member of the tribe, this knowledge is transmitted to other members secretly?

I heard the woman behind the bar saying 'That one can go?'

The man like Holofernes said 'Yes, that one can go.'

I thought – Well, bring his head along in a basket.

Lilia, of course, did look as desirable as an angel all in white: with her drawn sword above a battlefield.

I thought – It is instructions that are transmitted to each member of the tribe?

As I went out of the door I did have the impression, yes, that there might be someone looking down from a corner of the ceiling.

– Ladies and gentlemen, a fuse has blown: will you, or will you not, kindly leave the theatre?

There was almost no one left on the village green. There were cans and plastic bags and a few burst balloons. Policemen were still chatting in front of the gates of the airbase: on the horizon the noses of aeroplanes poked out above their lairs. I thought – This is the sort of landscape which depends on the chance of a bomb going off: people have to come to dead-ends in their ways through the maze.

Moving on my own, across this littered world, I had an impression of bits and pieces flying out from their box: splinters of light like flocks of birds migrating.

I was going towards the wood by the fence at the far side of the entrance gates. I had understood that here I would find whatever was left of the camp of the women. Here I also might find Eleanor and the child. I could not remember quite why I had felt so strongly that I had to do this. A splinter of light becomes lodged in your mind like a wingbeat, flying.

I have explained, haven't I (to you who bumps into this), about Eleanor. Eleanor is the Professor's wife, the old lady with black hair and bright-blue eyes that Jason talked about in his letter about the birth of the child. She was, yes, the witch-doctor of our tribe.

There has been this gap, hasn't there, of seven years. People came and went. Eleanor was not with the Professor much. She was there when you looked for her. She was like one of those eternal figures seated on the banks of the Nile.

It was not that nothing had happened to me during those seven years (there were times when what was happening to us, Jason, was like the knives of kingfishers' wings above dark pools of light). It was just that what was happening now, around and about this battle-area, was connected, I suppose, to what had happened to me that first time I was in London and also during my time in the Garden; there are these jumps, are there not, every seven years (at the end of each segment of the staircase?). You land, and you are ready to take off again; to take the lid off a further box, is it? (Where there are bits and pieces like light?)

I am so grateful still (prayers remain the same) for all of this: for the sheep like stars and the kingfishers' wings and the fishes that go back to the rivers where they were born. I am grateful to the chaos and darkness: to the sun and moon like gravity. I am grateful to you: to Bert; to the Professor: to everyone I have ever loved: to you and you who are with me now (who are you!). There are the other figures, statues, stories, around some corner. Walls fall down: birds whizz between openings in the maze.

There is myself walking through that wood; there is myself at the window writing this. The Professor is a little better today, thank you. Bert is coming to visit us. Eleanor was here the other day.

And where are you, Jason! Of course, it was right for you

to stay away. Things will sort themselves out. You will be, yes, with your child and Lilia.

But would you have written it like that, if you had not thought that you would one day come across me again!

The undergrowth on either side of the path through the wood had become trampled as if armies had passed there: among the trees there were mounds, or scrap-heaps, of ply-wood, plastic and sacking – the shelters of what had been the encampment of the women. I thought – Why are men so frightened of witches? is it because they fear the darkness in themselves – that of the hags in the temple, as well as that of the child?

But it is true that in those old dramas, when men came across women at their secret rituals in the forest, it was the men who were torn to pieces.

You used to say – What will happen when women come smiling out of the forest: then men will see that they have been their own terror?

I was going further into the forest. I thought – I am like Red Riding Hood going to visit her grandmother: of course Red Riding Hood knew her grandmother was a wolf! why else would she have gone to visit her?

In this strange wood there were bits of wool like knitting hung from the trees. I thought – Yes, but if women become gentle, authoritative, will there be networks like spiders' webs, like notations for music, hung from trees?

– Hullo, hullo, do you hear me?

In story-books things happen by chance, do they not?

In a further clearing of the forest there was a horse. The horse was standing with its reins hanging down. I thought – There was that figure riding on the edge of the battle-area?

Did not Lilia say that Eleanor had her horse?

At the back of the clearing in the forest was a Nissen-type hut with the door off its hinges. In the middle of the clearing there was the remains of a fire. The horse was standing by the fire with its reins hanging down. Eleanor was lying on the ground beside the horse.

I thought – Well, why should it in fact be more unusual that one set of things should happen rather than another?

Eleanor was lying on her back with her hands folded. She wore a long dress of rough material the colour of earth. I thought – Come on, where is that ring of fire!

Lilith used to lie on her rock? Brunnhilde was asleep for – what? – more than seven years!

I remember saying to you once – Don't you think it is ridiculous how travellers in novels of the eighteenth century keep on bumping into one another? and you said – Perhaps it was because there were so few travellers in the eighteenth century.

Do you think there are so few travellers in this dimension now?

Eleanor was this elderly lady with a pudding-basin haircut. I knew, yes, it was her custom to travel round on a horse. I knew she had been intending to visit the camp of the women. You see, I am on my guard: it is counter-productive to talk of luck?

I said to the Professor today – What is chance? He said – Chance is what you have techniques to observe but not to explain. I said – Such as what goes on in an atom. He said – Oh, for goodness' sake, an atom!

I sat on the fallen trunk of a tree some distance from Eleanor. If there is unheard music, and time has to pass – we can walk across a stage and sit upon ruined pillars?

Eleanor lay as if on a tomb. I thought – And a tree, I suppose, might grow out of her middle!

The Professor has been in some pain today. It was Eleanor who taught me to press upwards and outwards with my hands: to feel for the stone within the tree: to say – Is it here? Is it here?

We separate the earth from the firmament – in seven days: in seven years?

When Eleanor woke – old people, unlike children, wake as if they had never been away – she put out a hand as if to feel that her horse was there: she took hold of its bridle; the horse raised its head, and Eleanor was lifted by this into a sitting position. She said 'Hullo.' I said 'Hullo.' She said 'What's up?' I said 'I don't know.' She said 'I'm not surprised.'

Eleanor had these bright-blue eyes in a nut-brown face. She must have been about seventy at this time. She journeyed on her horse: she used to pop up here and there like someone in a mediaeval tapestry. (You thought I was going to say a fun-fair shooting-range?) One got the impression from her of a unicorn round some corner.

I said 'Lilia's lost her child. We thought he might be with you. Lilia's holed up with some official. Bert's got a story about a bomb being planted in the battle-area.'

Eleanor said 'How's Max?'

I said 'He's not too bad.'

'Is the pain any better?'

'Yes, I think it's better.'

The horse kept on pulling at Eleanor's arm as she held the bridle, so that her arm worked up and down like a pump.

I said 'And Bert got picked up by a helicopter.'

She said 'He'd like that.'

I said 'Yes. He'd climbed to the top of the façade of that building. I expect the helicopter belongs to his film company.'

She said 'Bert likes to feel omnipotent.'

When one talks with Eleanor there is often the impression of topics coming to an end: as if anything further would be over the edge of the paper.

I said 'I thought we should look for the child.'

She said 'Yes let's.'

I said 'He wasn't with you?'

Eleanor said 'No. But he might have been with me.'

I thought – You know the code; should you not know the message?

I said 'Where do you think he could have gone? He was on his bicycle.'

'You think he might have gone in to the battle-area?'

I said 'Why?'

She said 'You're anxious about this bomb.'

I said 'Bert used to tell him stories. He used to go there. When they were staying in the cottage.'

'Yes.'

I thought I might say – Why are you smiling?

She said 'Today would be a good day to go. Everyone will be out and around the airbase.'

I thought I might say – You know about the bomb?

I said 'Bert says they've got hold of this radioactive material.'

She said 'Why does he say that?'

I could not make out why, with the horse pulling so hard at Eleanor's arm, she did not stand up.

I said 'We must do something.'

She said 'Yes.' Then – 'I'm afraid I've sprained my ankle.'

I said 'Oh, I see.'

She said 'That's all right.'

I thought I might say – I can't live like this! I might stamp my foot on the ground and cry.

Eleanor said 'You could go on the horse, but I don't think he would leave me.'

I said 'I can't leave you!'

Eleanor said to the horse 'Will you go with this lady?'

The horse jerked its head so that the reins were pulled out of Eleanor's hand: it moved and stood at some distance.

Eleanor said 'What we need is some form of transport.'

She tried to get to her feet. I put a hand under her arm and lifted her.

There was the sound of a car, or lorry, coming through the forest: it was in low gear, grinding, querulous. I thought – It will be some monster, I suppose, that she has called up out of her head. Then – You do see, it is difficult to be like this. Eleanor seemed to be trying not to notice the noise. I thought – You make your mind a blank, then your number comes up on the wheel: but how with your mind do you make your mind a blank? And so on. Eleanor and I stood, arm in arm, with the horse drooping its head somewhere behind us. I thought – We are like a painting – of English country life in the eighteenth century.

It was a van, or minibus, that was coming through the wood: its windscreen was tinted so that one could not see inside. Eleanor said 'Or we could go to the cottage: he might have gone there.' I thought – What do you mean, we could go to the cottage? there is this frightful van or minibus coming through the wood: it is summoned up by witches.

The van, or minibus, came into the clearing and stopped. It was like an animal with antennae instead of eyes watching us.

I thought – You are supposed to wait, aren't you, till you see the whites of its eyes.

After a time the driver's door opened but no one got out. I thought – An object from outer space might look like a minibus in a forest?

Eleanor put a hand to her mouth as if she were laughing.

From the driving compartment a figure eventually emerged; it wore a khaki track-suit or battledress; it had a balaclava helmet over its head. It was difficult to tell whether it was a man or a woman.

The figure watched us. I thought – All right, Eleanor, now carry on with your manipulation of spirits!

The figure made a gesture towards us; it seemed to be telling us to go away. Or to come towards it. What do you do: smile and nod: offer it some sugar?

Two more people got out of the back of the van: one wore a balaclava helmet, and the other had a woollen cap and a huge profile that looked like a mask. It was difficult to tell whether they were men or women.

The first figure came towards us and made a gesture as if for us to go to the van. It still did not speak. This figure had a strange white face as if it were powdered; or as if it were an albino Negro.

Eleanor said 'What do you want?' Then – 'Can we help you?'

The figure took hold of Eleanor by the arm. The other two were getting something out of the back of the van: it was a stretcher on which was an object covered by a blanket. The object did not seem to be a body because it had no head nor legs. From underneath the blanket a piece of plastic hung down. I thought – This is nothing: not even ridiculous.

Eleanor was saying to the figure like an albino. 'You want us to get into the van.' Then – 'I've sprained my ankle.'

Myself and the figure helped Eleanor towards the van. The other two had gone with the stretcher into the Nissen-type hut with the door off its hinges. They came out without the stretcher: they tried to close the door. Eleanor said 'I did it when I was getting off my horse.'

None of the figures had spoken. The two from the hut had come to the van and we all helped Eleanor into the back. I thought – She is treating this as if it were an ambulance?

– But don't be taken in by this: it really might be an ambulance!

I said 'What about the horse?' Eleanor said 'What about the horse?' Then – 'These people seem to be giving us a lift.' In the back of the van there was a bench along either side and a small window through to the front. The side windows were boarded up. I thought – You know what you're doing? Will anyone, ever again, know what they are doing?

Then – These people are not speaking because they do not want us to recognise their voices? You mean, they might have guns?

I had begun to move away from the van towards the horse. The figure with the white face and the balaclava helmet came after me and took hold of my arm. I had the impression that it was a woman. Eleanor called to her 'You don't want us to have seen you?' Then – 'Indeed, it's not as if we have seen you!'

I thought – You mean, you think we might get away with this?

The woman with the white face led me back to the van. Eleanor was sitting on one of the benches in the back. She said 'The horse will find its own way.'

I got into the van and sat on the bench opposite. I thought – You think we will find our own way?

The other two figures had climbed into the van: the one with the white face shut the back doors. The second figure with a balaclava helmet sat between Eleanor and the door: he or she seemed to have a beard. The one with a profile like a mask sat between me and the door. I thought – Her face might be made of rubber; you pull it off, and there might be the same face underneath.

Eleanor said 'This was always happening to St Theresa.'

I said 'What was?'

She said 'Being picked up and taken somewhere and put down where she hadn't known she wanted to go.'

The van moved off. The ground was bumpy. We clung to the edges of our seats.

I thought – You mean, this is some experiment? There are people in white coats watching switches and dials?

– This is what people think who are mad?

– But if this is happening, who is or is not mad?

Eleanor had closed her eyes. I thought – She is meditating? She is in pain?

The van went over stony ground.

I thought – But might we not be like those people who just lined up on a platform to be shot?

Eleanor opened her eyes and smiled at me.

I said 'But letting things happen like this, mightn't it be like all those people who lined up on a platform?'

She said 'Well, for one thing, they did have an extraordinary effect.'

I said 'What?'

She said 'They altered the world.'

I said 'But they died.'

She said 'But the people who killed them were obliterated.'

The van went over a bump and the person with a profile like a mask hit her or his head against the roof. I thought – But I don't want to die!

Or – You mean, there was some resurrection?

The van was going through the wood. We could not see out of the windows. We were being shaken about like dice.

Eleanor said 'What no one knows is what would have happened if those people had seen what was happening.'

I thought – You think we see what is happening?

Then – But, of course, if one sees, one doesn't know the outcome of an experiment.

Eleanor said 'Some survived.'

The van seemed to get on to a road, or at least to where the ground was smoother. Eleanor leaned back and closed her eyes.

I thought I might say – You mean there are coincidences?

Eleanor would say – Yes, there are coincidences.

I could say – But you can't say – Some survived!

The van travelled smoothly for a time. The figure with a face like a mask held its head. The figure with a beard tried to rearrange the opening of its balaclava helmet. I thought – Perhaps they will take their heads right off, and have a look, and there will be those spikes going up inside.

I tried to make my mind go blank. How, even now, does one make one's mind go blank? Memories come in like the battle between the Lapiths and the Centaurs.

I thought – But there, outside the picture, are couples watching, in the gallery; their arms round each other's shoulders.

The van went off the road again. The figure with a mask hit its head against the roof again. The figure with a beard got up to help; he or she was bounced violently from side to side. I thought – Oh well, we are now inside this picture, we are agents being bashed about in occupied territory.

Eleanor said 'Have you ever done any of his experiments with dice?'

I said 'The Professor's? No, I never have.'

I thought – You mean, the one where you think you can influence the dice if you empty your mind of any thought that you can influence the dice –

She said 'But you know the one I mean – '

I thought – Here, what is happening is so empty that mutations might have a chance?

We seemed to be going across rolling countryside – the hills of Java perhaps, where some sort of consciousness had been born. I thought – If one emptied one's mind of thoughts, of plans, of memories, would there be figures in the clouds, reclining on one arm, looking down as if on a green baize table?

I said 'You know those skulls of primitive humans or pre-humans which had had holes knocked in the bottom of them in order to get out the brains so people could eat them?'

Eleanor said 'Yes.'

I said 'But they had holes in the bottom anyway for the spinal column to go up, so why did people want to knock another hole?'

Eleanor said 'Perhaps they thought they had to have two to get the brains out whole.' She laughed.

When Eleanor laughed her whole face lit up as if Catherine wheels were going round.

The van swerved so violently that this time it seemed about to overturn. I was thrown across and had to hold myself off the opposite wall with my arms on either side of Eleanor: we seemed to be saying hullo or good-bye. The figure with a mask had a knee in the groin of the person with a beard. The van seemed to have hit a rock, or the stump of a tree. It had stopped. There was the clatter of a helicopter overhead.

I thought – We are about to be rescued? To be shot? To be rolled out on to some strange planet like dice?

From the front of the van there was the whirring noise of the starter not working. The person with a mask was trying to open the back door of the van which had stuck. There was a smell of steam and scorching.

I said to Eleanor 'Are you all right?'

She said 'Yes, I'm all right.'

I thought – You can't mean, simply, that these people will destroy themselves?

The woman who was the driver had come round and was pulling at the back doors of the van. The person with a beard

263

kicked at the doors. They opened and caught the driver in the face. I thought – You are overdoing this!

The person with the beard scrambled out of the back of the van and started running towards a wood.

The driver shouted – 'Come back!'

She was holding her nose. I thought – But I wouldn't anyway have recognised the accent.

It seemed that what had happened was that the van had turned off a track which went over rolling countryside and had tried to get under the cover of a wood: this had probably been in order to get away from the helicopter. There the van had hit a fallen stump or log, and there had been damage to the bottom of the engine.

The helicopter was flying overhead – then just around some corner.

The person with a beard had stopped at the edge of the wood. The driver who was like an albino was helping the figure with the face like a mask to get out.

Eleanor said to them 'Go quickly!'

The helicopter was coming round again. I thought – Perhaps it is Bert: or that wild-haired girl with a sword above a battlefield.

The two remaining figures began to run, stumbling, towards the wood.

Eleanor and I were left in the back of the van.

I thought – Well here we are, when the sun comes up –
– *En plein!* Bingo!

I said 'But I know this place!'

Eleanor said 'Yes.'

I said 'I used to come here!'

Eleanor said 'He used to come here, too.'

I thought – You mean, all this time, we have been looking for the child?

The helicopter went on over the tops of trees.

Beyond us, where the van had turned off into the wood, there was a wide stretch of open grassland, bumped and pitted as if with shell-holes. Part of it, at the top of a slope, was enclosed within a wire fence – as so often in this empty countryside. There was a wooden hut within this enclosure. This was one of the places, sometimes a tourist attraction, where primitive men had dug for flints.

I said 'I'm lost.'

Eleanor said 'I thought you knew where you were.'

I said 'I mean – I don't know what I mean.'

I helped Eleanor out of the back of the van. It was a bright spring afternoon. I thought – Now be careful, on the edge of this strange landscape.

Eleanor said 'We'd better just go, now we're here, and have a look at those flint-mines.'

I thought – You become accustomed to this style? After a time, and if the ground is right, a mutation becomes conventional?

We were, yes, looking for the child.

I walked up the slope with Eleanor. I had my arm around her: we walked without much difficulty. I suppose I was to some extent taken over by Eleanor. She had a way of making even ordinary things seem extraordinary. So, I suppose, she made extraordinary things seem ordinary.

You don't know Eleanor all that well, do you? (You, not you.)

I had once gone to see Eleanor in order to talk about you, Jason, and Bert: this was when she was still working professionally. She had that room in Hampstead with her bits and pieces on the walls – her horses from China: her smiling figures from Etruscan tombs. I said I was in a muddle between you and Bert; I did not know what to do. I sat in a high-backed chair (there was her couch, empty, like a tomb) and she watched me with those all-things-bright-and-beautiful eyes. After a time, what I was saying seemed to have nothing to do with anything: I was saying what I was expected to say: but who was it who was expecting me? certainly not Eleanor. I mean – Of course Eleanor was expecting me to say these things, but this was because she knew that it was I who felt this was expected of me: and so on. So after a time I stopped. There

265

had been that sensation (we are surely becoming accustomed to this!) of all the lights coming on in a theatre. I said 'I don't know why I'm saying all this.' She said 'Don't you?' I said 'No.' She said 'You want me to know what an exciting time you're having.' I said 'Why do I want you to know what an exciting time I'm having?' She said 'You were the lucky one, weren't you, who was expected to have an exciting time in your family?'

With my mother and father, I suppose, at the place where those people had had the bottoms of their skulls bashed out – bashing each other's skulls out –

I had then thought – I will never be like this! I will never let my children feel so superior!

I had said to Eleanor – But that's terrible! Eleanor had said – Why is it terrible? I had said – That I have come here to show off to you! She had said – But I don't think it's terrible. Then – Though perhaps you won't always want to have that sort of exciting time.

With all the lights coming on, is it one's family who get up and leave the theatre?

It was just after this, I think, that Eleanor had said, as all of you at some time or other seem to say, that thing about what people are frightened of is not having too little but having too much.

Eleanor and I were moving up the slope towards the flint-mines. We were (I had to remind myself) looking for the child. Well, what have I told you about these flint-mines? they are quite well known: they are where some of the earliest traces of humans in Britain have been found. The best flints are ten or twelve metres below the surface; pits were dug with tunnels giving off at the bottom; the flints were lifted to the surface by ropes and baskets. With the discovery of metal, flints had been needed less and so the mines had been abandoned and had fallen in. They had been excavated some four thousand years later and one of them had been opened for tourists; there was a hut above it with a ladder going down.

Eleanor and I were struggling up the slope. I did not know

why I had not left her by the van. I did not know why, or why not, anything. Eleanor said 'He liked coming here.' I said 'Yes, I guess he would like coming here.' We came to the hut above the mine which was sometimes open to the public. It did not seem to be open now; perhaps because it was too early in the year. But the door was off its hinges.

I thought – What does it mean, it doesn't mean anything, these doors being off their hinges? Then – the people in the van were coming here?

I sat Eleanor down with her back against the wall of the hut. She smiled, and looked up at the sun. I said 'Will you be all right?' She said 'Yes, I'll be all right.' I said 'I'd better go down.' She said 'Yes, you'd better go down.' Then – 'I'm sorry.'

I said 'I expect there'll be nothing there.'

She said 'Yes, indeed, there may be nothing there.'

I did not want to go in through the door that was off its hinges. I suppose I was frightened. I tried to remember – What happens when you are frightened?

I said 'I wonder why they didn't speak?'

Eleanor said 'Then we can go on to the cottage.'

I thought – You mean, this is almost literally a journey through the maze?

This rolling green tract of land set around with fir plantations was not within the battle-area: it was on the edge: it was also quite close to what they referred to as the cottage.

I thought – This is some sort of initiation?

– You are blindfolded, go into holes in the ground, and there are people in masks like shadows on the walls – and all that rubbish?

– But even then, is it not true that you are looking for a child?

I said to Eleanor again 'Will you be all right?'

Eleanor said 'Of course I'll be all right!'

When I pulled at the door of the hut it came away in my hands. I thought – Why shouldn't I be frightened? those figures on clouds watching –

– This is a state of grace?

Within the hut it was dark. There was a counter where sometimes they sold tickets and postcards: there was a railing around the hole in the ground with the ladder going down. There used to be torches, I remembered, kept under the counter: I did not think that there would be torches now. Perhaps then I would not have to go down. I felt underneath the counter and there was a torch: I thought – If this is a ritual, it is some going down into the Pit? The torch was one of those box-like things with a handle; when it swung it made shadows on the wall; they came leaping out like tigers. I thought – Some sort of homage to those people in the cave? you sometimes have to go back, do you, in order to be out? It was conceivable, of course, that the child might have come this way. I began to climb down the ladder. The hole was about two metres wide. You remember when we came here that Sunday afternoon: you climbed down the ladder first, and when I got almost to the bottom you said – Wrap your legs around me and we'll go over the rim of the world. I said – God, you are boring! Why is it that when women are pleased, they often say to men – God, you are boring! I was climbing down the ladder with the torch making shadows on the wall. This was to do with sex? back to the womb? The child might have looked in here, fallen, on his way to the cottage: but you never truly know why you are doing things, do you? or how can you trust? and so what would be grace? There has to be just one thing after the other. At the bottom of the pit there was the level where primitive men had dug flints: and used them to bash one another's skulls in, probably; and eaten each other's brains. There was some burned wood and ashes as if people had been making a fire here: I thought – You mean, these people were amongst the first to make fire? Then – For God's sake, there have been people down here recently with a fire! Then – It would be a good place to shelter, wouldn't it, if there were a bomb going off? So, this is not ridiculous. There were five or six tunnels going off horizontally from the bottom of the pit: they were six or seven metres long and a metre high. I

268

thought – I suppose I have to crawl along each, one by one; it is no good my going on asking why. I got down on my hands and knees and started crawling; I thought – Or I am that sperm looking for life in a Fallopian tube: hullo, hullo, my little one. Down one of the tunnels, at the end, there were bits of old straw, and a suitcase. I mean there was a suitcase, closed, upright, at the end of one of the tunnels. It was like that enigmatic rectangular object in one of those space films. I thought – Well, what are you trying to tell me: or what am I trying to learn? Perhaps nothing. Or am I learning about nothing? I thought I should go quickly down the one or two other tunnels and then up and out again: I did this: then I had to go back to check that the suitcase was real. Well, you don't quite believe things, do you? or it is difficult to tear yourself away from certain mysteries? It was an old-fashioned leather suitcase with a handle on top: all packed up and ready to go. I thought – At least it is not wrapped in plastic. It is simply a dead-end of the maze. When I was climbing up the ladder again I felt I should go back even once more to make sure: but of what? that such things are ridiculous? I wanted to say – But will you learn, then, my little one! I went on up the ladder. I found Eleanor at the top still with her eyes closed facing the sun. I thought – Well, that was quite brave? Then – How brave are children to hang on!

I said to Eleanor 'There's a suitcase.'

Eleanor said 'A suitcase.'

I said 'Closed, with a handle, at the end of one of the tunnels.'

Eleanor smiled like fireworks again; like Roman candles.

I said 'What do you think it is?'

Eleanor said 'I don't know. I don't suppose it's anything.'

I said 'Do you think they left it here? Do you think they were coming to fetch it?'

Eleanor said 'Perhaps it belongs to the caretaker of the flint-mines. Perhaps it's where he keeps his clothes.'

A Land-Rover had appeared on the track by the wood along which we had previously come in the van. It had stopped.

There was the broken-down van just ahead of it in the wood.

Eleanor said 'You go on. I'll tell them. I'll stay here.'

I wanted to say to Eleanor – What I wanted to talk to you about was me and Bert! about whether or not we should marry!

Eleanor said 'There's a church with a broken spire. We used to go there on the horse.'

I said 'A church with a broken spire?'

She said 'Yes.'

I said 'I'll go to the cottage first.'

Then – 'I do love Bert, you know.'

Eleanor said 'Yes, I know.'

I began to walk across the landscape with the mounds and pits in it like old shell-craters. I thought I should have said again to Eleanor – You will be all right? But I wanted to get away before anyone saw me from the Land-Rover. I began to run. I thought – This is a strange life; but this is a strange old planet. I did not think that the Land-Rover would be able to come after me, because there were fences and woods between myself and the cottage: even if the Land-Rover went by the road, I could get there first.

I thought – What I am looking for is not only the child: it is also what would be the child's way of looking at things.

Then – It is not as if I were mad; it is as if I were looking down on myself moving freely among people who are likely to be mad.

I was out of sight of the Land-Rover. The child, certainly, might be at the cottage. You had been staying there last summer, had you not? Did Lilia say you had been there at Christmas?

When had my own child been conceived?

I should explain about this cottage: to you; to you.

The cottage had once belonged to Lilia and the Professor: then all of us took to staying there on and off. Perhaps it was somewhere where we went when we felt ourselves caught up by matters of love and hate and birth and death.

I thought – Is it death people run away from? But I have been down into that tomb!

I came to one of the fir plantations. There was a fence. Then there were those strange whisperings overhead. I thought – This is the path where you, Jason, and I once walked. Is it the plantation in your story where you walked with Lilia and the child?

What did make you write your plays and story like that? They were to be some nucleus, for a cell?

Soon I would come to the wild rhododendrons. They were unusual, you said, in this part of the country.

On Easter Saturday, when one does not die, does one go to visit shadows of the past? is this the Harrowing of Hell?

There are things about the past, of course, that I have not told you. Shall I tell you now? (To tell the truth, there has to be more than one letter, or description, or meaning, do you not think?)

– Oh happy fault, or whatever it was, that got us out of paradise, that Easter Saturday, and round to the back way!

When I came to this cottage with you, Jason, you met me at the railway station (where was Lilia? was it then that I got the impression that she did not mind? that she liked doing, as it were, her own thing?). I had always seen the cottage as something out of *Giselle* or *La Traviata:* there was wistaria and honeysuckle over the porch: if one could not imagine oneself innocent here – well, why build such a stage-set? Not just for sex: there is the movement of souls, is there not, in fairy tales. One falls in love, I suppose, as one might fall into a pool like Narcissus: but after this there is a vision beyond the walls of caves. You follow Plato's dark horse: you sprout wings: you are on the road to the gods again. I was going along the path through the rhododendrons: would the wistaria be in flower at this time of year? There, indeed, was the cottage in its clearing: it was more lonely than I remembered it: what do places exist as when you are not there? I remembered where the key was kept: you had said – If people want to break in they do not need a key: and I had thought – Do you break in, or do you have a key, when you have been right round the world? – and so on. The key was in its slot in one of the beams in the roof of the porch. There was the large brass knocker on the front door. I had thought – Knock, and it shall be opened: you are not burglars, if you are in love?

There was the chest with the telephone in the narrow hall; the door to the kitchen from which I had listened while you rang up Lilia. You had put on that terrible voice. What are the connections people think they know about between good and evil?

In the kitchen there was the scrubbed oak table where I had sat while you had cooked: you had said – Of course it's sensible to have more than one love: it gives security. I had said – Who wants security? You had said – So long as we both keep moving.

I had said – All men want to imagine women are like Judith! then they can think their heads are being chopped off, and so need have no conscience.

You had said – Only people who don't feel don't have to have pretences.

And so on. Why do people quarrel, do you know?

On the other side of the hallway was the sitting-room with the huge open fireplace. I had sat on the rug in front of the fire. You had drunk a lot of wine: why do you think men drink wine: so that they can get out of going to bed with women like Judith? I had said – But you and I don't have pretences: do we not feel?

I suppose I might have said – Please will you drive me to the railway station.

When we made love on that rug (it is not always easy to crawl back into that cave: that salt-lick is often the end of tears) it was as if there were some tending, yes, of whatever it is to feel and not to feel: to be both helpless and in control. How can you manage this: are these the fantasies or the realities of childhood?

It was the next afternoon, I suppose, that we walked through the rhododendrons to the flint-mines. You said – The part of us that looks down has to be kind to that terrible part that needs mothers – or children – and so on.

I said – Well, anyway, I love you.

272

When now I went into the sitting-room I found the curtains closed and the light indeed ghostly: there was that rug in front of the fire. What can I say now: there is that kindly part that looks down? In front of the fire – do you not call it the innocence of childhood?

You knew, did you not, about me and Bert? Why else should you have talked about our both going from one person to another? But you do not know, do you, that we had come here, Bert and I – not so long before you and I went back to India – to that rug in front of the fire? This is what I should tell you?

There is always some going down into the pit in making love: some Easter Saturday.

Such shadows pile in! it is like those people in the telephone-box. There are your dreams, your images of other people, your images of yourself. It is because of the embellishments, I suppose, that there is such glamour in love. But then what you find is some sort of unexplained suitcase there; some dead-end; some bomb; some package of babies' clothes.

Bert once made a film about this; do you remember?

There were two or more frames within the screen in which quite separate events were seen to be occurring: separate in place, that is: perhaps in time: the point was – in effect, what is separate and what is not? One frame kept nudging into the other. There was some crusader, was there not, who was away at war: he was in combat with an enemy: his sword was raised; he would either kill or be killed. In the other frame his wife, left at home, was about to take a lover. Something bulged out from one frame to the other: the lover's foot, perhaps, knocked against the elbow of the crusader so that it was he, unbalanced, who was killed. Or the crusader's hand, struggling for a hold, pushed against the wife so that for an instant she turned away on the bed: she had some memory, perhaps, of her husband: how sad she became! perhaps she pushed away, even, her lover on the bed. This was, was meant to be, like life: why does one do things, do you know? One is nudged by shadows; which one cannot talk about, because one does not know.

273

And it was like this, it seemed, in front of the fire. There was that rug: there were the things that you know and do not know: Bert's foot, perhaps kicking at us to make you go: well, why does one move this way rather than that? Why is one happy or sad? And then there was the Professor – why should I be telling you this now? because he might be dying? because he might be pleased at some nudge in honour of his life? I mean, I had come with the Professor once long ago to this cottage – the bodies piling up as if into that telephone-box – all those hands, feet, noses, pushing at one another; myself and you and Bert and the Professor: all going about our business of – what? getting out of the tin can? getting into and out of that box? helping each other up and out, might one even say, with an arm, a leg, a shoulder? There is always something wounding in love: if you are not wounded (that girl by the estuary) why should you want to get out (as you do)?

And what might be a father?

Is not this vision to do with what making love is – the acceptance of what might seem to be worms in a can; that by this vision, by its being beautiful, you may seem free? I mean, the acceptance is in the mind: so what would it be in reality? Well, there are those jostling, fighting, childish things, are there not: to gain identity, to lose it: sperms, to be accepted by the egg. But whether they are accepted, or are not, it is they who are lost: what is found, if anything, is the child. I mean something new might be born – anywhere. You take this chance, don't you? But the egg too is another dimension. You accept the bitching, the cheating, the pain, the betrayal – if you are the egg: if you are creating the child.

The room was still half in darkness. The curtains were not yet opened. I thought – It is not difficult to accept this.

Do you remember how you told me a story about Lilia – about the first time that you met her? She had said – I only go to bed with people I don't like: and you had said – Then that's all right, either we go to bed or else we like one another. Well, when I came to the cottage with the Professor he said – Shall I tell you a story about Lilia: the first time I met her she said – and so on. And I thought – Good: so what? and I think this now. This makes me love Lilia. Here we all are, these worms in the box: you take the lid off: why should we not also be bits and pieces of light?

Of course, the child was not in the cottage. There did not seem to have been anyone in the cottage for some time. I thought – Why not: too many of us have been here?

– We are all now out in the sun!

Bert said once – I came down here to see Lilia when she was pregnant. She had thought of getting rid of the child. I told her not to. I told her to marry Jason.

Is this true?

There is that empty nest in the dust.

I thought I would draw the curtains from the window. There would be the unmowed lawn, the hedge, the field across the plantation of fir trees. Beyond that was the battle-area. Of course, I had not gone into the battle-area when I had stayed here: I had only gone that once to the flint-mines.

I thought – So where is the child?

Did you not say that you had the impression, once, that he was looking down from a corner of the ceiling?

I drew back the curtains from the picture window. There was the lawn, the hedge, the field, the line of fir trees. Beyond that was the battle-area.

The window was made of plate glass. I could see behind me, half-reflected, the images of the room; not now only the shadows superimposed on the rug in front of the fire, but the chairs, bookcases, the dresser on the shelves of which bits and pieces of past lives were sometimes displayed – that pennant from the Spanish Civil War; Bert's machine for demonstrating Catastrophe Theory; the medallion you picked up from the sea near Masada. Also reflected in the plate glass was my own face: a face which seemed to contain – such was the effect – both the lawn and the hedge and fir plantations out in front and the room with its images of the past behind: containing these as if they were in some box, but now, indeed, with the lid half off; the light making everything semi-transparent, semi-opaque; but (again) what was light? I had been staring at my image in the window for some time.

There is a technique – do you know it? – to make your reflection disappear: you stare at yourself without blinking: you have arranged beside you a small source of light like a candle: after a while your face begins to take on shapes and sizes that you have never seen – those unborn might-have-beens of yourself, do you think, in their corners of the ceiling – and then in time you disappear: I mean your face in the glass disappears: in the place where it was there is simply nothing: or light. Well, I had been looking at myself like this for some time; and I had been thinking – You do not want yourself exactly to disappear! You say you love yourself: and now you love all those shadows in the room behind: so what you want, as usual, is to have everything all ways: to be yourself, to contain multitudes, and at the same time to get out. I thought – Well, all right, have I not said I accept just such prolifera-tion? And the danger of being burned outside, as if by the sun – do I not accept this too? I made a joke – After all, is not fire light? And at this moment the window – now you will not believe this; there may be several things here you may not quite believe, but least of all this; I mean, I don't really know if I believe it – the window broke. I mean, there was pressure going in and out against my eardrums, eyeballs, mind: the impression of a musical instrument being played but nothing heard because what one was involved with was simply vibra-tions: the light itself, like something material, seeming to go in and out: and then the window disintegrated, collapsed out-wards, in bits and pieces on the grass. I mean, there might have been explanations for other things that had happened this odd day: but not for just this moment, as I looked into the glass as if it were the wall of that cave containing shadows, and it dissolved so delicately, so precisely, like pieces of light. I mean, I had been thinking of that cave in which people were trapped and whatever it was stopped them from going out into the sun: and now – well, does there not have to be some chance coming in from outside? It became apparent quite soon, I suppose, that some sort of bomb had gone off: the glass had seemed to bulge outwards for a moment and then in and then out again; it had been like water breaking (well, yes, a birth?) then bits of light fell very gently to earth. I did not know where the bomb had gone off. There had been the pressure, and then the bang just after: the bomb must have been at some distance away. I went on trying to explain this to myself. The pressure did not seem to have come from in front; how had the glass fallen outwards? but how could it have come from behind, since the doors of the room were closed. And so on. Unless it had come from (another joke!) my mind. But would not that indeed be (and in what sense?) how a person in the cave might get out? – to the lawn, and the hedgerow, and the battle-area beyond. I thought – Oh well, if it has been the fear of death that has stopped us getting out – it is too late now to worry, surely, even if (or because) there has been that bomb. If we are to survive, if we want to survive, do we not have to say – So what? – to those bits and chances of death; to those portentous figures on clouds even: you think they want us not to want to get out?

There are breaking-points to substances, are there not? These are almost unexplained: they are called catastrophes: they are to do with birth and death: why are you laughing?

I could now step out into the sun.

There might be, of course, a real danger of being burned as if by some sun; if it was that sort of bomb that had gone off.

There was a column of smoke going up from somewhere in the direction of the American airbase.

I thought – The column, drawn by six white horses, rose to a height of several thousand feet –

Let's have one more effort at practical explanation, shall we?

There had been an explosion, at some distance, because of the gap between the pressure and the sound. There was no evidence that the explosion had occurred in the battle-area (though no evidence that it had not): there was evidence from the smoke that it had come from the direction of the airbase. There was no knowing why this particular window had blown: you can break a glass by singing, can't you? Perhaps someone had sung: perhaps some finger had come down: had I

277

not been singing in my mind: you do not call such explanations practical? You used to say – I mean everyone who arrives in this sort of area is accustomed to say – that there are states which are best described by metaphors. I stepped into the sun through the jagged splinters of light which were like glass. I thought – Perhaps what I am stepping into is, yes, a painting, a picture; the realisation of a metaphor.

Hullo, hullo, can you hear me?

I thought I would walk across the lawn to the small gate in the hedgerow. Perhaps the child had come this way.

The sun is death: the sun is life. I am practising.

I thought suddenly – Lilia, Bert, will be all right by the airbase?

The lawn was unmown; the gate through the hedge was on rusty hinges. I thought I should go out of the gate, across the field, and into the wood. And thus into the battle-area. Of course, I was looking for the child.

I wanted to go back again over what had happened – but you must not look back, must you, now you are here.

The experience does seem to be aesthetic. Have you not often said – One should know what to do, or rather do without exactly knowing, in the same way that one knows, or at least does, about a painting or a piece of writing? I mean by looking at it, having learned, you know you should do this or that (you can't always) but it goes if you try to explain it.

I used to say – Is not this also a characteristic of a madman?

You had said – The fact that you can say that, is not a characteristic of a madman.

Between the gate of the hedgerow and the fir plantation was rolling, pitted ground – this was another of the places where primitive men had looked for flints. And had found – what? – that in order to stay alive you had to eliminate this or that, as in a painting? –

I thought – But how do you bear this?

In one of the hollows of old pits there was a child's bucket and spade. It looked as if he had been digging.

I thought – One day, with other humans, we will stay alive without killing: or if we do not, what is the difference?

I did not think that the child's bucket and spade meant that he must just now have come this way: but it did seem to be some sign, as if it were a note of music hung from a tree, that I was following him.

You know the message: this sort of thing is the code?

– A fossil, planted by God, to remind you that the world might be recreated each day –

– A feather, from the wings of the bird that went its own way with an olive-branch in its mouth –

– Someone trying to dig a deep shelter through to the antipodes?

I was crossing the field to the line of fir trees which, I knew, was the boundary of the battle-area. This part of the boundary was distant from the ruined façade and the garden with a tomb: it was also distant in the other direction from the American airbase. In the latter direction the column of smoke bulged in the middle like some genie released from its bottle; perhaps those figures reclining on clouds were giving it a puff every now and then. At the edge of the field there was a fence with the usual notices: KEEP OUT and DANGER OF UN-EXPLODED BOMBS: there were the signs of the skull and crossbones. I thought – You need courage, do you, if you are facing the blank canvas of a painting? There was an old farm gate: a single strand of barbed wire along the top. I thought – Perhaps those angels with flaming swords are just the fear of appearing to have no hold on what you are doing; but then, if you know this, perhaps the hold is there. I prayed – I hope to God those others are all right.

I climbed the gate. I thought – I am one of those humans or pre-humans not quite yet down from the trees, setting out on my journey to the plains. My new-found language would be – silence? But I would not be all right if those others were not all right.

The silence in the trees was such that it was more than if you could hear it. I thought – Perhaps it was because those men could not bear silence that they invented speech; silence carried them like unheard music; it was this that did not seem to be in their control.

That tower that they were building up to heaven – the language of this had been silence? Speech had to come to imprison them: to give them the illusion of control?

I was over the gate and going through the fir plantation. I trod carefully: there were no paths: might there be trip-wires?

– Supposing the American airbase was a place where were stored the fruits of the Tree of Knowledge of good and evil (those missiles like snakes with death in their heads); of course here what we should now be looking for is the Tree of Life.

I mean, what child might be able to live in this strange territory?

Well, it has been said often enough, has it not, that there was a prohibition only against eating from the Tree of Knowledge of good and evil: there was no prohibition against eating from the Tree of Life. So humans, having language, ate the fruit of the Tree of Knowledge of good and evil. Language is counter-productive; they did not eat of the Tree of Life.

But a mutation (like a god) would know all this.

So the Tree of Life would then still be waiting round some corner – the child with its hand, as it were, on the collar of some fatted calf – or lamb?

I was treading carefully through the fir plantation. All this was in my mind. What is it that you can or cannot do with your mind: let it run: watch it? I was walking through the battle-area. I knew very little about the battle-area. I did not know about unexploded bombs or mines. I knew there was a sensation as if I were treading lightly on air a few inches off the ground: is this what people in Byzantine frescoes feel – that there might be trip-wires? You have been walking some time through the maze and then the bottom falls out: you hold out your arms: you are like a bird. I mean you are that which remains (are you?) when the rest has fallen through the grid, the riddle; which is the bottom of the maze.

Do you really think one is not mad if one can refer statements about this possibility back to oneself?

There were bracken and brambles underfoot: one had to step high to get through. I did not think the child would have come this way.

The battle-area was somewhere where men went to play games. They went there for no other purpose except for games: so – for once – there was no confusion. Men always play games; so in a place where there were no pretences, might there not also be something quite different – that which might grow apart from the pretences (and the predatoriness) of humans?

You once got us all into that cell, that stage: the cell was in our minds: we were in a theatre. We had to put up our hands and push against a wall – the front wall of the stage. This wall did not exist. Then we were to be hurled, like seeds, over the ploughed land of an audience.

The Tree of Life is something whose light contains its own shadow?

I was going through the wood with the light like bits of stained glass. Then ahead it became whiter. I thought – A rainbow is refracted back to its original sun. Or – A mutation might be something that would refract out, and back, and so be itself; and by this be more than itself.

I was coming to the edge of the wood. You do not see beyond the front of a stage unless the lights come on in the theatre.

Then the game is over.

By the end, the characters on a stage are often dead anyway.

But you could get up and walk about amongst an audience saying – Is it you? is it you?

Hullo, my little one.

I thought – Perhaps the child inside me will grow exposed to this strange sun and will live in its light-and-dark branches?

I was coming to the edge of the wood. It was here that the light was brighter. It was as if I were about to see through a further peephole of that box: then there would be, would there not, that bright-and-green landscape which makes its own light: and I should be able to walk amongst it.

The ground seemed to fall away at the edge of the wood. Of course, from that bomb, there might be little bits of death coming down: or seeds – you could tell the difference?

I sat on a tree-stump. What was it like when the child lay on the edge of that bed; do you remember?

You know how when you are writing or painting (have I said this before!) there is the impression that you are not creating but discovering what is already there: you have been going along in the dark for some time: is it here, is it there: then suddenly – what else is the excitement! You have been helpless for so long: well not quite helpless because you know (you have had these glimpses!) that what you are doing is uncovering; and so what is to be uncovered is there. The discipline is in the faith: you do not know what, but you know that: there has to be also, I suppose (how can you say this!), courage, skill; the skill being partly perhaps in knowing how to say – Ah, skill, how can you say that! So you let yourself go; with diligence, with pain: and then suddenly – by neither accident nor design; you have been blown round some corner – there is this extraordinary landscape.

The ground fell away into the rolling green parkland that I had seen before; in which light seemed to come not from reflection but from the objects themselves; in which trees seemed to contain their own shadows and sheep were dotted on the ground like stars. It was like the land of the hills beyond the estuary; the flowers like trees and the trees like large flowers; birds in the air like notes of music. It was also like that courtyard with the bird or finger coming down: also that place beyond the dust, I suppose, beyond the empty nest, beyond the frame, where no one except the child was looking.

The colours were vibrations; as was the music. It was indeed a landscape into which man might be said not yet to have come: because he came only to play games – and so he might be said deliberately not to have touched it.

There were thousands of lambs together with the sheep.

They were like those seeds, those chances of mutation, fallen on this ground, and waiting to see what might nourish them.

There was a road running through the landscape at the bottom of the slope – the road might almost be a river by the way it so much glistened. Or a snake – might it not be a snake? – coming down from a tree, and going for a drink along a road that could be a river.

You know that game in which you are supposed to find out, or test, the patterns of people's minds: you ask them to draw a house, a road, a river, a horse, a snake, a tree. And according to what story can be inferred from what they draw – the snake crossing the road towards the house: the horse cut off from the tree by the river – you think you can tell what is going on in their minds. But supposing there is in fact a house, a horse, a road, a snake, a tree: you have found out – what? – just that it is a sort of game that goes on in people's minds?

There was in fact a house, or what looked like a house, at the bottom of the slope, down by the road or the river. It was a house because it had four walls, a roof, a chimney: but it had nothing else; no attributes; no garden, path, outhouse, fence. It seemed as if it might be an idea of a house, before humans put anything on to it.

So – This is the nature of this strange territory?

Or do you think it was all to do with the angle of the late afternoon sun which was shining quite brightly now: like the face of a drunk man falling behind a table?

What one has to get used to, I suppose, is living and not just striving like this: chipping at the stone: being at home with what is there; watching with reverence in this strange territory. Not asking what it is – otherwise how can you find it? Of course the language is difficult. It has to circle itself: at the centre there is silence.

If one is able to walk at all in this strange territory (humans or post-humans coming down from the plains) would there not be the impression, yes, of its being precisely oneself and yet not oneself walking (the pencil or brush or whatever moving), this conjunction of what is one and what is the other being just what is emergent in the landscape – what one is discovering. And then one would know, yes, what is to be done as one knows this with a piece of writing or in a painting: just going along, in some sort of transport – of ecstasy or despair. You once said, did you not – Ecstasy and despair are the only two emotions worth having.

Or – The state of grace is where the two mean the same thing.

I was walking over the rolling grassland down to the house by the road. There were the trees dotted about like bright black holes or stars. There were not many sheep on the slope; they were farther down in the valley.

I wondered – What one cannot bear about the sun, perhaps, is simply the excitement.

Of course there might still be danger! Those bits and pieces of bombs like splinters coming down from a skylight –

The building that I was approaching – something that could be drawn in a second or two, perhaps: four lines and a roof like a hat with a bobble of a chimney on top – would be a diagram representing – well, what? the family as a statistical unit? whatever it is that is the average? the subject (or object) of an advertisement on television? Take the lid off and you would see – the family of four to six people round the breakfast-table; consuming the things they have seen a family like themselves consuming on television; smiling and looking rather daft as people do when posing for a camera. When I got close I saw that it was indeed a mock-up of a house: four walls and a roof but no doors or windows; these were just painted on; there was even painted, roughly, a figure of what might be a father or a mother or a child (or an enemy) leaning out of one of the windows. The construction had been used, obviously, in the games of war: in war you do not need real buildings; you like knocking them down, so why not have something you can put up again quickly? But was not this, indeed, somehow representative of the games of the family of four to six people around the breakfast-table? a board perhaps upon which two or more people try to occupy the same space at the same time;

on which someone succeeds, and someone fails, and someone is sent back to the beginning? I thought – Or perhaps the house has just been dumped at the side of the road like the Holy House of Loreto – come whizzing through the air as some encouragement or warning: the warning being just that this is, indeed, what families are like: unless – unless what? – you get away? whizz yourself like a bird over landscapes? There were perhaps, inside the house, my own father and mother arguing, complaining, cajoling: but I had seen myself in this, had I not? and forgiven it. All this was now like a stage-set. That one could move round it, through it, might be holy.

I walked round the building to find out if I could see inside: there might even be a further peephole: having taken the lid off the box, one might see beyond. One end of the construction was not bricked up: it was barricaded roughly with corrugated iron sheeting. There was indeed some crack or peephole through: at first I could see nothing. I thought – Don't be taken in by this! nothingness in the holy of holies? Then as my eye became accustomed I could make out – hay, fodder, racks for feeding sheep. I thought – Well, this is a bit corny: you mean just – Feed my sheep? The family of four to six around the breakfast-table? Perhaps I should go on? There was a board at the side of the corrugated sheeting which had on it in antique lettering 'The Old Mill'. I thought – Well, what might be a more recent dispensation?

The road went on towards the brow of a gentle hill. Everything was bright, and still, and exact: to do with the senses. The senses were not what interpreted the outside world: they were part of the outside world themselves: each composed, was composed of, the other. This was the at-oneness, the identity, that people longed for, I suppose, with drugs: but it was with drugs that the sun burned: in the state of grace I had gone round the sun, as it were, and here was the back way. I thought – It is as if we ourselves, now, through some further peephole, are bits and pieces of light.

The sheep and lambs were innumerable here. They were lying in the road; the road was warm to lie on; traffic seldom came. As I went past, the sheep watched me; they stretched their necks; they did not move to get out of the way. I thought – Even when people come to play games here, the sheep know that what they are doing is playing games.

The lambs stood sometimes and shook their tails so that little bits of light seemed to fall.

The column of smoke, in the direction of the airbase, was dispersing in a cloud. I thought – The tablecloth is shaken by those reclining figures; crumbs like bits of grey dust fall to the ground.

There were some strange blue flowers at the edge of the road. Their heads were like small sunflowers, their stems like trees. I thought – They are eyes? they are mutations? there is dust at the side of the road.

I came to the brow of a hill where the road went over to a valley. I stopped: there was the same, but different, landscape below. I could see much farther – to a whole world of planes, slopes, curves, lines, parkland. It was framed by the sky. In a hollow, not far away, was a village: it was of course a toy village: six or seven houses of the same kind as the one I had left – brick walls and a roof with doors and windows painted on: shadows out of the cave-box, for people to play with. And just beyond, on a slight rise in the ground, was a church. This seemed to be a real church. I mean, it was made of stone; it had a high wire fence around it; it looked derelict, destitute; which the other buildings, the toys, did not. I thought – You mean, it is one of those forbidden areas within the forbidden area, like the façade, the tomb? The church, I mean, had presumably been preserved because it was some ancient and sacred monument: it was one of those lumps beneath the skin: it was dead or dying: all its openings were boarded up. But it did have, yes – this was what Eleanor had told me to look for – a piece knocked out of its spire, which hung at an angle. I thought – You mean this X marks the spot? If it cannot be the spot itself (poor church!) it can be that cross: a finger?

It seemed that there must once have been a real village here – which had been knocked down, to be put up again as toys, so that people could knock it down and put it up more easily.

Also – The spire of that church is like the flailing arms of Petrouchka?

I went down towards the village. The houses were in a group round a village square; there was (surprise!) nothing in the square; it was one of those spaces from within which it seems that things are going on elsewhere. You know those pictures in which there are colonnades and arches; a statue on a pedestal, perhaps; smoke as if from a train round some corner: well, what is it round the corner? why is there an impression of fear? This is in our minds: what is it that we do not want to look at? I stood in the middle of the square. One of the buildings had its corrugated-iron covering at the end pulled back: just inside this opening there seemed to be – you remember fear? is it not like a bottom falling out? – just inside the opening there was what seemed to be a pair of legs sticking out: legs with no feet, covered with old sacking. I thought – But of course, if they were legs, they would have feet: in this place, of course, it is a toy. There were heartbeats going off in small explosions in my ears. I approached the building. The ground was dusty: no flowers grew: I thought – This is the nest of stones? Within the entrance, propped up with its back against the wall, was a dummy: you know those pictures? heads stitched up and stuffed with straw? It was wearing some sort of uniform – Russian or German or American or whatever: I mean a life-size dummy of a soldier, propped up against the wall just inside the entrance of the building as if it were on guard: a wooden rifle even across its knees; an old cap stitched on to its head; but no feet; I thought – In such circumstances, indeed, why should it have been given feet? The dummy was lolling sideways; it seemed to have been stuck through, at some time, with a bayonet. I thought – But who has placed it here now? What an enigmatic angel to be guarding the back way!

It was difficult to see inside the building because there was no light except from the opening in which I stood: so when you moved, it was yourself, as usual, who made the shadows. There was a faint smell: I had wondered – Perhaps I am going into some sort of charnel-house? But the smell was not of anything rotting: it was dry, acrid: of things that have remained the same for a very long time; almost of incense. When my eyes became accustomed to the dark I saw that this was, yes, a building where bodies were piled up and stored: the bodies, of course, were dummies: it was like the burial ground of some old king; a heap of heads and arms and legs – perhaps even those spectacles in piles – against a side wall almost to the roof: an atrocity, perhaps: but, as always here, for the purposes of a game. You remember those businessmen in Düsseldorf who bought flocks of plastic sheep and piled them into attics? I thought – Well here, in some storehouse of the mind, are businessmen who are kept as food for sheep? At the edge of the pile of bodies there was even a pram. I thought – What on earth would these people want with a pram? Except that, I suppose, if you want to play at killing, it would be quite fashionable to find some representation of children.

– And the child – he would have been looking up towards the leaves, the shadows?

– Or is he looking down at the temple where he might see himself being dismembered by hags.

I moved further into the building. At the end on the left (left as you look at it; right, do you think, if you are looking at the brain?) tucked away behind the pile of bodies as if it might be of old hair, teeth, spectacles, there was an area which had been cleared and in which some sort of order had been formed. I do not know, as usual of course, how to talk about this: but it does not seem too difficult. There had been set up, had occurred, a group of figures (of course we have been here before!) in a semicircle facing inwards: some of them were propped with their backs against the walls: one or two were wedged with their legs in positions as if they were kneeling: I mean there was a group of these stuffed dummies, three or four in uniform, one or two with sacking round their shoulders – well, do you not know where this is that we have been before? They were facing towards the centre where indeed there was, of course, nothing; or no more than an empty nest of stones. But one of the group of these adoring figures, as if in that painting in the National Gallery, was a sheep. I thought at first it must be a dummy sheep: it sat, or lay, with its legs underneath it so still: and I thought – But this is not quite right, is it? again a bit corny? But then I realised that the sheep was alive, and that it had two heads. This is a shock (you have thought you know where you are?). One head might have been growing out of the other: but each head seemed to be equal in relation to the other: it was as if each had grown to balance the whole – as if on some tightrope. As I approached, the sheep did not move. I thought – Poor old humanity! of course we are on some tightrope: if I move straight enough, you may be still. When I got close to the sheep I saw that, although one side of each head had a perfectly formed ear and eye and even a nose, in between – and it was this that was stretched like a tightrope – was a third eye. I suppose it was some conjunction of what might have been the other eyes of the two heads: an enormous eye, watery and flickering: some heroic attempt to attain that third eye – I mean, the eye of Shiva. This is the eye that looks inwards, isn't it? Perhaps it was just the strain of this attempt that made the third eye, in what was otherwise so still, seem always to be moving. I knelt down in front of the sheep. I thought – What can I offer you? – frankincense, love, myrrh? Precious humanity! You are at least honoured: you are, I mean, able to offer worship in terms of that painting. In addition to what seemed to be the semicircle of adoring figures, I noticed that there had been placed in front of the sheep, as if it had come from the place where the nest of stones had once been, a bowl of what looked like milk and a tray of greenstuff. I thought – Dear God, so where is the child? Then – You mean, he is, this is, somewhere just outside the picture?

When I looked into the huge central eye of the sheep there did seem to be both reflections of the building – the charnel-house and the semicircle of figures – and things going on within the eye: here were snakes, and networks, and notes of unheard music: here were the nerves and branches of a tree.

And I was sure that there was someone watching me. I did not want to look round. I thought – We are all in this painting: we will be getting on with whatever we are to be doing.

Then – The child is in the branches of the tree which is all around me.

What had he hoped for when he tended the sheep? that it would live? that he would help it to die?

I felt that the child might be up on one of the cross-beams of the roof. He would have hidden because he would not know who might be coming into this strange territory.

I thought – You mean, within the eye, there is that which we would discover: which is watching: which is also in the outside world all the time?

Lilia had said – Bert told him stories of a place where there is the Tree of Life.

I became aware – perhaps as a reflection of what was going on in those branches – that the child, in fact, was climbing down from one of the cross-beams that supported the roof; he had been lying there, I suppose, like the snake: no, not the snake! what was it that you thought was in the corner of the ceiling looking down?

Hullo, hullo, my little one.

He was seven or eight years old at the time. (Of course, you know this: you see, now, I am talking to *you*!)

He had a round face and fair hair. He was dressed in jeans and a football jersey.

Everything was happening at once. I felt I should not move.

When he had climbed down he came and knelt beside me and together we looked at the sheep. I thought – How long did this journey take? thousands of years – from the time when those first men came down from the trees?

He said 'It's called Hopeful Monster.'

I said 'That's a good name.'

I had feared that one might not be able to speak at all in this strange territory.

He said 'What is a hopeful monster?'

He pushed the bowl of milk towards the sheep.

I said 'It's when something is born which things outside are not quite ready for. Or perhaps they might just about be ready; that is the hope.'

He said 'I sometimes feel like that.'

I said 'Yes.'

He said 'Do you?'

There is something here that perhaps I should put in about the child.

You can guess how difficult it had been for me to see the child; I mean, because of Lilia. Then there had been a time when I did; when I came with Bert to the seaside to visit where they were staying (you see I am saying 'they' not 'you'!). In the afternoon we played a catching game among the sand-dunes: there is a catcher, and when you are caught you have to stand still until you are rescued by being touched. The child and I had both been caught: we were standing quite close; we were in a hollow of the sand-dunes. The main part of the game seemed to get farther and farther away – the catcher, I suppose, driving the baby turtles towards the sea. The child said – Can I ask you something? I said – Yes. He said – Why does Mummy hate you? He was at that time – what? – five or six. We were in this little grove of trees in the sand-dunes: old hags, I suppose, were dismembering a child. I said – There's often hate, somewhere, you know, where there is love. He said – Who does Daddy love best, her or you? I said – He loves her: he loves your mummy: he loves her far the best! He said – Then why does she say he loves you? We were in this sort of temple: the hags do go on and on, don't they? so methodically dismembering a child! I said – It's all a game: people do play games: you know this, don't you? He said – Yes. I said – What's not a game, is that your mummy loves you. He said – Yes. Then he shouted – Rescue! Then Bert came roaring over the sand-dunes like some great lion, and he touched us and we were free.

The child and I were now kneeling side by side watching the sheep.

I said 'Yes, I sometimes feel like that.'

He said 'Can I ask you something?'

I said 'Yes.'

He said 'Did Mummy want to die?'

There were two long shadows coming in from the door. I did not think they had been there before. They went past us, on either side of us, as if they were some contraption to hold us, to pick us up, like tongs. I thought for a moment that they might be our own shadows, but they came from behind us; then I thought, I do not know why, that they might be the legs of a horse.

I said 'No, she didn't want to die.' Then – 'People sometimes have to fight in extraordinary ways to live.'

He said 'That's not a game.'

I said 'No, that's not a game.'

He said 'She wants us all to live.'

He knelt down. He put his arms round the sheep. I thought – But it is you who are the Hopeful Monster!

The light coming in through the door behind us did appear to be strangely red and bright. I supposed it to be the sun beginning to set behind the trees. It made bars and networks through the cracks and holes in the corrugated doors; these spilled all over us, around us, in the air, on the ground. I thought – This is the grid, the riddle, through which we do not fall: it is the branches of the Tree.

Then I said 'Things are difficult not when you love too little, but when you love too much.'

He said 'Then that's all right.'

There was the sound of a horse's hooves on the ground outside. I did not think this possible, because the shadows on the ground did not move. I thought – But of course, those shadows are not the legs of a horse.

The child had put his head down by the sheep. He looked up at me. I thought – He is that third eye; for which conditions will one day be ready, to look outwards, on the world outside.

I wanted to say – But pray that the other people will have found the Tree!

I thought I should go to the door and look out. After all, a bomb had gone off.

I thought – We will get used to living like this?

Outside there was the make-believe village square: there was also someone, quite still, on a horse. I thought – That wild-haired girl, having come to an end of riding across battlefields –

It was Lilia, sitting with her head down, her hands on the horse's neck. I thought – She has rescued the horse; she has brought home her string of dragons?

The horse seemed to be Eleanor's. Lilia was looking at an empty place on the ground. I thought – She overheard me talking to the child?

Lilia was in her white clothes. She seemed, as usual, to be an angel. I thought – You mean, we have come on our long journey to this place in order to stay alive?

There was that cloud, like angry cherubs with arrows, drifting somewhere in the direction of the American air-base.

I thought – You mean, that is why we have been looking for the child?

There was an object that I had not noticed before; it was strange that I had not noticed it. Among the bars of light like a grid that ran across the ground of the square there were the two long shadows that I had imagined, impossibly, to be the legs of a horse: in fact they came from behind the horse, passing over and around it, with the strange red sun behind: they were from a large structure at the back of the square that was some sort of watchtower. I mean, it was extraordinary that I had not noticed it when I had looked down from the brow of the hill, or when I had come down to the buildings. It was a high wooden construction with four legs like telegraph poles; with a platform like a tin can on top. It was the four legs that made the shadows – two by two almost in line with the sun. Perhaps I had not noticed the watchtower because it was not in the same frame, as it were, as the rest of the village; I mean, it had been built not to be part of games, but to look down: presumably to be used by observers, judges, referees: like those beings I had imagined, perhaps, reclining on clouds. And so one might not have noticed it: until – what? – one had done whatever one was to do? and then were out in the sun again: and saw whatever might be the seeing of things together with their shadows.

The sheep was coming out of the doorway of the building into the sun. It was being led, or followed, by the child: he held on to the wool of its back. The sheep walked cautiously – as if on its tightrope. The child let go of it when it got into the sun. He stood in the doorway and looked at his mother. The sheep went on across the square. It seemed to move with its central eye like some gyroscope. When the sheep got to the far side of the square it lay down in a patch of sun. One head looked into the distance; the other seemed to be observing the scene in the square.

Lilia sat with the reins loose on the horse's neck.

The sun had become very red over the tops of the trees; giving the impression that the landscape was lit with its own light because it was burning.

Lilia was crying.

Her child said 'Mummy!' He ran to her. He tried to climb up on to her horse. He was like one of those figures in a cartoon film who run up a cliff on air. Lilia bent down to him.

I thought – We must not stay here too long: the air will run out in this bright atmosphere.

The child put his arms round his mother. Lilia held him.

Lilia said 'A bomb went off by that pub. On the green.'

I said 'By the pub?'

She said 'Yes.'

There was a ladder going up one of the legs of the watch-tower. I wondered if I climbed up I might see what was going on.

I said 'Were people hurt?'

She said 'Yes.' Then – 'One or two.'

I thought – One does not use the word 'killed'. Then –

That officer? That woman like someone in drag? Then – But not you!

I got as far as the foot of the ladder of the watchtower; then sat down.

I thought – But it's true we all might have been there if we had not been looking for the child!

The child said 'I wanted to see my sheep.'

Lilia said 'I told you not to come here.'

The child said 'I wanted to see my sheep.'

Lilia said 'I know.' She went on crying.

I thought – We need not cry! Do something: like climb up the leg of that watchtower.

– The watchtower might be that from which, in the outside world, the third eye can look out?

The child said 'Look! We are all right!'

I thought I might ask – What sort of bomb was it that went off? How did you get away from the pub and the green?

Lilia was saying 'Yes of course we are all right.'

The child was saying 'I found it easily. It was where I used to feed it.'

We were looking at the sheep. It was watchful, composed. It was looking this way and that: its eye in the middle.

The child was saying 'Do you think it will die?'

Lilia said as if to me 'In the end they believed me when I said that I had to look for my child.'

I thought – But of course we were looking for the child!

Then – So what if we don't know who a father is: we are all fathers and mothers who go across that desert with a donkey!

From where I was sitting with my back to the bottom of the watchtower there was this scene, growing slightly less lurid now as the sun went down behind the trees – these toy houses for families of four to six; the storerooms with bodies piled in memory; the circles of figures, inside and out, looking at places in the dust where there might have been nests; which might now be empty; from which birds have flown. Lilia and the child were on the horse. I was sitting by the watchtower. The sheep, like the rest of us, was something that might or might not survive.

I thought – Where is Jason? Up in some watchtower? Writing a book? Waiting for Lilia?

And you – Looking? Reading this? A bright light coming down!

The Professor is a little better today, thank you.

I had become aware, for some time, that there was the sound of a car, or van, or Land-Rover, approaching from somewhere in the direction of the church. From where I was sitting I could see only the top of the spire of the church because the view of the rest of it was blocked by the toy buildings. The noise of the engine stopped: then there were people's voices. One of the voices I recognised as Bert's. I thought again – I must get away: we have always said, haven't we, that what is not bearable is not too little –

While I was watching it, a bit off the top of the spire of the church fell down. Then I heard Bert's voice saying 'Boo!'

The child climbed down from Lilia's horse. He ran to the far side of the square. He picked up a bicycle.

I thought – All right, you can call this not bearable.

The child called 'Where are you?'

Bert said 'Here!'

The child said 'I've found my sheep!'

When Bert and whoever was with him came into the square, I was trying not to look. I was thinking – Oh yes, why should not Bert have been in that Land-Rover by the flint-mines: he would have been looking for the child –

Bert came into the square. The person with him, of course, was Eleanor. Eleanor did not seem to be walking with so much difficulty now. I did not feel I was yet able to get to the top of the watchtower.

Bert said 'I say, did you see me say Boo! and that bit of the spire fell down?'

The child said 'No, the spire fell down, and then you said Boo!'

Lilia said 'A bomb's gone off.'

Bert said 'Well it was nothing to do with me.'

Eleanor was crossing the square. I was thinking – But still, if we survive, how do we live with survival?

Eleanor said 'Are you all right?'

I said 'No.'

Eleanor said 'Well it was nothing to do with that hut in the woods. And there was nothing in that suitcase.'

I thought I might say – But is not everything to do with everything?

Bert and the child were looking at the sheep. He said 'Where did you find it?'

The child said 'It was where it was at Christmas.'

Bert said 'And now it's Easter!' He hit the palm of his hand against his forehead like a clown.

Lilia said 'Oh do shut up!'

Bert said 'Willingly.'

He came across the square towards the watchtower. Then when he saw me he stopped.

I thought – You mean, he had not noticed me before: it is as if I am in a different dimension, like the watchtower?

Bert said 'Hullo.'

I said 'Hullo.'

He said 'You've found it.'

I said 'What?'

He said 'The Tree of Life.'

I said 'Oh do shut up!'

Eleanor smiled. She put a hand on my hair. Then she moved away across the square to the sheep.

The child said 'Do you think it will die?'

Eleanor said 'They usually do. We'll see. One day.'

Lilia was getting down from her horse. Her child went and held the reins. I thought – He is like a mother seeing his child come home from war.

Bert said 'Are you pregnant?'

I said 'Yes.'

He said 'I thought you might be.'

We are all of us in this square. You are here, because you are reading this.

Lilia called – 'You might marry her!'

Bert called 'I want to be a surrogate mother!'

Eleanor sat down by the sheep. The sheep let her put her arm around it.

Bert went past me and began climbing the ladder of the watchtower. When he was half-way up he stopped and looked down. He said 'I'd like a girl.'

The child said 'Then I'll have someone to play with!' He left Lilia and the horse and began riding round the square on his bicycle.

Bert climbed to the top of the watchtower.

Well, how much more do you want to see of this?

My child, who is a girl, is asleep by the window as I write. So, hullo. Talk quietly.

You know the code. You know the message –

Love from Judith